D0936188

The DRAGONS OF NOVA

keymaster press

The DRAGONS OF NOVA

ELISE KOVA

Published by Keymaster Press

3971 Hoover Rd. Suite 77

Columbus, OH 43123-2839

Edited by: Rebecca Faith Heyman

Cover Design by: Nick D. Grey

Proofreading by: Christine Herman

Layout Design by: Gatekeeper Press

ISBN: 9781619845534

eISBN: 9781619845541

Library of Congress Control Number: 2017940126

Printed in the United States of America

Also by Elise Kova

LOOM SAGA
The Alchemists of Loom
The Dragons of Nova
The Rebels of Gold

AIR AWAKENS SERIES
Air Awakens
Fire Falling
Earth's End
Water's Wrath
Crystal Crowned

GOLDEN GUARD TRILOGY
The Crown's Dog
The Prince's Rogue
The Farmer's War

*for Robert
and all your colors*

Contents

Weuri
TEMPLE OF LORD XIN
EASTWIN
NAPOLE
VENYS
ABILLA
XIN MANOR
Ruana

ARIANNA

It wasn't that she didn't trust Cvareh piloting the glider, it was that she valued her life a lot more than a superfluous notion like trust.

His hands, the color of the blue-gray sky that stretched above them, clutched the handles of the vessel with less than inspiring certainty. They shook as though they held birds or writhing snakes, not gold. His magic flowed through the metal and into the glider beneath them, filling the air, giving lift and speed, before discharging out behind the glider's bat-like wings as a full prism's worth of color.

Arianna clutched his waist, pushing her own magic under her heels, rooting herself to the glider in a battle against gravity. The contraption was not built for two and she had to manage her magic carefully to avoid interrupting the flow of his—a fate that would send them spiraling back earthward toward a near-certain death from the fall. His magic was fluctuating at best; the man had clearly never been taught how to pilot a glider and didn't even understand the basics of how magic was channeled through the gold to give it lift.

It would be easy for her to assume control. He was powerful, but she would have no reservations and a firm understanding of how the glider functioned.

Arianna grit her teeth and kept her magic wound tightly around her feet. She let him struggle silently. Piloting a glider was something that, as far as Loom was concerned, only a Dragon could do. Even a strong Chimera couldn't sustain the magic required to give it stable lift for very long. Which meant that there was no way Arianna should be able to.

She *could*, however. She could pilot it more gracefully than the Dragon she was pressed against and the fact made her dangerous. It was a secret so great it would make her both revered and hunted should it ever be discovered. So Arianna kept her mouth shut. She remained the Chimera, the White Wraith, and nothing more.

Her eyes drifted down behind them at the diminishing earth. Loom spread out beneath her, smaller and smaller until the tallest trees in the forest looked like toothpicks, and the coastline was nothing more than the teeth of a cog she could fit in the palm of her hand. Down there, was the Alchemists' guild hall, reduced to nothing more than a speck, and in it was Florence.

Her dearest friend, her ward, her Florence, had set out to change the world. The girl had challenged Ari to do the same and dream again as she once had. But the birth of dreams stained reality. Dreams charted courses beyond the line of possibility that the present drew. They turned that forbidden threshold into an invitation, one that offered no absolution to those who boldly ventured into its alluring unknown.

Arianna knew this all too well.

She had dreamed. She had carved her infamy from the impossible. The dreams had wrapped reality in a sweet illusion that had turned sour with betrayal. If she dreamed again, she would no longer dream for the world. She would not risk leaving another mark on such a scale. She would merely be a player in other's dreams—like Florence's.

When the girl awoke this dawn, Arianna hoped she would understand. There wasn't room for goodbyes between women of action. It would be wasted words. If Florence wanted to assume the post of a visionary, she had to weigh the importance of deeds before the importance of words, not just from Arianna, but from the whole world.

"Brace yourself!" Cvareh shouted over the gusty currents.

The winds howled with greater ferocity the closer they got to the thick clouds that perpetually engulfed Loom. Ari grabbed her elbows at Cvareh's sides, locking muscle against muscle as she pressed into the taller man. The closer they were to each other, the less possibility for drag or for a rogue gust to get between them and knock her off.

His magic washed over her in pulses that increased in frequency until they were a sustained force across the entire glider, including her. Surviving through the clouds required a hefty amount of protection—a corona. This was the second barrier that prevented a Chimera from piloting a glider. Built into the handles Cvareh gripped were golden channels designed to funnel magic into a protective shield. Even if a Chimera could manage lift, it wouldn't be enough to sustain a suitable corona that would protect against the wind.

Light sparked across them, shining like scales, as the wind battered the magical force-field. Ari's refined goggles were whitewashed from the magic and clouds, her ears nearly deaf from the roaring wind that echoed through the magical barrier—a paper-thin separation between them and certain death.

But she never closed her eyes.

She remained alert, poised to take over should Cvareh falter. She would not die this day and certainly not due to someone else's incompetence. Arianna waited, her breaths shallowed with nerves, until they broke through the line that separated the world she knew below, and the world of Dragons in the skies above.

Magic snapped audibly as they crossed the threshold between worlds. Ari blinked into unfiltered sunlight for the very first time.

Her eyes had no trouble adjusting. They had been cut from a Dragon and implanted in her sockets. Her irises closed to thin slits and adapted instantly. But her mind rejected the blinding light. It was a struggle to process, like a ribbon of magnesium exposed to flame.

How could anything be so bright?

The sunlight illuminated every nook and cranny of the world that floated before her. It defied all logic, hovering in the empty air in violation of every scientific law that formed the load-bearing walls of the structure of her life. *Nova*, the homeland of the Dragons. She was loath to admit it, but the sketches in books hadn't done it justice.

Diamond-shaped islands drifted like icebergs through tides of wind. Inverted towers and honeycombed living quarters had been carved into the shade of their underbellies. Sunbeams winked through the hollow spaces where gardens thrived and waterfalls fell into the nothingness below, spilling a seemingly infinite amount of liquid into the void as if it were tithing for an unknown god.

Smaller masses floated around the larger oncs, like islands to continents. The glider rose higher and higher, giving Arianna her first glimpse of the tops. The land was as colorful as its people: purple mountains offset against emerald trees, gold splattered atop grasses as if the sun itself had been poured out. Every building was painted and adorned on all possible surfaces. Not one had escaped the artist's brush or sculptor's touch. *Every. Single. One.*

"What do you think?" Cvareh shouted over his shoulder.

Arianna wanted to quip back with some scathing remark. It was tacky. It was over the top. It was too much of everything. There was no appreciation for the beauty of simplicity. But her tongue had gone soft and spongy, and her usual wit hadn't caught up with her.

"It's not what I expected." She wouldn't give him the satisfaction of more than that. "Now focus on not getting us killed."

He must've agreed with the sentiment, because Cvareh said nothing further. Ari could feel his magic thinning. Bruises were beginning to form on his skin as his body broke down from the exertion. Arianna had no doubt he had a large mark around his torso where she'd been gripping for her life. But the man had yet to speak a word against her potentially painful proximity or hold on his person.

The glider banked. Carved into the far side of the mountains, she could see the outlines of a grand series of structures that defied all sense of logic and necessity. They were suspended in the air, connected by gusty bridge-ways and narrow spiraling stairs. Cvareh tracked them to a large building above it all at the top of the mountain.

"You need to slow us," Ari cautioned nervously, realizing he intended to land on a flat alcove just on the other side of the structure.

"I'm working on it."

"Work on it more urgently." They were coming in far too fast for such a narrow ledge. Numbers flashed through her head, estimations based on estimations, but in every scenario they were splattered against the back wall of the wide-mouthed cavern.

Cvareh tugged on the handles, his magic straining in spite of his obvious will. "You want to try flying this thing?"

The question was obviously meant to be rhetorical, but Arianna had to bite her tongue from answering a resounding *yes!*

She waited until what she estimated to be the last possible second for Cvareh to pull himself together and get the glider back under his control and on a proper trajectory. He met her expectations of failure. Ari pushed her magic into him, into the glider through her feet. It wasn't possible to assume complete control without gripping the handles, but it had the desired effect. His magic was vastly weakened by the dominant influx of her own, resulting in the almost total arrest of the vessel's momentum—and thus knocking it off the suicide course it had been propelling them along. Arianna mentally accommodated for the falter by adding extra lift beneath the wings.

They skipped like a stone on water, skidding to a stop with a crash that crumpled one wing and sent them both tumbling from the glider. Ari's ears were ringing from the sharp *bang* of metal crushing against stone. She winced at the sight of the technical masterpiece that was a Dragon glider reduced to half a heap of scrap.

"Are you all right?" Cvareh drew himself to a seated position, taking note of her expression.

"Takes a lot more than that to fell me." Ari quickly checked for any rogue cuts or scratches she'd need to hide.

"Isn't that the truth?" He stood. "We need to get moving."

"To where?" Ari was already in step behind him.

"The Temple of Xin."

Arianna had studied Dragon culture enough to know of the culture's pantheon—the twenty needless gods they prayed to for everything from love to peace to luck. She could list off a good fifteen, maybe even all twenty, but Arianna could only align three to what they were said to be the gods of—and Xin was one of them.

Lord Xin, the death-giver and patron of the House of his namesake—Cvareh's family's House.

"Unless you can sprout actual wings on Nova, I doubt we'll be going anywhere anytime soon." Arianna shuffled toward the edge of the cavern, looking up and down. The walls were sheer and frustratingly smooth. Climbing would be a trick. Her mind was already turning around what they could salvage from the wreckage of the glider to help them scale the face when magic popped faintly around her companion.

Cvareh murmured softly to himself in Ryouk, the language of the Dragons. Arianna's ears picked up half of the conversation, but he spoke too softly for her to catch anything substantial. She stepped closer and his hand promptly fell away from his ear.

"Wings are coming."

"What does that mean?" She raised her eyebrows.

He laughed. The infuriating Dragon had the audacity to laugh at her as though she were a child inquiring about how water turned to ice. Arianna narrowed her eyes at him in warning.

"You'll see." He leaned against one of the side walls, folding his arms over his chest.

The Dragon had become bolder around her and Arianna hadn't done enough to discourage the disdainful behavior. His mannerisms were his own, but every now and then she saw the shade of someone else in them. Someone that gave her pause even when she was at her boldest.

"I'd rather you just tell me." She leaned against the wall at his side with a hefty sigh.

"By the time I did, you—"

The air from the flapping of large wings buffeted the side of her face and Arianna turned as a loud screech nearly deafened her. A giant bird-like creature had been saddled with an ornate leather seat like those intended for horseback. Her fingers closed around the hilt of her sharper dagger.

A Dragon the color of pale sea foam sat poised on its back as the bird perched with ease on the ledge. The rider had golden eyes not unlike Cvareh's, but his hair was a darker shade, closer to the color of fired brick or wet clay. He ran a hand through his shoulder-length locks, smoothing them from the ride. His eyes drifted to her instantly.

"You brought a Chimera?" Disapproval radiated from the man's pores.

"The ends, Cain." Cvareh's tone had a cautionary punctuation, the words strung together with a vibrato of authority Arianna had never heard from him before. It made her look sideways at the man she'd traveled across Loom with.

"Looking forward to hearing more of those." Cain shook his head. "Come on then. Petra'Oji wants you in the Temple post haste."

Cvareh made a start for the bird, Arianna at his side. He stopped her with an arm. "You need to wait here."

"Excuse me?"

"The boco can't take more than two riders at a time."

"Then leave this petulant Dragon and take me." Arianna motioned rudely to the man named Cain. Cvareh had earned his name; all others would as well.

"What did you call me?" The man on the boco growled.

"Peace." Cvareh held out his hands between them. But amusement was alight in his eyes—amusement for her.

Bloody cogs, first his boldness and now she was endearing to him? She was losing her edge.

"Wait here. Time is of the essence and I can't explain now. Cain will come back for you," Cvareh said.

"If he doesn't—"

"He will," the Dragon cut off her threat. "Trust me, Ari."

She rolled her eyes and leaned against the side wall again, arms folded across her chest to communicate her general displeasure at the situation. Cvareh shook his head, squeezing awkwardly into the saddle behind Cain. She watched them depart, questioning the choices that had led her here.

Arianna drew her dagger and commenced flipping it in the air, attempting to take her mind off the fact that she had just willingly walked into the Dragon's den.

PETRA

P etra walked the tightrope of treason. On either side were
the voids of failure, an oblivion from which there was no
escape. Dangled at the far end before her was the title of
Dono, Queen of the Dragons, glory of House Xin. The
sight of it was enough to keep her toeing a line that even the most
suicidally ambitious dragon wouldn't dare to walk.

She grinned madly into the wind, baring her canines to an
invisible foe.

Islands of Nova flashed beneath her, reduced to green blurs
by Raku's speed. She fisted his feathers and altered course slightly.
The other three bocos behind her followed suit.

She had the Dono and two riders in tow. Their magic sparked
with aggression, but only one held weight. Yveun Dono, King of
the Dragons, barely held his emotions in check. She knew when
his eyes fell on her back by the ferocity that lit the wind between
them.

He knew he'd been played. It had been a plan years in the
making, ever since Finnyr had slipped. Petra had cut it from the
cloth of knowledge given to her by her elder brother—the King's
financial adviser for Loom. That knowledge of the Philosopher's
Box would be the pattern for the tapestry of her ultimate victory.

She'd moved carefully, sending Cvareh to acquire the documents and entrusting him to get them to the resistance on Loom. Her younger brother was underestimated by the whole of Nova. She'd kept him in the wings, cultivating his skills when no one watched. When the time came he was overlooked and slipped through the cracks, just as expected.

Her years of patience were now paying dividends. She knew he was stronger than anyone gave him credit for, but even Petra had not expected her brother would be the one to slay the King's Master Rider. Poor Leona; for all her airs and appearances, she was felled by sweet little Cvareh. Not bearing witness to her ultimate demise had already become one of Petra's few regrets.

Now the King sought justice for his slain bitch. He wanted Cvareh's head in recompense, and that was a price Petra wasn't going to pay. When Cvareh arrived hours ago, Petra had lifted the baton on the next movement of her orchestrations. Her brother was seen to the Temple of Xin. The Chimera he'd brought...well, that was an unexpected deviation that she had yet to attain a full explanation for.

Petra shifted in her saddle. *One thing at a time*, she reminded herself. The Chimera was hidden, for now. She'd deal with the creature later when she didn't have a King in tow.

Her shadow zipped across the God's Line far below, jumping on and off smaller islands as she crossed above them. The isle of Ruana, twice the size of House Rok's Lysip, came into view. Mountains curved on the far ridge-line, spilling bountiful plains and fertile farmland in their shade. It was impossible for Petra to keep a smile off her face when her home came into view. No raging Dragon King could damper the way her soul soared alongside Raku as she crossed the threshold of Xin land.

Far on the horizon, at the highest peak, was the Temple of Lord Xin, the Death-bringer. It shot upward, like a sword spearing the land itself, in a single column: a pointed obelisk that both unified and severed earth and sky. Against the morning light, it was awash in ominous shadow.

Petra adjusted her grip on the boco. She feared no mortal man, but the gods were another matter. She would repent to the Death God in triplicate when this was over for using his temple in her fight against Yveun Dono. In the meantime, she could only hope Lord Xin turned his eternal gaze upon her fondly. Petra would believe that she was truly his chosen daughter, so if there were to be death dealt today, it would not be her or Cvareh's.

With a chorus of flapping, the boco quartet landed on a nearly too-small ledge at the base of the temple. A yawning entrance, simple and unadorned, waited before them, cut and smoothed from the gray mountain stone. Petra dismounted alongside the others, silence their fifth companion.

She toed to the threshold of the entrance, the bright daylight cut in a sharp line of shadow. Petra closed her eyes and covered them with both palms, a sign of servitude and respect. One knew not what waited in eternity; the crossing happened only when one's eyes closed for the final time.

Petra stepped into the temple.

Her eyes adjusted quickly to the dim lighting. Not a single candle burned and the world beyond cast long shadows over the twenty sculptures that lined the long hall. Nineteen alternated placement on either side, visages of every other god and goddess in the pantheon. Lord Tam held out scales, Lord To cradled an open manuscript with the delicacy of a babe, Lady Che held her trumpet of truth to her lips—the statues stretched on and on, atop their ornate daises.

There was one variation to the statues found in Lord Xin's temple: they all wore a large veil atop their faces. The shroud of death was settled upon every brow, including the sculpture at the very end of the Lord of Death himself. Lord Xin's visage had been carved with such elegance that his layered robes seemed to move with ethereal grace, even in stone. His veil was stretched taught over unknown features, pulled by an invisible wind. He looked as though he could at any moment become flesh and steal the life from any of his divine brethren.

Some worshipers took note of the unorthodox party as they traversed the hall. They offered bows of their heads to the King, though Petra was certain the gestures were far less than the prostrations he was accustomed to on Lysip. But the King's demeanor was unchanged. Yveun Dono was either humbled into muted silence in the presence of the Death bringer, or he was too upset for his magic to hold any further aggression.

Petra led them back behind the statue of Lord Xin and into a narrow stair. Darkness engulfed them, so thick that even her eyes couldn't penetrate it. She slid her hand along the wall, recognizing every subtle shift of the craftsmen's work. Her feet knew the exact spacing of every step, memorized over years of pilgrimage.

One of the Riders stumbled, the noise breaking silence's purity. Petra withheld a snapping remark, not wanting to shame her Lord further by doing the same herself. Still, she bared her teeth at the blackness behind her.

It would be in her right as the Xin'Oji to kill any who shamed her House's patron without need of a formal duel. Yveun Dono certainly knew this, and his measured steps were barely audible; even his breathing was hushed. Certainly, his magic sparked violently, but he kept his physical manner in close check. He would never make it that easy for her.

The weight of the stone grew suffocating as they continued to spiral upward. Silence stretched into infinity. Darkness tore at the mind, turning seconds into hours.

The Riders' breathing became labored, and not from the strain of the stairs. Petra didn't turn or offer them even a thought of pity. Yveun Dono kept pace and didn't falter.

Slowly, the sound of wind whispered freshness to them. They took one more wide curve and arrived at the apex of the obelisk. A single oculus cut through the darkness like a triumphant banner. It offered the temptation of a world beyond, a lone portal and no more.

Upon the floor was a circular divot, recessed as if the light itself had worn away the stone in time. Cvareh was curled within it like a snake in an egg, taking up nearly all available space. He was as naked as the day he was born. His palms covered his face and his body was still. His barely moving shoulders betrayed that he was alive at all.

Petra crossed over to her brother. His months-long meditation had been pretense, but now that he was swaddled within the embrace of Lord Xin, she would observe convention— and not just for Yveun's sake. She knelt down at the rim of the recessed area, covered her eyes with her palms and brought her forehead to the floor.

"End bringer." Her hushed whisper sounded like a shout. "Your child beseeches you, return Cvareh to us. Return him in both body and soul with your infinite wisdom and eternal truth."

Three breaths, and Cvareh stirred. His breathing quickened to a normal pace, his muscles rippling under his powder-fair skin. With painful slowness he rolled forward, his face still covered by his hands in a position that mirrored Petra's. His back straightened, each vertebra clicking into place. His head tilted back, and he finally pulled away his palms, blinking into the light.

She sat in tandem, opening her eyes as well. The relief that flooded Petra didn't need to be faked. It surged through her at the sight of her brother, powerful and whole. The Lord of Death had not taken his soul yet from her side, not down upon Loom, not now as punishment for using his temple in her maneuvering against Yveun Dono. He rose again, and again, stronger than ever.

Cvareh's blood-colored eyes finally drifted to her. They shone like two golden disks in the sunlight. She had whispered the plan to him as she organized it on her way to the Rok Estate. He had known she would be there, but a tangible joy pulled at his expression, tugging it into the realm of inappropriate given their current venue.

"Forgive me for pulling you from your meditation, brother." She pushed through the moment. There was still work to be done. "Our divine King has demanded to speak with you."

Cvareh played his part just as she'd instructed. Her brother was the perfect soldier. He never questioned and he was always attentive when she spoke.

"Yveun Dono—" Cvareh cleared his throat, as though he had not used it in months and it troubled him to speak. "It is an honor to be sought by you."

"Cvareh Xin." The Dono could not keep a growl from his voice. He stalked across the space with restrained and measured steps. "Where have you been these past months?"

Confusion furrowed Cvareh's brow. "Forgive me, Dono, but I fear I don't understand your question." He lowered his eyes demurely, radiating nothing but subservience to the King looming over him.

Yveun leaned forward and Petra reminded herself to breathe. She'd instructed Cvareh carefully on what he needed to do. A scrub of perfumed salts until he bled, a wash of boiling water; when his skin had knitted he was to cut it again and smear his blood atop himself. And, by all the gods, he was to do it nowhere near the Chimera or anything else of Loom.

The King inhaled deeply. Petra knew she had won from that single sniff. His mouth pressed into a line and he breathed again in quick succession.

"Do not play dumb with me, child," Yveun growled. "I know you have not been in this temple."

"Has it been weeks?" Cvareh's face paled on command. He turned to Petra and then looked back at the Dono in false confusion. "My King, I've been seeking the words of my Lord. Time has escaped me... If you called on me and I did not answer then—"

"Do not lie to me, you thief." Yveun's claws shot out from his fingers. They gleamed in the light, sharpened by grating on bones from years of duels.

Petra stood slowly. Her own claws itched for release. If she could goad Yveun into a mistake now, she could claim the throne.

"Yveun Dono... We are in the Temple of Lord Xin, Patron of my House. As his mortal hand and protector of all Xin, it is my duty to defend my kin." She drew her height. Petra was three fingers shorter than the King but she felt evenly matched as she threw her magic against him without fear of repercussion. Cvareh could handle two fresh Riders if he could slay Leona. The King would be hers. "I have tolerated your affronts against

my brother and have violated my Lord's sacred code to bring
you here. But if you maintain these slanderous claims before
man and god, I will evoke the Deathbringer and demand your
atonement for them."

Her claws finally unsheathed to punctuate her words in a
sweet release. It was the first time she had bared them before
Yveun and doing so was a thrill unto itself.

Yveun's lips curled in a snarl, exposing his canines. But he
didn't attack, and he didn't speak further. While preserving all
the dominance he could, he stepped away.

His retreating magic left a bittersweet aftertaste, a surge of
power that Petra craved. It was delicious to feel it shrink before
her and she wanted to feel the sensation again and again. At the
same time, she wished it had been the first and only time she'd
feel such a thing. For if such were the case, then the title of Dono
would be attached to *her* name.

"Caution, Petra." The King dropped her title, slapping her
across the face with words. Petra remained mentally fettered. "If
you continue down this path you shall evoke the Death-bringer
indeed. But it shall not be my atonement he seeks. Do not let your
ambition blind you to your ideals."

Yveun Dono stepped away, knowing he'd been beat. With
Cvareh in the place she claimed, acting so perfectly, not a scent
of Loom on him, the King had no proof—for now. To challenge
them would require the King to own up to his shames—Cvareh
having bested both him in stealing the schematics from under
his nose, and his Riders on Loom. She would see the sun and
moon rise together before she expected Yveun to imbibe on his
own humility. Petra watched as he departed back down the bleak
descent of the Temple of Death, knowing it would not be the last
time their tensions would rise to a near boil only to be iced again.

She relaxed her hands, claws retreating *for now*. "You are mistaken, Yveun," she breathed. "Ends before ideals."

CVAREH

Cvareh would trade his soul for a well-tailored pair of trousers and tastefully matching shoulder adornments. It was ice cold atop the mountain and he fought shivers as the air nipped at his bare skin. It was still tender from healing after the abuse he'd put it through at Petra's request.

Petra.

He followed his elder sister down the long staircase he'd sprinted up only an hour before. He couldn't see her in the darkness, but he could feel her. She was bright and sharp. Her magic smelled crisply of pine. Her steps were measured and even, the lithe, sinewy muscles in her legs betraying strength hidden from the casual eye. Her breathing was even, unlabored, unfaltering. She'd met the Dragon King and walked away as though it was a matter that caused her no more concern than choosing what to wear in the morning.

Meanwhile, Cvareh's knees still trembled. Yveun Dono was an imposing force. He was not to be trifled with and made no hesitation in making it known. Cvareh had enough experience to last a lifetime fighting against his Riders; the last thing he was inclined to do was fight the King himself.

But he kept himself together in Petra's presence. He worked to mimic her stoicism. His sister was far more devout to the Lord Xin than Cvareh was, and he would do nothing to offend her faithful sensibilities to Lord and House.

She didn't so much as look back at him the entire length of the hall. Cvareh noticed the occasional curious glance, and the knowing look from worshippers, but no one commented. He mirrored Petra's movements as she covered her eyes with the heels of her hands and crossed the threshold into sunlight.

His sister took a deep breath, spreading out her arms as if to invite all of Ruana into her embrace. The sunlight danced along her golden curls, striking against the midnight blue skin of her shoulders. Petra was nearly the same height as Cvareh, but her body was cut and primed. She was born to be the Oji he adored—alongside everyone else in House Xin.

"Cvareh!" Without warning, a switch flipped in her demeanor. She spun on her heel and pulled him in for a bone-crushing embrace. "How I have missed you, little brother."

"And I, you." He had missed being enveloped in the scent of pine, the familiar feeling of her muscles beneath his palms, the pleased hum that thrummed across their magic when they were in the other's presence. Petra was born to be Oji, and Cvareh was born to be her Ryu.

"I insist you tell me everything." She pulled back, leaving space for business to come between them.

"I must insist on clothing first." He let himself shiver in the wake of a mountain gust for emphasis.

"Very well." She started for her boco. "Come home. It has been too long since you graced the halls of the Xin manor."

"I see Raku put on weight while I was gone." Cvareh patted the boco's side as he situated himself behind his sister. Riding a saddle without trousers was bound to be a positively miserable experience, and he'd turn his thoughts to anything else.

"Muscle," she insisted.

"Of course." Cvareh grabbed his sister's waist as they took to the air.

Ruana spread out like a lover beneath him once more, inviting and familiar. This time he could appreciate the splendor of his homeland. For now, it appeared as if they'd evaded Yveun Dono, which meant his life was secure for a little longer.

In the distance he saw the towns of Abilla and Venys, sprawling toward the largest city on Ruana, Napole. He imagined the soaring vocals of the last opera he'd seen there drifting to him on the wind, and was instantly set to wondering what was playing now. Cvareh felt like a Dragon seeing the upper half for the first time. Everything was wondrous; everything felt new. The sights and sounds he had taken for granted all his life were now shining in the eyes of a man who had resigned himself to the real possibility that he might never see them again. The eyes of a man who had seen nothing but steel blended with bronze and steam for months.

His sister tilted and Raku banked. Cvareh moved with them as their course altered. They no longer tracked along the sloping valley, but aimed instead for a smaller mountain nestled between the grasslands and the Temple of Xin.

"You've made progress," he observed.

"The winds have been kind to the workers," Petra affirmed.

Cvareh had been born in a smaller estate much closer to the heart of Napole that was now used to house the Kin and Da of House Xin. When Petra killed their father, assuming the Xin'Oji title, she had deemed the older estate unfit for the current House Xin. She'd hand-picked the best architects from across Nova, pulling them in on the most ambitious project to date. Any who deemed her vision impossible met an ill fate.

Petra's methodology had reaped rewards, as it so often did. Now, the Xin manor was the jewel of Ruana. Its spires defied logic as they curved and wound together like mating snakes. Rooms hung as freely as ripe fruit on the vine in the free air. Tunnels burrowed into the mountain itself, opening into cavernous meeting spaces, only to be rolled out like lapping tongues to meet the illogically suspended towers.

A smile thinned his lips. He wondered what Arianna and all her Rivet sensibilities would make of his wondrous home.

"That's a new feeling." Petra glanced over her shoulder, catching him in the act.

"What is?" He tried and failed to play dumb.

"That pleased pulse across your magic. That coy smile."

"Hardly."

Petra laughed like song bells. "Cvareh, your efforts to conceal the truth to me are futile. You whispered to me about a woman—the White Wraith no less. Now, you bring a Chimera home to me whom I can only assume is one and the same."

"I promise I will tell you everything once I have clothes on." He shifted uncomfortably in the saddle, ready for Raku to land on the waiting stretch of stone beneath them. "What's the style of the day?"

"Magenta seems to be quite popular among the tea house socialites," Petra answered over Raku's fluttering wings, easing them back to the earth.

Cvareh made a gagging noise. "Rok's influence no doubt." The color would clash terribly with his skin.

"You'll pull it off fine. Or, there is always the tried and true Xin blue," Petra consoled, seeing straight through him. "For now, indulge me and wear last year's fashions so that we may catch up."

"If I must." Cvareh sighed, already half dressed.

Servants had met them on the platform, preempting their needs. As soon as Cvareh had dismounted, his feet were in the wide legs of lounging trousers. While Petra had been speaking the help had woven a delicately embroidered shawl around his arms and across his shoulders. The final adornments were affixed about his neck, a silver chain with many loops, black stones reminiscent of the Rider's beads weighting their apexes.

Those same servants disappeared back into the shadows and off even the edges of Cvareh's subconscious as he followed his sister into their home. The floor of the main entry hall had been done in glass, save for a stone lip on the outer edge. The mountain beneath it had been carved away and radiant sunlight from the clouds far below filled the room. Petra walked boldly across it, Cvareh following in her steps.

She settled on a raised dais as the doors closed. A throne of stone, simple yet imposing, its angular lines cut into the hazy light projected upward from the floral-patterned glass. Cvareh wondered if Yveun Dono had yet to see his sister's hall. The statement it made was hardly subtle.

"Now, tell me all that has transpired." Petra's tone changed the moment she sat upon the throne. Gone was his adoring little sister, overwhelmed with excitement and relief at the sight of him. In her place was the Xin'Oji, the deadly and fearless leader who had desired nothing more for the entirety of her short life than to be Dono.

Cvareh approached, settling himself cross-legged on one of the wide lower rungs of her dais. He remained poised with his back straight, instinctively answering her unspoken demand by assuming his place. If she was to be the Oji, then he was to be her Ryu.

"Flying the glider proved to be more of a challenge than expected. I didn't get far before crashing in New Dortam, the Riders close on my tail..."

The words spilled from him as he watched the events of the past months replay before his eyes in double time. Things had grown hazy, especially at the onset. Details had faded into the obscurity of unimportance, shrouded by the more pertinent and immediately relevant parts.

One shining element remained in crystalline focus. At every turn and twist, he could see Arianna perfectly. He could recall with ease the expression she wore the first time she'd driven him to stop time. He remembered the contours of her face when her gaze softened as she looked at him on the ship crossing to Ter.4.2, the first moment he had seen beauty in the unique skills she possessed. Cvareh's memories were painted with her, making their mere recollection an unparalleled delight.

His tale wrapped up with the Alchemists' Guild. It was the most somber note of all he said. Despite all the progress he'd recounted, he and Arianna had left Loom at a place of tension and strangeness. But when he spoke his last words, the taste of honeysuckle tinted with cedar filled his mouth, evoked by the mere memory of the imbibing they had shared following the airship crash.

Petra hadn't moved the entire time he spoke. She remained still and contemplative. Her magic was withdrawn tight to her body, betraying nothing.

"How long will she stay?" his sister finally asked.

"I don't know," Cvareh confessed. His summary had hardly been short, but it proved impossible to explain that he found himself in no place to question Arianna. "I presume she'll want to leave as soon as she is confident in your leadership."

His sister shifted, drawing her fingertips to her lips in thought. "This is an amusing little Chimera, isn't it?" The corner of her mouth curled. "She has you quite ensnared and now designs to make me submit before her as well."

"She is not one to be underestimated."

"Oh that much is well apparent. Anyone who could kill the King's bitch shouldn't be." Petra laughed with glee at the mere mention of the former Master Rider's demise. "Leona, felled by a Chimera. Lord Xin can be delightful at times." His sister straightened, pulling herself from her musings. "You know this woman—"

"Not quite," he corrected, noting his sister's tone.

"Then know her better." Petra smirked. "Tell me, Cvareh, what must I do to earn her trust?"

He was still figuring that out himself. Cvareh stared at the decorative hem of his pants, patterns of leaves woven and cut into the edge. He debated quietly with the fabric until he had a decent answer. There were only two things in the world Cvareh could say with certainty were important to Ari. Two things that would prove someone an ally of the woman who called herself the White Wraith.

"Prove to her you love Loom."

"I hold no love for that dreary rock."

He knew it to be true, and instantly felt foolish for phrasing it as he had. "Prove to her, then, that you are aligned with Loom's interests."

"I know not what those are and furthermore, I don't care."

Cvareh closed his eyes a moment. Petra was a force unto herself, and now he had Ari to grapple with on Nova in addition to her. The idea of praying to Lord Agendi for luck grew more appealing by the minute.

"If you do not care, then assure her Loom will have sovereignty." Cvareh met his sister's eyes. "For all you care about the title of Dono, Arianna cares for Loom."

"If she believes this, she will make the Philosopher's Box for me? She will hand me my army?"

"For Loom, there is nothing she wouldn't do."

FLORENCE

Beads of sweat rolled down Florence's cheek, sliding slowly over her outlined Raven tattoo. She drew breath slowly through her nose, hissing it out between her teeth to keep them from chattering. The room was frigid. Her blood was boiling.

She held a golden canister between her index finger and thumb, blinking at it through the goggles. There was a small mountain of gunpowder at her right, and a half dozen reactive chemicals at her left. She could be blown five ways to eternity with one wrong move.

"Adding mercury..." she breathed, entirely to herself. With deliberate movements she reached for the beaker she knew held the element in question, lifting it precisely to the canister in hand. She watched as the liquid metal flowed into the concoction in the golden tube.

Magic pulsed from under her fingers in uneven bursts. Controlling it was like trying to hold lard with her fingertips. Every time she thought she had a grip, it slithered from her grasp, leaving only remnants. It left her struggling to clasp it again, to find the same weight she'd held it with mere seconds before.

If she messed up now, she'd kill herself and blow out a wing of the Alchemists' guild hall with her. One wrong move, one improperly measured powder or chemical, one second of too much stabilizing magic, was all it would take. A tiny smirk graced her lips as she eased the beaker back down to the table.

This tension was what she lived for. It was one half of a whole, scales that tipped with her every movement. She spent minutes—hours—creating, only to reap destruction tenfold with her products. It was what had drawn her away from the Ravens guild, the transportation experts of the world, to the Revolvers.

A sharp, metallic scent filled her nose. Smelling chemical reactions taking place was a new sensation. Naturally, large-scale or prominent reactions might be discernible to any chemist. But this was different. Her senses had been changing since she had become a Chimera. Her whole body was adapting to the introduction of Dragon blood. In the two weeks since she had changed, she'd grown half a finger taller. She slept less and ate less, but had far more energy.

As loath as Arianna would be to hear Florence say it, she did see the benefits of being a Chimera—of being a Dragon. It had become easier to understand why the Philosopher's Box was so sought-after. A perfect Chimera—one that could have all the Dragon organs at once without the magic corrupting their mind, rotting their body, and turning them forsaken? Such a thing would change the world.

But Florence couldn't make such a box. That skill set rested solely with the woman she had called friend and mentor. And now... now Florence didn't know what she was to that talented inventor.

She set the canister into its slot on a stand. Her hands had moved through her thoughts. The distraction made them steady and certain rather than clouded by too much focus weighted on a single task.

Arianna had left without a word. They'd fought, she'd been aloof for about a week, and then vanished beyond the clouds above. Everyone seemed to expect Florence to have some insight as to Arianna's methods, but she had none. She'd never had any. The trappings of the woman's mind were an enigma Florence had never been fit to unravel.

Florence capped the canister with certainty.

She'd not been entirely honest with the Alchemists. She couldn't quite fit her suspicions about Arianna's departure into words, not in a way they'd understand. It was a feeling more than logic. After their last conversation, if all she knew to be true about the woman held fact, then Arianna had left to do what needed to be done. Florence marveled at the notion that it might have been her words that compelled Arianna to do so, but only at night when she waited for sleep.

By day, there was work to do. Arianna was above the clouds with Cvareh, hopefully not killing every Dragon she saw on sight—*that* would be bad for relations with the rebellion. Florence remained on Loom, helping those same rebels whom she now fancied herself part and parcel of.

She reached for her latest modified revolver. It was heavier than the standard issue due to all the gold she'd used. Along the barrel were etched Alchemical runes. Not more than six months ago, those same runes were nothing more than grooves beneath her fingertips. Now, they tingled across her flesh, begging for magic, whispering back to her of the power she'd stored in them. It was an interesting sort of science that had to be felt as much as it was learned.

Florence grabbed her pea coat and slung it over her shoulders, venturing into the heart of the Alchemists' Guild.

It was quiet in the early hours of the morning. Most still slept and the golden elevators were silent. She no longer needed the assistance of another to make the lifts move. With a thought, she reached out to the metal magically, forcing it downward. The gears beneath the platform groaned to life. Their teeth slotted into grooves on the wall, clicking down the length of the tower that served as the heart of the most secretive guild in the world.

She ventured out into the Skeleton Forest, as hazy as the impenetrable layer of clouds above Loom. Ghostly wisps wove around trees and obscured shrubs. Magic singed across the back of her neck, alerting her to all the traps the Alchemists had placed to ward off the deadly Endwig. Florence was careful to avoid them; if the traps were mighty enough to slay one of the haunting creatures, they would no doubt render her to a pulp in seconds.

Just beyond the edge of the traps' territory was where she'd made her range—a decent winding walk from the guild hall. Florence didn't presume her activities had gone unnoticed. Her detonations weren't exactly subtle. But she hadn't expected to find a trike waiting for her.

A man lay out in the seat of the vehicle, his knees draped over the handlebars. His hands were folded behind his head, their obsidian skin nearly blending in with the iron of his hair in the dim light. He wore a loose shirt, barely decent enough to be counted as a dressing for bed, and loose pants that were nearly the same shade of brown as the bronze of his vehicle.

Florence was accustomed now to Derek venturing about in such a lax state of undress, but it had been the cause for much surprise the first early morning they'd worked together.

"I was wondering when you'd show." He beat her to the first word.

"I might have never. I don't come out here every morning." Florence continued onward, narrowing the distance between her and the trike positioned right at the start of her makeshift shooting range.

"You come out here every morning you get up early to finish a canister." He peered at her with one golden eye. It was a dark color, nearly smoldering red. Against the dark ash of his skin, it looked like an ember that remained in wait for the chance to spark fire again.

"I didn't know you paid that much attention to my work." Florence rounded the large tires of the vehicle. On the other side was a long stretch of bare forest. Holes of upturned earth marked the spaces that Florence had used as testing grounds for bombs. A tree wider than four of her rested perpendicular to her line of sight. Countless pockmarks pitted its surface from rounds long past. Whole chunks had been reduced to sawdust along the stretch of trunk. Today, if Florence's round worked as she hoped, there would be another gaping maw in its bark.

"I've paid attention to your work from the first time I saw it."

That wasn't untrue. Derek had always heeded Florence's input. But only when it came to the things that were important to him. She'd been all too eager to help the rebellion however she could, and with her connections in Ter.4's Underground through Will and Helen, and ties in Mercury Town, that meant assisting with getting the Alchemists the necessary supplies the Dragon King had been trying to throttle.

To date, Florence had only very minor successes on that front, and she could tell that it was beginning to grate on the nerves of the powers in the Alchemists' Guild. Florence opened the hinge on her revolver in frustration. No matter how much she explained otherwise, they saw the tattoo on her cheek— the outline of a raven—before listening to her about where her skills lay. She knew nothing about how long it would take to get supplies across the world. She didn't understand the nuances of seafaring. And train schedules made her eyes blur over. The Alchemists needed a true Raven to accomplish what they wanted; Florence could make the right introductions, but she was useless beyond that.

"You're going to break the gun if you keep loading rounds like that." Derek drew in his feet, sitting upward in the seat of the trike.

"Actually, this is an alpha model. The hinges are more durable than the beta versions, cast in high heat steel." Florence held up the gun, inspecting it in the light. "I've also reinforced the locking mechanism and tightened the springs. It's meant to hold up under the strain of active combat, so it can take a bit of abuse from canister loading."

Derek was silent, but she could feel his eyes on her back. There was a certain type of power that came from knowing she had done something to earn stiff-lipped respect. Eventually, she might even get through to him and the rest of them that her value extended far beyond the marking on her cheek.

Let him watch, Florence thought as she pushed small piles of dirt on either side of her feet to assume a wide firing stance. She wanted him to see the fruits of her labor. To respect her ingenuity like she had respected Ari's for years.

Power surged though her arms. It was leeched from her blood like sweat from pores on a hot day. It oozed through her hands and flowed in a perfect channel to the runes along the barrel. It wrapped around the canister like a constricting serpent.

Her finger curled around the trigger. That was always her favorite moment: the half second when her skin first came in contact with the trigger of a gun. It was a surge of power. Judgment encased in metal, welded together with the ability to change the world with the merest twitch of muscle. In that breath, everything else faded away, and Florence felt like the universe hung on her will.

The last rune along the barrel lit up. The charge was too slow, but she could work on that later. Florence took her aim and pulled the trigger.

The gun exploded in her hand with a rain of shrapnel. She tumbled backward, half in surprise and half from force. A clumsy beam of energy shot forward, radiating outward and carving a ditch into the earth underneath the line of its shot.

She hit the ground ungracefully, bringing a hand up to her stinging face. Bits of metal were lodged into her cheek. The pain was ringing in her ears and the exhaustion from her magic working overtime set in, forming bruises along her legs as it tried to heal the cuts on her face.

"You're going to kill yourself," Derek muttered.

Florence hadn't heard him move, but he was now squatted before her. One hand curled around the more intact side of her face. She blinked away the haze as his other hand began to pick out the bits of metal. Even when he wasn't trying to be graceful, his movements held a surgical precision. Her eyes settled on the tattoo on his cheek: two solid black triangles, one pointing up, the other down, connected by a line.

"It wasn't a bad attempt." It was clear his compliment was nothing more than placating. *No, it was a positively miserable attempt.* Embarrassment stung the back of her throat, becoming more potent with the taste of blood.

"Then I never want to see a bad attempt of yours." Derek knew she was lying, his chuckle told her so. But the statement was void of any sting.

Her magic had set her face to knitting at the expense of some burst blood vessels. That was the way of magic. Florence had always known it, but this was the first time she was experiencing it. When magic was overused it turned the organs it lived in—which, in Flor's case, was her blood—brittle and necrotic. If too much magic was used, the body was pushed beyond repair.

She looked with clarity and a heavy sigh on the broken remnants of her revolver. She'd need another, more gold, more chemicals… She wasn't looking forward to another trip to the armory.

"Up with you." Derek took her hands, pulling her to her feet. "Nora wasn't up late last night. She'll be awake soon and wondering where we are."

The man relinquished her fingers and walked back over to the trike. Florence stood in limbo. She felt trapped between the failure of her passions and the weak successes of a duty she'd never wanted.

"Flor?" Derek called from atop the vehicle.

"Coming." She left the remnants of the gun in the dirt. Failure was a missed shot; quitting was never reloading the gun. She was Florence, student of the White Wraith, and she did not quit.

ARIANNA

"Hold on."

Arianna immediately took issue with Cain's tone. "You think I can't figure that out?"

She settled herself on the back of the giant purple flying chicken, hating the feeling of a living creature under her rather than something mechanical. She'd nearly prefer the busted glider over the bird. At least it didn't have a mind of its own that could rebel when she was in the open air.

"Well?" He drew out a long pause at the end of the word, looking over his shoulder.

"You don't think I'm actually going to touch you, do you?" Arianna gripped the back of the saddle with both hands for show. Her legs pressed tightly on either side, stabilizing herself.

"Technically—" His eyes darted down to where her hips were pressed against his backside by virtue of the shape of the seat.

"I don't want to hear it, Dragon." Arianna narrowed her eyes and reached for her dagger. "Cross me and I will cut—"

"Suit yourself." Cain shrugged and snapped the reins.

With a mighty caw, the bird lurched off the ledge. Arianna's stomach was instantly in her throat. She held on with white knuckles and all the determination that came from being keenly aware of how vulnerable she presently was. Arianna had absolutely no control: not of the bird, not of the man before her, not of where he was taking her.

"Where are we going?" She needed to take something back from him, even if it was just knowledge.

"The Xin Manor." Arianna hadn't actually expected him to answer. "The Dono will be on Ruana soon, and we need to try to scrub the stink of Loom off you before he arrives."

"Dragon—" she half snarled.

He jerked the reins and the bird banked hard to the right around the mountain. Arianna's grip slipped and she teetered in the seat. Still her hands didn't seek out the stability of his form. She righted herself, collapsing the muscles in her stomach, compressing those in her back, and weighting herself in the seat.

Cain gave her another quick glance. "You're a stubborn one, aren't you?"

Arianna fantasized about all the ways she could peel his green-blue skin off his bones the second they landed.

"My name is not 'Dragon'." He turned forward again with a self-righteous squaring of his shoulders. "It's Cain Xin'Da Bek."

She rolled her eyes dramatically at his back. "Cvareh told me much the same when we first met."

"That's Cvareh Soh to you, Chimera." She'd struck an obvious nerve as his tone shifted.

"So defensive," Arianna mock-praised over the howling wind. "Cva would be so proud."

Cain gave a sharp whistle and the bird dropped into a free fall. Arianna's shoulder muscles strained from the tension she put them under as she worked to hold onto the saddle rather than giving in to the Dragon. She'd show him that Fenthri were not to be underestimated. That *she* was not to be underestimated.

Just when she thought she'd go deaf from the howling wind, he pulled again, leaning into the curve of the mountain. Arianna learned fast and moved with him. The centrifugal force held her in place.

"Cvareh had to earn his name, as do you." Arianna didn't miss a beat when the bird leveled again.

Cain laughed at the sky. It was different than the way people laughed on Loom. This sound was loud, full-bellied, a half-roar of mirth.

"Twenty gods above, what *are* you?"

Arianna leaned forward, finally placing her hands on him. She wanted him to feel her there. To feel the power in her fingertips, to feel her magic. The smell of earth after rain—the scent of his magic—tingled her nose.

"The White Wraith," she whispered.

Three simple words evoked such shock in the Dragon that she thought his neck might snap from turning to look at her. Arianna curled her mouth into a wide smile, baring her teeth. His golden eyes tried to dissect a lie from her proclamation where there was none.

Good. He'd heard of her.

Cain turned forward rigidly, his whole body tense under her hands. Arianna relaxed away, resting on the saddle once more. She was more dangerous when her palms were free to grip her daggers at will. Not that he expressly knew that, but she'd relish keeping him guessing. Predictability was the death of fear.

The gray stone of the mountain arched beside them, unfurling like a grand banner. And the gem of that banner was what Arianna could only assume to be the Xin manor. She worked to keep her face passive, just in case Cain turned to face her. She had only a glimpse of the mountainside structure during her harrowing flight in. Now, it grew before her, inviting and impossible.

Stone arched and curved, spinning around towers and lacing between walkways. There were stretches of woven masonry that served no other purpose than aesthetics, as they were clearly too thin and brittle to be supports or walkways. Raw crystal or glass had been cut into it, filtering the sunlight into rainbows upon the walls.

The boco banked again, beginning to descend. Numbers upon numbers whirred in Ari's head as she stared at every arch and tower. The calculations kept coming up as impossible, time and again. This structure shouldn't be standing. It should crumble under its own weight, or be toppled by one of the mighty gusts that ripped around the mountainside.

Arianna lived in a world of calculation on Loom. She understood the laws of nature, what could and couldn't be done. But she was no longer on Loom. She was in a land of endless waterfalls, flying bird mounts, inverted mountains, floating islands, and castles of stone that were held aloft in the sky with the same ease as a paper plane in a breeze.

She dismounted with purpose, her legs steady despite her knees having turned to gelatin. She was Arianna, the White Wraith; the hem of her white coat flapped around her calves, and she would walk like the bloody god she was, come to pass judgment on this backward land. As if sensing her mental declaration, the Dragons who were waiting to greet them in the jeweled courtyard they landed within hovered in the shade of an upper galley. They looked uncertainly from her to Cain, begging silently for some kind of explanation for her presence.

Just for effect, Arianna lifted her goggles onto her forehead, showing off her pilfered Dragon eyes like rare and coveted gemstones.

"Cain'Da." A woman was the bravest among them. *No surprise.* She kept her eyes turned downward as she approached, cloth draped over her arm. Arianna watched as the sapphire-skinned woman peeled his fitted riding jacket from his bare chest, holding a coat void of sleeves as an equally pointless alternative.

Arianna folded her hands over her chest. "Can't even dress yourself?"

"Come, Chimera." Cain looked at her sideways.

"Arianna." She didn't budge.

"If I must earn my name, you must earn yours," he snarled, baring his teeth.

Arianna curled her lips in reply. She may not have the fearsome canines of a Dragon, but she knew how to speak their language. One of the servants balked at the sight. Unfortunately, it didn't have the same effect on Cain.

"Do you think you can intimidate me?" He strolled over nonchalantly. "Do you know how many I've killed?"

"Forced to guess, I would estimate the number to be less than not nearly enough to make me scared." A hand curled around the hilt of her dagger. "You've heard of me, so you must know what I do to Dragons."

"And yet here you are, on Nova." Cain motioned to the air around him. He waited for a retort she was loath not to have. He took a step forward, encroaching on her personal space. "That's what I thought. I don't know why you're here, *White Wraith.*" More than one Dragon waiting in the wings visibly tensed. Even in Fennish, her moniker was known to them. "But you're in my home now. And while you are here, you will be an obedient and obliging guest."

He reached for her chin. To do what, Arianna didn't know. But the motion felt sickly condescending following his declaration. She didn't hesitate to draw her dagger. The golden blade was still ringing from its sheath when it sliced into his flesh. Sharp and precise, she cut off the tip of the offending finger before it could touch her.

Every Dragon around them, all five of them, had their claws out in an instant. They lunged from the shadows with snarls and growls, like dogs let off their chains. Cain held up his still bleeding hand, the fingertip already re-growing. The world seemed to hold its breath with his singular command. All except for Arianna's heaving chest.

"I admire the ferocity. But if you turn your blade against me again, I will not stay my talons."

"You can't kill me." She called his bluff. If Cvareh was to be believed, his sister—the head of House Xin—needed Arianna a lot more than she needed them.

At least, that's what she'd let them believe.

The truth was, if Florence's rebellion was to succeed, they needed the Dragons' help as much as the Dragons needed theirs. The rebellion needed Dragon organs, the ability to transport things quickly, fighting power and an established base on Nova. And a certain resource for the Philosopher's Box that Arianna was determined to find in her time on the floating islands.

"I never said anything about *killing* you. You're the White Wraith, aren't you? I'm sure you can use your imagination as to how I would occupy my time instead." He grinned wildly, showing his teeth again. "Now, will you come with me to the baths? Or do I need to drag you there by force?"

Arianna regretted her decision to come to Nova more and more by the second. She was outnumbered tens, hundreds, to one. Individually, the Dragons might fear her, but as a pack they had her trapped like a wounded hare. With all the dignity she could muster, Arianna sheathed her dagger and straightened from a hostile crouch.

"Lead on," she forced through gritted teeth. If she couldn't keep a combative advantage, she'd keep her pride.

They walked into the shade of the gallery and penetrated the castle's innards. Led through back halls and side passages, Arianna did not see another Dragon outside their group. But she could sense them, smell them, feel their magic rippling through the currents of the air. It was loud, like a hundred people speaking all at once. Her senses were constantly flaring with recognition of them, trying to understand and catalog every magical signature. Arianna could only assume that living on Nova brought the Dragons more success at filtering their senses than she was able to muster. She hoped it would prove a learned trait, otherwise the sensation would drive her mad long before she sized up this Petra she had come to meet.

The servants said nothing. They kept their eyes down and their lips pursed. For the most part, they even contained their curious glances. All except for one.

"Why does Cvareh'Ryu bring a Chimera into our home?" the woman from earlier asked Cain in Ryouk.

"The ends justify these means," Cain replied vaguely. He clearly didn't have much more of an explanation himself.

"She smells," the woman whispered, but not quietly enough that Arianna couldn't hear.

"She will be better once she's washed." They continued on as though Arianna was none the wiser to their discourse. She

held her tongue, avoiding speaking in the Dragon's language
and giving up the game.

"All Chimera reek, rotten blood."

"I know, Dawyn'Anh," Cain conceded, as if heartbroken
by the fact that he would have to endure her scent for another
moment longer. "But our Ryu has spoken with the support of
the Oji."

That silenced the woman, though Arianna could still feel her
radiant frustration. The mention of Cvareh put both the likes of
Cain and this Dawyn woman into submission. Arianna failed to
stifle a chuckle, earning a confused look from her companions
that was abandoned when it became apparent she had no intent
of elaborating on the source of her sudden amusement.

The idea of Cvareh scaring anyone into submission was
laughable. She had put the Dragon in his place too many times to
think of him as anything more than... *than*... Arianna paused,
struggling to fill in the blank for an all-too-long second... *than
Cvareh.*

They finally rounded into an airy room—yet another space
constructed upon a foundation of impossibilities. Steam hung
thick in the air, clouding around the aromatic scent of the
wildflowers floating in the wading pool. An entire wall was
made of rippled glass—or some kind of clear quartz, Arianna
had yet to decipher which. She hoped it was the latter, because
the former made her question what exactly the builders had
been thinking using such large panes of glass to stand against
such violent gusts.

One side of the pool was made up of the clear wall, giving
the illusion that the water stopped mid-air. The tile surrounding
it was set in a chevron pattern and glistened with moisture.
A small stool sat out by a bucket full of steaming water and

an array of tools that were either for washing or stripping off skin—she couldn't tell which.

The entire group remained, two Dragons on either side of the door. Cain leaned against her only escape nonchalantly. The woman—Dawyn—approached her.

Arianna took a step away, avoiding her outstretched hands.

"I will help you." She spoke in a rudimentary attempt at Fennish, a thick guttural accent over top.

"Help me with what?" Arianna knew exactly what she was implying. But she'd stall to underscore her sour opinion of the implication.

"Wash."

"I think I've managed well enough on my own so far in life."

Cain sighed. "Stop being so difficult. If we wanted you dead, you would be."

"As if you could kill me." She kept up her facade. The second she showed weakness would be the second they'd have her. Even if she was outnumbered, she wouldn't act it. "I don't particularly want an audience for my bath."

Confusion marred Cain's face.

Rusty cogs. Realization hit her with the grace of a steam engine. Dragons were not known for their modesty. Half of the people staring at her now were in what she considered various states of undress. They truly didn't, and couldn't, understand why she wouldn't want guests during her ablutions.

Arianna had only been naked around two people: Eva and Florence. She had reached a level of comfort with her long-dead lover and still-living student that surpassed propriety and convention.

But this wasn't Loom.

She had ventured above the clouds in pursuit of new opportunities, old truths, and scores still waiting to be settled. Arianna locked eyes with Cain as her hands began unclasping her harness. He didn't even blink as the metal of her winch box and spools hit the tile floor with an echoing clang, chipping one of the ornate tiles. She started on the fastenings of her coat.

He acknowledged the silent challenge, amusement dancing with fascination in the deep gold of his eyes. She would show them all that she could rise to any occasion—on Loom, on Nova, in this world or the next. One by one, the scraps of her clothing fell and the heat of the room dotted her bare ashen skin with beads of moisture.

Cain's eyes never left her face.

YVEUN

The Dragon King oozed displeasure from his very pores. He felt it seeping out of him, simmering hot, elevating the temperature of the room. He was alone, which was an unfamiliar sensation. Leona had been a figure at his side for decades and now it was as though the woman had never existed.

She'd had her faults, as they all did, but her loyalty was only matched by her ferocity. And, for the most part, she could manage to temper the fire that burned under her skin even when her frustrations struggled to get the better of her. It was a fire he'd stoked in all the right ways, until it burned white-hot and only for him. Nurturing Leona's radical worship of him had been the rare duty that was also a delight.

Now, years of work had been lost in what seemed like a blink on his lifeline.

Yveun sheathed and unsheathed his claws, raking them against the wall of the room he'd been pacing like some lowly caged animal.

It was one of his secret habits. The Dono, the sky ruler, the overseer of the land below, chosen one of the Life-bringer, for all his sweeping palaces and grand rooms, preferred the comfort

of a tiny space to think in. A space with only one way out. A
space so confined that just the thought of being trapped within
it set his heart to racing.

In that heightened awareness of his own mortality, he found
clarity. It was as though the stone walls that surrounded him,
marred from years of claws scraped against them, were the only
thing solid enough to contain the torrents of his thoughts. It was
a place where the feeling of lowliness growled for dominance in
his stomach once more, and when he ascended, he returned to
the world like a merciful god.

Leona and Coletta were the only two who knew of his secret
lair. Coletta never came down; she had her spaces, he had his,
and they issued the utmost respect to each other in preserving
those barriers. They were three times as effective because they
maintained that separation, and the world regarded them as a
split entity.

Yveun smiled wide, pure delight filling him at the very
thought of Coletta. He and his mate, moon and sun. They were
two halves that orbited each other and only very rarely touched.

But Leona... She would wait at the top of the narrow stair
that led back into his private chambers. She would grant him
his privacy, and say nothing of the clawing or howling that no
doubt echoed up to her from time to time. She thought herself
mightier for it, for knowing the King's secret. Yet another
suggestion of Coletta's gone well, only to be wasted by Leona
throwing her life away on Loom.

Yveun snarled, his claws straining against his skin as he
gouged them into the wall. *Cvareh Xin.* He thought only Petra
would be able to elicit a raw, emotional response from him.
But it seemed she'd taught her younger brother in much the
same fashion. How that meager slip of a man had bested his

Leona was a mystery. Seeing the Dragon-child emerge from his supposed meditation only proved the point further.

Cvareh was not a laughable specimen, but he was no exemplar of the Dragon form. Not even the will of the twenty gods should be able to sway the cards in his favor in a duel against Leona. Yveun retracted his claws and folded them over his chest, walking faster.

Sybil, Leona's sister, had said that Cvareh had help upon Loom—a Chimera and Fenthri. Yveun had seen Leona turn Fenthri into ribbons and reduce Chimera to no more than sharpening posts for her talons. Logic told him it was highly improbable for such meager prospects to be a threat to his Master Rider.

But logic had run its course, and here he was—less several Riders, and his Leona gone well before he intended her removal. Cvareh was alive and upon Nova once more. No schematics for the Philosopher's Box returned. An Alchemists' guild gone rogue—or going fast. And no answer for any of it.

When the probable had been exhausted, the only explanation that remained was the impossible.

Yveun launched himself forward with wide steps. He needed more information and there was one way he knew how to get it with any measure of certainty: he needed a Dragon on the inside. Fortunately for him, he had just the blue-skinned worm for the job on retainer.

The world materialized beneath his feet as he left his unorthodox sanctuary. He envisioned that nothing existed while he was in that tiny claw-scratched room, that the gods themselves held their breath and halted everything for the sake of his thoughts. When he emerged, the world shone with their magic, pulled back together in a new shape that carved a path for him to progress.

Yveun pushed against the wall at the top of the stair. It gave and he emerged from the passage that closed to form the back of the large hearth that dominated one wall of his chambers. They were a glittering contrast to the dark, rough-hewn passage he'd just been in. A large platform bed stood adorned with silks. Pillows were tasseled with beads cut from jewels. The desk alone had taken three craftsmen four months of non-stop work to carve.

It was a collection of all his favorite things, arranged only for him and the few he deemed worthy to rest their eyes upon it. Yveun was in no mood for it. He wouldn't soil the essence of his room with his present ferocity. He'd return when he could rest knowing that action was being taken.

Waiting for him in the hall was the man-child he'd been forced to choose as his new Master Rider. Yveun did not even lay eyes upon the boy. He was barely twenty. His age made his three beads more impressive, but all Yveun could see was how scarce they were compared to Leona's.

He needed to call a Crimson Court soon and test the mettle of his Riders. A few would fall, and a few unexpected upstarts would distinguish themselves from the pack. Yveun would pluck them from their humble beginnings for a place on the top of Lysip. He could only hope a woman would emerge from the lot as a potential candidate for Master Rider. He had a much easier time manipulating a creature he could leverage sexuality against.

"Finnyr?" he demanded.

"In his quarters, I believe." The Rider endeared himself to his lord by knowing exactly what Yveun sought in nothing more than a word.

Beads clicked softly around Yveun's neck as he walked, holding a decorative plate that bore the symbol of House Rok over his bare chest. The silver contrasted brilliantly with his wine-colored skin. Around his waist was a simple sash, holding in place a draped cloth in both front and back. Otherwise, his physique was apparent, cut muscle rippling ominously with each aggravated stride.

Even the Rider gave him an extra half-step of space. Nervousness flashed across his magic, assuring Yveun that his choices in how to present himself were well founded. He leveraged his sexuality against his female riders, his physical presence against male riders. In both, sheer dominance prevailed.

In the end, Yveun didn't care if his subjects loved or feared him, so long as the emotion was an all-consuming one.

"Dono," a green-skinned man greeted him and stepped to the side. He was a Kin from House Tam, a ward of the Dono's to assure the other House's loyalty to their sovereign. But, just having him on Lysip wasn't enough.

Around the man's neck was a thin gold chain. The tempering on the metal whispered familiarity to Yveun, assuring him that his magic was the only force by which the metal could be controlled. Keeping the most important family members of the two subservient Houses might have been sufficient for some other, less King, but Yveun preferred adorning his wards with nooses he could tighten with a thought.

Above all else was his dominance over Loom and Nova.

The Rok Estate opened up on the north side, spilling over the hillside in wandering arcades that connected smaller chalets. The Dono smiled, inhaling the potent scent of wildflowers and subservience.

This was where his *most loyal* subjects lived. Chosen Kin of Xin and Tam—immediate family to the Oji and Ryu of the Houses. The Dono invited them to the Rok Estate and gave them some of the most lavish accommodations in all of Nova. They ate like kings and slept like brothel masters. They were given honors of state and management of affairs both on Loom and Nova. It was a life that many could only dream of.

And all he asked for in return was their unyielding and unquestioning loyalty.

He strode past his subservient subjects on a mission towards one of the middle homes. Yveun did not even knock before crossing the threshold of a stately one-roomed chalet. Just the man he was looking for stared, startled, from behind a desk that could nearly rival Yveun's in quality. *Nearly* rival.

"Dono." Finnyr stood only to fold at the waist in a low bow. "I was not expecting you this morning."

"Weren't you?" Yveun folded his arms over his chest, widening his stance.

"My lord?" Confusion shone true from Finnyr's face into his magic. He clearly had not consulted the whisperer for House Xin. Or, more likely, Petra hadn't sent any word of the King's venture this morning.

Yveun let the accusations drop. "Finnyr, where do your loyalties lie?"

"My King, they lie where they have always been, with you and House Rok." His brows, the color of tarnished gold, knitted together, drawing lines in his powder blue flesh.

"I have no room for question in this." Yveun crossed the remaining distance to the desk opposite the other man. "The Guilds on Loom still resist me. Those that do not outright have yet to fully embrace the structure which I am attempting to impose upon them—structure that is the only thing standing in the way of the world below being lost to their own devices as they leech off the earth past the breaking point."

"None have understood the gravity of this more than I."

Finnyr was a smart and resourceful man. What he lacked in physical prowess he made up for in mental fortitude. It was the only thing that had kept him alive for the past decade. He was certainly of no other use to his family. Though Yveun had found creative ways to apply his talents.

"I cannot fight battles on two fronts. I cannot give Loom the attention it needs when I am being picked apart from within."

Finnyr paled to nearly the white of a Fenthri. He'd heard all the layered meanings in Yveun's words. They had not been on entirely good terms since the schematics were stolen.

"How may I serve you, Dono? You are our one true King."

"I hope you believe that," Yveun pushed.

"You are everything."

That the Dono believed. Without him, Finnyr would long be dead. And Yveun knew that he held the key to the future Finnyr sought. It was a shameful bargain for a Dragon to make, to seek power and prestige through a means other than sanctioned duels. But Finnyr was a Xin, and the Xin put their ends before the means used to achieve them. They would cut out their own eye and sell it to a Harvester if it benefited their goals, and that was how Yveun had ended up in this predicament to begin with.

"See that I am, Finnyr, and you will have that which you desire someday." The man's eyes were alight at the prospect. Finnyr's very existence rested in Yevun's hands. But the King's future was stacked precariously on the lesser Dragon's shoulders. The brother of Petra'Oji, the man who would inherit House Xin by blood and rank should he somehow best his sister in a duel, or if Petra and Cvareh were suddenly and mysteriously found dead. "For now, I need you to speak with your dear little sister. I need answers."

Finnyr paused. Petra's was one entity that still deflated him with a mention after more than a decade. Shame was a seeping wound and Yveun pressed upon it to get what he wanted.

"What do you want to know?" the Dragon forced through his all-too-dull canines.

"I want to know how Cvareh survived the Riders. I want to know what happened to my schematics." Yveun's claws unsheathed at the mere mention of the drawings that held the most substantial progress made on the Philosopher's box to date. "I want to know what Petra is keeping from me."

"My lord, my sister, she—"

"No excuses and no half measures, Finnyr. You were born in the month of Lord Rok. Show me where your true heart lies." Yveun rested his hands on the desk, his claws raking long lines across its surface as he stepped away. He'd have Finnyr flayed for an hour if he buffed them out of the resin. Yveun wanted them to last as a threat to the man until the whole catastrophe that had been the past three months was behind them. The Dono paused at the door. "Succeed, and I will forgive your prior lapse in judgment in even *mentioning* the schematics to your sister. Fail, and I will not let you live long enough to try again."

Yveun sneered widely, showing off his wicked sharp fangs. He left the man fighting trembles, but felt immensely better himself. There was more to be done, but it was progress for now.

As loathe as he was to see powder blue skin, it had paid off to have the loyalty of Finnyr Xin'Kin To, eldest son of House Xin.

ARIANNA

I t didn't take long for Arianna to grow bored.

The room she'd been thrown into was uselessly lovely. She circled it a few times, staring out the tall windows to try to get her bearings. It was somewhere in the center of the castle's x-axis, on western side, judging by the increasing brightness that streamed through one wall. She guessed she was somewhere in the middle of the y-axis as well.

Through both windows, she could see the curve of the carved stone, other colored glass portals dotting its surface. Those out the west-most facing window were far and the wall was sheer and smoothed. However, her other window was within an alcove of sorts. Relief carvings of sweeping birds across the face of the castle would make easy hand and foot holds, and it was sheltered from the gusts that regularly rattled the other window.

Why there were carvings on the *outside* of a castle, where only a select few with windows could see, escaped her. But seemingly everything about this place served to confound and enrage her, from the decor choices to the very Dragons living among them.

The bed had no less than ten pillows. *Ten.* As in, the number she would have to use two hands to count to. The fireplace burned cheerfully for a race of people who had skin as strong and thick as leather. Shelves were cluttered with all manner of paintings, bobbles, and strange devices that Arianna could not fathom a purpose for.

Cain had first had the audacity to refuse her winch box and daggers, claiming she was now under the protection of House Xin and such things were no longer needed. Arianna had cut a chunk from Dawyn's throat with a straight razor in an effort to get to her effects before Cvareh's "friend" did.

That had been the man's first mistake. His second was when he threatened to burn her clothes due to the "stench of Loom" on them. Arianna had nearly painted the floor of the bath gold with Dragon blood before she finally submitted. She was outnumbered and it was a battle she'd never had a chance of winning, especially naked and needing to avoid every nick or scratch from the Dragons' sharp talons. But her viciousness had forced them into a compromise—her clothing would be washed and boxed and hidden until it was decided what they were "doing with her."

The satisfaction of backing them into a compromise was short-lived as they, in turn, forced her into the most offensive articles of clothing she'd ever worn. They were trying to make a fool of her with the garb, that much was obvious. Two-thirds of the shirt was literally missing and the skirt was utterly impractical. Arianna was a heinous seamstress, but necessity was the mother of invention and she understood the mechanics and principles behind tailoring.

It'd taken her nearly an hour of muttered curses but she'd finally modified some found garments in the room she'd been locked in into something that suited her a little better. Loose trousers belled around her knees, cinched at the waist. Over top, she wore a long tunic dress, split at the bottom much like her White Wraith coat. Just feeling the hem at her calves brought back reassurances in triplicate.

Dressed and harnessed, Arianna opened the window she'd selected, pushing it against the near-constant wind to be open flush against the outer wall. She placed her palms on the sill, leaning over. Nothing stared back up at her, the hazy clouds fogging over the world of Loom below in shifting degrees of opaque. If she didn't know it was there, she wouldn't imagine there could be anything solid beneath that impenetrable line.

But Loom waited. A resistance brewed. And Florence had cast in her lot with those rebels. Meaning Arianna had no choice but to align herself as well.

She stepped up onto the sill, the wind rising to meet her. Taking a deep breath, she grasped the clip of her golden line firmly, charging it with a jolt of magic. It jumped from her fingertips. The cabling spool on her hip whirred, golden line funneled through the gearbox without resistance, propelled by magic. It shot across the narrow chasm between her room and the stonework by the opposite window. The clip looped around the sculpture at Arianna's silent command, magically fastening to itself.

She gave the line a firm tug, feeling the tension through her harness. There was a moment's hesitation, a second where her throat tightened. Her feet shifted against the sill and then, nothing.

Her stomach shot to her throat and her harness tightened reassuringly as she dropped in free fall. Arianna had used her winch box to perform such a maneuver hundreds—thousands—of times, from heights that would mean her death if she miscalculated distance or the security of her line. But this felt different. The vast nothingness that yawned beneath her rose with alarming speed, threatening to consume her like nothing more than an irrelevant speck of sand in the hourglass of time.

She gripped the line tighter, pushing magic into her winch box with almost violent intent. Her descent slowed as she neared the arc of her jump. Ari felt herself rising upward toward the window and toward the security of established hand and foot holds.

Fear was nothing more than staring into the mirror known as death and seeing the reflection of your own transience, a visage far too intense for many to look upon. But, for Arianna, it was nothing more than an instrument in her toolbox. It had a handle worn from years of grabbing for it time and again. Fear was familiar from taking it into her own hands and using it as deftly as if she were the personification of time's judgment upon all mortal men.

Weighted against the wall, she grabbed for one of the two daggers settled at the small of her back. The blunt, thin tip of one fit nicely into the narrow groove of the window. The locks were simple tension latches; nothing more than a twist of the wrist, and mechanical precision Ari possessed from years of practice, was needed to render it useless.

The window swung open, and she helped herself into the quiet hall before shutting the pane behind her. She hadn't known Cain for very long, but she was already savoring the idea of the arrogant Dragon guarding an empty room. Arianna knew she'd be discovered eventually, or would choose to expose herself. But for now, she'd wander this floating castle on her own terms.

Arianna pulled her own magic in tight, winding it like a ball around her core. She silenced its pulse as much as possible, limiting its ability to radiate from her with each breath. The stillness it created was prone to disturbances from other magic, and Arianna avoided any unwanted encounters with relative ease.

For a castle of stone and glass, it was alive with the scents of earth. Notes of moss blended with fresh dirt and the sharp smells of cedar and sandalwood to create a palette that was slowly becoming definable as distinctly "Xin". Twice, she thought she picked up the scent of woodsmoke, and edged toward corners expecting to see Cvareh on the other side. But it was never him, and she was left to label the emotion that charged through her as relief.

It would be an immense inconvenience if Cvareh discovered me now, she insisted. She certainly had no need of the Dragon.

At first, Arianna tried to make notes of the individual Dragon scents, but it quickly became impossible. Every Dragon's aroma seemed unique on Loom purely because there weren't many Dragons. But on Nova, the scents became repetitive and Arianna began to focus, instead, on filtering out all scents but the ones most important to her: woodsmoke and cedar.

No longer concerning herself with logging every Dragon in residence, Arianna shifted her focus to the residence itself. During her schooling in the Rivets guild, she had learned about architecture. It wasn't her forte, but she understood the basic principle as any good Rivet would be able to. With every project, the first thing a designer was taught to look at was the function of the space, followed by allowances for land and materials. The result was a blissful logic across Loom. Everything had a purpose, and the reasoning behind that purpose was simple to see.

She could not see the purpose in half the decisions the architects made here.

Hallways led to nowhere. Rooms materialized in the least logical places she could fathom. Alcoves with what must be months' worth of embellishments on their stonework were tucked away in obscurity. There were switchbacks and odd connections that made it nearly impossible to map the palace in her mind.

After nearly an hour of wandering, Arianna knew the only way she'd be able to find her way back to her room would be to let herself get discovered by one of the wandering occupants. It only made her resentment for the Dragons grow. Of course their way of life would prove as aggravating as their very existence.

She was about to give herself over to the next Dragon she encountered, when the scent of woodsmoke tickled her nose. It sizzled with familiarity she couldn't deny. *Cvareh*. The man was close.

Like a bloodhound, Arianna tracked the essence of magic through narrow corridors and wide thoroughfares alike. Her ears twitched as the scent grew. The familiar tones of his speech, muffled yet from distance, echoed like an invisible whisper tether between them. He had imbibed from her and she from him; there was no place he could hide now where she wouldn't find him, and the fact wasn't nearly as repulsive to her as she thought it should be.

"... She will hand me my army?" an unfamiliar voice echoed from behind the door she'd tracked to.

"For Loom, there is nothing she wouldn't do," Cvareh replied.

Arianna dulled the sharpness of her anger at the idea of Cvareh *correctly* describing the design of her mind to someone else with the curiosity of what else he might say about her. If she knew what he told others about her, she could adjust her actions accordingly when the need to be subversive arose. She stilled her hand over the latch of the wide door, exercising patience.

"Very well," the female voice continued after a long pause. "I will tell this Chimera what she needs to hear."

"Arianna will know if you lie to her."

Laughter erupted at the notion. "Brother, did your time on Loom dull your senses? You think I cannot handle a Chimera?"

Brother. That meant the speaker was certainly his sister— the woman Arianna had come to meet.

"She is of Loom, but do not underestimate her for it. Heed my counsel on this, Petra."

"I fear no Dragon, so I hold no more concern for Chimera or Fenthri. I will sing the song she wishes to hear and she will thank me for it. Then I will have my army."

Arianna rolled her eyes and pushed down the door handle. Loathing seared through her veins and she did little to temper it. She had come up to the Dragon's world, allowed herself to be bare before strangers and treated like a simpleton. She had to draw a line somewhere.

"Your song will fall flat, I fear, since I have heard the truth of its melody," Arianna seethed by means of greeting.

At one end of the wide room, Cvareh sat in surprise on the second level of a dais. Above him was a woman who looked as though her skin was made from the deepest blue ocean waters. Hair the color of Dragon blood spilled from her head in thick tresses. And, instead of shock or anger, she smiled widely, baring her canines.

Arianna replied in kind.

"I was told you had been sequestered." Petra's eyes had a nearly identical color to Cvareh's, but they were similar in no other way. There was a savage edge to their shape, and they regarded her with a ravenous desire to consume every scrap of courage Arianna might even attempt to muster.

Arianna would reveal no seams in the iron walls of her resolve. She was the opposite and equal of this woman. She bent before no man, woman, king, or queen—and most certainly no Dragon. Folding her arms over her chest, Arianna leaned against the door, making no effort to cross the room. Foremost, she wanted to make it clear that she would not approach like some groveling mortal before an idol.

But not having to cross the floor was also appealing.

What builder would ever think it was a good idea to make the floor of a suspended castle from glass? Arianna deeply hoped that the multi-colored design was, in actuality, crystal or stone. Something, anything, stronger than liquefied and hardened sand. But she had her doubts.

"Were you also told that I cut a chunk from one of your servants' necks? Or bit the ear off another?"

"Those details were neglected." Instead of anger, there was a twisted sort of amusement playing between the woman's words.

"Arianna, you should—"

Arianna shot Cvareh a glare.

"Silence, Cvareh," Petra echoed Arianna's sentiment, much to her surprise. "I am told that you have come to *assess* me for our negotiations with Loom's rebellion to proceed."

"That's one way to put it." Arianna relaxed her hands, placing them behind her, ready to grab for her daggers in an instant.

"Cvareh tells me you seek assurances for Loom should I rule. I will gladly give them."

Arianna snorted. Did the woman really think her words would mean anything after what Arianna had just heard? "And what do you think your assurances are worth?"

"The word of an Oji? Very much."

Well, Petra certainly believes her words, Arianna thought silently. She was shaping up to be exactly what Arianna had feared. The Dragon would be another ruler that saw herself seated above the world, who paid little attention to the plights of Loom and cared even less.

Which meant Arianna might need to course-correct. If she wouldn't get anywhere with Petra, she would need to secure a way on her own to get the materials needed for the Philosopher's Box. To give Loom a fighting chance in the power struggle to come. Let the Dragons fight among themselves, kill each other off. If they turned their eyes to Loom, Loom would be ready. There were options before her, still, and she would consider them all for Florence's sake.

"We don't have Oji—" Arianna tried to form the word so carefully it bordered on mocking, "—on Loom. So it means nothing to me, Petra."

The claws shot out from the woman's fingers so fast that Arianna was surprised they didn't launch from her hands. Dragons were predictable. If one didn't give in to their excessive system of titles and decorum, they lost all patience. Arianna would push until she exposed the truth of this woman's nature.

Cvareh was an anomaly among Dragons. As was the fact that Arianna found him tolerable. The fact that, in some impossible way, she truly believed he harbored no ill will toward Loom. But it ended with him. All other Dragons thus far had proved just as she'd expected.

"I must remind you that you are not on Loom any longer, Arianna." The woman continued to smile with murderous intent. She stood, unfurling like a sail, her ego ballooning on her magic to a size that was greater than her physical frame. "You are in my House. You are under my protection. Your presence is a liability to the wellbeing of my family, should you be discovered by the Dragon King. You are alive because I permit it. And for all this, you will call me Petra'Oji."

Arianna shrugged. "I'll call you as I please."

The woman stepped forward. Cvareh rose as well, but made no attempt to impede his sister's progress. Certainly, Petra had told him to stay out of their squabble, and Arianna echoed the sentiment. But the fact that he didn't struggle to resist even the slightest urge to rise to her defense told Arianna everything.

He stood behind his sister, at home on Nova. She stood as a foreigner in a strange land on behalf of a Fenthri girl. No matter how close they'd become on their journey, an impenetrable line was still drawn between them. It had been foolish to think the chasm could ever be crossed.

Arianna drew her dagger. Her other hand hovered over the clip dangling from her winch box. Petra stopped in the middle of the room, the glass floor illuminating her from below as though she stood in the sky itself.

"Sheathe your blade. I have no interest in spilling blood here."

"Certainly fooled me." Arianna didn't oblige the command.

"Cvareh told me of your ferocity. He told me you killed the King's Bitch, which tells me two things, Arianna the Rivet." She held up two clawed fingers. "One, that we are not enemies. Two, that killing you would be a waste. If you are not my enemy and you are a fierce fighter, then it would be a shame to see you die needlessly."

Anger flashed like gunpowder in the priming pan of her emotional arsenal, but it was short lived. For, as frustrating as it was to see, Cvareh's suspicions echoed true. She and Petra seemed to hold something in common, for Arianna had used much the same logic when it came to deeming who was worthy to kill.

"You have yet to prove that you are not my enemy. And you are doing a poor job of endearing yourself to me if you wish an ally." Arianna sheathed her dagger.

Petra smiled. It was an arrogant look, but not sinister. Arianna couldn't shake the condescending feeling of it, however. The Dragon began to walk again, making her way toward a different door.

"My family has been fighting the Dragon King for centuries. A few more days, weeks, months, years, will not hurt me. Time to wait for you to come around is something I have." Petra paused in the open door frame across the room, staring Arianna down for one last long moment. "The real question is, do you?"

Arianna wanted to gouge out the knowing gaze from her eye sockets. The Dragon would live more than six lifetimes of the average Fenthri. Arianna could threaten with the Philosopher's Box all she wanted. But the woman could stall until long after Florence was dead.

Petra hummed softly at Arianna's silence, a purr of victory. "Cvareh, escort our guest back to her chambers before she makes a scene."

Arianna watched the Dragon leave, walking as though she already owned the world.

FLORENCE

I'm telling you I need more." Florence balked at the Revolver who was in charge of the Alchemists' armory. "I'm telling you, you're not getting any." The man was old; Florence guessed he was nearly thirty-eight. His black hair had begun to twist in weird directions, haloing thinly around the crown of his head. It was salted with gray almost the same color as his skin. The dark symbol of the Revolvers tattooed on his cheek sagged. She'd never met a Revo as old as him before. It wasn't usually a profession that boasted particularly long lifespans. Perhaps being assigned far from the guild hall in Dortam had helped spare him from the Revolver's suicidal groupthink.

"Not a day ago I counted that you had at least two barrels of sulfur. I know charcoal isn't hard to come by, and you don't need much graphite…" He was back to ignoring her as she spoke, counting and checking off quantities behind the gated shelves. "Why are you being so stingy with the gunpowder?"

"Because you're wasting it." He didn't even turn.

"I am not wasting it. I'm trying to help you."

The man shot a look over his shoulder that told Florence exactly what he thought of *that* claim. Florence put her hands on her hips, trying not to deflate. Certainly she'd had some failures... a lot of failures. But she was making progress. It was just difficult to explain that progress to anyone who hadn't seen the implosion beam she was trying to recreate based on what the Riders had used to attack the airship she'd ridden on weeks ago.

"You fashion yourself a Revo." He punctuated the statement with a sigh, finally giving her his attention. "But it shows that you have not had proper training."

"I had ample tr—"

"I looked through your notes."

"Y-you went into my laboratory?" Florence stuttered. There was no more sacred place on Loom than the halls of research. It was more private than a bed and more secret than a bath. She would rather parade naked through the guild than think of someone poking through her research.

"I did." He was utterly unapologetic. "I've been letting you leech off our supplies for weeks. I wanted to see the fruits of your labors... or lack thereof."

"My research wouldn't make sense to someone else. My shorthand isn't common."

"You're right on both accounts. It doesn't make sense to someone else because you are chasing rabbits without knowing the first thing of the hunt. And your shorthand is uncommon for a youth like you, but the style was fairly popular twenty years ago."

Florence pursed her lips, taking issue with his tone.

"The Wraith taught you, didn't she?"

"She did," Florence affirmed proudly. Ari had quickly become infamous among the Alchemists. She'd only been there about two weeks before flying to Nova, but in that time she'd worked the Vicar into a fit, claimed to be the creator of the Philosopher's Box—a *real* Philosopher's Box, and produced so many clockwork locks that half the initiates couldn't get into their rooms after they quickly forgot the complexity of Arianna's designs.

"The woman is half monster and half master. I can't deny it," he continued before Florence could correct him in Ari's defense on the former. "But she is a Master *Rivet*. I've no doubt you benefited from her tutelage. You ask the right questions and you've been trained to think beyond what is there to what could be. You are young but you have the foundation of one truly raised on Ter.0." Sadness lined the man's eyes at the mention of the lost continent, a way of life that had been destroyed by the Dragons. "But she is not a Revolver. She cannot teach you the skills of follow-through on those theories. And, to that end, you are lacking."

"Then you teach me."

The man scoffed, brushing away the notion with a wave of his hand. "If I'd wanted a pupil I would've remained near the guild hall chasing my circle. I've not the time, energy, or interest for a student."

"Then give me the gunpowder so I can continue to learn on my own."

"No."

Florence felt like she was stuck in a loop. "How am I supposed to improve?"

"Go back to the Revolvers, have whomever you claim was teaching you—despite your being a marked Raven—continue to do so."

"Even if I could do that..." Florence didn't actually know if she could. Her teachers likely stopped going to their meeting places when she'd stopped showing up. Arianna had been the one to forge those relationships. "I want to help the resistance."

"Then help us, and don't be a leech on our powder."

"I—"

"Go away, girl. There's nothing more to say." The man turned his back on her again.

Florence couldn't help herself; she shot one nasty face at his ugly salted hair before storming out of the armory. The guild continued on around her. Initiates worked on magic, reagents, pharmaceuticals, and a half dozen other things with all the help and support of a guild behind them. Florence was the only one adrift.

She slunk back to her tiny laboratory with her tail between her legs in the hope of licking her wounds in relative peace. She had only about twenty minutes of quiet before her door opened for two Alchemists. Nora and Derek helped themselves into her space, crowding around her table without invitation.

"You weren't at dinner." Derek dropped a plate before her.

"I'm not hungry."

"Do you know how quickly your body will go into starvation mode if you don't eat?" Nora leaned forward, resting her elbows on the table. "The second it does, it starts breaking down your muscle for energy because it's the densest source in your body. It also destroys your ability to process—"

"I get it. I get it." Florence hooked the plate and pulled it toward her. She *was* hungry, she just didn't want to be around people. But it seemed she had an audience despite her efforts. And, if she was going to be miserable either way, she may as well be miserable and full.

"What has you so upset?" Derek asked after she tucked in.

Florence offered them both a quick summary of her encounter with the armory master.

Derek leaned back and folded his arms, listening thoughtfully. Nora hummed and nodded along, picking off the vegetables that were too bland for Florence's taste. The other girl was the first one to speak when Florence finished her tale.

"He has a point."

"As do I." Florence frowned.

"His is more valid," Nora insisted. "You haven't done much here."

"I'm working on making long-term change."

"At least by blowing up trees in the forest," Derek added dryly, earning him a sharp look. He remained unapologetic. "You two go through reagents like water. And I've seen how quickly chemicals disappear when you're working on something new."

"But we're Alchemists. This is our home, our guild," Nora reminded her, as though she could've somehow forgotten. "It isn't the place for you to run your... whatever tests you run. You should go home for that."

Florence rolled a canister across the desk as Nora spoke. If she hit it too hard it would blow up the three of them. Though she neglected to mention that fact about the "tests" she ran. "I thought the resistance believed in the old ways of Loom? The notion that men and women should choose to study what they please. That there's more to be learned from working together than apart?"

"We do. But if our resistance falls, it doesn't matter what we believe."

Florence bristled at the implication: the idea that she would do something to contribute to the fall of the resistance, rather than its success. She kept her face emotionless as Ari would have. Or tried to.

"Why don't you just focus on something that will actually help us? Like trying to pin down those friends of yours who can get guns and clockwork through Ter.4?" No matter how many times Florence reminded her, Nora never seemed to fully grasp that she wasn't a Raven at heart despite what was on her cheek. And that getting in touch with Helen and Will was harder than turning steel into gold for someone who didn't understand all the tunnels and transport systems.

"I am trying to actually help you." Florence's plate was empty and she greatly missed the forced breaks in the conversation that came from eating. "But I need more gold and more explosives to do that."

"And I'm telling you that you're not going to be getting any more."

"Have you tried speaking with the Vicar about these matters?" Derek stopped Florence mid-breath. Which was likely for the best, as her patience with Nora was running thin.

"No… Do you think I should?" Florence hadn't properly been in a guild for nearly three years. Additionally, she'd just been an initiate in the Ravens and it had been made clear to her then that appealing to the higher powers simply wasn't done. The Vicar Raven always had the Dragon adviser at his side, and Florence had always heard he was strict about adhering to certain expectations about hierarchy.

But Florence had never seen a Dragon in the Alchemists' Guild, not counting Cvareh or corpses.

"You could try pleading your case." Derek shrugged.

Florence regarded him skeptically, wondering if he was trying to get her into a worse spot by bringing up her losses with the Vicar.

"Or don't." He stood. "It's your choice. But your options seem to be growing thinner."

Derek held out a hand to Nora, which she took. He helped her to her feet, lacing his fingers against hers. The two left Florence alone to her thoughts.

She knew better than to pick up any of her remaining chemicals or powders. When her mind was so wild, she'd only produce greater mistakes. That stress had certainly not been helpful over the past few weeks, when her failures were the only thing keeping her ledgers company.

Florence flipped through her notes, wondering what the Revolver had seen in them. He was a journeyman of the Revos, his tattoo completely filled. He had years of practice ahead of her, and was willing to impart none of it.

She snapped the book shut.

Loom was like a mirror that had been cracked by the Dragons' first descent. Spider-web fractures stretched across its surface, turning a single image into smaller pieces. They were all parts of one whole that fit together, but no longer joined cleanly at the seams. For one dark moment, she wondered if it was a wound that could ever be healed. By what magic could Loom be put back together into a single, flawless piece?

And then Florence made her way to the Vicar Alchemist. She wasn't one to sit in place contentedly. Ari had taught her better than that. Even now, from above the clouds, the woman known as the White Wraith challenged Florence to be better, do more.

She received a few curious stares as she boarded the elevator that went directly to the Vicar's laboratory, but no one stopped her. It seemed to be an accepted practice in the Alchemists that there were times when one needed to speak to the Vicar. At least, that was what Florence hoped. If not, everyone was about to have a good laugh at her expense.

"Enter," a voice called from behind a door emblazoned with the symbol of the Master Alchemist, following Florence's knock.

Florence entered, her heart in her throat. Sophie, the Vicar Alchemist, straightened away from her work table. She pulled the refined goggles off her eyes to get a better look at her visitor.

"I wasn't expecting a little crow."

"Little bullet would be more appropriate," Florence corrected tiredly. Sophie arched her eyebrows in surprise and Florence added, carefully, "Just a suggestion..."

"We'll settle on Florence." Sophie smiled thinly. "Why has Arianna's student come to visit me this day?"

Florence scraped together every rogue bit of boldness before speaking. "I need your backing on some experiments I'm running."

"My backing?"

"Yes, as the Vicar. I'm working on some things to help the rebellion but I need more gold and more gunpowder, at the very least. I've been refused."

"I know." Sophie continued to smile and, in that moment, reminded Florence of King Louie. There was nothing physically similar between the capable looking Vicar and the bony man of Mercury Town. But their eyes, their mannerisms, suddenly overlapped so strongly it set off warning bells between Florence's ears.

"Then you should know exactly why I'm here." If Sophie was like Louie, then Florence would treat her as she would the little king of Mercury Town. The only difference was that she no longer had a White Wraith nearby to keep her safe.

"We're skipping the small talk then? Excellent." Sophie's mannerisms shifted and she returned to managing some bubbling beakers on her table. "Your answer is no."

"Vicar, I need—"

"Whatever you need pales in comparison to the needs of my Guild and this rebellion I'm trying to build."

"I want to help the rebellion."

"Then actually help us." Sophie gave her a challenging stare.

Florence knew that look. It was so similar to the ones Arianna had given her, it was eerie. It reminded Florence, yet again, how little she knew of Arianna's history.

"Let's cut a deal." Part Ari, part Louie, Florence knew how to navigate this personality. "You know better than anyone the needs of guild and rebellion. You know what I need and what I can do. Tell me how I can help you."

"And in return you want access to your resources."

"Naturally."

"Very well." The conversation picked up speed like a locomotive down the tracks. "You want more gold? Go and fetch it yourself."

"Where is the nearest refinery?" Florence didn't know the first thing about stealing, but she'd figure it out if she had to. It's what Arianna would've done.

"Ter.1."

"Ter.5 has no refineries?" Florence balked.

"The Dragon King didn't want us to have such easy access to gold or reagents." They both took a silent moment to curse the King's pragmatism. "We have an allotment that comes along the main tracks through the Skeleton Forest. But it's not enough."

"So you need another shipment."

"One outside of Dragon sanction," Sophie affirmed. "There's another route, but it's never used. It was shut down for winding too deep into the forest and too close to endwig haunts."

"I'm not a Raven." Florence was ready to tattoo the words on her opposite cheek.

"I have secured a Raven to run the engine. I have Alchemists to speak on my behalf. I have a Rivet to ensure things run smoothly along the way."

Florence knew where she was headed before Sophie even finished.

"I do not have a spare Revolver to fight off any who might seek to sabotage the mission. It is not called the Skeleton Forest for nothing. I would not like to see this costly excursion reduced to bones in the woods."

It was neat, tidy, and convenient. Sophie won either way. If Florence succeeded, the Vicar would have more resources and a goal accomplished. Giving Florence a little gold in return was nothing in the wake of that particular victory. If Florence failed, she would be one of those corpses, reduced to nothing more than bones licked clean by the Endwig.

"Do you think I can do it?" Florence was compelled to ask.

"Of course," Sophie praised brightly. "After all, you're the multi-talented Raven, not Raven but Revolver."

Florence took a deep breath and gave Sophie the benefit of the doubt. Florence's failure would mean the death of her Alchemists. It made no sense for her to be hopeful for it or indifferent to it.

"Then I'll do it."

"Wonderful. Plan to leave within the fortnight. I'll spread the word that you're to have everything you need to prepare."

Finally, a gear turned smoothly for Florence. "Thank you."

"Oh, and Florence," Sophie stopped her just as she was about to depart. "I think it goes without saying that this is quite a dangerous mission."

Florence knew that, but she nodded anyway.

"Should you fail, it will mean your death."

There was the whisper of a threat ghosting around Sophie's words, a certainty that couldn't be known unless a promise was being given. Florence kept her suspicion to herself, not wanting to unreasonably accuse the Vicar Alchemist of telling her outright that her options were to die on the mission, or die upon her unsuccessful return. Florence searched Sophie's eyes for something more, something else. But there was nothing beyond careful calculation glittering in their depths.

ARIANNA

rianna wished she had Florence's penchant for explosives. If she did, she would've long since slipped a small disk bomb into Cain's pocket. For one, she liked the man about as much as she enjoyed chewing on rusty nails. But more than that, she couldn't stand the monotony their days had fallen into. It was a very Revolver notion for her, but stripped screws, she'd blow it all halfway to Ter.5 just to see something happen.

Breakfast came promptly with the dawn. Cain hand delivered it, seemingly the only one authorized to interact with her on a personal basis. The first few mornings he nearly scared her into a rage at the sound of someone entering her room. The next few mornings, she began to sleep through his arrival, offering no thank you nor note of his efforts on her behalf. The forced lack of appreciation became more normal with each passing day until sleeping through his coming and going became natural.

Ari still stirred at the sound of someone entering her space. Her hand closed around the hilt of her dagger that she kept under her pillow on instinct. But ritual won out the second the familiar scent of wet earth filled her nose, and she relaxed.

Cain never did anything that would warrant her drawing her weapon.

Around lunch, he would come to her and weave a tight illusion over her that shifted her appearance into the colors and more extreme angles of Dragon skin and bone. Arianna would stare at her brightly colored form in the windows and mirrors of the Xin manor as she explored with Cain in tow. It was an unnatural shade layered atop her, a weightless shroud that was nearly suffocating to all that she was.

But it was the only way she could escape her room. Cvareh had made Petra's will clear the last time he'd delivered her back after her second escape; Arianna's wandering would not be tolerated, given the secret nature of her presence. And, as much as she wanted to delight in putting the Dragons in their places, the truth was she had no ground to stand on for the matter. If Arianna fought, she would only make it so far before being violently subdued.

The foolishness of her impulsive decision to come to Nova weighed on her more with every passing hour, crushing her with each day. She had no route back to Loom. She knew little of the Dragon's society and couldn't even navigate without causing a fuss for no other reason than the shade of her skin. Escape on her own wasn't enough; she wouldn't leave after spending this long on Nova without some kind of success, and if she was to accomplish anything she needed to regain some of her sovereignty.

Arianna vowed to do just that nearly a month into her virtual imprisonment.

"Take me to Cvareh," she demanded of Cain, awake with the dawn to greet him.

The man stared at her for a long moment, then continued his morning rituals as if she hadn't woken at all. Arianna stood. She would not be ignored.

"I wish to speak to Cvareh."

"And if the Ryu wished to speak to you, do you not think he would've come to do so himself?" Cain stared at her from the opposite side of the small table in the center of her room.

Arianna laughed. That Dragon rank and file nonsense wasn't about to work on her. She was born of Loom, and she didn't kneel before any man or woman simply because they wished her to.

"He doesn't know I seek him."

"Then I shall deliver your message."

"I don't trust you," Arianna snapped back. For a retort that required such little thought, it stilled Cain by a satisfying margin.

"I am a Xin'Da, I would never—"

"That means nothing to me." She rolled her eyes with a dramatic sigh, sitting heavily on the bed. "All that matters to me is action."

"Action?" Cain tapped his fingertips on the table, claws sheathed. "And what have my actions done to earn your mistrust? I have gone out of my way for you. I have attended to you daily. Were it not for my magic, you would be trapped within this room in perpetuity."

Arianna scowled viciously, as if to scare away the truth.

"Do you think I do it because I enjoy being around you?" he scoffed. "Quite the opposite, I assure you."

She stared at his hands as they thrummed against the tabletop, her mind made up. "Very well, Cain. If you will not take me to him, bring Cvareh to me."

He snorted, crossing over to her. The Dragon stared down his nose at her with his molten gold eyes. Arianna met them fearlessly. Cain cocked his head to the side.

"Why are you here, White Wraith?"

She rose to her feet, drawing her full height, but the crown of her head only came up to his mouth. Nevertheless, Arianna stood as though she was eye to eye with the Dragon. She would not be made to feel small. She would not be relegated to the space he deemed her worthy of.

"Does it bother you, not knowing why you're ordered to attend to me day after day?" She could only assume he was under orders to oversee her. "The great Cain Xin'Da Bek, reduced to nannying a Chimera. To bringing her food and tending to her needs."

Arianna knew just what places to prod. She knew enough of Dragon society to be offensive when it suited her. Cain narrowed his eyes.

"Now, bring me Cvareh."

Cain moved and Arianna fell backward. His hand grasped for the empty air where her face had just been. She collapsed onto the bed, one hand on the hilt of her dagger. The pillow burst in an explosion of feathers as her dagger tore through it; they floated through the air between them as he landed atop her. One hand supported him above her, the other reached for her face again.

Her dagger rose against his palm, gold dripping onto her shoulder where it bit into his flesh. Arianna scowled. Cain snarled in reply.

"You think you can order me, *Fen*?"

"I do," she sneered in kind at the slur for her people. "Because if you could kill me, you would've already."

He pressed his hand forward, the dagger meeting bone. Arianna's muscles strained against the force, keeping it at bay. Blood fell atop her like raindrops, smelling sharply of the fresh scent of wet earth.

"Why are you here?" he repeated. "Why have you ventured to my home? Why do you insult my Oji and still walk? How do you make demands of my Ryu as though he breathes for you alone?"

There was the root of it.

"Bring me Cvareh," she demanded again, quietly. So quiet that his dripping blood against her shoulder was louder with each dull *splat*.

Cain snarled once more, then pushed away. Arianna pushed back, giving him purchase against her dagger and digging it deeper into his flesh. She laced the slash with magic, stinting his healing and slowing the knitting of his skin. The Dragon looked at it curiously.

"You act as though you are truly a Wraith—mighty and untouchable." He clenched his fingers into a fist, blood oozing between them. "But I have seen your flesh." The words stung, reminding her of the impropriety she'd endured before him. "I know under the armor of words and talons of sharpened gold, you are no more immortal than I."

He left quickly, denying her the possibility of a retort. Arianna was set to pacing, her mind racing. It spun like clockwork assembled around every possibility, tooling for every outcome. At the core of the gearbox of her mind, Florence remained.

Arianna crossed over to the window, staring at the clouds below her. Not for the first time, she wondered how her apprentice fared. She'd sought redemption in Florence's eyes, but in doing so had left the girl alone with the one woman whom Arianna had nothing but bitter feelings toward.

Lost in the labyrinth of her mind, Arianna was startled when she heard the door open once more. She half expected to be faced with Cain and some excuse of why she wasn't good enough for his Ryu's time. But the man she sought closed the stately portal behind him.

Cvareh regarded her warily. *As he should*, Arianna seethed quietly. They had not spoken since he last condemned her to the proverbial prison she had been trapped within for the past few weeks. He hadn't so much as sought after her once as far as she knew.

But would she have wanted him to? She owed him nothing, and he owed her nothing but the yet unrequited boon. That was hardly anything significant to pull them together outside of a magical transaction. And yet, she couldn't deny a hurt sort of yearning for it.

"It's good to see you." He startled her by speaking first.

"If that were truly the case, you would've looked in on me sooner." Arianna rolled her eyes, dismissing the sentiment.

"Well, you're not exactly the most approachable woman in the manor." He sat at one of the chairs by her table, glancing at the cooling food. "Is it not to your liking?"

"Nothing is to my liking." She narrowed the distance between them. But the advance felt nothing like it had with Cain. There was a different sort of tension between her and Cvareh, a sort of ebb and flow they both could acknowledge but had been strung along in the current despite. He made her quiver with tension. His presence elicited a physical response as her breath held and muscles tensed. But, unlike her body's response to Cain, it was not her dagger that her hands wanted to reach for. She felt *safe* around this Dragon. It was a welcome sensation that seemed to be magnified by how long it had been since she had last seen him. "I am trapped within these walls, a prisoner of your sister's. But she does not seek me out either. I will not hand the Philosopher's Box to her in a fit of boredom."

"I had never thought otherwise."

"Does she?" Cvareh's silence told Arianna everything. She pulled the chair opposite him around the table to sit before him. Arianna folded her hands, resting her elbows on her knees. "Cvareh, you know that will not work with me."

"I've advised Petra thusly."

"And yet your words haven't worked." Arianna shook her head. This is why she didn't depend on other people to get the job done. "I want to return to Loom."

"What?" Cvareh drew back, his magic fluctuating. "Petra would never allow it."

"I'll find a way out or I'll jump to my death and take the knowledge of the box with me."

"You wouldn't."

"Do you want to test me?" Arianna grinned faintly at the notion. The man clearly thought she placed more value on her own life than she did. She leaned back with a sigh. "Or, perhaps, I'll wish for you to do it."

"That's not what you want the boon for."

"You know nothing about me," she cautioned.

"I know more than you think."

Arianna wanted to refuse him. She wanted to shut him out violently and without remorse. But the door had been opened too wide between them. His mouth on hers ghosted upon her lips, reminding her of the un-crossable lines they'd traversed together. Lines that she might dare walk again if she had the chance. Arianna focused on the curve of his mouth for too long a moment.

She wouldn't let herself give into frivolous distractions. "Here are your options: Tell Petra that I seek passage home without hindrance."

"Or?"

"Or, I demand a pair of hands."

Cvareh's brows knitted in confusion only to untangle with shock when he realized what she was asking. He sputtered, trying to build momentum behind his words. "That's something that isn't done. I can't just—"

"Those are the options, Cvareh. Either would give me my freedom, and therefore her trust in my future actions." Arianna stood and turned her back to him. "If Petra seeks my acquiescence, she must treat me like an equal. Or at the very least, a worthy opponent."

PETRA

There has been another contact from Finnyr'Kin,
Oji." A weathered, ancient woman reported from the
side of the room where Petra dressed in her riding
leathers.

"And does my brother have anything worthwhile for me?"

"He seeks to return home." The whisperer had the sense to
pass no judgment on the message she'd received, merely report
the facts.

Petra waved the slaves away and busied her hands with
buttoning up her knee-length riding trousers with a heavy
sigh. Finnyr had gotten it in his mind that he needed to return.
She had no doubt it was in some way Yveun's influence; her
brother wasn't known for having his own thoughts. Either the
Dragon King had made Finnyr's life torturous as a result of
Petra's actions against him, or he had ordered Finnyr to seek
information on the truth of Cvareh's supposed prayers to Lord
Xin.

Either way, it made no sense for Petra to let her brother
back into her home. Finnyr would be put in a harder position
to feed lies to the Dragon King if he were here. At the Rok estate
he could continue to collect information for her on the King's

scheming, even if it was an intolerable place for him to be.

"Tell Finnyr he has more to offer House Xin by continuing to express his loyalty to our Dono." The words were sickly false. But the whisperer wouldn't betray that to anyone. It was one of the sacred rites of becoming a House whisperer: no secrets were repeated and all messages were verbatim. All Dragons respected this as much as they respected the other innate laws of their world.

"As you command, Oji." The whisperer gave her a low bow.

"And, Shawin," Petra stopped the woman in the door frame. "Also tell Finnyr that when I do see him again, I am looking forward to tales of all his time at House Rok."

"Of course." The woman departed.

When it came to matters of House, Petra felt as though she were trapped on a stationary wheel that spun and spun without progress, no matter how hard she pushed ahead. Finnyr was as useless as he'd always been, offering little more to her than his position as a pawn in the Rok estate that freed up Cvareh to remain at her side. Cvareh had returned, but his help was relegated to the shadows as it had always been. He was worth too much to her to risk parading his strengths before any member of the Crimson Court.

And then there was the Chimera.

Cvareh had reminded Petra time and again that threatening the woman would be of little use. But every moment lost due to her stubbornness was another that scraped away at Petra's patience—and she wasn't known for an excess of that to begin with. Petra kept enough of her head to recognize that losing it over the woman's antics would be akin to defeat. She chose to focus on the things she had direct control over, instead, and today those matters were hidden on the far side of Ruana.

She fastened a tight circle of leather around her bosom, draping emerald strips of fabric over her shoulders and fastening them to cuffs at her wrists. The cuffs appeared to be leather on the outside, but their inners were gold, enough to support a corona should she need it. She'd had to leverage the defense four times in her life, and she was not afraid to welcome a fifth if the world so designed.

Men and women stepped aside as she strode through her manor in the waking dawn. Servants, slaves, Anh, and nameless—those for whom Petra didn't even need to spare a sideways glance. On occasion, a Da was about, and Petra would give their bow a small nod of her head. Otherwise, she gave them no heed.

She loved her house like a wolf loved its pups. But she did them no favors by coddling them or tempering her demands. The world would burn under her heels if her designs saw the light of day. Only a strong House would able to rise from its ashes. If she failed to set the example, they were all destined for death.

Raku milled about in a high courtyard. He cooed the moment his giant eyes caught sight of her and Petra smiled in reply to her trusty steed. He was saddled at her request, her favorite oxblood colored seat. Petra wasted no time, mounted, and took to the skies.

Ruana shrunk beneath her, smaller and smaller with each flap of Raku's wide wings. The Temple of Lord Xin rose from the mountainside, shading the farmlands below. The cities and towns speckled the countryside like gemstones in a mine only to cluster together in determination against nature to create cities and centers of art and culture. They were children of earth and sky, birthed from sunlight fractured into a thousand shining colors.

From this vantage, Petra could see all that she fought for. Her home, her father's home, her father's father's home, and all the way back hundreds of years to the great fall of House Xin to House Rok. This was the land where the Dono was meant to sit. And she would see the mantle returned.

Banking across cliff faces and weaving over treetops, Petra made her way around the mountains that curved across the back of the Isle of Ruana. Nearly opposite the Xin estate, tucked behind imposing sheer mountain peaks, was a series of work houses situated atop a slowly blossoming network of mines. From the air, it was easy to mistake as nothing more than a snowy, barren valley. The smokestacks had been carefully tunneled through the mountain itself, hiding the real work of Ruana's first refinery.

Petra tugged on Raku's feathers, clicking a command with her tongue and teeth. The beast curved through the sky, spiraling downward. He landed nimbly on a narrow ledge, well trained to seek the safest footing.

She swung down from the saddle, her long toes curling through the thick snow and seeking purchase against the frozen rock beneath. The wind was icy and bit with savage numbness into her skin. Every pinprick made her feel alive.

She waved her hand at Raku, and the boco took to the skies. He would hunt, or roost, or mate—whatever satisfied his wild nature that morning. Petra allowed the beast to indulge his whims as long as he always responded to the shrill whistle that demanded his presence once more. He was one of the few beasts in the wide world who had yet to fail her.

"Oji," a man greeted her from the shade of a sheltered window. "It is a pleasure to have you in our presence."

"You flatter me, Poiris'Kin." Petra jumped down into the hall where he stood. Despite having no glass or shutters, it was so warm that the snow melted on the windowsill.

"Never flattery, merely truth." The Kin walked forward, knowing why she was there without an explanation. "We are making good progress. Spinning iron to steel is becoming a simpler task by the day."

"The help you demanded?"

"Has been invaluable."

Poiris was a smart man, enough so that Petra had placed him in charge of one of the most important tasks involved in laying the foundation of her new world order. He was leading the charge in assembling the refineries she needed to produce House Xin's own gold. Doing so would free the House from under Rok's thumb. He who controlled the gold, controlled Nova. Once House Xin had their own refineries working, they would no longer need to depend on small allotments or what limited back-winds trading could be done with Loom.

Of course, it wouldn't be enough. Not even close. Petra still needed Loom and the depths of their mines, the extensive capacity of their refineries, the efficiency with which the Fenthri operated. But even small steps were progress. Change did not happen overnight, birthed from plots of wishes. It grew from the grit of sacrifice and blood.

"Have they presented any problem?" Petra asked.

"Quite the opposite." She gave him a look that demanded elaboration. "They tell me we treat them much better than House Rok."

"So even Fen have sense." Wicked satisfaction pulled on Petra's cheeks, drawing her lips taut in a satisfied smirk.

"More than we give them credit for, on the whole," Poiris affirmed.

"Don't go too far." Petra couldn't help but think of the woman Cvareh had brought home. She fashioned herself as clever, but all Petra had seen was a child. She had been too easy to break, sitting quietly in her room, only walking the courses that Petra had designed for her to be led along. She had expected more from New Dortam's infamous White Wraith. "Show me your product."

Poiris led her inward to a great room of whirring mechanisms and molten metal. Petra surveyed it like some fire god. She didn't understand the first thing about how it worked, but she commanded it nonetheless. Chimera stood in the corners, sweat dripping off their faces, as they spoke to Dragons who walked unfazed through the overbearing heat. Giant buckets poured liquid iron into other containers.

"We have the air lance situated to remove impurities in the iron." Poiris pointed overhead to a long tube. "But we are yet working on the reagent lance." He shifted her attention down to the bottom floor far below, where a similar golden tube was being fashioned by a number of laborers.

"You are slowed by gold," Petra observed.

"We believe with what we can attain, we should have it finished within the next six months."

Slower than she wanted, but nothing could be done. A solution was offered and her men were hard at work. She could demand nothing more from them. When a boco was flapping its wings with all its might, it served little to push it harder. That was how riders got thrown from their saddles.

I have time, she reminded herself. There were decades of history behind her. She would not sacrifice all her work in haste. At the least, she delighted in the knowledge that she was quietly siphoning off gold and resources for the refineries she claimed to be assisting Rok in building.

"Show me."

Poiris led her back into the hall from the observation deck and they wound down through the refinery's innards. It was simple, rough, and raw compared to the luxury of the Xin manor. But there was no time to fit it with things of beauty. She allowed those living here to bring their own artistic sensibilities to bear, and fashion furniture as they could without raising suspicion, but could do no more for them. It was a pitiable existence, but it had to do. Somehow, the Chimera didn't seem to mind in the slightest.

They had almost reached the ground when a Dragon, unknown to her, came bounding down the stairs behind them. Petra turned with fluid grace, her claws tensing on instinct but not unsheathing.

"Oji, the Ryu has arrived," the man reported.

Petra glanced between the messenger and Poiris.

"You may use my office," the Kin offered.

"See him there," Petra ordered the other Dragon. "Lead on, Poiris'Kin."

They traversed upward on a secondary set of stairs to a homely office. Poiris was notorious for favoring practicality over fashion, but nothing betrayed him more than his working space. It was humble for a Kin and reminded Petra that she had risen him from an Anh. After his work at the refinery was finished, she'd see him situated in a lavish room in the Xin manor. No more rough fur carpets, no more worn desks; Poiris would have the trimmings yielded by the gold he helped create.

"Thank you." Petra gave Poiris a pointed nod as Cvareh was ushered in, and the two were promptly left in peace. Petra placed her hands on her hips expectantly.

"Arianna has some demands." Uncertainty dulled the scent of Cvareh's magic.

Petra did not ease her expectations for Cvareh. Out of everyone, he, as her Ryu, needed to be fearless before her. "Tell me."

"She is restless."

Petra snorted. "I am not made to amuse her."

"She wants to return to Loom."

"Unacceptable." Petra wouldn't even entertain the thought. She had the crafter of the Philosopher's Box. She would do whatever she must to gain the information of its machinations.

"I had a feeling you would say that." Cvareh sighed heavily, running his hand through his blood orange hair. Petra watched it fall over his face time and again as he repeated the motion.

"So you have an alternate solution?" He wouldn't have come to her if he didn't.

"She wants to return to Loom... Or have hands."

Petra considered this for a long moment. "She wants to make her own illusions."

Cvareh nodded.

"Can she sustain the additional magic without becoming forsaken?" Petra knew of the plagues that would set in on Fenthri bodies pushed too far with Dragon magic. She would not be responsible for the woman's death. At least not prematurely.

"I don't think she would've asked if she couldn't." Cvareh was certain in Arianna's self-awareness, Petra noted with amusement. "She wants a shade similar to her skin, light blue, steel blue..."

"A shame you cannot make illusions," Petra stole his thoughts and gave them sound. Another note was made when she realized that Cvareh was truly disappointed. *Her brother would've given the woman his hands.* Cvareh was loyal to their House above all else, of that Petra had no doubt, but no Dragon savored the notion of cutting off their body parts for Fenthri gain. They should loathe it. The fact that Cvareh not only seemed willing, but gleaned some sort of delight at the idea of pleasing her was worthy of note in the slowly evolving dynamic of their relationship.

"No matter, she will have the hands she needs."

"Truly?" Cvareh was shocked.

"Yes, truly. I gain more by appeasing the woman, and a set of hands means little to me." Petra started for the door. Progress churned within her, the feeling of a great wheel beginning to spin forward once more. Yes, this was the White Wraith she'd been expecting. She'd give the woman free reign, she'd give her space to challenge the narrow parameters Petra had put her in—if she dared, and she'd see if the gray Chimera was made of steel or steam. "Fortunately for me, I have two brothers."

Petra grinned to herself. Finnyr had been so eager as of late to help their House. Well, now she really needed him to give a hand... or two.

ARIANNA

"Which one do you like the best?" She nearly startled Cain out of his skin when she spoke. He stared at her as though her illusion had melted away like ice in the sunlight of a summer's day. "You always pause here. Which do you like best?"

"The one on the far left is Lord Xin." He motioned to the painting of a veiled figure wielding a sword.

"That's not what I asked." It didn't matter which one he liked or why. But time had whittled away at her. Time, and silence, and more time. It persisted, encasing her mind insistently and eroding her resolve to hate Cain. She was stuck with him and he with her, for the foreseeable future. They may as well put aside the determination to be at each other's throats.

He seemed to have arrived at much the same conclusion over the past week.

Cvareh had proved himself worthless, and a Dragon to the core. He'd not returned with hands nor a glider to bring her back to Loom. Arianna shouldn't have expected differently. So she waited, and bided her time carefully.

"Isn't it though? I am of House Xin."

"And that dictates your favorite will always be Xin?" Arianna asked incredulously.

"Would it not?"

Arianna laughed and shook her head. "You Dragons accuse Loom of being mechanical, but you are nothing more than automatons competing for the distinction of being most suicidally loyal."

"Gird your tongue." His jabs had been slowly losing their edge with each passing week.

"Cain, we both know we're at a stalemate. You'll do nothing to me because you can't—I'm too precious to your House. I'll do nothing to you because, even if I could take you down, I'd never get out of here alive." She gave him an opening to refute the claim, which he didn't, because he couldn't. "Drop the bravado already. I'm not questioning your loyalty. I'm merely asking for your opinion."

He looked back at the paintings with new consideration.

"The one of Lord Xin is magnificent. It truly is... However, I find the one of Lord Pak calls to me more."

"Lord Pak?" Arianna studied the painting to the right of the veiled god. It was done entirely in grays. If she tilted her head to the side, she could perhaps make out a face, not quite Fenthri, not quite Dragon. It was familiar and unknown, a depth that threatened to embrace but never relinquish.

"The Dark-wielder," Cain clarified. "I was born under his month."

Before the clouds had been breached, Loom had no concept of sun or moon. The idea that a glowing orb of light floated across the sky was still unnerving to Arianna each morning she rose to look upon it. The large moon was no better in its pale and contrasting glow.

Beneath the clouds, the light was muted, diffused. Once in a rare while the clouds thinned enough to betray a potentially circular source of light, but what it was had every Guild guessing for hundreds of years. That said, Loom still knew of the moon's cycles. There were periods of bright nights and periods of dark nights. Arianna remembered the first time she'd looked upon sketches of the moon's phases, thinking about the inexplicable sense it made for some sort of hanging heavenly body to change its shape.

As a result of the "dark nights," the evolution of Loom's calendar had developed a similar pattern to Nova's. Twenty cycles of the moon making up twenty months in a year, the end and beginning punctuated by a full day of light.

On Loom, the months were merely numbered—a simple, logical system of ordered progression. On Nova, the months were named like everything else, difficult to remember and seemingly random.

"What number month is that?" Arianna asked.

Cain regarded her cautiously, as if the question could have some sort of veiled meaning. "The tenth."

She grinned madly.

"What?" Cain frowned, obviously expecting her to make a joke of some aspect of his culture.

"You and I share the same month."

"We have the same Patron?" Cain seemed aghast at the notion.

"That seems to be the case." Arianna delighted in his discomfort about them having anything in common. "What day were you born?"

"The tenth."

She inwardly cursed: couldn't have been lucky enough to have the same day. That would be enough to drive the man mad for months. "The seventh." Perhaps it was a mark of the overall improvement in their relationship that she didn't lie to him. They began walking again and Arianna let the conversation shift. "Why are there only three Dragon Houses, if there are twenty possible patrons?"

"There were more, thousands of years ago. But the others were killed off until only three remained. House Tam proposed a system to keep things equal among the Houses with one overseer and two Houses to keep them in check. A sort of peace treaty," Cain explained. "Once every decade or two, some bold upstart works up the notion to have his own House, supposedly called to task by some Patron."

"But the three in power never let that happen."

He gave her a nod of affirmation, and silence passed between them once more. She began to steer them in a new direction. Each day she'd used the conversation to distract him long enough to let them wander somewhere new. They strayed from what she'd come to suspect was the "approved path," into new areas of the Xin Manor. Arianna had yet to find the glider, but she would eventually. And, once she knew the route, she would not be long for Nova.

"How did you learn Fennish?" They had yet to speak in the Dragon's tongue. It served Arianna better for him to think she couldn't understand his whispered Royuk to servants about her and her care, or the conversations she could pick up as they passed through the halls.

"Petra'Oji wants all Da and higher in the House to be educated in the ways of Loom."

Arianna snorted, earning herself a sour look. "If you are as 'educated' as Cvareh was before he came to Loom, then your understanding of Fenthri ends at a rough attempt at our language."

Cain considered her a long moment. Arianna held his golden gaze, unafraid and challenging. Let him try to dissuade her. Let him speak one word counter to her point.

But he remained silent and—dare she say it?—thoughtful.

Shortly after, Cain realized they'd strayed from the course and promptly returned her to her room. No further words were exchanged on the way, but Arianna had learned enough. Judging from the scent, the halls they'd traversed were near the kitchen, and that was not what she was looking for. She needed to pick up the metallic tang of gears and oil. But perhaps that was looking for something that couldn't be found on Nova. They seemed to have everything but workshops and laboratories.

"Is there something else?"

Cain lingered after he'd released her illusion. Two of the fingers in his hand had broken from holding the magic for so long and they were slowly knitting back into place. "Why have you not yet tried to escape?"

"Escape to where?" If he had a genuine answer to her question, she wanted to hear it. "I can't fly, I have no glider, no boco—"

"You escaped your room the first day."

"Only to be returned here."

"Then you escaped again."

"Only to be returned here *again*," she reiterated.

"I took you for bolder."

Was there genuine disappointment in his tone? "I'm merely biding my time," she threatened with a smile.

He faltered. That was the thing about effective threats: they must possess a grain of truth. In this case, it was completely transparent.

"Whatever you're planning, it will not get past me."

"Like you didn't let me escape either of the other times?" Arianna bared her teeth at the man.

His claws shot out but retracted just as quickly. She'd punched a nice nerve. "You no longer have that machination. You will need to depart through the door—a door I guard."

"You should pray to each of your twenty gods that's not the case. Because if it is, it will only mean that yours will be the first heart I cut out when the time comes."

Cain growled. Arianna's hand was limp at her side, ready to summon her dagger to her palm. If he wanted a fight, she would give him one while there were no others to interfere. His magic flared brightly, assaulting her senses with the smell of wet earth.

But it diminished quickly, fading into nothing more than frustration and a fearsome scowl. The Dragon retreated, slamming the door behind him like a petulant child. Arianna sighed heavily, turning to the window.

She had yet to tire of staring at the sun. For all it hurt her eyes and seared her vision, she was fascinated by its circular presence.

It was also a reminder: Arianna was very far from home, and understood little of the world surrounding her.

FLORENCE

The engine that was going to propel them through the dense and dangerous wood known as the Skeleton Forest had seen better days. Better years actually. Long, *long-ago* years. It was an old and rusted thing, paint peeled at every corner and orange lines of oxidation ran down its sides. Florence didn't have to be a Rivet to know that the make and model dated before she was even born.

It should be in a museum, or an artifact graveyard, not the overgrown tracks they were supposed to be traveling on.

Even with her minimal training as a Raven, Florence could see the signs of wear that time had abused into the exposed metal. The cranks between the wheels looked brittle and the pistons were in no better shape. The actual Raven of their group, Anders, had been tearing out his hair over it for the past week trying to get it up to par. Florence wished he looked a little more confident now, running his final checks.

"Where did we even find this thing?" Derek asked no one in particular.

"I feel like some questions are better left unanswered." Nora threw her rucksack into the car that would be their moving home for the next few weeks as they traversed down through

Ter.2 into Ter.1. The train was only three parts long—the engine, the tender, the car—and no two parts looked as though they'd come from the same machine yard.

"Flor, come help me with this!" Anders called from the front.

Florence glanced between her chests and the direction the voice had come from.

"We'll load it up," Derek offered.

"Carefully," Florence cautioned. "Or you're going to blow us straight to Nova."

"If there's anything that temperamental in here, we have no chance of making it to Ter.1. I doubt this is going to be a smooth ride." Nora grabbed for one side of the chest.

"Still, be careful," Florence called over her shoulder, making her way up to the engine. "Anders?"

"Flor, pass me a wrench." The man held out a hand from where he was wedged under the engine. "There's a small disconnect here to the cylinder I want to fix and Rotus is up bothering with the whistle. Not that I know why we even need a whistle. If we encounter another train on these tracks we have bigger problems to worry about…"

Florence passed the Raven his tools as he muttered commands. She watched him tinker and toil, remembering all the times she'd seen Will and Helen do the same when they were younger. Florence wondered where her friends were now, what vessel they were currently obsessed with.

"This is almost on tight… Can you check up on the safety valve while I finish up?"

"I don't think you want me doing that…"

"It'll save us time, and I want to get well down the tracks before midday."

"Yes, but I'm not—"

"You were born in the Ravens, no?"

"Yes, but—"

"How long were you there?"

"Fourteen years. But—"

"More than enough time to understand a safety valve," he insisted.

"I left for a reason." Florence chewed the inside of her cheek to keep herself from chewing out Anders and creating tensions before they'd even started on their journey.

Anders paused, sticking his head out enough to inspect her properly. "Do you understand it or not?"

"Not confidently…" The truth was Florence *did* understand it, in principle. But she didn't want anyone depending on her work when it came to anything but guns and explosives. And even when it came to those, she didn't have the best resume for a gunsmith.

"We all understand things a little better when our lives depend on it." Anders passed her a tool and Florence reluctantly accepted it before climbing up to where the safety valve was located at the top of the engine.

Her handiwork appeared to be sufficient, and within the hour they were chugging down the tracks, set along a southerly course. Florence, Nora, Derek, and Rotus took turns helping Anders manage the engine. For the most part, that involved shoveling coal and calling out numbers on gauges.

It was shocking to Florence how ineffective purely steam-based travel was compared to magically augmented vessels. The train was so old that there wasn't a speck of gold on it, and the metal was too rare for the Alchemists to have invested in attaching some before they left. But Anders was an older man,

Florence would guess in his late twenties, so he was raised in a time on the fringe of the wide proliferation of magic. Where Florence was unnerved, he was relaxed behind the wheel. Or as relaxed as one could hope to be in a rattling death trap.

Florence was surprised the train held itself together well enough to grind the wheels to life and pull the two cars day after day. It was an imperfect process that changed regularly. Things broke, and repairs had to be creative solutions. She was continually selected as the extra set of hands over Derek or Nora. Anders reasoned it was because of her birth guild. Rotus reasoned it was because she'd studied under a Master Rivet.

After the first week, she stopped all form of protest. She had worked with Arianna enough times on various clockwork gadgets to trust herself when given direction. Each morning she'd get up early with one of the two men and help them with any daily maintenance.

The trees towered around them, encroaching tightly on the untended tracks. Florence watched them whiz by in the fading light. Her eyes lacked focus that reflected her blank mind.

"What is it like in Ter.5?" Derek asked as he plopped down next to her, ungracefully due to the swaying of the train.

"The trees are smaller." They passed the hours doing almost anything to stave off boredom. This was the carbon copy of a conversation they'd had before. But they'd have it again over the endless symphony of chugging metal and grinding wheels. "The land isn't really flat, not unless you're by the coast."

"And Ter.4?"

"More flat land there." Florence tried to dredge up memories of the Territory she was born in, but all that came to mind was the great, moving guild hall of the Ravens. A perpetually changing, ever-moving structure from all the tracks and raceways that curved through its many levels. "Though I haven't ever really explored it."

"Just the Underground?" He already knew the story.

"Just the Underground."

"What's that like?"

"Dark and terrifying." Florence had no good memories of the Underground. She'd almost died both times she'd ventured beneath Ter.4.

"I can't imagine anywhere more terrifying than the depths of the Skeleton Forest." Derek followed her blank stare out the open door of the train car to the whizzing trees. Darkness remained nestled within them, uninviting.

Florence shook her head. "There's light here. There's sky, and up, and down, and headway to be made. In the Underground there is simply blackness. Inky, endless, blackness... and Wretches."

"Perhaps the endwig are nothing more than forest Wretches?"

"You'd know better than I, Alchemist."

"We don't regularly find them in a state we can dissect. Or we would."

Florence inwardly cringed at the idea. Her hands were kept busy with the revolver in her hands, diligently oiling it. Every day it had its turn, following the rifle slung over her back. "What are the endwig like?"

"Nightmare given flesh." Derek's tone was instantly grave.

"Have you seen them before?" Florence studied his face with fascination. It was an expression she knew, one of world-shaking horror—a death shroud pulled taut over one's features, even if they escaped its clutches. She knew the answer before she even asked the question.

"Only once, from a distance. They hunt in the twilight hours; it was my mistake for even being out then."

"What happened?"

"A nightmare."

Florence knew she would get nothing more from him, and she didn't pry. It would be like someone asking her to recreate the sound of the Wretches' pincers, or describe the glow of their mutated saliva as it cut through the darkness like the most ominous beacon one could possibly imagine. She wasn't that cruel.

The conversation faded with the light and the train's steam. They coasted to a stop along the tracks, not risking wearing down their brakes for no good reason. By the time they jumped out of the nearly immobile vehicle, dusk was nearly upon them.

Nora made the fire that they would all sit around. Anders and Rotus were exhausted from managing the train, and did little. Derek kept Florence company as they ventured into the silent woods in search of game, hastily avoiding the impending twilight.

His hearing was better than hers. Pointed and ruby red, he had the ears of a Dragon instead of a Fenthri. Even though Florence found her senses heightened since the introduction of magic—years of ringing from explosions smoothed away due to the healing powers of her new blood—her aural acuity was nothing compared to his. They stalked quietly through the brush in the direction of a water source.

Derek would collect the water while Florence hunted their dinner. She was the best shot of the group and had yet to fail them. Creatures crowded around the streams and brooks that wound through the forest. She'd never hunted before this excursion, but it proved no more difficult than target practice.

Point, aim, shoot.

She adjusted her grip on her rifle, scanning the brush for any signs of life. A fat hare, a small deer, a wild boar—it made no difference. With her gun in hand, they were all made equal.

The rush of water over stones permeated the foliage, blending with the sound of rustling leaves. They broke through the brush and crossed onto a rocky bank. Florence scanned the edge of the small river they had come across.

"I don't see anything." She sighed heavily. "I'm going to track upstream a bit."

"Don't go too far, it's almost twilight."

"Just around the bend." She kept her voice low to avoid scaring off any potential quarry in the distance.

"I'll wait for you." He slung the water bladders off his shoulder and they fell to the ground with a dull splat. Derek began to unscrew them, his skin almost the same shade as the dark leather in the fading light.

"I won't wander," Florence promised. She knew the dangers of wandering. It was what had separated her and Arianna in the Underground. She would only stay along the stream.

Derek vanished behind her as she trekked onward. Time and again, Florence ran her hands over the hinges of her rifle. She felt the tension in the trigger, assuring her that it was cocked and ready. She needed just one creature, and she could return back victorious.

With a grand stroke of luck, a pheasant made its way along the bank with an enticing little coo. Florence dropped to her knees, gun at the ready. The noise of her footfalls was covered by the sound of a nearby waterfall, seemingly the font of the river.

It rushed down around craggy rocks, determined to smooth over the rough hillside in long white strands that seemed to glow in the pale twilight. Florence brought the gun to her shoulder, adjusting her crouch so that one knee was up and the other was planted firmly in the river rock. She lined up the notches down the barrel of the gun, tracking it over the bird.

Florence took a deep breath and fought the urge to close one eye. With the bird securely in her sights, she brought her finger to the trigger and held her breath.

The creature raised its head suddenly, turning in surprise. Florence hadn't heard what spooked the animal, but she didn't hesitate; she took her shot.

With a crack, the bird was dead.

Satisfied, Florence stood, slinging the rifle over her shoulder. It wasn't as much as she'd bagged previously but it would be enough for a night, even split five ways. So relived was she that Florence never bothered to heed to what had nearly scared the bird away from its watering hole.

She didn't realize she wasn't alone until she had the pheasant's clawed feet in her grasp.

The sound of the water rushing over the rocks began to fade. Her head filled with a numbing white noise that set her inner ear to spinning. Florence blinked, turning, looking between the darkness of the trees. She grabbed for her revolver, waiting with heart-pounding dread for something to emerge.

Movement caught the corner of her eye and Florence looked up to the top of the waterfall. Long, clawed, horribly joined and gnarled fingers curled over the edge of the rock. Cresting the edge was a set of horns woven like frozen flame. They were attached to a skeletal face, skinless and pointed in a sharp-toothed snarl.

Eyes like those of a Dragon glowed in spite of the darkness. White on a field of obsidian sockets sunk far into the depths of the creature's head. It was all arms and legs and sinew, a monster that looked as though it had woken from a thousand-year slumber and now sought its first meal.

Its low breathing dulled her senses. There was a wicked sort of magic at play here. Not like the Dragons, not like Chimera. This was a creature born of malice and murder...

And it was not alone.

One by one, horned monsters crested the rocky bluff. Each sang their sense-dulling requiem. Their eyes turned to her with instinctual purpose.

Florence's sweating palm slipped off the handle of her revolver. Her legs had been disconnected from her body. Her hands didn't move as commanded. She could hear nothing other than the mind-numbing, low breaths of the monsters. She could see nothing other than their glowing eyes.

In the fading twilight, she stared at a nightmare made flesh.

ARIANNA

The sun and moon were not even close to the same thing. While they both gave off light for nearly equal portions of the day, one was bright and painful to stare at, while the other was muted and ghostly. Arianna had known this before arriving on Nova, but even after nearly two months of her useless tenure in the Xin manor, she remained fascinated by the moon's shifting phases.

The sun was constant. Every day it shone in its perpetual orb-like manner. Bright, blinding, and filtering down through the clouds onto Loom below. But the moon shifted. It went through its phases with no regard for any who might be depending on its light for guidance through the dark night. And once every month, it winked out of existence entirely, as if to remind the world below that they were lucky to have it at all.

Arianna had been forced to be like the sun on Nova: constant, present, dependable. On Loom, her true nature was that of the moon. She could be an evolving creature, growing with every turn of the calendar.

The stagnancy she found herself in was nearly coming to an end.

She'd moved the small table over to the western facing window so she could watch the moon trail through the sky. Arianna enjoyed its ghostly play on her papers, the way it set her firm black lines of ink against the white. She kept diligent records of everywhere Cain showed her, adjusting her map regularly.

There was something in the rock of Nova, Arianna had decided, that made it defy gravity. The islands floated, that much couldn't be argued. Why they were floating she had yet to fathom, and likely never would. Magic was as good an explanation as any. But even magic had rules it must follow, and if *some* of the rock could float, then why couldn't all rock float?

Arianna continued to push the question aside, focusing on what was of most direct importance to her.

The second she'd wrapped her mind around accepting that rock could float, she threw out the parameters she'd been relying on for her mental reconstruction of the manor. If there was no need of support beams, load bearing walls, or secure foundation, the structure could indeed evolve in whatever way the Dragons saw fit. That led her to her next string of logic: What way did they see fit?

Cain had been hard to unravel, but unravel he had. Day by day, Arianna had prodded and worked her way under his thick skull to try to understand what was important to him and the other inhabitants of this world. It was surprisingly simple from there.

Gods. Hierarchy. Beauty before reason.

It was a language Arianna didn't speak, but she was learning. And, in the process, she'd nearly zeroed in on where she suspected the glider was being kept. Her pen paused mid-stroke, the detailed blueprint forgotten.

Her nostrils flared, her mind trying to process the thick scent assaulting her nose. She knew it from all similar aromas like a lock-box that could be fashioned by a thousand Rivets but bore a single maker's mark. It was familiar in the worst of ways. One whiff and a hundred memories assaulted her with vicious purpose.

Arianna stood slowly, reaching for her daggers, sliding them out from under her pillows. She gripped them tightly, her eyes focused on the door as she rounded the bed. The scent grew.

It couldn't be this easy. Her lips curled back, baring her teeth in a ferocious snarl. Bloodlust churned through her veins with every mechanical beat of her heart. Her mind screamed for death—for vengeance.

The door lock disengaged and the handle turned. Arianna flipped her dagger into an ice pick grip and reared back. The door opened and the scent clouded every sense. She lunged forward and… stopped short.

Cvareh stared back at her, wide-eyed and caught completely off guard. The edge of her dagger rested between his eyes. Blood headed around its tip, cutting the smell of cedar with potent woodsmoke. In his hands he cradled a box, one whose contents were so important that he clearly did not risk dropping it even for the sake of defending himself.

Arianna panted, her mind clearing slowly. She blinked and her eyes darted with every close of her eyelids, trying to find the source of the offending scent. They landed on the box.

"What do you have?" she hissed.

"Only what you asked for." Blood ran down his nose in a thin golden line. He had yet to step away from or move aside her dagger. The Dragon placed a foolish amount of trust in her to assume she wouldn't plunge the blade straight into his brain.

"What I asked for?" She was slow on the uptake, slower than she'd ever been previously. But her mind put together the pieces with ritualistic precision in spite of her vertigo. "The hands?"

"Yes." Cvareh rubbed the bead of blood on his forehead the second she pulled away the blade. "Is that how you greet Cain?"

"Only if he's earned my ire." Her jest fell flat. Arianna's mind was entirely on the hands. "I smelled the blood, thought that maybe there was some kind of combatant…"

Her words trailed off as she continued to focus on what he was bringing her. For now, she bit her tongue and kept herself from asking him where he'd acquired them. She would guard that particular question until she was ready to act on its truth. Until the time of her vengeance was right.

Arianna set her daggers down on the table and motioned for Cvareh to place the box before her. As soon as he did, the Dragon took a full two steps away from the vessel in question. The whole idea of what was about to transpire clearly set him on edge. It was enough proof of the box's contents that Arianna didn't feel the need to verify it with her own eyes just yet.

"I trust you know what to do with them?"

"I do. I will need three stand mirrors, thread, needle, and bandages."

Cvareh looked to the door frame and Arianna followed his gaze. She shouldn't have been surprised to see Cain there. She shouldn't have been surprised to see every Dragon in the Xin manor standing there to investigate the potent stink that was now wafting from her room.

The sea-foam blue Dragon looked on in disgust. "You can't possibly—"

"Fetch them for her," Cvareh ordered. There was no space for questioning between the sharp clip of his words.

Cain's nostrils tensed, arching upward in disgust and anger, but he left as commanded. Arianna got a wicked sense of pleasure from his discomfort. The night was shaping up in unpredictable ways. Her plans were changing before her eyes, a new set unfurling like a scroll of truth that had been kept from her until just that moment. Patience was paying off.

"What can I do to help?" Cvareh asked.

"Nothing."

"But—"

"I said nothing." She glared at him, wondering what about a singular word could possibly be confusing.

The Dragon blinked back at her. He didn't understand. He wouldn't understand the source of the rekindled flame of her rage. If anything, his confusion assured her enough to keep him alive, to prevent her slamming him against the nearest wall and skinning him over and over and over until he told her what she wanted to know.

"I know what you are about to do, and you cannot possibly intend to do it alone."

"I do intend, and I will." Arianna was spared further exhausting affirmation by Cain's return. At least someone among them was competent enough to do as she asked and then leave her be. The other Dragon departed with a pointed glare, the supplies deposited haphazardly on the opposite edge of the bed as though he could not be coaxed into entering her room more than necessary under the present circumstances.

Arianna began setting up the supplies on the table. Her hands moved with the certainty of practice. She had done this before with Eva. She had done *worse* before. It was not a delight, but it was not something that was cause for fear. *It was science*, as Eva would say. And science existed beyond right, wrong, and fear.

"Let me help."

"Do you really want to be involved with this?" Her violet eyes met his gold ones as Arianna attempted to burrow under his resolve. It was a plant with shallow roots, easily felled when the earth around it was overturned. She could feel his magic waver before his stare did. "I didn't think so."

Cvareh opened his mouth to speak, but Arianna wouldn't let him.

"I commanded you to harvest one of your own. I am going to cut off my hands, and stitch these on, and use them forevermore as though I was born with them." Arianna tilted her head to the side. "The blood of your kin is already on your palms. Do you want to take that further?"

He was completely disarmed, and that told her everything. Arianna didn't know the depth of the truth yet, but she would find out in time. She would find who the original owner of the hands had been; she'd just confirmed the man she had known simply as "Rafansi" during the last rebellion was someone of House Xin.

"I have been here for weeks, and you could not be bothered with me," she reminded him. The pain was real and bright and angry like a fresh wound. It hurt more than she thought it would, and that only flared her temper further.

"I have acted in no way that was not on your behalf, or in your best interest," he insisted. "But I have had other things to attend to. I couldn't let myself be distracted, and when I am near you… There were matters of my House."

"I understand," she said quietly, letting the clasps of the box falling open ring louder than any single word. "Because you are Cvareh Xin'Ryu Soh, peeled from the blue of the sky itself. I am Arianna the Rivet, steam given the shape of a woman. And our priorities only overlap as much as it behooves your sister to seek my help."

He had the sense not to try to object. Though his face was tormented by enough conflict to make her very briefly question what, exactly, was going through his head.

Arianna put the hesitation aside with a smile, an expression somewhere between an exhausted triumph and a bitter sneer. "So, pretend this is nothing more than what it is: you earning my trust. And get out."

His claws shot from his fingers and an equal measure of hurt and anger was fresh on his magic. It dotted his pores like a midday sweat. She wanted him to fight, she realized. Arianna wanted him to tell her she was wrong and insist that there was some purity beyond simply overlapping desires that strung them together.

Instead Cvareh retreated. He left with wide, hasty steps.

She paid him no further mind. The truth of her words had made them pointed, not the bitterness that had been building in her chest at the weeks of being saddled with Cain. She was here for a purpose, a shifting, changing, elusive purpose, but a purpose all the same.

Arianna walked over to the door, dragging the spare chair behind her. She sat heavily in it, placing some of her makeshift tools in her lap. Running her fingers over the lock like a lover, she made quick work of the panel. She was Arianna, and she would be kept nowhere she didn't wish to be. She'd do nothing she didn't wish to do. She'd let the Dragons think otherwise for weeks, but now it was time to remind them that she was a force of her own.

Within a few minutes, and a few precise movements, she'd dismantled the lock into the engaged position. Arianna stood and swung the chair around, wedging it under the door handle for good measure. She didn't think anyone would have even the slightest bit of interest in coming to her side, especially not after she warned off the one Dragon who could—for some inexplicable reason—have half a mind to do so.

But she could take no chances.

She was about to be in the most vulnerable state imaginable. She was about to spill her secrets upon the table with every drop of blood. And she would risk no witnesses.

Like a ritual, Arianna drew the curtains over the windows, candlelight the room's only glow. It was more than enough light for her Dragon eyes to see with precision. She sat heavily at the table, her reflection a flickering visage in the polished mirrors. Purple eyes stared back at her from every angle.

Arianna remembered when her eyes had been black. She remembered when they had been violently gouged out. She remembered losing all sight, and the moment of stomach-churning terror when she thought she might never see again. She remembered coming to peace with the notion that the face of the woman she loved could well be the last thing she ever saw.

Her eyes had opened again. Sharper, clearer, more precise than she could've ever imagined. Now Arianna inspected her hands. They were the hands that Master Oliver had trained, hands that could dismantle a Rivet lock like it was nothing more than a simple bank vault.

Arianna rested her palm on the table and reached for her sharpest dagger. Her chest tightened. Nature fought against what she was about to do. Her mind flooded with endorphins as it fought against itself. Instinct commanded she jump from the table and drop the knife. It struggled with her hand, trying to force it to shake, wanting her movements to suffer so much that she gave up on them entirely.

But Arianna was stable. She kept her churning stomach quelled. She kept her breathing even.

The knife pierced her ashen flesh. It gouged sharp and true, bit to bone. Arianna bared her teeth, gritting them so hard they ached straight through her jaw and into her neck. Golden blood pooled across the table, mixing with marrow as bone splintered.

Two hands waited for her, the same color as her ears. They held the same scent as the man who had given her organs in a gesture of trust, only to turn and betray all that she loved. Arianna's lips curled back. Her body shook. But she remained focused. She would take his magic once more. She would use it to find him.

She would kill him in blood more frigid than snow.

Arianna repeated it over and over in her head, uttered it like a violent prayer of the darkest variety. She did it again and again to keep the agony at bay as her magic fought to heal her body, to keep her mind right in the wake of shock.

She was Arianna the Rivet. She was the White Wraith. And she would not scream.

CVAREH

He could hear her.
He could hear every labored breath. He could hear every drop of blood splattering the floor. He could hear each dull thud of flesh that served as a chilling auditory reminder of what was happening behind the door he faced.

Cvareh hadn't moved since being cast out. He had made no motion when he heard her quiet tinkering with the lock. He did not attempt to force entry by breaking the door frame and smashing the chair she'd propped against the latch.

She had not wanted him there. She had chosen to endure the self-surgery on her own. It was as foolish as it was brave. It clouded his emotions with both admiration for her ferocity and aggravation at her persistence that every burden be shouldered alone.

But that was Arianna. That was the torrent that pulled him under every time his eyes rested on her. And it was no wonder why he had purposefully avoided seeing her. Every complex emotion combined with the draw of the boon was too much for him. For weeks he'd wanted to run from it, and now that he was faced with her once more, literally carrying a reason to loathe her, he wanted nothing more than to be by her side. He wanted to tell her that she didn't have to be alone.

Cvareh sighed heavily, closing his eyes. He pressed his forehead to the door. He could smell the bright, unique signature of her magic. It was overwhelming, no doubt from all the blood being spilled from the process of severing her own hands.

He licked his lips.

Clawed fingers curled around the door lever and Cvareh considered how much force he'd have to apply to earn entry. But even if he did, what then? What could he possibly do? He knew nothing of the ways of adding new parts to a Chimera. And somehow, even one-or no-handed, he suspected Arianna would have enough rage to still be a force to be reckoned with.

"Will you wait there all night?"

Cvareh's eyes regained focus, peering through the dimly lit hall at the man who leaned against a far wall. Cain stared back at him, inquisitive. The question hadn't been rhetorical.

"Perhaps." Cvareh didn't really know what he would do. Not when it came to Arianna. Just when he thought he'd figured it out, the woman elicited a different response from him.

"Why?"

Cain wouldn't understand. All Cain saw was the Chimera from Loom, a wretched amalgamation of Dragon and Fenthri that was now stealing magic from one of their House. Cain had not been there on Loom for all the days spent journeying with the brash and beautiful woman.

"Because we need her."

"More that you need her." Cain crossed the hall with measured steps; his walk betrayed both his boldness and willingness to turn at dismissal. It was a delicate dance that only a Dragon could manage. But Cain had earned boldness around Cvareh. The two had grown up together nearly as brothers, and in the dark halls of the Xin Manor with no eyes upon them, Cvareh fashioned them closer to equals.

"Both are true," he confessed.

"Why? What do we need with her?" Cain focused on the House first.

"She can make a Philosopher's Box." Confusion crossed his friend's face, forcing Cvareh to elaborate. "A mechanism that will make perfect Chimera. It will give Loom the ability to stand against the Dono."

"Do we want that?" Cain asked uncertainly.

"It will shift the tides for House Xin."

"And then we will be faced with Fenthri who are emboldened against us."

"We will let the Fenthri govern themselves. Petra has never wanted to be the Dono of Loom. In our great history, House Xin has never governed the world below. Our ends are entirely Nova. We don't need to dirty ourselves with the rock—" Cvareh's appeal to Cain's distaste for Loom was cut short as Arianna let out a sharp gasp. He leaned against the door, listening carefully, holding his own breath while he waited to hear the continued sounds of her labors.

"Petra should be Dono of the world below and above." Cain's loyalty was unwavering.

"She will be the Dono of nothing if we do not gain an advantage over House Rok." Cvareh had sat through too many discussions with his sister to entertain alternatives. They had turned over numbers, hypotheses, plots and plans every which way. Barring the Dono making some grave error—which

Yveun was not known for—gaining strength from Loom was their only way to tip the scales and force House Tam's hand.

"I trust you both." Of that, Cvareh had no doubt. "But this does not sit easy with me." Cain motioned toward the door. "You gave her your brother's hands. Of all who would make that sacrifice for the House, she will have the magic of the direct blood of the Oji."

"And it was the Oji's choice." Cvareh neglected to mention that she had already had the direct blood of the Oji from imbibing off him.

Cain sighed.

"I would think this would delight you, as it will mean you no longer need to waste your time illusioning her."

"Am I pleased to be free of that burden? Yes." Cain didn't even bother denying it. "But that means she will walk freely among us. You have given her the ability to pass among our brothers and sisters, to mingle so long as the illusion can be maintained. I don't trust her in my home."

"Then trust in me, and the trust I place in her."

Cain's eyes, nearly a reflection of Cvareh's own, studied him. He kept his height and didn't waver. If he did, weakness would poison the waters of his authority. It was something Cvareh could not afford to have happen. Even though Cain was like a brother, the distance Cvareh held as Ryu needed to be maintained. Petra had worked too hard in crafting it; he could not let his sister down.

"The ends best be great, Cvareh." The other man pushed off the wall he'd leaned against. "Because you are charting a dangerous course." Cain rested a hand on Cvareh's shoulder, a familial motion that showed his sincerity. "Keep both eyes open about this woman. She will gut you alive if it serves her."

"No one knows this more than I." He had seen Arianna's ruthlessness first-hand on multiple occasions. "I'm the only one among us who truly sees her. I am the only one on Nova who knows anything about this woman."

Cvareh looked to Cain with a silent challenge. Would the man think that the time he had spent with Arianna had given him more insight into the woman than he himself possessed? Cain narrowed his eyes slightly, but stepped away with a small bow of his head—deferring to Cvareh's assessment.

Cain disappeared into the darkness, his figure fading in the diminishing light of the oil lanterns that lined the hall. As much as Cvareh wanted to defend Arianna further, he knew he couldn't. Cain's assessment was pointed, as an experienced tactician's should be. But Cvareh still wondered how he'd gathered so much from the seemingly short and tumultuous relationship he'd had with Arianna.

An unusual emotion crept up on him, a jealousy of sorts for Cain's unexpected awareness of Arianna—though it had been Cvareh's decision for him to look after her in the first place. Cain was the only one Cvareh trusted to not be completely overrun by Arianna's mannerisms, which seemed to hold true. Cvareh had thought he needed space from her to clear his head, but now regret for the decision to let anyone else stay at her side was sudden and swift.

The woman had been quiet for some time, but a sharp hiss of pain brought Cvareh's attention back to the door. She continued on. His watch continued alongside her.

He sat, the back of his head resting against the barrier that kept him from her. He closed his eyes and listened to the sounds of her labor. Behind his eyelids, he remembered the first time he'd watched her hands work on the ship they rode to cross the inner sea between Ter.4 and Ter.5. They'd moved deftly, fixing engine problems with fearless precision.

Those hands would be gone, in their place something new. Cvareh had never thought about it quite under the same circumstances, but Fenthri had the capacity to change, to grow. Being a Chimera, adding new organs, they became something more. He had been born into his skin and he would keep it with him until the day he died.

But she was something more now than she was a mere few hours ago.

She was always something more.

His memories played like a soft lullaby in dark harmony with the sounds of her labors. Sounds that, for all their gruesome truths, told him she was still alive. A morbid peace took over him as he waited away the night.

Shifting stirred Cvareh from an unexpected sleep. He blinked his eyes open, wondering how and when he fell asleep. The echoes of Arianna's labors played in his ears and Cvareh tried to make sense of when they'd quieted enough for him to slumber.

The hallway was illuminated with the brightness of dawn, windows cutting beams of light in the quiet corner of the manor. Just as his mind was shrugging off the haze of sleep, the door behind him opened. Cvareh toppled backward, catching himself at the last second with an elbow, nearly colliding with the pair of legs that waited on the inside of the door.

They were a pale blue color, not unlike his own. Leather shorts, similar to what Petra would fashion herself in, hugged mostly bare hips. Strips of crossed fabric bound over her breasts, the dark wine color offsetting the hue of her exposed skin in a way Cvareh would've never himself attempted. And yet, he must commend her for it, as there was something quite striking about the color contrast. Her eyes were the same purple color, but her hair had gained a more golden shade, framing the only thing familiar about the woman staring down at him.

"Since you seem to be suddenly insistent on keeping my company, you can be the one to take me out of this place."

The voice was distinctly Arianna. Nothing could change her tone and cadence. But it was a strange disconnect to see it coming from a Dragon's mouth.

"Up with you." She nudged him with her foot. "I want to see this Isle of Ruana."

YVEUN

Yveun tapped his quill mindlessly upon the desk as he looked out over the wide balcony to his left.

The world had been quiet, almost quiet enough to give the illusion that all was right within it. But Yveun knew better. He did not appreciate the silence from his guild advisers down on Loom. He certainly knew better than to think the relative silence from Petra meant the woman had given up on her foolishly grandiose ambitions.

But those were two areas over which he had no control. His advisers on Loom were doing the best they could, considering the current climate within the guilds. The one he'd sent to get a hold on the Alchemists had been put off time and again, enough so that Yveun was nearly at the point of applying force. And Yveun had never boasted a measure of control over Petra, which was part of the problem.

He looked back down at his papers, rubbing his temples. If he looked at the balcony, he saw the ghost of Leona, reminding him of his immense failure in losing one of his greatest assets. If he looked at his work he was reminded of the guilds on Loom and all their troubles.

It all left only one frustration for him to focus on: Fennyr.

The elder brother of his enemy had been given what Yveun considered a simple task. Sniff out some information, *any* information. It couldn't possibly be difficult. But his lack of results reminded Yveun why, despite being older than Petra, Fennyr was not the Oji of House Xin.

Still, Yveun had cause for hope. Fennyr had finally been invited home by Petra. The Dono rarely let his wards return to their respective islands, but he was all too eager to make an exception in this case.

He had been patient, but his patience was finally running out. The man had been gone for three days now, and Yveun wondered what could possibly be taking so long.

He tapped his quill again.

He lamented over the state of Loom.

His mind tortured him with the need to find a suitable replacement for Leona.

He could even smell the stink of the Chimeras House Rok kept deep below from where he sat, wafting up to his wandering mind like a foul potpourri that perfectly complemented his rotten state.

The distractions were unkind and it took Yveun nearly twice his usual time to attend to the resource allocation of both Loom and Nova. It was a delicate balance, one that was getting marginally easier with time, albeit no less tedious. Now that Fenthri were raised and kept in the guild they were born into, there were more exact counts on what each guild needed to sustain itself. Enough years had also passed that it was becoming clearer how many would survive, on average, the guild tests at Initiate and Journeymen to then become part of the general population.

Before, the land below was running through resources like wildfire, uncontrolled and unabashed. Had contact with Nova not been made, Yveun doubted they would have been able to sustain themselves for much longer before reaching their limit. And yet the Fenthri remained ungrateful to the good changes he was trying to implement.

Yveun stood from his desk, gathering his monthly updates. Not much changed with each cycle of the moon, just small shifts in how he wanted to see trade managed. But year after year, progress was made.

Lossom, his current Master Rider, waited outside his room. Yveun had yet to allow the man into his space.

"Tell me of the happenings beneath Lysip," Yveun demanded as they walked. There were precious few hours in the day to waste any. He had yet to grant the young man quarters in the great Rok Estate and, for the time being, it meant he would also serve as Yveun's eyes to the underside of the island.

"There was a dispute between some no-titled and some Bek." Such was par for the course. Two of the lower rungs of society fighting tooth and nail. "A Veh chose to involve himself."

"A Veh?" Yveun was actually interested now. "Why would a Veh bother with no-ranked squalor?"

"Because the no-titled slew all the Bek and proceeded to feast on them before their families."

Yveun considered this. When Lossom had originally said "some no-titled" he had assumed his Rider to be speaking of multiple people—not a single person whose name he merely did not know. That made it all the more interesting.

"And did the Veh put this no-name to rest?"

"The Veh was killed, Dono."

Even after feasting on the hearts of fallen foes, for a no-name to defeat a Veh... This no-name had Yveun's interest. "What does this no-title go by?"

"I do not know." Admitting as much made Lossom nervous. Nothing pleased Yveun more.

"Find out," Yveun commanded. "Or better, bring him to me."

"Her," Lossom corrected.

Her.

All the better. In Yveun's experience, women were fiercer fighters than men. He had a list of theories longer than his claws on the why, but it made no difference. All he had to look at was the evidence around him: Coletta, Leona, Petra, Camile, and a handful of other Riders he'd seen come and die. Women approached every battle as though it was their last, and they had nothing left to lose but everything to prove.

"Bring her to me." Yveun would be truly impressed if the man could. It was likely a matter he would pass to Coletta and her quiet flowers, whose unassuming roots ran deep.

"As you wish." Lossom bowed, holding his position as Yveun entered the Hall of Whispers.

It was a long corridor with doors on either side. Emblazoned on every door was a plate that bore two names. The first was the occupant of the room; the second was the person with whom the occupant shared a whisper link. The Hall of Whispers served as the main communication hub for Nova and Loom, and it was entirely under Yveun's control.

Yveun first went to the whisperer who had a link with the Harvesters' guild, explaining the message that was to be delivered down to Loom. He repeated the process for every guild but the Alchemists. Yveun had been hoping that by throttling their resources, he would finally force the guild's hand into accepting his advisement and oversight, but they remained as persistent as ever. They would not relish the alternative methods he would employ if forced.

He was halfway back to his quarters when a slave of House Rok stopped him with all the etiquette that could be mustered for one so lowly.

"Dono, Fennyr Xin'Kin To has returned," the prostrating man reported.

Yveun's triumph spread across his face. Finally, Fennyr had returned and he would have some answers. The slave held his reverence the entire time Yveun was visible. If he hadn't, Yveun may well have killed him in a fit of delight.

The wildflowers of Lysip were in their second bloom. Their potent scent masked all others, effectively clouding magic and blood alike. It was one of the many reasons why the old Donos of House Rok had chosen this spot on which to build the estate. All manner of horror could be hidden behind the lovely petals of dragon snaps, lavender, honeysuckle, and the magical properties of Lord Agandi's Flowers.

He entered Finnyr's home without so much as a knock. The man nearly jumped out of his skin at the sight of the Dono. Finnyr was pale, almost Fen-like in his overall pallor. Even his muted gold hair seemed to lack some of its luster. More disconcerting were the bruises that dotted his skin.

Yveun closed the door slowly behind him, assessing the frightened man-creature. He wasn't concerned for the man's well-being out of any friendly obligation. Finnyr was a tool in a greater game, a useful pawn and a powerful player when deployed properly, which meant Yveun cared about the picture all the signs added up to make. Some kind of trauma had clearly occurred, and Yveun wasn't about to let any more of his chips be taken from him by unknown sources.

"Does Petra know?" Yveun asked foremost. If the rival Oji had ascertained Finnyr's true loyalties, much would change.

"K-know?" Finnyr shook his head, pacing. "No, but her continued belief in my loyalty despite sleeping under your care has come at a new price."

Yveun didn't care what Petra charged her kin for their loyalty. "Did you find out the truth of Cvareh's trip to Loom?"

"Not quite." Finnyr spoke hastily as Yveun began to vivisect him with his eyes. It would be mere minutes before he was doing it with his claws. Given Finnyr's generally depleted state, Yveun wasn't sure how long the other man would survive. "She is suspicious of me, of my loyalty still. She *tests* me still. She doesn't want me to return home often because she says I am more valuable to her here. But she does not give me any information on what is happening in the Xin manor."

"Finnyr, I am not a man who has time for excuses," Yveun snarled.

Finnyr wrung his hands, over and over and over again. "I know one thing."

The fact the Yveun had yet to gnaw on his sinew and bone was encouragement enough for Finnyr to continue.

"She demanded my hands."

"Your hands?" Yveun narrowed his eyes.

"Mine, specifically. She said she needed them, for the glory of the house."

"You mean...?"

"To harvest," Finnyr clarified weakly.

Once more, Petra affirmed what Yveun knew to be a fundamental truth about women: they did not hesitate. They waited for none to spoon them their desires. They took what they deemed theirs gratefully, forcefully, unapologetically, gracefully, or viciously. It didn't matter so long as it rested with them when the day was done.

He admired them for it. Not a dawn rose that he didn't envision how he could be more like his wife in that respect.

"Why?" Yveun asked himself as much as he asked the Dragon before him. Finnyr had magic in his hands, but so did many other Dragons. Many, no doubt, under Petra's direct supervision. She didn't need to call back her brother simply to harvest a pair of hands.

"Because it's Petra and she delights in my displeasure?"

Yveun was loath to admit that he and the Xin'Oji had anything in common, so he let the remark fade. "That's not enough for Petra. She called you from under my care... She wanted *your* hands."

"Cvareh told me nothing else quite matched their specific ends." Finnyr scowled at the mere mention of Cvareh's name.

Yveun had no doubt the careful phrasing was chosen by Petra herself, so he turned it over again and again in his mind, trying to make sense of it. *Matched.* That was the odd word out. "Did you smell a Chimera on him?"

"On Cvareh?" Finnyr clearly couldn't fathom why Yveun would even ask. "I doubt my younger brother knows even the first thing about Chimera."

They were getting nowhere. While Yveun wasted time trying to turn Finnyr into something he wasn't, Petra was clearly unfurling more banners to lay claim upon the edges of Yveun's control. He had stalled enough.

"No more half measures," Yveun muttered to himself.

"Dono?"

"How long has it been since the last Crimson Court?"

Finnyr blinked at the sudden shift in conversation, but recovered quickly. "Perhaps four years? No more than six…"

"I think it is time I summon my nobility together." Yveun grinned with malicious glee, a new plan unfolding before him. There was one way Petra could not keep Finnyr out, or him, or half the noble Dragons upon Nova. "Contact your sister. Be thrilled that you will be the first to tell her that I am holding a Crimson Court."

"When should I tell her this will take place?"

"A fortnight." Yveun wanted to waste no time. He started for the door to return to the Hall of Whispers; there were preparations to be made. "But you did not ask the most important question, Finnyr. It is not when it will take place. It is *where*."

Finnyr was slow on the uptake, but his eyes widened as he suddenly understood the source of the King's mirth.

"Tell her that she has the delight of hosting the Crimson Court on the Isle of Ruana. And I expect every man, woman, and child under House Xin's care to be in attendance, regardless if they are usual Court members or not."

He would root out the truth himself. He would see the blood of every member of House Xin stain the ground if that was what it took. He was Yveun Rok'Oji Dono, and he did not operate in half measures.

FLORENCE

The endwig crawled over the precipice. They nearly floated down around the face of the waterfall like wraiths in the darkness. Florence's eyes were locked on them, their glowing white orbs staring back at her.

They would consume her soul, and her sanity, before they started on her flesh.

The monsters continued their approach, humming in their dark and mind-numbing way. Florence's fingers rested on the hilt of her revolver, though the world around her seemed to be moving under water. The weapon was a steely reminder of the truth: she was about to die. Her brain would be sucked out through her nose and the endwig would fill her mind with its black poison. It would control her. It would use her as a lifeless puppet to draw them back to her friends. To get close enough that their whispering siren song could fatten their stomachs further.

Florence gripped the gun. The noise grew to a crescendo as the creatures fought against her will. They uttered their dirge of self-preservation while Florence's hand shook, struggling to draw the weapon from its holster. The weapon fell to her side like a block of lead, her arm useless.

Sweat dotted her brow despite the chill air. Florence tilted her wrist. The creatures stalked through the water, but all she heard was the incessant humming. She would grin if she could, but it took every ounce of concentration she possessed to squeeze the trigger.

The gunshot was like lightning between her eyelids. Its crack broke the deadly repetition of the endwig, and the searing pain that followed it scared away the thick shadows that had been clouding the edges of her vision. Florence saw the monsters with horrific clarity, her senses her own once more. Twice the size of a Fenthri, hunched over and pale as electric light, they growled at her through dagger-like teeth.

With a roar, the first endwig charged forward. Florence moved to run but skidded to a stop along the river rocks. Her hands moved for her belt, knowing one canister from the next on pure memory. She plucked an explosive round and had it in the revolver in one fluid movement.

By the time the muzzle of her gun was aimed at the endwig still scaling the waterfall, the alchemical runes along the barrel were alight in the darkness. Florence didn't hesitate, taking her shot. Derek said all she had been good for was exploding the forest around the Alchemists' guild; if she survived this, she would make sure he appreciated the irony of the situation as the rocky bluff collapsed, taking the endwig with it.

Florence didn't waste time. Two endwig had already alighted on the ground when she took her shot. They were on her tail and she sincerely doubted that a five-peca fall would kill the rest.

Inky blood dotted the ground behind her as she ran. It diminished with every step, her magic healing the gunshot wound she'd used to break free of the endwig's song. Florence sprinted along the bank, hearing the scraping of stone and the bestial snarl of the creatures behind her. They were gaining, and fast.

She cut into the trees.

"Derek!" Florence screamed into the darkness. His Dragon ears should pick her up clear back to the train. "Derek!"

"Flor?" A familiar male voice echoed back to her.

Relief flooded her chest. He was safe, which was more than could be said for her at the moment.

The swipe of a long, clawed hand whizzed over her head. It sunk into the bark of the tree, narrowly missing its mark. Florence rolled along the forest floor, seeking purchase on the dead brush and leaves.

The second endwig materialized out of nowhere. Its long fingers wrapping around her shoulder, drawing both blood and a scream. Florence dropped two canisters into her weapon and pressed the muzzle of the gun into its neck as it leaned forward to bite off her face in one crunch of its gaping jowls.

Blood exploded the moment she pulled the trigger. Florence didn't know much about the endwig, but she had learned all she needed to from the Revolver at the Alchemists' Guild Hall. She knew the one thing she would care about: how to kill the bastards.

The endwig were tough creatures with bones of near literal steel. Their rib cages protected their hearts by forming an impenetrable barrier not unlike a Dragon's. But at the base of the neck was a soft spot. With the gun angled just the right way, one could fire in through the top of the ribs.

Florence didn't expect she would have the opportunity to make a clean shot that exploited their seemingly one weakness very often.

As she pushed off the creature's corpse with a grunt, the other endwig was on her like a dog lunging for a discarded bone. Florence didn't have a chance to even take aim. The canister singed her flesh as it exploded against the endwig's face in close proximity, stunning it.

Scrambling to her feet, Florence began sprinting once more. Her shoulder oozed lifeblood onto her shirt and vest, her face streaked with flesh-curling burns from the proximity explosion. But the magic that Cvareh had given her by virtue of his blood held true. It healed her wounds and poured energy into her fatiguing muscles. It met the demands she placed on her body and then some.

"Flor!" Another cry rose up through the night, a woman's this time. "Flor, get your Revo ass over here!"

She wished it took something more than an endwig assault to inspire the use of her chosen guild.

The flickering light of Nora's campfire streamed through the trees in shifting beams. Florence's ears picked up the chaotic charge of the other endwig tearing through the forest behind her. Ahead was the small train, already hissing with steam.

"What do you think you're doing?" Nora screamed as Florence broke through the tree line that was almost on top of the tracks themselves. She held out her hand. "That type of explosion is sure to draw out the endwig."

"What do you think I used 'that type of explosion' on?" Florence screamed back. There wasn't any need to speak so loudly or violently; Nora's face was less than half a peca away from hers as the other woman hoisted her into the train car. But it certainly felt good to do.

"Are you all right?" Derek asked.

Florence was relieved to see her split-second judgment call of not heading back to where she'd last seen him along the river proved sound. The man was too smart to wait for her and it blossomed a newfound appreciation for him in a hot flush against her chest. The feeling was equally a product of the near-death situation and her adrenaline, but she knew she'd truly been ruined by Arianna when cold pragmatism was suddenly the sexiest thing in the world to her.

"We're not going fast enough." Florence reached for the leather strap of canisters and explosives wrapped around her body, her mind whirring with all the ways to fend off the endwig. "They'll be on us." She handed them each disk bombs. "Press, throw, push magic in to make heat."

There wasn't time to explain the mechanics of using magic to heat molten gold and start a carefully calculated chemical reaction. She just needed them to do as they were told. Florence had sat back long enough. Life or death: this was the line she was meant to walk.

The first endwig launched itself from between the trees, springing off them and leaving dark grooves in the bark. From the vantage of the train car, Florence had just enough height to stare down the barrel of her gun at the monster's outstretched neck. It was sent tumbling on the ground, all momentum lost, as she killed it with a pull of the trigger.

"Good shot." Nora's praise was lost.

"Derek, bomb!" Florence barked, pointing to where she wanted the explosion. He followed her order as two other endwig lunged from the darkness. The moment his hands were free, she passed him the rifle. "Load it with canisters from the green box."

"Which green box?" he called back.

"The one on the left." Florence fired another shot from her revolver.

"They're coming from the front!" Nora screamed over the crescendo of the engine gaining speed. On cue, the train lurched as an endwig was splattered to a bloody mess on the point of the engine's pilot.

"Bloody cogs," Florence cursed. The Vicar Alchemist had sent her to protect the mission as the Revolver, but one of her wasn't going to be enough. "I'm going to the engine."

"What are we going to do?" The usually self-sure Nora had the face of a cornered hare.

"You're going to fight." Florence passed her a weapon.

"I've never shot a gun before."

"Now is a great time to learn."

"I'm an Alchemist!"

Seriously, Florence was a breath away from shooting the woman herself. "You're dead if you don't adapt! There's three more bombs exactly like the ones you just used, right there. Just fend them off until the train gets up to speed. But don't use any other disks."

Florence had no more time to waste as the train lurched again. They just had to survive until the train reached full speed. For all the endwig were, they certainly couldn't keep up with a locomotive.

She hoped.

The wind whipped her hair around her face as she stuck her head from the train car. Florence reached out for the ladder to the right of the door, scaling up before another endwig could emerge. She swung up just in time as an explosion nearly blew her foot clean off.

"By the five guilds, you two only had three bombs!" she screamed over the wind, not knowing if they could hear. "Ration them a bit!"

Standing, Florence looked in horror at the tracks ahead. Dozens of endwig lined the path, running eagerly to meet the train. She loaded six canisters at once.

Jumping to the tender, Florence lost her footing atop the moving train car. A nail snapped clean off as she sought a grip that would prevent her from being thrown to certain death. If she fell now, she would never get back on the vessel. She'd be torn limb from limb.

Gritting her teeth, Florence rose to her knees, shooting two endwig in the process. She wedged herself between two grooves on the top of the tender. Blood pooled around her shins as she dug them into the metal for a grip where there was none, but she was stable enough to take aim, and that meant she could open fire.

Five shots down, and Florence reloaded her gun. Endwig came relentlessly like a never-ending nightmare. But the train didn't gain any more speed. She repeated the process, waiting for the vessel to be like her bullets, whizzing through the night at deadly speeds.

"Anders, now would be a great time to open her up!" she screamed.

There was no reply.

"Anders, Rotus, we need speed, get us out of here faster!"

Five long claws curled around the door of the engine in answer. Florence watched in horror as the white silhouette of an endwig, dotted in the black blood of a Chimera, pulled itself from the engine room. Florence swallowed hard.

They were without Rivet and Raven, stumbling through the darkness, enemies at all sides. She raised her gun slowly, looking fearlessly at the face of death itself. Her revolver was steady over the rocking of the train.

"You think I'm not used to this?" Her mouth curled into a mad grin. "I've been fighting my way out of the darkness my whole life. And you're not going to stop me now."

Gunshots echoed through the forest.

PETRA

She'd kill the bastard herself.

Petra rolled, a tumbleweed of claws and teeth. The man atop her responded with delightful viciousness. Fine-twitch muscle fibers spasmed as she dodged his attack; a claw caught on her neck. Petra raised a leg, propping it against his stomach, and twisted with enough force to send him skidding off to the side.

She found her feet, panting, sweating, stinking of her blood and the blood of a handful of others who had already been subdued beneath her. Yveun Dono did not fight; it was beneath him as the King of all Dragons. Wylder Tam'Oji To did not fight his lessers either, not unless challenged, following Yveun's lead.

Petra was a young Oji with boiling blood that screamed to be set free in a pit. She was met with upstarts on every front, challengers twice her age who continually questioned her merit as Oji. Petra bared her teeth and lunged forward, freeing the man's skin from his bones.

Only the Oji could sanction duels within Houses, save one exception: the Court. Called the Crimson Court due to House Rok's current power, it was the time when all grievances in upper Dragon society were aired. Petra had no doubt that a Court on Ruana proper would hold a countless many challenges for her title as Oji.

Her claws pressed into the man's chest beneath her; fangs raked against the soft flesh of his throat as she mounted him. In one bite she could gouge out his jugular and carve his heart from his ribs.

Petra's claws retracted, her palm resting lightly on his chest. She carefully withdrew her teeth, avoiding puncturing the skin. If she tasted his blood, she would be forced to kill him. There was no other option when one imbibed from the living.

"I need you twice as fast before the Court." Petra stood, her legs on either side of the man's waist in a position of dominance. "If you can't manage that, then dive into the Gods' Line before the first blood."

She stepped away, letting him find his feet. Petra ignored the cerulean man as he scampered off into some hole with his proverbial tail between his legs. Once an order had been given, she didn't engage further; doing otherwise merely invited questioning from her lowers.

"Cain." She caught the eyes of the tall man at the edge of the observation ring, leaning against the wall underneath a sunshade that was nearly the same color as his skin.

"Oji." He bowed and held it, saying nothing more, offering her his complete submission.

Slaves stepped forward from the woodwork, stripping off her soiled clothing. They toweled her with damp, perfumed cloths, wiping away the remnants of combat. A clean robe was draped over her arms and cinched at the waist. She wore it mostly open, the scars that crossed over her chest and stomach from failed attempts on her life on display as a warning to all.

"Walk with me."

He did so in silence, waiting for her to have the first word. Petra led him into the manor, straying past the main thoroughfares and onto the more private halls. Heavy tapestries draped the walls, overbearing and cluttered, one on top of the next. They splashed bright patterns between careful needlework that depicted the famous temples and landscapes across the floating isles of Nova.

It was Petra's favorite form of artwork: carefully built with the patience of thousands of single stitches. Delicate in that all it took was one tear to ruin. And surprisingly functional when it came to muffling conversations.

"You have heard?"

"Of the Crimson Court to be held on Ruana?" She nodded in affirmation. "I have."

"Yveun no doubt plans to use the guise of the Court to cut down our forces, and I have every expectation he will encourage dozens of duels against my person."

"Myself and countless others will step forward for you."

Petra snorted. "It is just us, Cain. You have no need to prove your loyalty to me and I know better than to demand it of you with words. I am a far more competent fighter than you."

He gave no rebuke.

"The more duels I can take, the better for all of Xin. It will send a message to Yveun that my claws are the ones he need fear above all others, while saving most from death in the pit." Petra rolled her shoulders, already beginning to mentally prepare for the beating she knew she would endure in the coming month. She tried to keep herself in shape, but general upkeep and preparation for a Court were two wildly different things. "I need you to gather the most competent fighters and train them well."

"Understood."

"And Cvareh," Petra added. "At night, as you have done before."

"No one will see him fighting."

Petra didn't want her brother to be challenged. The longer he was seen as a useless Ryu, the longer she could move him with relative ease, free of suspicion. But it was foolish to think he would escape public challenge during a Court on Ruana. And if a challenge came to pass, Petra wouldn't step forward for him. As much as she wanted to keep all skills he possessed both in and outside the arena secrets, she needed his position to remain unquestioned.

"I could step forward," Cain spoke, as if reading her mind.

"I will think on it," Petra relented. She didn't have a good answer yet, but had some time to figure one out. "For now, know that when there is a call, I want House Xin to speak first against Rok, always. I don't care how insignificant the grounds for a duel are; it's a Court. Most things pass and Yveun knows it."

"Understood." Cain stopped walking as she did, pausing at one of the intersections.

"Send Cvareh to me," Petra finished dismissively. "I will need to speak with him about all this, and we will need to start assembling the grand pit for the Court."

"I will tell him to seek you out first thing when he returns."

Petra stopped. "When he returns? Where has he gone?"

"He left early in the dawn. With our... guest." Mere mention of the Chimera still made Cain uneasy, despite Petra's endorsement of Cvareh's decision to saddle them together.

Cvareh went off with the Chimera. Petra swirled it in her mind like wine in a glass. "Where did they go?"

"I don't know."

"Then it would be rather hard to find him." She shrugged nonchalantly. "The moment he returns, tell him his Oji commands his presence."

"Gladly." Cain gave a low bow, but Petra paid it no heed. She was already turning over the notion in her mind. It seemed her brother was mending some of the tensions born of her first meeting with the Chimera. Perhaps something good could come of the day yet.

ARIANNA

S he was more stable on the boco the second time around. It also helped that she had a lot more faith in the man controlling the mount. Her hands rested on Cvareh's hips, her legs tensed alongside his for stability, flush against the taut muscles in his thighs. They moved far more effortlessly together than she and Cain did, a sort of innate understanding between them that she didn't expect to be there but knew better than to question by now.

The two fingers on her left hand had been tied together. It was a bit of a trick to get a grasp on illusions, quite literally. It was a new sort of magic, slithering and amorphous—like trying to form and harden steam into diamonds. The magic was all in the hands, and she found that so long as she held her fingers in a particular position, she could maintain the illusion. Eventually, the bones inside would snap from the strain. Based on what she knew of magic, Arianna suspected that if she forced it long enough, the fingers would begin to rot and die. It would be a fine line to walk, but she'd tight-roped thinner.

So she'd trained the fourth and fifth fingers on her left hand—her less dominant hand—to hold the illusion. Then, once she had it, she fashioned a simple splint to hold them in shape. It was freedom born of binding, and Arianna quickly forgot about the lack of mobility in part of one hand altogether.

Ruana spilled out beneath her as the boco gained height like a bright splotch of paint atop the canvas of clouds below. Arianna tried to use the height of their trajectory to her advantage. There was a possibility that the glider was still in that alcove, unmoved. She suspected a few locations, but it was hard to make out the exact path she and Cain had taken between the mountain peaks when they'd gone to the manor.

"Where does the water come from?" Arianna leaned forward, her chin resting on Cvareh's shoulder to speak over the wind.

"The water?"

"I assumed 'water' to mean the same thing on Nova as it does on Loom." She spoke the word for water in Royuk for emphasis.

"I know what water is." Cvareh pushed back into her in exasperation, their bodies flush for a brief moment. "We drink from the streams and rivers."

It was her turn to nudge him. "I meant, where does it come from to feed the rivers?"

Cvareh was quiet for a long moment. She knew what he was going to say before he said it. "I don't know."

"No one has investigated?" Arianna pointed to a tall waterfall that poured from the side of a far cliff. "If we went in there, where does the water come from?"

"A spring, I presume."

"And what feeds the spring? How does it not run out of water?" She was suddenly reminded of speaking to young initiates in the guild as they struggled to grasp the most obvious of concepts, teaching them to learn through questioning.

"I don't know."

"How do you not know?" she asked incredulously.

"I've never looked." He glanced over his shoulder, seemingly equally confused by her line of inquiry.

"Hasn't anyone?"

"I doubt it."

"Why? Why not? What if it runs out? What if you are a week away from not having any water and you don't know it? There could be a large glacier that has been melting for hundreds of years, trapped in some far mountain valley, and it's soon to be exhausted."

"I doubt it." Cvareh shrugged. "Lady Lei gives the Dragons all we need to survive. She wouldn't have our water run thin before the end of days."

"Lady Lei, the Caregiver."

He looked honestly surprised she knew the Goddess's title, meriting a turn of his head.

"I've been talking with Cain."

"So it would seem." Cvareh tugged on the boco's reins, pulling left. The creature banked away from the mountains and toward the sloping hills that flattened across the island. "Hearing him start to speak of you was a surprise."

"I had to speak to someone or I was liable to go mad." Arianna bit her tongue, holding in the rest of her thought: she was driven to speak to Cain because Cvareh had not come to visit her once. She would not sound so desperate.

"The surprise came more from knowing he was speaking to you in return. He holds no love for Fenthri and even less for Chimera. And, from what I hear—and saw first-hand with a dagger at my forehead—you have done little to endear yourself to him."

"And why would I?" She snorted. "I gathered we weren't going to be friends from the first time he laid eyes on me."

"You seem friendly now."

"Apparently the word 'friends' does have a different meaning on Nova and Loom." She would describe her and Cain more like begrudging allies in their current state.

Cvareh chuckled. "Do you prefer his company, or mine?"

"I haven't had much of a choice in the matter," she reminded him.

"Even still?"

"Yours." There was little thought in the answer, even despite the confusion and annoyance Cvareh had caused her across the past few months.

It sparked a pulse of delight in his magic that set the palms of Arianna's hands to tingling.

Honestly, talking with Cain for the past few weeks had been nearly as thrilling as cutting off her own hands the night before. Arianna flexed her fingers, instantly regretting the analogy. They still felt strange, like phantom limbs given substance.

She had yet to confront Cvareh about their origin, but she let the matter stew. There was time yet. Now that she had freedom on Nova, she had more time for everything. Not much—Florence still needed her—but time enough. The fact that he produced hands that matched her ears connected a few dots for her all on her own, however. She was closing in the lines that explained how he'd even known of, not to mention acquired, her schematics. It meant the man who took them was somewhere close.

Arianna bared her teeth at the notion. The Dragon known as Rafansi was so very near, and she would find him.

Cvareh hissed loudly, jolting forward. "You have claws now."

She retracted them, not even realizing she'd unsheathed them at the mere thought of the man who had betrayed her and the last resistance. "That comes with the territory of having Dragon hands."

"Yes, well..." She saw Cvareh's profile as he considered her hand on his waist. There was a note of recognition, a familiarity in the way he regarded it. He continued before the questions about its origins could spill from her lips. "I suppose it also comes with the territory to know how to pull your claws. You will attract unwanted conflict if you go waving them about, or digging them into people's sides."

"Are you going to *duel* me, Cvareh'Ryu?" she teased. Cain had told her in various brisk snippets—as most of their conversations went—about the importance of Dragon duels.

Cvareh laughed. It was loud and seemed to echo off the hills below and swirl like raw color in the wind. It was a different sound than he'd had down on Loom. Arianna regarded the man thoughtfully. She certainly hadn't acted the same on Nova as she would on Loom. She was out of her element and outnumbered— an unwanted person in a foreign land. It would make sense he would've acted strangely on Loom in the same circumstances.

Which begot a new curiosity. What was he like here on Nova? What was the real Cvareh, and which did she favor?

"Cvareh'*Ryu*?" His mirth was uncontrollable.

"That is your name."

"It is, but twenty gods, I never thought I'd hear you address me with any formality."

"I was hardly being formal." She'd used the title for ironic emphasis.

"That much was obvious. Still, a strange treat to hear it from your lips." A smile was in his words, one Arianna didn't quite understand.

"Where are we headed?" She changed the topic as the landscape beneath her began to give way to smaller towns that only grew against the far horizon.

"That down there is Abilla. They're known for their millineries and cobblers. Some of Nova's finest textiles come from their looms."

The rooftops were shingled with wood, the houses made in all shapes and sizes. Arianna saw large windows and small. Bridges stretched between some; over others, ivy crept across to create a leafy walkway. The streets were cobblestone, or gravel, or packed dirt, winding like gnarled roots around the homes.

They were each coated in plaster and washed in some kind of ink, or paint, or clay. Yellow houses stood against purple ones, trimmed in vermilion or edged in ruby. The gears of her mind created smoke that clouded her head as they tried to find a pattern or logic in it. But if there was some rhyme or reason, it eluded her. It looked as though a child had spilled an architect's models across a mossy surface, then proceeded to draw tall, thin, trees between the shorter balls of foliage connected by spindly trunks.

"See, look there." Cvareh pointed to a river on the edge of town that had flowed down mightily from the mountains they'd started in. "They're washing the inks from the fabrics."

"I know what it looks like to wash ink from cloth." Arianna rolled her eyes dramatically.

"Really?" He sounded genuinely surprised.

"There's a science, you know, to getting the right color and getting it to stick to the fibers. I learned it during my basic schooling on Ter.0."

Cvareh was silent an acceptably somber second following the mention of the demolished Territory on Loom. "I wouldn't have thought you studied something like dyeing fabric."

"Why? There's a practical methodology to it. Furthermore, sometimes you need different colors to mark things like ships or cautionary areas."

"Practical methodology," he repeated thoughtfully. "It would be something like that."

"Let me guess: you do it for these impractical, gaudy rags you call clothes." Arianna picked at his love of fashion and his clothing in the same breath.

He snorted. "For once, I can't disagree with you. These are gaudy rags, nearly a full year old."

She was utterly lost as to why his clothing would have some sort of expiry.

"That's why we're headed to Napole!" Cvareh turned forward with elation. The wind swelled beneath them, carrying them higher.

If Arianna hadn't understood the logic behind the builder's plans of Abilla, she was utterly hopeless when they arrived in Napole. The hills continued to slope downward to the island's eventual end, and houses piled atop them precariously in such a way that reminded her of the castle and its ignorance to all form of logic. The structures leaned against each other for support like jolly drunkards, spires drew long shadows across rooftops, and archways reached down to bustling roadways.

As they descended, Dragons paused, shading their eyes with long fingers to peer at the boco headed earthward. A few raised their hands and even more dipped into low bows, the motion barely visible from their height. Arianna glanced at her forearm, worried her illusion had somehow slipped and garnered the attention. It hadn't.

"Are you that well known?" she asked when Cvareh took note of a genuflecting group.

"I am the Xin'Ryu," he said it as though it should have been obvious. "The Isle of Ruana is Xin's. Everyone here is a Xin."

That was startling. Ariana had been struggling to grasp the notion of family since it had first been introduced on Loom by the Dragons. Two parents rearing a child seemed vastly more ineffective than the communal arrangement of Ter.0 that she had been brought up in. But the size of a single Dragon family now seemed impossibly excessive. *How did they even keep track of it all?*

"There are red and green Dragons here," she observed, the colors blurring together as their shadow cut across rooftops.

"There are. A Dragon's skin color is determined by the island they're born on, their native House."

"So two red Dragons can give birth to a blue Dragon?"

"Technically, though I have no idea why two of House Rok would ever move to Ruana."

"That makes... absolutely no sense." Arianna's head hurt already from the lack of reason surrounding her. If she were an Alchemist and possessed more than rudimentary knowledge of biology, she'd likely be having a conniption.

"Why?"

"Because children take after their parents. It's why strong, healthy Fenthri were selected to breed on Ter.0, before the Dragon King mucked up the system and forced this ridiculous notion of families."

She thought he stiffened at the mere mention of "breeding," but perhaps it was her imagination reading overmuch into the shift of his body as he navigated the boco onto a wide platform. Other birds milled about, pecking from troughs and cawing at each other in a way only they could understand.

Here, too, there were silent keepers who materialized from the shadows. They were an omnipresent reminder of the hierarchy Nova steeped itself in—a system that inspired a discomfort in Arianna she struggled to shake. They brought trays laden with fruit and heavy glasses filled to the brim with a liquid the color of Fenthri blood. Cvareh took a glass and refused the fruit. Arianna followed suit, operating under the assumption that Dragons would never willingly drink the blood of a Fenthri.

"Cvareh'Ryu!" A woman strode out from an overhang that was bursting with flowering vines. The sunlight didn't hesitate to expose the bareness of her chest. Everything was too bright on Nova. "It has been some time."

"I've been at prayer to our Lord in the mountains," Cvareh kept his lie.

"So the rumors say." The lie was clearly well known and as flimsy as it sounded, judging by her tone.

Arianna averted her eyes from the exchange, bringing the glass to her lips. She had yet to fully acclimate to the Dragons' way of dressing—or lack thereof. Even as Arianna had donned the fashion, she felt consolation that the illusion would be placed over top her bare skin. Every breeze was a chilling reminder for all the fabric she didn't wear. But donning the guise of a Dragon made her feel oddly less exposed.

She sniffed the contents of the goblet. It had a strange aroma, like grape and sulfur, heady, with a sharp edge unlike anything she'd encountered before. Arianna took a sip, and was overcome by an instantaneous coughing fit the moment it burned her throat.

"Dear me, is your companion all right?" the woman asked.

"Fine," Arianna replied for herself before Cvareh could speak. Royuk was heavy on her tongue, as Arianna was more accustomed to listening than speaking, but her mouth still formed the sounds with the confidence of years of tutelage.

Her accent must have been passable, as the woman didn't comment. "Is the wine not to your liking?"

"It's fine." Arianna had no idea what else to say. She glanced at Cvareh, hoping he'd explain somehow what "wine" was and how she was supposed to respond.

The bastard broke out laughing. "Forgive her." He took a step closer to Arianna. An arm slipped around her waist, long fingers palming the bare skin of her side. "This is Ari Xin'Anh, and recently, Bek."

"So you are new to the upper side of the isle." The woman smiled, flashing her teeth.

Arianna was new to Nova. She was still attaching textbook learning to practical meaning. But she knew when someone was trying to intimidate her. She smiled wide in return and wondered if she'd made her canines long enough in the illusion she'd crafted.

Apparently she had, as the woman broke eye contact first and turned back to Cvareh. "A personal Anh, I take it?"

"Indeed." Cvareh had yet to remove his hand from her person and Arianna was ready to remove it herself. The only thing that prevented her from doing so was the determined grip he had, the swell of his magic at her side that felt as if it were trying to engulf her.

"You are so lucky, Ari'Anh." Arianna instantly didn't like the way her name sounded in the woman's mouth. "To have been noticed by the Xin'Ryu."

Arianna said nothing. She just kept smiling. And drinking her wine.

"How long will you be in Napole?" the woman asked.

"The night." Cvareh guided Arianna inside, earning himself a questioning glare. He didn't change his demeanor. "I trust you have lodging?"

"For you? Always." The woman smiled, thinner, subservient to Cvareh.

They were led down a long hall. A swirling ribbon carved into the wood on either side of them created a dizzying pattern from one end to the next, breaking away from the wall to become the banister for a wide stairway. Arianna stretched her fingers against their binding. Her fifth finger had gone completely unresponsive, the bone likely shattered to dust from magical exhaustion.

"Will this be suitable?" The innkeeper opened a wide door that had the motif of a bird painted across its surface.

The room itself shone like freshly oiled clockwork. Wooden floors were polished to a mirror shine, reflecting light off the many portals that had been bored into the far wall. Silver lined them, curling like tiny serpents that seemed to wriggle in the sunlight, connecting every window to a grand mirror on the ceiling—of all places. A perfectly square bed jutted against the unnecessary curves of the room, its linens softening the hard lines of its wooden base. Arianna narrowed her eyes at the furniture.

"It will do." Cvareh hardly seemed impressed.

"Do let me know if you need anything." The woman bowed, her breasts hanging erotically.

Arianna kept her eyes anywhere else. The woman had a nice figure, certainly. But such a sight should be earned. If given to everyone, it held no excitement and therefore lacked interest.

"I will, Xillia." Cvareh dismissed the woman, shutting the door in haste. He turned to Arianna, and they shared a long look. "I thought you might need to relax your illusion and rest a moment."

Her whole body tensed instantly at the notion. He had preempted her status. Arianna placed her wine down on a nearby table, grabbed for the splint, pulled it off, and let the illusion fall away with the same gritty feeling as a rain of sand. "Could you smell it in my magic?"

"Smell what?" He seemed confused.

"The illusion beginning to turn." Arianna held up her hand. Her fifth finger was completely limp, almost like gelatin encased in flesh; bruising turned the blue of the hand dark. Her fourth finger hung at a painful angle. She snapped it back into place with a small grimace.

"No, your magic didn't smell any different than it normally does."

"Then how did you know?" Arianna needed to dissect the weaknesses in her illusion. While she was confident in her ability to take on most Dragons, especially now with claws at her disposal, she didn't want to be put in a position where she had to.

"Call it intuition." He shrugged.

Arianna scowled at him.

"And what have I done to offend you now?" Cvareh chuckled lightly.

That only served to sour her mood more. "'Intuition' makes no sense. Intuition is merely a collection of past evidence compiled in your subconscious. There's a reason you thought that. Just like there's a reason for, for this." She motioned to the windows.

"For what?"

"For why they're spaced oddly, and circular—do you have any idea how much effort it is to make a circle that perfect architecturally?"

He appeared to be really considering it, as if for the first time. "They're prettier that way."

She was going to literally tear out her hair. Arianna spun on her heel and stalked toward the bed. Her magic was exhausted and recovering slowly while her fingers finished knitting. She grabbed a fist full of pillow and threw it over her shoulder.

"Now what?" Cvareh leaned against the door, an amused pull at the corner of his lips. She was going to carve that look off his face if he kept it up.

"I'm told there's a bed under here." She continued to cast aside the offending cushions. "I intend to make use of it so my magic recovers faster."

"It's more comfortable if you actually sleep *on* the pillows, you know."

Arianna paused with a dramatic sigh. "Cvareh, no Dragon, Fenthri, Chimera, or creature on Loom or Nova or anywhere else needs this many plush objects to sleep upon. A glass doll would call it excessive."

"However you like it." He held his hands out in a motion of forfeit, but his magic still sparked with amusement.

She turned her eyes away from him, not wanting to see the shine that seemed to almost visibly spark around him. Magic held no light, unless channeled through gold. She really was losing her mind in this backwards land if she began to believe otherwise.

"Yes, remember that." She fell on the bed with purpose. "For I am going to sleep just long enough to recover my magic, and then you shall show me this Napole in earnest."

"If it pleases you, Ari." His voice was nearer. The mattress, in all its softness, betrayed his weight as he sat on the edge of the bed.

Arianna wanted to tell the Dragon that his encroaching presence was unwelcome. That despite whatever kindness he showed her, whatever familiarity his magic held, whatever warmth she could find in the tones of his voice, she simply did not want him there. She had not given him express permission to share her bed. But she couldn't see to bring herself to deny him either.

She *wanted* to lash out at him ferociously. But her magic was more exhausted than she gave it credit for. Her eyelids felt heavy and the bed—even the remaining pillows—were more comfortable than she'd anticipated. She heard Cvareh settle among his cloud of cushions, the plush articles creating a barrier between their bodies. Arianna closed her eyes and did nothing to remove his familiar presence from her side.

CVAREH

His enigma slept.

Nova was different when Arianna was upon it. Familiar societal norms were suddenly cause for concern as potential interactions that could expose her for what she was. *For what she was.*

The thought turned over in his head again and again as he remained poised in such a way that he could watch her sleep. He didn't move out of fear of disturbing her, his arm prickling and then going numb from the strange position. It wasn't the first time he'd seen her sleep, but something felt different without Florence snuggled against the woman's chest.

She was still dressed in Dragon clothing, and her body was on display to him for the first time. The Arianna on Loom had always been buttoned up tightly, reserved and withdrawn. Here his eyes could draw lines up her thighs, trace the hard muscles that cut across her abdomen, the swell of her biceps draped across her covered breasts. They rested on dark marks etched into her skin. Tattoos, but not like the one that should be emblazoned on her cheek. Script-like numbers scrolled across her right wrist, just off to the side of her modest cleavage, upon her left shoulder.

He wanted nothing more than to delicately trace his claw over them. To learn their locations with his eyes, his hand, his mouth...

This woman should be his mortal enemy, and here he was admiring her. Cvareh finally eased onto his back, staring at his reflection in the ceiling. He certainly looked the same, but something had changed on Loom.

The reflection blurred a moment, clouded by the memory of Finnyr's face when Cvareh had told him he needed to remove his hands. He had harvested his brother. Conflict clouded his chest. Sure, Petra had blessed it, even ordered it expressly as the Oji—and there was no questioning nor going back when such an outright decree had been made. Furthermore, him and Finnyr had never been particularly close. After Finnyr had lost to Petra for the Ryu position and was shipped off to Lysip, it was hard to foster a particularly deep bond with his brother. Cvareh had tried, but when Petra had chosen him as her Ryu, rather than Finnyr, it had only exacerbated the problem.

Still, Finnyr was his brother. He was the direct blood of House Xin. And Cvareh felt more conflict over his lack of feeling conflict than he did actual turmoil over harvesting him.

Cvareh smiled to himself. Petra would be proud.

The moment Arianna stirred, she donned the contraption she'd designed for her fingers. It was brilliant, really. And with that alone her illusion settled atop her, weaving like a thousand strands of light to form a perfect facade. It was all a testament to her ingenuity and strength, and Cvareh discredited her with his internal disappointment at seeing her as a Dragon rather than in her natural state.

When they left, he made it a point to put his hand on her hip once more. The proximity marked her as his. It affirmed to all Dragons that she was claimed by the Xin'Ryu himself. However small the measure of protection was, he would give it to her gladly.

"How long do you intend to touch me?" she muttered, clearly not sharing his sentiments about the contact.

"Would you trust me if I say it's for your best interest?"

"Hardly." Her head turned as her eyes remained glued on a stall selling wind chimes. Cvareh briefly debated if the word meant she thought he was doing so because it delighted him. "What are those?"

"They make sound as the wind blows."

"I can see that." She peeled her attention away long enough to roll her eyes at him. "Is it for wind storms of some variety? A warning?"

"No, just because they sound nice."

All her questions were in the same vein. Arianna asked why some walkways were suspended and why some were on the ground. He remembered the Raven city, and how each level served a separate purpose. But there were no such motives on Nova. Things were as they were because someone was compelled to make them that way.

Her displeasure mounted throughout the day. Cvareh tried to take her everywhere that made him happy. He took her to his favorite sundries shop, his tailor, to see the best performers in all of Ruana. But Arianna merely continued to withdraw.

He was exhausted, and he wasn't even cultivating an illusion.

They ducked into one of his favorite tea parlors in a quieter area of town. Usually he haunted more fashionable places to see and be seen. But Cvareh avoided them today. He didn't think he or Arianna could handle the expectations of a highly public appearance. And besides, his tailor had yet to cut him anything befitting of the current season. He would certainly not be seen wearing clothes from a year ago—though the fact had likely already reached the ears of the gossips.

The parlor's patrons bowed their heads as he entered. Herbs hung from thick beams that drew lines across a plaster ceiling. They perfumed the air and clouded the nose with promises of brews that would be even more delightful than their aromas. The tea master from behind the bar gave a nod of recognition as Cvareh led Arianna back to an iron gate that served as the parlor's back door.

It opened into the shop's private garden. A delightful nook of Napole with wafting lavender, sunny chamomile, leafy tea plants, and—Cvareh stilled. His favorite scent hovered above them all in a carved arbor that framed the lone table nestled among the greenery. Vining honeysuckle was heavy in the air, the sweet floral notes at once an invitation and a comfort.

He looked suddenly at the woman next to him.

"What?" Arianna was expectedly oblivious.

"Nothing..." The taste of her blood was across his tongue at the mere thought. Had he known all along? Had he sensed it from the first moment he'd met her, the faint aromas that always lingered upon the woman by the very essence of her magic? The smell he so loved was within her veins.

It didn't matter what he knew before. He needed her *now*, more than ever. He wanted to sink his canines into her flesh. He wanted to smear her blood across their flesh, mingling with his. He wanted to drown in her magic. He wanted—

"What may I get started for you?" The tea master was a welcome interruption.

"Whatever is in season," Cvareh mumbled by means of reply. His eyes were on the woman who was easing herself into one of the three seats around the table. Cvareh closed the distance between them once more, pulling his chair slightly closer in the process of sitting. "Do you understand tea?"

"Brewed herbal remedies for colds and other such things are found on Loom."

He couldn't help his laughter, even though he knew it was going to draw out her ire. "This is purely for pleasure, not for medicinal purposes."

"Everything the Dragons do seems to be for pleasure." She stared at the garden and while he would've hoped for a spark of interest or inspiration, the mounting confusion that'd been lining her brow remained. "You build for beauty before function. You spend countless hours on adornments. You make noises with your mouth and tools, calling it song, moving to it and calling it dance, but it serves no greater design." She shook her head in frustration. "You don't even know where your water comes from."

He'd nearly forgotten about that anecdote from the morning. "You're not wrong about those things."

"But what do you *do*?" she pressed. "Loom has given the Dragons Gold, gliders, science, mathematics, a true way of understanding the world. We—"

"That is untrue," he interrupted. "Nova understands the world in a way Loom does not. We understand it through the Twenty Gods above. We understand it through magic." She pursed her lips together as he continued. "You're right, we do not craft engines of steam or write arithmetic that can lift people to the skies. But we understand life, a richer meaning for it than on Loom, and we create joy."

"Xin'Ryu." A young girl with Tam skin delivered steaming mugs of amber colored liquid. Arianna stared so intensely at her that the child was nearly startled.

"Thank you." Cvareh dismissed her, sparing her from whatever had Arianna's vicious interest.

The girl bowed and turned, happy to flee.

"I see where the notion came from," Arianna whispered.

He couldn't fathom what she was on about until the woman raised a hand to her cheek. Cvareh hadn't even noticed the mark. He'd not paid it any credit as he hadn't his whole life. It was a part of his world, as inconsequential as the icy peaks of the mountains or the never-ending waterfalls. He hadn't had cause to look at it differently until a Chimera forced him to see it through her eyes. "The tattoos are how we know when someone has left their native House," he explained.

"Tattoos should be choices, not brands." She tried to pin him down with a deathly glare.

"These are choices. They *choose* to leave their house and join a new one. It's how I and everyone else here knows they are friendly, that they are kin. It is their decision." He reached out and grabbed her wrist, speaking before she could pull away, "Just as these are."

Arianna stared at his hand a long moment where it fell over her own tattoos. If her eyes were actual daggers he'd be cut from thumb to cheek. "Unhand me."

"Explain them."

"Unhand me," she repeated, a little louder.

He acquiesced, but only because he did not want to make a scene. His hand was cold in the wake of her warmth. "I had never seen them before. I want to understand."

She looked away sharply, as if he would vanish because her eyes were no longer on him. He didn't. And so she was left to gather herself to speak. "We call them link marks. They signify a date of importance regarding... a person."

And she had three. For whom? He could guess Florence would be one. Her lost lover another... Was another lover the third, perhaps? Even with a short life span and no notion of family, how a Fenthri could forge such a deeply amorous connection with so many people was lost on him.

"You saw when I dropped my illusion." She massaged her wrist lightly where he had touched it.

"I did. I think they're beautiful." He operated on instinct, offering encouragement when in doubt.

She found amusement in that decision. "They are, because they are significant." Arianna's purple eyes met his and Cvareh felt helpless in their gaze. "They were choices. For nothing touches my body that isn't my choice."

What did that make him?

Cvareh opened his mouth to speak and was interrupted by a velvet-clad man. "Cvareh! I did not expect to find you in the city, my friend."

"Zurut." Cvareh stood, embracing the man in greeting. "It was an impromptu trip."

"Seeing the tailor, no doubt." The man picked a ribbon on Cvareh's shoulder with two fingers as though the color that had gone out of vogue could somehow stain his quite lavish and luxe design. "Are you trying to make a new statement?"

"Hardly. You couldn't be more correct, it was time to visit the seam masters." Cvareh mentally cursed Petra, again, for not ordering clothes to greet him upon his return.

"And what a time it is! I was just there myself ordering a new jerkin to wear to the Court."

"The Court?" Cvareh repeated, certain he'd misheard his friend.

"How have you not heard?" Zurut was in shock. "The Crimson Court will be happening on Ruana within the fortnight. It's been all the talk across the city this afternoon." His friend's eyes drifted toward Arianna. "Though I see your attentions have been elsewhere."

Cvareh had always known that choosing a mate beyond superfluous play would result in quite the talk. It was natural as the Ryu, and sometimes the tea parlors on Ruana were hard up for gossip. But today was not one of those days.

He muttered off an introduction, his mind elsewhere. He couldn't even be certain what name and title he'd given Arianna, if it was the same as the one he'd fabricated before. He couldn't be bothered.

A Crimson Court on Ruana.

The Dono intended to wash the streets gold with Xin blood. There would be no harbor, no excuses for why key members of their House could not attend. They were being cornered and led to slaughter. And now he had exposed Arianna as his potential mate, a Xin'Anh, easy fodder for any woman who had sought Cvareh's fondness and the prestige it gave for herself. Cvareh swallowed hard. It was likely to be his first court in the pit.

"Ari." She stood at the tone in his voice alone. "We need to return to the Xin Manor. Now."

He was worried for himself. He was worried for maintaining Arianna's illusion. But his mind remained focused on one thing: his House. He had to return to his sister.

YVEUN

Underneath the main continents of Nova, there was the "below". The underbellies of the iceberg-shaped islands had been carved out and hollowed into a reversed anthill of maze-like passages, freezing alleyways, and the seedy abodes where all manner of business was conducted. It was the type of commerce that could only happen in a place where the sun didn't shine.

Below was a place where the threads that bound the structure of Nova together would barely hold knots. Here was where the Anh and lower Da of Houses were sequestered. Further down were the Bek. And further down, still, lived those who barely had a name. Close to the Gods' Line, close to the vulgar world of Loom where only first names were used and all elegant social structure was lost.

It was a place a King should never venture, for it was far, far beneath him.

But it was in these places that he dredged up gold from among the rock and raw metal of his society. Leona had come from these chilled and dank halls. He had been given whispers and guidance regarding the woman he would find down here from Coletta, and Yevun had pulled Leona into the sunlight, molding her into something that truly shone by obliging his whims. Once again, this would be how he would find his next Master Rider.

Hooded and robed, he kept his face downward, focused on the smooth, sinking stairs that wound around a building. Wind whipped against his left side, intent on pulling him from the perch and tipping him into the abyss below. Graffiti stretched against the wall under his palm, glazed with moisture from the perpetual chill. Xin swords and books were painted atop Rok crowns that dwarfed Tam scales.

Blood was thick in the air. He could almost see it alight in the alleyway he turned into. A fruit cocktail of the scents of Dragons who had died from illegal duels.

How many organs were fed to the Fen below from fights gone awry? It was a wonder that the race below the clouds hadn't learned of Nova sooner. It was all chance that their world and the world below had been separate for so many years. It had been chance they had connected at all.

He'd been following the blood for hours now. It led him to illegal pits and questionable feeding halls that engaged in the darkest sort of trade one could imagine on Nova—imbibing off the living. It was said that when a Dragon had a taste of a living host, nothing could satiate the hunger that followed other than more blood. It ensured the feeding halls stayed in business with a slew of loyal patrons. It also drove Dragons to madness with the craze that set in when they had gone too long without their last taste.

Still, it would be in one of these places that he knew he would find her. His current Master Rider had about as much tact as a battering ram and, unsurprisingly, turned up nothing when he'd ventured under to ask questions. There were things

Yveun knew he would have to do himself if he wanted them done at all. He couldn't send another to do it, for that was no better than a half measure in the worst sort of way. The best foe was one slain with one's own claws.

Revelries and betting flooded his ears as he neared the fighting pit. Yveun entered, unhindered, to take his place among the crowd. The runner of the ring sat at its side before a low table, deciding fighters, calling odds, and taking bets. It reminded him that was a role he still needed filled before the Crimson Court was to happen, lest Petra get the notion that she may suggest one of her own with the Court happening on Ruana. Unsurprisingly, the woman who ran the pit here was a Tam. The balance keepers of Nova were unparalleled in ensuring the best fights by sensing the skill of the fighters involved.

In the pit, two Dragons tumbled. A blue Xin with the symbol of House Rok emblazoned on his cheek and a green Tam with the same. It was a battle of underdogs, and no matter who won, all the red native-born Roks would be pleased with the outcome.

Yveun watched five fights. No one shone. No woman who stepped into the ring fought with the grace and blood lust he assumed his target to possess. Yveun departed in frustration.

He continued on until the clouds below began to turn purple with the first light of dawn. Still, the woman eluded him. Perhaps it had merely been rumor, a grand underdog story those beneath delighted in telling of a no-name, no-rank, rising above and felling those with title and prestige. It wouldn't be the first time, or the last.

Yveun wound upward, climbing questionable ladders and precarious stairways. As he neared the upper side of the island, the conditions steadily improved, but the weight of the world above them only grew heavier. The whole of the rock that supported Lysip was trapped beneath a nearly palpable weight, as if the whole expanse of the island above could suddenly drop its heft into his very lungs. A physical reminder of the world above that was so close and so far at the same time.

All roads funneled into one main tunnel that cut through the island. It was gated and guarded at all times. Yveun made for it with the ease of nearly being home, pulling his hood from his face in preparation to meet the Riders who manned the portal.

A hand shot from the darkness. It wrapped itself around his neck, claws pressing into his throat. Yveun only smiled.

"There you are," he whispered.

"Tell me, Dono," a deep and feminine voice husked into his ear from behind. "What happens if I kill you here? Do I become the Dono of Lysip?"

"Not quite." He made no motion away, assessing the power in the woman's forearm, the tension in her magic, the skill required to hold him in place using her claws while not drawing blood that would alert his Riders with a scent. "Coletta'Ryu would be come Coletta Dono, as this would not be a sanctioned duel."

"So killing you will be for bragging alone." Her fingers tensed.

"How did you know it was me?" he asked.

"Your walk." She inhaled deeply. "Your scent."

"How do you know those things?"

"We know of the sun here below, even if we never see it," she retorted. He'd allow her to keep her secrets, for now. It betrayed her cunning. There were ample plausible explanations: She'd seen him in a past Crimson Court. She'd worked at the estate. She'd been taken as a personal Anh for one of his To. She'd worked with one of Coletta's flowers. It all mattered naught to him.

"Do you wish to see it? The sun?"

She gasped laughter, keeping her mouth by his ear. "You think you can buy your life with pretty things? With shiny baubles and the promise of ruby hallways everyone so lusts after in your grand palace?"

"I hope not. Or you are not the woman I am hoping for." She remained silent, letting him speak. "I hope to buy your life with the promise of the one thing I hope you crave more than all else."

"What do you think I desire?" she purred, her fingers tapping against his throat.

"Blood. More blood than you can gorge yourself on." Dragons didn't become as strong as this woman by remaining pure and not imbibing. She clearly cared naught for taboo and he wouldn't shun her for it. He'd feed this little monster if it made her his pet.

"How will you give me that?"

"Come with me. Come as my new Master Rider, and I will see you have all the blood and carrion your claws and fangs would ever desire."

She let him go. Yveun turned. The woman was cloaked as he was, hooded, and Yveun could only make out a strong chin and hooked nose from the shade of her cowl, but he could not recognize the shade of her skin in the low light. A smirk adorned her mouth, and Yveun was certain he'd won.

"I will think it over." She turned, as if her sole intent was to prove him wrong.

"You would be wise not to disobey your King," he cautioned, claws jutting from his fingers.

She merely glanced at them. "I gave you your life, you tolerate my disobedience. A fair exchange, Dono."

The woman gave a small wave, dropping off the side of the wall and into the depths below. He didn't hear her land, her movements more precise than that of a cat's. Yveun bared his teeth into the darkness, frustrated and delighted at the same time.

He hadn't even learned her name.

FLORENCE

Florence was quite literally running out of foul language. She spat vulgarity with the same reckless abandon as she pulled on the throttle. The train went faster when she cursed at it.

She turned to the pressure gauges, only about three-fourths of which she could actually boast an understanding of their numbers. And of that three fourths, she only had a rudimentary working knowledge. Ari would have been driven up a wall. Helen and Will would laugh at the mere sight of her behind the engine. But none of them were there now.

Florence didn't have an endless supply of numbers that spewed from the depths of her mind, only some vulgar phrases. She was certainly not one of the most gifted Ravens to walk the guild hall in Holx, just a little crow on the run. She had her wits, a basic amount of education in a number of areas, two dead bodies, and a lot of endwig as motivation for some quick thinking.

The train rattled and shook as it gained steam. Embers spit out from the engine gate, singeing her clothes and skin. The vessel lurched violently, sending her scrambling for some variety of hold that wouldn't leave her tumbling out the side of the car. The clamp of teeth echoed by her ear as an endwig nearly missed her shoulder.

With a grunt, she righted herself in the engine room, her hands finding the levers again. Endwig were now splattering against the side of the train. Their attempts at a hypnotic hum were drowned out by the sound of the wheels on rails, the squeal of steel on steel as they rounded a corner in the wood.

It looked like they'd gained enough steam—*finally*—to outrun any real threat from the monsters. Florence still pushed the train hard, like a bullet from the chamber. This wasn't the Underground, where the next move was to proceed with quiet and caution. The endwig slept during the day and fed in the twilight hours. She would take them past the dawn and into the only "safe" time they had now.

They. Florence hoped it was still a case of "they" and not just "her". Nora and Derek only had to fend off the endwig for a short time before she'd gotten the train up to speed. After that it was just a matter of not falling out. Florence began to ease up the steam. If they couldn't handle staying on the train, she really had no hope of helping them all the way to Ter.1.

The train coasted along the track, slowly losing momentum. They'd wasted a lot of coal on their flight, and she'd have to make what was left stretch. That meant using the brakes as minimally as possible and squeezing every last bit of heat out of the steam that it had to give. It was nearly midday by the time they finally ground to a halt.

She collapsed, exhausted, still sweating from the heat of the engine and the stress. Florence leaned against the wall, her head tipped back. She took in long, luxurious breaths of air and savored the silence. The blood of Anders and Rotus was caked on the floor around her. She'd ditched their bodies at some point in the early dawn in the hopes they might draw away the endwig. But their blood remained, and likely would for some time.

The train sighed softly with motion from the back. Florence heard footsteps nearing the engine door. She pulled her revolver, holding it up at arm's length.

Lined up in her sight was a pair of familiar coal colored eyes. Derek slowly raised his hands.

The gun was heavy in Florence's palm. It was like she lifted a cannon made of pure lead, not a revolver. Her finger tensed on the trigger. The hammer struck on the gun.

And nothing happened.

"Bang." Florence had run out of canisters three hours ago. "If you were an endwig, you'd be dead," she lied.

"Good thing I'm not." Derek seemed to have the sense not to point out the falsehood of the weary Revolver's claims, seeing as she'd just saved his life.

"Good thing." She dropped the gun with a loud clang as it met the metal floor and closed her eyes. "Did Nora make it?"

"She did."

"I felt one of your explosions. Damn near knocked me out of the engine," Florence muttered. Exhaustion crashed down on her all at once. She never wanted to open her eyes again.

Derek stepped up into the engine, approaching her without hesitation or question. A hand slipped under her knees, the other rounding her back.

"Don't," she commanded as he tried to lift her.

"Nora is already asleep. I'm taking you back to the car with us."

"No." Florence shook her head. "We're too close to the endwig. I need to sleep in the engine in case we need to make a sudden and unexpected escape."

"Are you our Raven now?"

"And your Rivet. And your Revolver." Florence grinned, opening her eyes halfway. She felt drunk off fatigue and high on the remnants of adrenaline. "It doesn't matter what you want to call me. I promised the Vicar Alchemist I would get you to Ter.1, and you can bet that's what I'm going to do."

Derek rolled on his side, settling next to her. She watched him until her eyelids were spent and her neck was too exhausted to fight gravity a moment longer. Her head tipped onto his shoulder and Derek kept his arm around her.

They both stank of perspiration and blood, but neither cared. He tilted his head, resting it on hers. "Don't be an Alchemist next."

"Why?"

"Then you won't need Nora or me."

She huffed at the notion. "I don't need you now."

He chuckled by way of agreement.

"But I like having you both around," Florence confessed. The two had been annoying for her, but it would be lonely without them on the journey. There was comfort to be found in the warmth of another, and the radiant heat reminded her for a moment longer that she was not alone.

CVAREH

The wind was still under his heels as Cvareh sped through the halls of the Xin Manor. Arianna was back sequestered to her room, only placated with the promise that he would return later to explain the Crimson Court in full. Ever since Zurut informed him that the Court was coming to Ruana, all he could think about was what he had to do to help Petra and his house.

For all the urges he felt toward Arianna, Cvareh would not let his loyalty to Xin be shaken. She was a new presence in his life, and he was loath to admit that she would likely force herself to be a temporary one. But his House would be his family forever. It was his home, his legacy, the greater picture of which he was only one small part.

He ignored all others, focusing on the one place he expected to find his sister. Up a curving stairway, he ascended to the heart of Xin Manor. The ancients lined the walls. Dragons with mighty bat-like wings and mouths filled with pointed teeth hovered overhead, sculpted with lifelike precision. Candlelight flickered over their faces, slowly diminishing into nothingness.

Cvareh emerged from the smothering blackness into a room of pure light, feeling like he had been born again in the process. His eyes narrowed to thin slits, adjusting to the sudden change in brightness. They found the room's focal point. Not any sort of art, but a woman. Muscles bulged from her skin, fueled by frustrations that Petra had yet to relinquish. Her eyes were locked on the Temple of Lord Xin, visible in the far distance through the glass windows that made up more of the walls than the stone.

"Brother." Petra shifted slightly on the pedestal where she sat.

He accepted her invitation, sitting on the opposite edge. He leaned so their backs and heads would touch. One mind, one body, one unit that existed for House Xin. Cvareh closed his eyes and readied his ears for the words of the Oji.

"Yveun seeks to root out weakness in our House."

"He does."

"I informed Cain that all are to be ready, that we are to be the ones to fight duels. We will open our land to his Court, but I will not give him our blood easily."

Cvareh expected no less. "I will seek out Finnyr for potential challenge opportunities."

"Let it be done."

None could ever say that Petra hesitated. In moments she could assess a situation for an opportunity and decide upon the best course of action. It was more than Cvareh could do in hours some days.

"I cannot keep you from this Court." Her voice shifted slightly at the mere notion of him.

Cvareh gave the world a tired smile. "We knew this day would come."

"I cannot stand for you."

"I understand."

Petra could stand for nearly anyone in House Xin, but not Cvareh. He was her brother and the chosen Ryu. All eyes turned to him to defend the House in her name and carry the title of Oji should she be felled in some form of misfortune other than a sanctioned duel. He would have to defend himself, or he would never be accepted as the Ryu again.

"How many could you kill?"

Cvareh considered it a long moment. The first time he'd really put training to application was on Loom, and that had been a failure overall. Though using any combat against Arianna was entirely unfair... Responsibility suddenly crushed him, the supports that held it over his head breaking the moment he awoke to the real truth of his standing.

"No more than three beads." He put it in the perspective of the King's Riders—a somewhat universal standard for the might of a warrior.

Silence was Petra's way of screaming her displeasure. "You must work with Cain."

"I will."

"Daily."

"I will."

"Cvareh." Her body was so tense he was surprised her muscles had yet to snap her bones from the strain.

"Petra."

"You must not die on me. That is an order from the Oji to her Ryu." The room was so silent he could hear her swallow. "We did not come this far together for you to fall to Rok scum. Go beneath the surface, find duels, gain practice killing."

Unsanctioned duels were something the Oji should discourage at all costs. Yet here she was, doing the exact opposite. The ends would come before the ideals sacrificed to reach them. They were Xin.

"I will."

A different sort of quiet passed between them. A comfortable separation of realities where Nova existed elsewhere and they were the only people in the world of Petra's meditation tower. Cvareh played with Arianna's name in his head, trying to figure out how best to broach the topic.

"Out with it." Petra sensed his turmoil.

"Arianna and I… We went into Napole, and she wore the guise of a Xin."

"Good. I could not handle dealing with the common populous knowing we harbored an odd Chimera."

"I introduced her as an Anh."

Petra didn't move; she hardly seemed to breathe. "You are truly an idiot, brother."

"I did not expect a Crimson Court."

"No, and you wanted to make it known you had found a potential mate." Petra's tone was stretched between amusement, frustration, and exasperation. "She could have been nothing more than a slave, and yet you chose to give her a name of our House."

Was that what it was? Cvareh wondered to himself. "I was merely trying to protect her."

Petra broke the room's stillness with unabashed laughter. "From what you tell me of our Chimera, you should be more worried about protecting yourself. I do not think the woman wants nor needs you to fight her battles."

"You know her surprisingly well for someone who has spoken to her once."

"Cain tells me things."

It was Cvareh's turn to tense. It was no secret that Cain delighted in his sister's happiness. They weren't a poor match, either. But Cvareh didn't relish the notion of any man with Petra. Furthermore, the last one who had aspired ended with a few holes in unexpected places and a gouged out throat when he had ultimately displeased Cvareh's sister. And Cvareh actually liked Cain.

"You've introduced her as your own. If she's challenged, you'll stand for her." Duty pulled the command from Petra's lips.

"She won't be challenged," he offered hopefully, not wanting to linger on the fact that Petra had just all but said that Ari's life would ultimately be worth more than his. "Those who know she exists won't care enough to interrupt the flow of the pit with all the duels we will be challenging in Rok. It would be against the spirit of the Court."

Petra hummed in mild agreement, unconvinced. "Just make sure she stands out no more than she already will as the first by your side."

Cvareh straightened away and Petra did the same. As comforting as it was to linger on one another, they both had work to do. Cvareh descended first, winding his way back to Arianna. His thoughts were gray and clouded, not unlike the Gods' Line in the sun's fading light.

He wandered back to the other woman who had given purpose to his days. Cvareh went straight to her room first, before even changing his clothes for proper evening attire.

He gave the door a soft knock, waiting for permission before entering. Arianna was positioned at her table by the Western facing window. He would've thought it would be too bright for anyone to sit in the sun like that, but there she was, day after

Elise Kova

day. For the first time, Cvareh wondered if she was even happy on Nova.

"Have you attended the Oji?"

"The Oji? You're beginning to sound like a Dragon." He closed the door behind him, crossing over to her desk.

She turned stiffly. He'd heard the sarcastic tone in the way she'd used Petra's title. But Cvareh knew it would irk her more to play into it than make a fuss of it. The assessment seemed to hold true.

"What are you working on?"

"Hypotheticals," she answered vaguely.

The schematics held a weird sort of beauty. Dark wound against light as ink on parchment. Seemingly chaotic conceptions became definite shapes punctuated with calculations that were a language all their own. And, if Arianna wasn't going to decode their meaning for him, he was certainly not going to decipher it by himself. So Cvareh was left to quiet admiration, seeing the form before the function.

"You owe me an explanation," she reminded him.

Cvareh caught her eyes, the demand in them apparent. "I do." He sat back onto the bed and Arianna turned to face him. "The Crimson Court will be held here on Ruana in a fortnight. It is usually held on Lysip, home of House Rok and the current Dono. But Yveun has decided to have it here on Ruana."

"This is significant."

He could see Arianna trying to piece together the parts she'd been handed, but—likely to her annoyance—she had too many knowledge gaps still to truly comprehend the gravity of the situation. "It is. All named members of the hosting House must be in attendance. Usually, Rok is all too happy to have the advantage of their own turf and the inevitable outnumbering—"

"But this time they want to corner you."

Cvareh held his tongue that it could be a literal "you," as he was notorious for avoiding the Court. "Petra and I believe so, yes."

"So what is the real concern? A noble court hardly sounds like cause for too much agony. Worried you won't have the most fashionable garb there?" She snickered, but the smile slowly faded from her mouth at his solemn expression.

"The Court is not some place that we all gather and gossip; we have the tea parlors and wineries for that. The only way for people to advance in Dragon society is by killing the rank above them. To keep things orderly, these duels must usually be sanctioned by the Oji, except during the Court. Then, nearly all duels are heard and seen out... One exception being if the Dono himself decides to intervene."

Arianna stared at him for a long, hard moment. She tapped her nails on the table in quick succession and glanced over her shoulder at the fading light outside. Her magic was as silent as her lips, her thoughts locked away in some place he couldn't reach.

She turned back to him with the look of resolve he associated with overt danger. "You're going to be challenged."

"I have no doubt of it. It's possible you will be too."

"Me?" The idea shouldn't have delighted the woman nearly as much as it did.

"I introduced you as a Xin'Anh today. It's not impossible some woman who had been craving the idea of being my mate could challenge you in an attempt to earn my favor."

As Arianna considered this, she folded her hands behind her head. Her grin only continued to expand. "Someone craving you is almost comical."

Cvareh rolled his eyes, slightly stung from her words. Not overly so, but just a bit more than he'd want to admit. "I am something here on Nova." He would never dismiss the title Petra had given to him, what it meant to his House.

"You are," she agreed easily with a small spring to her feet. Arianna's fingers were like wriggling worms attached to her palms. "And that's why you deserve a real woman, should a woman be your desire."

Arianna advanced on him and Cvareh leaned back, his palms spreading against the heavy duvet that covered her bed. She straddled his knees, looming over him. It was imposing and dominating and it made him want to wrestle her to the ground. It made him want to submit.

"How do you define a 'real woman', Fenthri?" His voice had shifted to something he was barely familiar with. He liked the molasses quality of it as it coated his throat and honeyed his tongue.

"One who doesn't lurk in shadows waiting for opportune challenges because they know you would otherwise never support them at your side." She spoke as though the fact should be obvious, but it was a somewhat foreign notion to Cvareh's Dragon blood. Foreign, but not unwelcome.

Cvareh straightened some, closing a hand's width of distance between them. Arianna was too smart for him to assume she wasn't aware of what she was doing. But what was she doing? Cvareh didn't know, but he wasn't bound by her logical mind. He was a man who could savor beauty and relax in knowing something was because that was how it should be.

When she was near him, like this, everything was how it should be.

"So, when do we begin?"

"Begin?" He swallowed, the word having application to a seemingly infinite number of meanings.

"I may be challenged. You *will* be challenged." Arianna held out her hands.

No, my brother's hands, Cvareh reminded himself. The idea sobered him some. This entrancing woman who seemed to hold a universe of possibilities on her tongue—if she deigned to share them—was made of the pieces of his kin.

With far too much focus, claws jutted like magic from her fingers. Arianna's mouth curved into a wild snarl, the somewhat sensual woman from before lost completely to a wild and equally thrilling side. Cvareh's magic heightened as he was aware in a very new way that she had him trapped between her legs, every vital spot within a hand's reach.

"I need to learn to use these." Arianna turned over her hands in utter fascination. "Why don't we help each other?"

"You want to spar with me?"

"I can always twist Cain's arm into it," she said, as lightly as if the proud Dragon had already agreed to the matter.

Cvareh placed his hands on her hips. They were wide with strong bones underneath the muscle and flesh. He pushed her away just enough to stand. Face to face, a breath apart, he kept her in his grip far longer than what was necessary, just to feel her pulse under his fingers.

She didn't step away; she let him hold her there. That fact he was somehow keenly aware of, despite having no reason to know it. He nor anyone else would ever touch her, hold her, keep her, unless she willed it so.

"We begin at sundown every day." Cvareh fought the urge to pull her the rest of the way to him. To press her so tightly against his body that they no longer knew where one of them ended and the other began.

"It's sundown now, Cvareh'Ryu," she observed quietly.

"I suppose it is." Though he had long been admiring the way the sunset lit her white hair afire. "Are you ready?"

"Am I ever not?" She gave him what Cvareh would dare call a coy grin.

It was a question he delighted in not being able to refute.

PETRA

etra ran her claws along the unfinished banister that led down from her personal roost in the Xin Manor. Let it never be said that she didn't make sacrifices on behalf of her House. She had reallocated all hands and tradesmen from finishing different parts of the manor for the sake of building an amphitheater for the Crimson Court.

It had been a couple hundred years since the last Court had been held on Ruana, long ago when House Xin was still in power and the gathering was known as the Cobalt Court. A crumbling reminder of the long-ago glory days of House Xin, the amphitheater had suffered from disuse. No Xin wanted to lay eyes on it, like a shameful scar that would never stop weeping blood.

Petra was determined to see the place resurrected not just to its former glory, but even better than before. The laborers would work non-stop until the Court to complete her grand designs. But they would make the usual venue for the Crimson Court on Lysip look humble in comparison. She wanted retractable sunshades over the stadium seating. Cushions, special just for this Court, made for every seat. Running water, box seats, food and wine service throughout—nothing would be spared.

If Yveun was going to hand them the Court, she would show everyone why they deserved it.

"How does the construction proceed?" Cain waited for her at the bottom of the stairs.

"Slower than I would like." As was usually the case. "But well enough. The foreman assures me that we will have it completed in time." There were only two weeks left before the Court would begin.

"Gathering offenses on House Rok has proved no real difficulty."

She snorted, as if it would have.

"Any word from Finnyr on the matter?"

"He's handed me some good bits of information. I have those who can make the claims already working on ways for them to 'uncover' these offenses on their own." Petra trusted Cain. She trusted him as much as she trusted any other man—the length of her arms and the depth of her claws. But he'd proved a loyal leader within House Xin and a faithful friend to Cvareh. For those two things, she found herself able to appreciate his brisk mannerisms and focused nature.

"Finnyr has proved useful."

"By some miracle," she agreed reluctantly. By far the most helpful information she'd ever worked out of Finnyr was the knowledge of the Philosopher's Box schematics. Petra had heard about the box from the snippets of details she'd managed to attain from the last rebellion. But it wasn't until one night when Finnyr was well in his cups that he boasted he'd seen such plans with his own eyes.

After that, it was simply a matter of more wine, sending Cvareh to visit his brother more often, and patience. Thoughts of Cvareh shifted her attention.

"How do my brother and the Chimera fare?" Petra hadn't been terribly surprised when Cain had informed her Cvareh had elected to work with Arianna over him. The woman had a certain *appeal* for Cvareh that Cain did not. And Petra was inclined to allow Cvareh his desires, so long as he was still ready for the Court when the time came. She'd set Cain to ensuring that much.

"Surprising progress." Cain motioned for a nearby stair, and Petra nodded.

They progressed silently upward, the stairs leveling out upon a high arcade. From the vantage, they could look down upon a private pit she had seen set aside for use of her immediate family. There were few windows that oversaw this pit, and Petra knew who had access to every one of them. She cast her eyes downward.

It was the first time she had seen the Chimera's Dragon illusion. It was skillful, tight upon her and smooth. There wasn't a single kink in it and no bizarre ripple of magic. The pulse that radiated from it was nothing more than what one would expect of a Dragon's magical aura in general. There was nothing about it that would alert even Petra to its presence if she hadn't known it was there.

Arianna spun widely around Cvareh, bringing her fingertips into his neck—a kill. Petra watched as they backed away and lunged for each other once more. The woman tripped up Petra's brother, stumbling him and grabbing for his throat in the process—a kill. They separated again and were soon tumbling, head over heels, until the Chimera had mounted Cvareh like a broken stallion with her fingertips pressing over his heart—a kill.

"She's quite good, isn't she?"

"She is known as the White Wraith," Cain begrudgingly admitted. "At least she seems to have earned her infamy."

Petra watched them round each other, again and again. The longer she watched, the more unsettled she became. It was not just because Cvareh clearly needed to develop considerable polish in the short time before the Court. There was an odd shadow puppetry before her; it ran deeper than the illusion and more mysterious than the woman's apparent skill.

"Why do they not use their claws?" The woman was all teeth and snarls and pure attack power. Yet neither drew blood.

"Cvareh tells me it was her decision. A caveat to their arrangement."

"Did he say why?" The notion seemed far too tender for the woman before Petra. She couldn't imagine Arianna's demand stemmed from mere sentimentality.

Cain shook his head.

Petra continued to stare, trying to make sense of what she was seeing. There was something amiss. She could almost, almost... smell it.

"There is something... *off* about her." Cain gave Petra's thoughts sound. "I thought it the first day she came. I'd mistakenly attributed it to merely being a Chimera, but it's deeper than that."

"Explain." Petra would not rake her brain against something Cain had already begun to make sense of.

"She moves like a Dragon, she acts like a Dragon."

"She's clearly well educated." The woman had designed the Philosopher's Box, after all. Or so Cvareh claimed.

"She's taller than the usual Fen. Her body is stronger. She has true weight to her." Petra held her refute, allowing Cain to continue, hoping he would tell her something more meaningful than mannerisms and muscles. "She doesn't smell of rot."

Petra inhaled deeply, as though she could smell the woman in the pit far below from their obscure vantage. *That's what it is,* she realized. All the Chimera she had ever encountered smelled fiercely of rot, of muddled blood and stolen organs. Arianna had no such scent about her.

"Even when she attached Finnyr's hands... There were no rags of blood in her quarters. She burnt them along with her severed parts. The stink from the procedure should have been enough to set half the manor fleeing to avoid the smell."

"Was there no mark of Chimera blood in her room?" Only Dragon blood disappeared tidily in the air. Chimera and Fenthri blood stained, much like their very existence.

Cain shook his head. Petra considered heading there herself just for the sake of checking. "There was a blood trace, but it was unlike anything I've known—Dragon or Chimera. It smelled of both Xin cedar, like Finnyr, and Tam honeysuckle."

"The room would smell of Finnyr," Petra reasoned, thinking of her elder brother's severed hands. But that didn't explain the crispness, the purity. "What do you think is the cause?"

"I don't know..." Cain struggled with the evidence set before him. If looks could kill, the Chimera who was still besting Cvareh far below them would be struck down and begging for release. "But I do know she has at least four Dragon organs."

"Four?"

"Eyes and ears were visible from the start, even if she's capped her ears with metal so they do not grow into points."

Petra couldn't stop herself from touching her own ear, horrified at the thought of such mutilation of one of the most striking features of a Dragon.

"Hands, now, thanks to Finnyr," Cain continued. "And her stomach."

"Her stomach?" Petra repeated expectantly. That wasn't information that could be encountered casually.

"I saw the addition of holly peas into her food."

Red and unassuming, the holly pea looked similar to any other brilliant berry. But it caused severe indigestion in both Dragon and Fenthri alike. Consumption of just a small amount was usually followed with a day of vomiting and diarrhea. Non-lethal, but severely uncomfortable if one did not possess magic in their stomach. "How very underhanded of you, Cain."

"Forgive me." He avoided her narrowed eyes.

Subversion was something Petra didn't tolerate; it was an affront to their ways. But the matter was done, and the woman in question wasn't a Dragon anyway. "Do not make a habit of such deceptions. You are above it."

"I would not." He looked horrified.

"Good." Petra let the conversation continue, satisfied. "She was unaffected?"

"No sign of troubles."

"There was no way she could have removed them?"

"If she even knows what they are? No. They were added to a strawberry jam."

"You are truly ruthless." She bared her teeth in an appreciative smile. This was what she needed from Cain. She needed someone who was so loyal to their House that he would risk her ire for the sake of its defense.

He gave a small bow of his head. All delight faded when Cain turned back to the pit. Arianna had just bested Cvareh again. "Petra'Oji..."

She wasn't familiar with hesitation from Cain. It made her give him all the more attention. "Be careful with this one."

Petra narrowed her eyes to slits. "You think I cannot fell her?"

"I do not doubt you." The *but* was felt before it was spoken. "But she is something different. She has that many organs and has not fallen. Think of what she might be like with more. More magic? More power? She—"

"You have been heard, Cain," Petra dismissed him abruptly. She would not tolerate dissent or questioning in her ranks. Cain had earned himself good will for investigating the woman, an odd mix given his unconventional methods of doing so. She wouldn't want to see him squander it.

Cain gave a short bow and descended the stairs gracefully. Petra's eyes remained locked on the woman far below. Cain didn't know it, but what he feared was a Perfect Chimera. A creature that was so mighty it could even challenge a Dragon.

Petra grinned madly.

One man's fear was another's salvation.

YVEUN

The skies were filled with boco as Dragons of all colors flooded Easwin, the easternmost town of the Isle of Ruana. It was impossible to look in any direction and not see scarlet, cerulean, or viridian. Yveun surveyed the generally unassuming town from his current perch. It was unorthodox to be anywhere but Lysip for a Crimson Court, but it was too late now to question his play.

"How many people worked on getting the amphitheater up to par?" he asked over his shoulder. Slaves silently dotted and lined his exposed chest with a thick paste that would temporarily tattoo his flesh.

"Petra told me she had over five hundred workers at all hours." Finnyr was seated awkwardly in the center of the room behind Yveun. He was appropriately ignored by the slaves, their focus on their master—as it should be. Yet the fact that Yveun had not dismissed him was its own form of honor. Yveun kept Finnyr trapped in the "between", a place few Dragons ever found themselves in thanks to their society's strict hierarchy.

"How did she find the craftsmen?" It annoyed Yveun to no end that Petra had managed to scrape together the sort of display that towered against the distant horizon. The girl was an annoying little gnat, impossible to squish and always flying around where she didn't belong. A gnat that aspired to be a wasp and already fashioned itself thusly.

"She told me she took all hands from progression on the Xin manor. Some others were in Napole still after the initial construction. The rest? Nameless from below, I believe."

"So desperate is she to display her strength that she leans on the shadowed nameless." His insult was for no one but himself. Finnyr was already his obedient servant. The slaves who attended him had no names themselves and therefore no souls and no purpose. Nevertheless, letting out his displeasure into the very air on Ruana sated him some. "I will let you return to her tonight when the day's duels have ended."

"You will?" Finnyr's voice started shrill before he managed to control his emotions.

"Is that a problem, Finnyr?" Yveun held up a hand, stalling the servants' work. He turned to look at the Xin's face. It was harder for a man to lie when you were actively trying to spoon out the truth through his eyes.

"N-no, Dono..." He went pale. "After last time, my sister was adamant that I stay with you."

Yveun keenly remembered the man's bruises from having his hands harvested. He wanted to slice Finnyr up himself and force him to watch his organs being fed and connected to Fenthri as punishment for his cowardice. His voice was a low growl that rumbled over the jagged stones of his aggravation. "I held this Court on Ruana so I might finally learn the truth of what happened on Loom, and the extent of how far Petra's power reaches into the land below—how it may even be increasing here on Nova. You will play your role and return to her as a relieved prodigal child, blessed to be home. You will prove your worth and give me the information I seek."

Finnyr lowered his eyes submissively. "Of course, Dono. I live to serve you in no half measures."

Satisfied, Yveun turned forward again. "I want you to find whatever information you can on Cvareh—of his trip to Loom, of the schematics he stole. Speak to slaves, servants. Offer them a better life on Lysip with the favor of the Dono if you must."

He would never actually allow Xin hands who had served Petra directly to attend him. But they didn't need to know he would see them dead the second they set foot on his home. Their surprise would be delicious.

He locked eyes on the grand, stone amphitheater in the distance. The streets were already filled with music and cheers. Laughter harmonized with song as men and women danced together. The Court was a celebration of life, and death, and everything that hung in the balance between those conflicting yet beautiful forces.

He rode in a litter to the Court. It was a wide platform with low railings and a pointed roof covered in red clay tiles and edged in silver. The wooden base and poles were a fine mahogany, stained to a deep wine color. Textiles the colors of fire shone, silks glinting with sunlight. Sixteen men carried its bulk through the streets.

It stood in stark contrast to the lake blue pennons and people of House Xin that parted like waves around his metaphorical boat. Yveun kept his eyes forward, or on the woman who lounged next to him.

Coletta Rok'Ryu To was thin for a Dragon. She had never quite grown out of her girlish years, her face remaining soft and her cheeks rounded. Her ears pointed more outward than upward and her nose was thin and narrow, cutting between two eyes that looked all the larger for it.

She was his cherry woman. She smelled of the fruit and perfumed herself with it for added effect. Her flesh was creamy-orange, hardly red at all, but it reminded him of the sweet cherries that could be cultivated in the spring. Her hair was the bright red of a candied fruit of the same variety. But her eyes were truly striking, dark orbs that shone with the depth of a rich wine. The kind that could absorb a man whole.

Those same eyes looked listlessly at the world around them, as if it were all more trouble than what it was worth. For Coletta, it may well have been.

"Ruana has not changed much since the last time I was here," she said softly. She was a humble and unassuming counterpart to the loud and dominating presence that was Yveun.

"And how often do you come to Ruana?"

"Too often, in that I come at all." She lay back. Gossip-mongers would continue to perpetuate her weak and sickly state. But all Yveun saw was the visage of a woman who was nothing more than fiercely bored.

"I appreciate your indulgence, Rok'Ryu." He spoke sincerely. Coletta wasn't one for leaving her gardens or... diversions. But she had packed and mounted her boco without question upon hearing that the Court was to be held on Ruana.

"You should never have any doubt." The words were almost threatening, on the off chance he sincerely had.

"In you? Never." Truer words had yet to be spoken that day.

"Besides, you need me." Her mouth pressed into a thin and knowing smile that Yveun could never deny. "So, what role am I playing by day while we are here?"

He was the sun, and she was his moon. Forever in orbit, perpetually watching the sky while the other slumbered. Thus, by day, she operated by his wants and rules. By night, he by hers. "The same role you usually do. No one will challenge you if they think it will be a poor, shameful duel with a sickly Ryu."

Coletta laughed softly. When she smiled he could see the gray of her gums, turned to ash with her secretive and underhanded business.

"Let them challenge me, Yveun, and see how long they live."

Yveun smiled back at his mate, baring his teeth. If anyone did ever challenge the Rok'Ryu, they would answer to him. Yveun would never let another touch his queen. They should *hope* to answer to him. For, if Coletta had her way, the death would be infinitely more painful and drawn out than anything Yveun could devise.

The amphitheater was even more impressive up close. Every fifth column was the sculpture of a Dragon—ones he did not recognize but could only assume were important to House Xin. Wide, bat-like wings extended behind them, supporting the second tier of seating and arcade windows that let in the breezes from above. Sapphires as big as his head made their eyes, shining keenly at all who entered through the archways below.

They were met by a tall man with skin the color of sea foam. His name faded away from Yveun's immediate memory into the realm of unimportance, but Finnyr seemed to recognize him. The two exchanged a tense look before the man led them up a quiet stair.

"The Xin'Oji has prepared this viewing platform especially for you, Dono." He bowed, motioning for Yveun and his party to continue.

The balcony was high, the highest in the amphitheater, laden with fineries and draped in chiffon that danced upon the wind. It was a box befitting of a king positioned among the nameless and slaves.

In all other instances, he would insist on being the highest in a room, the better to loom over all that was his. But at the Court he wanted to be in the thick of it. He wanted to be so close to the pit that blood could splatter his cheeks. He wanted to be—

Yveun walked over to the edge of the balcony.

—where Petra was sitting.

The woman raised her glass of Xin wine with a thin smile. It was a restrained motion, but a quiet jab all the same. Yveun waged an internal war. He could demand her position, but then he would look like the insecure ruler who needed a place to solidify his prowess. Tam would certainly trade him; their platform was in the middle of the arena. But the spot was fitting for those who kept the balance. Furthermore, he was the Rok'Oji Dono, and he *would not* rely on a Tam.

"Wine," Yveun growled, holding out his hand. He didn't even see who supplied it.

He raised his own glass to Petra, staring down the woman for a long moment. She sipped, and he did the same. Yveun turned and stalked to his seat, virtually out of sight for the masses below. No, he asked no man or woman for pity. If he was to be seated above them all, he would appear like a god to rule over life and death and the Dragon Court. He made concessions to no man or woman.

The man who had escorted them to the box departed. Finnyr, Coletta, Lossom, and two of his most trusted Kin remained. Coletta stepped forward, dropping her voice to a hush meant only for his ears.

"She seeks to make a fool of you, Yveun."

"Doesn't she always?" He took another healthy drink from his wineglass.

"You have walked into her home to let her do it." Coletta rarely guarded her tongue to anyone, Yveun included.

"She will be the fool before the day is done," Yveun swore.

"See that she is, Dono." Coletta gave him a cautionary stare. "I grow tired of this game I've let you play."

A growl rose from his throat as his mate walked to one of the plush seats. It escaped as a roar that echoed throughout the amphitheater. A third of the seats were still empty, as the upper echelons of Dragon society slowly flowed in from the revelries outside. But Yveun was done waiting, and they all functioned at his behest.

He threw down his glass. Wine arced through the air like crimson rain before splattering between shards of glass in the pit far below. The very wind itself seemed to hold its breath for his decree.

"I did not travel from Lysip for wine." His voice boomed, echoing off every pillar and person. "I traveled for blood. I traveled to thin my fattening Court. I traveled to see which of you are deserving of your names and which of you have yet to grow into the titles you were born for."

No one spoke. No one breathed.

"Let the Crimson Court commence!" he shouted so loudly the very heavens rumbled. "Who will be the first challenger?"

A man stood, eager for the honor of being the first in the pit, to be the one whose feet would touch that hallowed and unsoiled ground. Yveun bared his teeth in utter delight that the man was one of House Rok. Unsurprisingly, he called against one of House Xin for an offense of cheating committed in his card room.

The two leapt over people and empty stands, descending into the pit as claws and teeth and rage. With no objection from Yveun, they collided. Gold splattered the walls, the smell of freshly cut grasses filling the air from the Xin. It mingled and soured against the smell of huckleberry from the Rok. The two scraped and scrambled for a long few minutes, shredding each other to pulp.

But, as Yveun expected in all things, the man of House Rok eventually won the upper hand.

He tore the Xin man's heart still beating from his chest. He held it up with a primal cry, golden blood running down his arm and dripping onto his face before slowly evaporating into the air. The Rok man brought the heart to his mouth and took a glutinous bite.

Rok and Xin battled into the afternoon. For every one Rok challenge, there were two Xin. Tam may as well have not even shown up. It was clear who was fighting for dominance in this Court. Yveun missed half the fights, his seat positioned too far back and too high for a good view. But every time he graced the edge of the balcony, the Rok fighters below battled twice as hard and went for increasingly vicious kills.

As a result of this poor positioning, it was afternoon by the time he finally realized the House Xin box had been filled. Yveun's blood ran hot at the mere sight of Cvareh, the lying bastard brother of the bitch who pursued his demise as though she had nothing else in the world to worry over.

"Lossom," he summoned his current Master Rider. The man was at his side in an instant. "Challenge Cvareh'Ryu."

"Dono, I have no cause for a challenge against the Xin'Ryu..." Lossom's hesitation was almost enough for Yveun to kick him face-first into the pit below and let whoever desired tear him limb from limb and lick his bones clean.

They had cause a hundred times over. The death of each one of his Riders on Loom would be more than enough for Yveun to order any Rok to challenge Cvareh. But that would first require admitting that the Riders were on Loom to begin with. Yveun growled, caught in a snare of his own shadowy invention.

"Invent one."

"But—"

"I am the Dono, Lossom. Comprehend what that means. If I support your demand for a duel, none will permit him to back out." Yveun walked away from the edge, and toward his beacon of sanity lounging in the shape of a woman.

Cheers erupted from the duel ending. The runner of the ring, one of House Tam for all their love of balance, called for the next challenger. Yveun waited expectantly.

"I, Lossom Rok'Anh To, Master Rider to Yveun Dono, challenge Cvareh Xin'Ryu Soh as a liar, and for disgraces against the Dono's name in the presence of a Rok." Lossom didn't flinch, completing the fatuous challenge with bold confidence. "Let he whose merit runs deepest through his veins live for the night's revelries. Let he whose merit is a facade be reduced to blood upon the ground and shame upon his House."

The arena had fallen silent. Every ear hung on Cvareh's response. Yveun waited with a smirk. Cvareh could not back down. If he questioned the legitimacy he'd look like a coward, for they all knew Yveun was going to allow the duel. It was time for the Xin'Ryu to finally enter the ring and be put to rest, out of Yveun's concerns once and for all.

"I stand for Cvareh'Ryu." An unfamiliar woman's voice rang out loud and clear.

Yveun stood slowly, walking to the edge. He had not expected anyone to stand for Cvareh against his Master Rider. To do so was the most foolish display of suicidal loyalty the Court had ever seen. Because if the one who stood for the accused fell, the accused was also put to death.

Far below, a pale blue woman stood with eyes like late sunset and hair the color of morning's first light. She cut her place in the world with foolhardy arrogance, standing as though she were the personified herald of the Death Lord himself.

ARIANNA

"I, Lossom Rok'Anh To, Master Rider to Yveun Dono, challenge Cvareh Xin'Ryu Soh as a liar, and for disgraces against the Dono's name in the presence of a Rok."

Cvareh tensed next to her. His eyes were locked in a grim sort of determination against the crimson man who stood at the edge of the King's box. Arianna could practically hear the echo of the words repeating themselves in his head as the challenger still spoke them.

"Let he whose merit runs deepest through his veins live for the night's revelries. Let he whose merit is a facade be reduced to blood upon the ground and shame upon his House."

Cvareh didn't move. It was as if the man who called himself Lossom had woven a netted spell that trapped him to the spot. Arianna made quick work of sizing up Lossom. Judging from her angle, the height of the amphitheater, and his perspective size, she knew he was larger than Cvareh both in muscle and height.

Her eyes fell on the beads that dangled by his ear. He had called himself the Master Rider. It seemed Yveun had been forced to go with a less experienced combatant after his other Riders had never returned from Loom.

She knew what was about to happen; she'd seen it enough throughout the day. Cvareh would stand, accept the challenge, and they would descend into the ring. No others of House Xin stood. It was a matter for the Ryu to defend his title, and judging from their practice sessions leading up to the Court, Ari had minimal confidence in his ability to do so.

"I stand for Cvareh'Ryu." Arianna jumped to her feet.

"What are you doing?" Cvareh hissed.

"Saving your life."

"This isn't done." He grabbed her arm, trying to pull her back down. "Dragons don't stand for their Ryu or Oji."

Arianna leaned forward, meeting him halfway. Her mouth found his ear as she spoke "Good thing I'm not a Dragon, then."

"Who are you?" The King's voice echoed across the silence.

She turned to address the man who gave face to all her nightmares, the formless evil who stood atop Loom like it was a tailless scorpion beneath his boot. She had watched him all day, studied him in every way she knew how. All evidence pointed to a singular truth: The Dragon King was nothing more than a man.

And men could be killed.

Men could be pinned down and ripped apart and tortured until they begged for release—release that would *never* be given to them.

"Ari Xin'Anh Bek," she recited.

His head turned, looking to Petra. Arianna followed his stare as well, catching Cain's eyes. They were as round as saucers and sparking with anger. She gave him a toothy grin. The man still thought she couldn't speak Royuk. *Well, now he knew.*

Petra glanced at her from the corners of her eyes but said nothing. Ari's play had worked. Petra couldn't speak against her without calling their whole facade into question. She couldn't give Ari any more care than she would any other Dragon. She had to ignore the fact that Arianna was the Fenthri who held the design of the Philosopher's Box in her mind. Cvareh could not stand when someone had stood for him. And that meant she was about to head into the pit.

"Very well, Ari Xin'Anh Bek. You fight with both your life and title as well as that of Cvareh Xin'Ryu." The Dono gave his blessing with amusement, already writing off the duel, and the Rider launched himself onto the stands nearby.

When Lossom was halfway down, Arianna set herself into motion as well. She'd seen enough of his mannerisms to gain an overall understanding of how fast he could move. She'd meet him in the pit.

The scent of blood and magic assaulted her the second her feet touched the packed ground. With no air or wind, it sat trapped on the surface, smothering her senses with the remnants of gore.

Arianna tightened the splint on her fingers one clip. They would be cut off before her illusion would fall.

She sprinted forward, determined to pounce on the Rider the moment he landed. But he sprung off the wall, spinning through the air and landing nimbly behind her. With the advantage she'd sought lost, Arianna was instantly on defensive.

He swung wide and she ducked, jabbing for his side. The edge of her claw caught against his lined and dotted skin, spilling first blood.

Lossom snarled, reaching for her with a clawed hand. Arianna fell backward, rolling away. He squinted in confusion.

Dragons were strong creatures, that much Arianna could not—and never had—denied. Their magic made them formidable. But it also made them predictable. When nearly any wound could be healed in moments, making very few cuts lethal, it meant their fighting styles favored close range and tight jabs. They shouldered wounds gladly that Arianna avoided desperately, and that made her erratic dodges unpredictable to them. It made her method of fighting as sensible to them as their fashion was to her.

She would win this fight without him drawing blood.

She had to.

Arianna lunged forward again. She leaned and spun, his claws whizzing over her back in a near miss. She would give nearly anything for her lines and daggers, but all that was permitted in the pit were claws and prowess. Weapons, coronas, gold, and magic—beyond healing—were all against the rules. Cvareh had taught her that much, to Arianna's dismay.

She sidestepped in and brought her hand up to the man's chin. Startled, it caught, stabbing right through to his tongue. Blood ran down her forearm and cheers erupted from above.

Arianna had never fought with an audience before. All her work had been done at night and in the shadows with the least number of eyes possible on her. She had never felt the thrill of screams and cries of encouragement. She had never fought for sport.

There was something about it, something...*thrilling*. Her heart raced faster and her feet moved with more confidence. She wanted to give the people a show. It was illogical, utterly illogical. Everything lacked meaning, and in that, there was joy. Joy in death, in life, in doing just to do.

Lossom's claws swung closer and closer. Every near miss pushed her forward. Blood still evaporated off his chest from where she had wounded him, from the new cuts she gave him.

She was faster, stronger, more skilled, and far more fearless than this Dragon would ever be. He could not kill those he loved for the sake of the survival of an ideal. He could not cut open his own chest and turn himself into a living machine for the sake of science.

But she could. She could because she was not Fenthri, or Dragon, or Chimera. She could because she had, and would again if fate re-dealt her a cruel hand.

Arianna kicked the Rider squarely in the chest. He stumbled, and she caught his ankle with the top of her foot, pulling it right out from under him. Off-balance, his attacks were thrown wildly. Arianna lunged into them. She pushed him downward and buried her hand in his chest. He struggled against her, his claws digging into her wrist viciously. Her blood mingled with his as it bubbled from the wound she was inflicting.

His heart beat frantically against her palm. For a brief second, she held his life and future in her hand. And then she ripped it from him.

Arianna stood with the man's heart. The arena's momentary shock was only half as deafening as the cheers that followed it in a rush. Her eyes found the Dragon King's high above, but not so far that he was untouchable. Not as far as he should want to be from her.

She stared at him as she buried her teeth into the Rider's heart, and envisioned it was his.

FLORENCE

The land had changed.

The Skeleton Forest had thinned and the dominant pines that oppressed their senses at every waking hour of the day had become scrawnier. As the train barreled down the winding pathway, they swerved out to the coast, giving Florence her first glimpse of the tall, rocky bluffs that made the Western side of Ter.2 impenetrable by boat.

The majority of Ter.2 was an imposing place—tall and shadowed, full of harsh rocky outcrops and the forest that boasted some of the most dangerous monsters in the world. But they had eluded the endwig, and lived to see the land change from the cold north to the more temperate, flatter south.

Tall grasses grew like in Ter.4, but the terrain was mostly flat, not hilly. It lacked significant features to the point that Florence wondered how the oceans had not just swallowed it whole. She watched it blur by as they continued on their tiny, overgrown track.

Nora and Derek alternated helping her. She had forced them to learn. She would shoulder as much of the burden as she had to, as they needed, but she could not do it alone. Will only went so far; skill was always required to make up the remainder.

They were begrudging at first, but not as much as Florence expected. She was too tired to question why, and thankfully the reason became apparent soon enough. She had earned an unexpected amount of respect from her companions after the night of the endwig. Her unconventional upbringing had served a purpose.

"How do you know how much coal to add, again?" Nora asked from where she was manning the grate and shovel.

Florence tapped the gauge next to her. "This meter. You want this to stay out of the high and low levels here and here. Ideally, it should sit around fifteen."

"Why?"

"For an engine this size, that amount of power seems to clip us along without wasting power. There's only so fast we can push her, or should…" Florence thought back to the sloppy repairs she'd made across the train following their frantic flight, and especially those she had less faith in holding. At least she'd had some training in the Ravens, but all her knowledge as a Rivet came from watching and helping Arianna.

Arianna. The name sat within Florence's heart, still encased in love. The months apart had shown Florence that much. She loved Arianna as the teacher and guardian she had been. The recognition of the fact made the distance, surprisingly, more bearable. It dulled the harsh words they'd spoken to one another and quietly assured Florence of Arianna's intentions. She knew the woman, and she knew that her venture to Nova was for the right reasons. And she knew that when Arianna returned, they would embrace once more and Florence would again be crafting canisters to help both the revolution and the White Wraith.

"What is most important to a Raven?"

Florence used the rattling of the train to mask a heavy sigh. She was always going to be seen as a Raven before anything else. She'd delighted in it when it had served her, when it had made people unassuming of her canisters in Mercury Town or her skill with the revolver. Or when it had helped her blend in at the port of Ter.5.2. But she was quickly learning she would give such things up for the sake of choice.

"Speed, mostly." The echoes of trikes whizzing through the streets of Holx echoed in Florence's ears. "Suicidal speed."

"And for a Revolver?"

Florence paused in surprise. She glanced over at Nora, who stopped her inspection of the gages long enough to search Florence's face.

"You'd know that too, right?"

"Explosions." Florence gave the woman a small smile.

"And Rivets?"

Florence had to think about that for a moment. While Ari was a Master Rivet, she was also not the most conventional of her guild. "Mathematics, perhaps?"

"That sounds terribly dull." Nora scrunched her coal dust-coated nose.

Florence grinned. "I think so too."

They slept together, all three of them, in the back car during the day while they were in the Skeleton Forest, and transitioned to sleeping at night in Ter.1. The air itself in the southern territory was thick; it made the hair on her neck stick without any effort. Florence much preferred working through the day when she would be uncomfortable in the engine anyway, than struggling to sleep in the moist daylight hours.

The nights were cooler, and it made huddling together all the more pleasant. There was a different sort of comfort among them than she'd found with Arianna. When Florence had lain in bed with Arianna, even snuggled together, there was a relaxed ease about it. But with Derek and Nora the pressure sat in her stomach, closer to her abdomen. It was the first time she'd felt such tension. She was smart enough to understand lust, but she wasn't fully aware for whom it stirred.

In all, the trip was mostly peaceful. There was still the stress of maintaining the train and managing the coal, but the old track they rode on was in good enough condition that Florence was confident it'd been used to smuggle things more recently than anyone let on. It was an overall straight shot with only two dead-end switch-offs until they reached Ter.1.2.

The train's terminal was an abandoned yard and they subsequently left it behind. Florence, Nora, and Derek continued on foot. Despite their brands, they were far enough from the Alchemists' Guild hall and past the territory border that they could move without any major concern. Derek carried two large trunks, Nora one, and Florence managed hers and a small case of their remaining powders onto the final train that would take them the rest of the way to Faroe.

They paid into a simple car, huddled with other patrons in bench seats. It was quite unlike her last train ride with Arianna when they had their own cabin; this trip lacked all sort of privacy or grace. Harvesters and others piled into the car, taking all available space, and they found themselves sharing their benches with three others.

Florence was pressed against the window for the two-day ride, and she watched as the land continued to change. The fertile middle ground between the end of the Skeleton Forest and the far end of Ter.1 became rocky and barren, void of life.

"What's that?" Florence squinted at a hole in the earth far in the distance. It looked as if someone had taken a spoon and carved out the land, removing it for some unknown reason.

"A strip mine," one of the Harvesters—Powell—replied.

"That's a mine?" Florence tried to reconcile what was before her. "Aren't mines in mountains? Tunnels?"

"They can be," Powell whispered, trying hard not to wake their sleeping companions squashed into the bench together. "It depends on the mineral we're mining for. If it occurs naturally in large pockets, we strip mine it. If it's in veins, tunnels may be more effective. Some can only be found in mountains."

The Harvester was quiet for a long moment.

"You lived far from home."

"What?" Florence asked, startled. They'd barely spoken more than courtesies, yet he had somehow known that about her.

"There are no mountains in Ter.4, little crow." The man gave a knowing smile. "Which leads me to believe you've spent some time in Ter.5."

Florence pursed her lips.

"Well, wherever you come from, you're far from home." He looked out the window.

"I don't know where home is." She didn't, not anymore. Florence longed for the flat she'd shared with Ari in Old Dortam. But it no longer fit them. Too much had changed. And, if the smaller flat in Ter.4.2 was any indication, Ari had no problem abandoning homes to move on when life demanded it.

"You're young enough that home should be Holx."

"It should be."

"But people are rarely what they should be." The man was older than her, perhaps nearing twenty-five. Older than

Arianna, at least, and that meant old enough to know of the time before the Dragons. "Why do you head to Faroe?"

"I'm taking my friends." Florence nodded at Nora and Derek, slumbering the hours away across from her.

"It's your first time in Ter.1?"

Florence nodded. The man leaned back in his chair, his gaze still focused on the mine in the distance as they slowly plodded along past it. Even packed in close as they were, they swayed slightly, shoulders brushing and sides flush.

"The land has changed much, in my years." Florence tried to decipher the somewhat somber note in the man's voice. "The Guild Initiates and Journeymen your age know it only as it is…"

"What's wrong with it?" Florence asked, still hearing the haze of regret that floated through the man's words.

"How long will you be in Faroe?"

If Florence wasn't so accustomed to Arianna, the questions answered with questions might have been grating. But there was a tranquil similarity in the obscured truths and hidden meanings. "I'm not sure."

"Then it will be long enough for you to arrive at your own opinions on these matters."

Florence heard the finality in the statement and rested her head on the glass of the window. The strip mine was now out of view, but she kept her eyes forward as the train swayed in determined progression to the home of the Harvesters. More and more mines dotted the surface of the land as they neared Faroe. Deeper and wider they ran, until the train traversed suspended bridge-ways that spanned a mine directly below them.

She stared over the ominous edge, keenly aware of the thin pieces of steel that separated the train from the seemingly infinite oblivion stretched deep into the earth below. Men and women worked on spiraling walkways on the outer edges of the mine, so far below her that they looked like flicks of dust floating in the mine's smoky haze rather than actual people. So, *so* far below that the explosions they set off were nothing more than flashes of light and dull reverberations.

It was as if the Harvesters had peeled back the surface of the earth to find its soul. And its soul was the very lifeblood of Loom: iron, minerals, oil, and coal.

Faroe was perched in the center of these seemingly endless mines, like an island among an empty sea. Its towering buildings and compact construction was unlike anything Florence had ever seen. Buildings made of concrete had spires of brick built atop them, foundations made from the carved stone left from long-ago mining. Like an impenetrable wall, it was all connected. One city, one guild, every peca of space used. She wondered if Arianna had ever been to Faroe, and if so, what the Rivet's take on the architectural choices were.

The train ran into a station underneath the city. Powell, in his kindness, offered to escort them to the guild hall. Florence was thankful they accepted when he led them through a rat maze of tunnels and tiny elevators that served as the city's only means of getting around.

"Faroe built up when it could no longer build out," Powell explained. "The problem with situating itself at the world's richest mineral deposits meant that most of the land needed to be committed to mining. The Rivets tried to make sense of it, but the Harvesters ended up doing what we do best." He knocked on the rough, bare stone wall next to him. Pick marks still pocked its surface. "We tunneled our way through."

Within the city proper, Florence felt an omnipresent weight. Rock and steel, brick and concrete hovered over her. It compressed Florence's lungs, and she was suddenly reminded of the last time she'd felt such a sensation.

"The Underground," Florence said boldly. It was a taboo subject in Ter.4, and, judging by the rise of Powell's eyebrows, it was known as such in Ter.1 as well. "Did Harvesters help with that at all?"

Powell considered it a long moment, encouraging in that he didn't immediately refuse the subject. "At the time the Underground was first being conceived, perhaps. We did grant them some of our explosives long ago, pre-Revolvers even, to help blast deeper after the ground was broken. But the limestone of Ter.4 is prone to pockets and holes, and the Ravens seemed impatient and determined to make the place their own. Moreso after the Dragons' regulations on the guilds."

The man's tone differed from Ari's at the mere mention of the Dragons. There was no bitter bite, no longing for the past. Instead she heard quiet acceptance. His eyes reflected... appreciation?

The weight was lifted as they ascended to the guild proper. A disk shape at the very top of Faroe, the hall's outer walls were all windows, permitting the gray sunlight and a view of the barren earth beyond. Florence set her bag down slowly, her hand numb from carrying it. As if in a trance, she crossed to the nearest pane of glass. Five times her width, three times her height, it felt as if the view could swallow her whole.

With the flatness of the land she could see for veca upon veca. She saw the dusty clouds that plumed off the ground between the mines. She saw the far explosions that broke into the earth farther and deeper. The mines she'd seen from the train had only been a small part of a much, much larger system.

"What do you think?" Powell asked.

Florence jumped, startled. She hadn't heard the man approach. Pulled from her trance, she immediately sought out Derek and Nora, but they were nowhere to be found.

"They had business on behalf of the Vicar Alchemist for the Vicar Harvester. I saw that they spoke with the right people to get them where they were going."

"Thank you," Florence said sincerely. "You've been quite kind to us."

"You are guests in my home." Powell smiled in reply. "Ter.1 may not be what it once was, but it is still home and I will still love it and see it is shown in the best light."

"You said that before," she noted. "That it's not what it was."

He nodded, but offered no more explanation this time than he had the last.

"Do you mean before the Dragons?" she pressed.

"I do."

She followed Powell's stare, looking out at the land. "What was better, then? How has it changed?"

Powell shook his head and chuckled. "The Dragons changed a lot, overseen directly by the King." Again, unlike Ari, there was no bite at the mention of their oppressors. "Not much was better in my lifetime. We've been on this suicidal path for hundreds of years. If they hadn't come when they did, Loom would be in a difficult spot now."

"What do you mean?" Florence couldn't comprehend what the man before her was saying. There was no path of logic that let her get to his point until he spelled it out.

"The Dragons, Florence. They saved Loom."

CVAREH

The blood shone like liquid metal, caked upon her skin. It picked up the sunlight like some horrible truth that his mind, in all its efforts, could not fathom. Arianna had killed yet another of the Dono's Master Riders. That should be the fact his mind circled around relentlessly.

But it wasn't.

He stared at where her flesh had been punctured by Lossom's claws. Gold streamed from the wound, mingled with the drippings of the heart she held up in victory. But it was clear enough with every pulse of her heart, clear as Lady Lei's springs and rivers. For the first time, it was as if he was seeing the real woman behind the name.

"She actually did it," Cain said in awe from Cvareh's left.

"This court just got interesting." Petra clapped her hands in appreciation from between them. His sister turned to him, summoning Cvareh from his thoughts. "You should go to the new Soh. She did stand for you, after all."

Cvareh's gaze swung to Arianna, but her back was to him. The woman had her eyes locked on Yveun Dono's. If she wasn't careful, she was going to challenge the King himself.

He moved, jumping down the short distance to the pit. Arianna tuned sharply, but relaxed visibly at the sight of him. Men and women shouted and cheered. Challenges flew above their heads, the Court whipping into a blood frenzy at the upset.

Cvareh's eyes rose from her forearm to meet hers. "Come." He held out a hand and she hesitated, the potent dissonance of the emotions in his magic giving her pause. But he had no hope of reining it in, not until he had explanations. "Come, Ari Xin'Anh Soh."

She finally obliged, and took his hand.

Sweat glistened off her, even through the illusion. A perfect crafting, he realized, because she was already so close to a Dragon. She was stockier than most Dragon females, but she had the height and the speed of one of his kind. She had the eyes and the claws. The ears—if she ever removed the metal caps. She was more Dragon than he had ever given her credit for, than maybe she had ever realized.

And that fact was surprisingly disappointing. It was like everything that made her shine was losing its spark. The picture he had painted in his mind of her was losing all its complementary colors at the idea that there was something so important about her that she had knowingly kept from him. He hated his distance from her, and grew weary of the feeling of her keeping him at arm's length.

They walked out of the light and into the dim of a hall, only to be greeted by other victors and the bold applause of servants. Arianna kept her eyes forward, oblivious to it all. The metal of the splint on her fingers pressed against his skin. Even with the surge of power from imbibing, holding the illusion must be tiresome...

"Where is an empty parlor?" he demanded.

"This way, Xin'Ryu." A servant stepped forward, eager to appease. The girl led them down a side hall and into a modest sitting area, a room of rest and recovery for the victors in the pit. It was perfumed with lavender, incense, and the ripe smell of fruit and cheese that had sat out for an hour too long.

Cvareh dismissed the girl with a curt nod, eager to close the door behind her. The world shut out, there were only the four walls that surrounded him and the woman who had become his enigma. There was no one to pass judgment and no one to bear witness beyond themselves. Ari had yet to face him, yet to confront the truth that she undoubtedly knew he'd seen.

He took a breath, readying himself to speak.

"You're welcome," she interrupted.

"Pardon?" he nearly stuttered in surprise.

"I assume you were about to say thank you." Arianna pulled off the splint from her fingers with a glance at the bolt engaged in the door.

The illusion fell. Her color faded to gray and white. Her tattoos were visible, inked back into existence by an invisible hand. The woman who should have been familiar seemed as false as the Dragon who had been in her place moments before. Her forearm betrayed no marks from the wound, yet Cvareh's eyes were still glued to the spot.

"What are you?" he whispered.

She couldn't have hidden her reaction if she tried. All his senses were honed on her. Cvareh practically heard the spark of tension through her muscles at the question.

"You know what I am." She squared against him as if the room had become a new pit, and they were about to do battle.

"Do I?" Cvareh curled his hands into fists so that he would not unsheathe his claws in frustration. If she wanted a sparring partner, he would rise to task. And this time, he would not stay his claws against her.

"Do you?"

"Don't be circular," he growled. "I saw it."

"Saw what?" She drew her height, coming nearly to eye level with him. "Me stand for you? Me fell your enemy? Me further prove that—" Arianna faltered. "That despite all the reasons I have to hate you, I clearly cannot bring myself to do so?"

The confession was virtually lost on him in his pursuit of the truth. She was trying to shift his focus. He wasn't going to let her, even if it teetered on the verge of words he so very dearly wanted to hear.

"I saw your arm. I saw the blood."

"What of it?"

"It was gold."

"Of course it would be, I had just killed a Dragon. Dragon blood is gold." She took the tone of one speaking to a small child.

Cvareh didn't even let the disrespect sway him from the truth he desired. "Dragon blood *is* gold. So why is yours?"

"You are confused."

"I am not." He didn't remember crossing the room. He didn't remember advancing on her. He didn't remember her taking steps backward, allowing him to do so.

But there they were. There he was, holding her in place with a power he didn't think he possessed. It filled the space behind his ribs, blowing out his chest. If he let it unfurl his sails large enough, it may just be enough to touch her.

"It was an illusion." She stood straighter, trying to not to lose her ground. But she'd long lost the advantage in the encounter. Cvareh wasn't going to give it back.

"That might work on others, Arianna—it likely has. But it will not work on me." He grabbed for the arm in question, holding it up. "I know your blood. I know it like my own. I know it because its very scent torments my waking hours almost as much as your mere visage."

"Then you should regain your head," she snarled, baring her teeth. "For you may be drunk on magic if you think my blood was gold, if you cannot tell the difference between an illusion and—"

His claws jutted forward. They dug deep into her flesh for the first time. They tore through her gray skin to expose the meat beneath. Honeysuckle and cedar filled the room, more potent on his nose than the finest wine he'd ever drunk.

And, sure enough, gold flowed between his fingers.

"You bastard." Arianna went to move but he was faster this time. He pushed her against the wall, grabbing for her other wrist.

"What are you?" he repeated, his voice deepening in resonance to an almost-growl. He had her pinned in place, but likely only due to shock. He'd healed too many bruises and seen her fight too many times to think she wasn't about to throw him off and flay him like livestock. "Arianna, tell me: what are you?" Cvareh's voice broke on the plea. He begged her. The scent of her blood was dizzying, and his entire body and mind desired her and her alone. "Close this gap between us. Let me help you as I want to."

"And what do you want?" She curled her lips.

"I don't know, not truly." He used her breath as fuel for his words, tasting her. "All I know is that I want you."

The snarl fell from her mouth and Arianna searched his face with her brilliantly lilac eyes. He had never held his breath with such anticipation of a woman's judgment—of anyone's judgment. But she held all he was in that moment. She formed his future with her tongue and lips and she was going to destroy him if what spilled from them wasn't everything he needed—not wanted, *needed*—to be for her.

"How do you want me?" she raised her chin slightly, the woman was powerful even while prone.

"Ari..." He was losing momentum. He was losing his footing. The tides were shifting under him, pulling him deeper into her, and she had yet to show any inclination to save him from the swirling depths.

He would drown in her, if only she would let him.

"Tell me, Cvareh. Tell me and I will tell you."

It was a deal too good to be true.

Cvareh leaned forward, slowly. Slow enough that she could fight back. That she could resist. That she had ample time to utter a word of protest. His hands didn't restrain her; instead they caressed her ashen skin like he would the finest of silks in Napole. His fingertips sought out the calluses on the pads of her hands. All his lust, all the lust in the world, would be nothing if she didn't burn for him in return.

His nose brushed along her jawline. Slowly. Tracing the strong curve to her ear. She smelled of dust, sweat, the remnants of Rok blood, sun, and his most favorite scent of all: the sultry notes of honeysuckle. It was a perfume sweeter than any he'd ever been exposed to. It was all he wanted to inhale.

"I want you for my lover, for my mate. I want to lay you down and take you to the pinnacles of delight. I want you... even while not knowing if you could ever grant me your favor." Mentions of her former lover echoed in his mind. Cvareh didn't actually know if Arianna even took a liking to men. He acted on hope, and her lack of refusal—physical or verbal.

"Will you want me still after I kill your King?"

He chuckled darkly. "I will want you all the more for it."

"Will you want me if I refuse your sister?"

That demanded consideration. But desire and love and forever were all separate mistresses. And right now, all three were courting him as one combined. "I will want you even then." His teeth graced the soft flesh of her neck as he spoke.

"Will you want me, even knowing I am a Perfect Chimera?"

The heat in his veins cooled by a small enough margin that he could straighten and look her in the eye, attempting to root out any forced boldness in the claim.

There was none.

The gold blood. Bones strong as steel, as strong as a Dragon's. Her height. Her muscular structure. It made too much sense to be a lie. She had developed and grown with the strength of Dragon blood coursing through her veins.

"Nothing, Arianna. Nothing in your world or mine, or the next, would make me want you less."

She grinned, the flat line of her Fenthri teeth showing. "You're a fool, Cvareh."

"I am," he agreed with a grin of his own.

Cvareh closed the gap at last, and found her lips with his. His chest was flush against hers and his thigh pressed between her legs. He held her fingers with white knuckles, as if to hold in place the tension he was struggling to let out only a moment at a time, savored like sips of the most perfect wine, held on the tongue to embolden the flavor.

Her tongue probed his mouth, pressing into his canine. Blood wet his palate. She smothered a groan.

The sound shot straight through him, forcing his hips further into hers. Her magic, her essence, flooded him. The dam holding the tension between them shattered, and Cvareh grasped her hips, pushing her up further against the wall. Claws shredded against the bindings across her thighs and up into the cloth that covered her groin.

Twenty Gods above, restraint be damned. Cvareh would know all there was to know of her before the day was done. And if he was lucky, he would do it again, and again, and again.

PETRA

"What has you so pleased?" Cain asked from her left. He'd been silent for hours, clearly mulling over something. Petra wondered if the obvious small talk would be enough to bring it forward, because her patience only stretched so far and he was already beginning to pull at it.

"The sun is warm, more Rok blood has been spilled than Xin, Yveun has remained mostly tucked out of sight, and my brother seems to have escaped the Court." She stretched her fingers, her claws digging into the chair. She'd only had to stand for two people so far, and while that would permit her to excuse herself from the remainder of the Court if she desired, Petra remained. After all the trouble it was to see the Court to daylight, she wasn't about to step away.

"He seems to have escaped for quite a while," Cain muttered.

Petra laughed. "Does his fondness for the woman bother you so?" Cvareh was certainly a gossip with all his visits to Napole's tea parlors, but she'd never taken Cain for such habits.

"Why doesn't it bother you, is the better question?" As if realizing his own boldness after the fact, Cain glanced around quickly, taking note of any who could've overheard. Lucky for him, the only other guests in the box were close Kin who Petra had no cause to worry over.

"Cvareh is loyal above all to House Xin. If someone is fond of him, then they must also be fond of his House. Their relationship is an advantage to us. Ends before ideals."

"Ends before ideals," Cain repeated.

"Have a little more heart in that," Petra cautioned.

"Forgive me, Oji. It is only, the notion of our Ryu with a... thing... like that woman." Conflict was apparent in both Cain's voice and expression. He believed in the motto of House Xin, but the matter bothered him to an immense degree—enough that it seemed to rattle his very core.

Oh well. It doesn't matter what he thinks. There were certain benefits to being Oji, and never having to explain herself was one. Cain would come to his senses sooner or later, or Petra would forcefully remove all conflict on the matter for him.

"Petra, her blood..."

"Was as it should be." Cain was too smart for his own good and had been around the woman for too long. Petra needed to stop this speculation where it was. "It is none of your concern."

"You must have seen it, smelled it. There was something *off* about that illusion. I don't think—"

"I do not need you to think," Petra interrupted abruptly. "I need you to do as I say for the good of Xin."

"That is what I am concerned for, Oji."

"Cain, that is what *I* am concerned for. If you wish to be so concerned for it, then you wish to be the Oji." Petra turned to him, baring her teeth. "Would you like to step into the pit?"

"Never." Cain lowered his eyes and face, submissive.

"Good."

The duel before them finished and a long stretch passed before any challengers shouted forward. It had been an aggressive first day, but they were all becoming overwhelmed with bloodsport. Half the stands had already retired and even the Rok versus Rok duels held less joy for her.

"There is someone I need to see," she announced upon arriving at a decision in her head. "Cain, stand for someone if they're of particular import."

"Understood, Oji." His eyes betrayed his curiosity, but his tone and body language were obedient. She hoped he had learned his lesson sufficiently.

Petra descended into the busy halls and walks of the amphitheater. With most of the stands emptying, many a Dragon worked their way to the town below. Petra did not blend in. The masses parted for her with small bows. Members of House Xin delighted in their genuflections. Tam were pleased to keep the balance, respecting the Oji of another House.

House Rok stepped to the back of the lines that formed on either side of her. They gave nothing more than the obligatory bow of their heads, regarding her with shadowed eyes and mouths pressed into thin lines. Their subservience and respect was drawn from them with force.

The Court had only served to make things worse between the Houses, she decided. The bloodshed had singed their nostrils and reminded them that Nova was not one Dragon family. They were factions, divided and vying for the circumstances that would give them the most power. What was "best for Nova" was defined entirely by what was best for any one individual House.

Petra turned, disappearing through a curtained hall and onto a shaded balcony. The sticky scent of fruit that had been baking in the sun all day upon silver platters created a masking perfume to the carnage that happened in the pit. Petra's eyes fell upon two lounging couples—luckily Xin and Tam.

"Out with you," she commanded. "I require this space."

The Dragons exchanged a look. She could sense their displeasure at the prospect of being uprooted. But they obliged her, every last one.

Petra turned to the slave who stood in the corner by the table, a scrawny little Tam with the symbol of Xin emblazoned upon her cheek. Petra had made sure that all the slaves and low servants were wine-or forest-skinned Dragons. She wanted Tam and Rok Dragons to look upon the men and women who had left their Houses and now wore Xin's mark forever. She wanted to test the slaves' loyalty. She wanted all to see Dragons that were previously Rock and Tam now under her claws, and serving her as the picture of obedience.

"Bring me Finnyr Xin'Kin To," Petra ordered. "You will find him with the Dono."

The servant nodded, departing in haste. Petra walked over to the un-railed edge of the balcony. The sun was starting to dip low in the sky. If Court hadn't been formally ended, it would be soon.

The Crimson Court was always between dawn and sunset. The priests taught that Lady Luc, the Light-herald, was born each morning by the hand of Lord Rok. Each night, she was slain by Lord Xin, to make room for his brother, Lord Pak the Dark-wielder, to overtake the sky. Lord Rok fought against Lord Pak until the dawn… when the cycle repeated.

House Rok held the Crimson Court during the hours of their patron's Lady. Long ago, when it was the Cobalt Court, duels were held at night. Petra tensed her claws, relaxed them.

Her mind filled with the fantasy of midnight blue Dragons swirling through the pit like wraiths made from shadow and death, illuminated by the moon, and fighting for House and glory.

"You summoned me."

Petra turned, her thoughts pushed back into the far recesses of her most delightful fantasies. Finnyr stood just inside the still-swaying curtain. Petra tried to remember the last time she'd seen her brother as she assessed him.

He was still small; his time at House Rok had put no might on his bones. It was further affirmation that nothing about Rok or Lysip was inherently mighty. Petra had narrower hips and shoulders than her brother, but her muscle held twice the raw power and her magic was overwhelming in comparison.

Finnyr, her pale-skinned brother with his tarnished hair. The child of House Xin that should never have been born.

"Come, Finnyr." She smiled, displaying her canines, and motioned for the spot next to her. "It has been some time since we last spoke face to face."

"It has." He obeyed, standing in the spot she selected for him.

"You appear to be well. Has House Rok treated you properly?"

He snorted. "As well as can be expected from House Rok."

That was an acceptable answer. "And the Dono?"

"He gives me no cause for complaint."

"Unfortunately," Petra lamented. She would always stand with her House first, but there would be something quite convenient about Yveun abusing her brother, giving her enough cause to challenge the Dono outright.

"He has never harvested any of my parts."

Petra folded her hands in front of her abdomen to keep her claws from unsheathing. Finnyr was familiar enough with the motion that he visibly tensed, realizing what he'd done. Petra took a half step away from the ledge, toward Finnyr's back.

"Brother, who is the Xin'Oji?"

"You are."

"And what House do you belong to?"

"House Xin."

"Therefore, what must you never do?"

Finnyr sighed heavily. "Petra, I was not questioning your decision, I was merely stating—"

Petra's arm shot out without even half a thought behind it. Her claws extended beyond her fingertips like magic daggers. They hovered at the edge of his throat.

"Finnyr, your very existence happens at my allowance," she growled. "You are not to think, you are not to hesitate. It was these traits by which you lost your place as the rightful heir to House Xin. Have some shame and work to make yourself useful."

She wanted to love him. She wanted to embrace her brother as a fellow warrior. If he had been strong, the responsibility of Xin would've never fallen to her. Not that she'd minded, of course. But he was an embarrassment of a brother and had been the shame of their mother and father. His weakness continued to be a blemish on the opinion of their House from the rest of Nova. Unlike Cvareh, it was not a calculated play. Finnyr was truly inept.

Fear colored his magic, even if he didn't let it show on his face. Petra kept her claws at his throat.

"Now, tell me of the Dono." Anger singed the edges of her consciousness.

"I know nothing more than I've told you before."

"You didn't know of the new Master Rider?" Petra scowled.

"I did, but—"

"You did not think to inform me?"

"I did not think it was of note." Finnyr held up his hands, showing that his claws were still not out despite Petra's being at his throat. "You must have assumed, with Leona's death, that the Dono would find a new Master Rider. And with all the other Dragons that perished hunting Cvareh on Loom, the Dono didn't have many choices. Lossom was no one of importance, and a Dragon without much experience."

Petra took her time reasoning through this. The logic stood. If she *had* committed a moment's thought to it, she likely could've reached the same conclusion herself. She eased her hand away from Finnyr's throat.

"Now, sister, *you* did not tell *me* you had such a fierce fighter you were training up within House Xin." Finnyr spoke lightly, as though she hadn't just threatened his life. All was forgiven to the Oji of the House when the Oji had only acted in the best interest of the Dragons whom she sought to protect.

"I prefer to keep many surprises." Petra would not give Finnyr the knowledge of Arianna. She, Cvareh and apparently Cain had managed to keep the truth of her to themselves, and she would see it remained so.

"How many others do you train?"

"Enough to see this Crimson Court to its bloated conclusion."

"Enough to fight against House Rok?"

Petra scowled at the horizon. "No."

Far out there was the Isle of Lysip, the largest island on Nova and the most overrun with fighters. Floating between them was the Isle of Gwenri, home of Tam. And another House's worth of Dragons who would fight for the sake of keeping the status quo.

"Such numbers will never be found on Nova."

"On Nova?" Finnyr knew her too well. He knew where the important parts of her phrasing lay.

"Tell me more about the Dono."

"There is not much to say."

Useless. "You live in his home. You eat his food. You mingle with his other To and you gossip in Lysip's tea parlors. There must be more to say."

"The Dono is his own Oji as well. He keeps people at claw's length and only tells them of his plans and movements when he deems it essential for them to know."

Petra stared down Finnyr from the corners of her eyes. "You have done well enough making yourself so small that things are said in your presence without concern. Learning of why there was always a Rider stationed at that records room has paid well in dividends."

Finnyr remained silent.

"You must have heard something else of use to our House."

"I did hear that Yveun went beneath Lysip not more than a month before the Court."

"*Beneath?*" she emphasized for clarity. "Why would Yveun lower himself to such measures?"

"I don't know."

Petra cursed. "Find out."

"It would be easier if he trusted me."

"Then go back and earn his trust."

"I am House Xin, I will never earn his trust." Finnyr sighed heavily. "Unless…"

"Unless?"

"You give me something I could use as a bartering chip to do it." Finnyr seemed determined to toe dangerous lines. She ground her teeth together, reminding herself not to rip out his throat. "Give me something small, something that changes nothing. I could spin it into a lie, even, but the best lie has a grain of truth. Tell me how you are training Dragons like this Ari—for he now knows you have the means for warriors such as her. Tell me of your work on the refineries; are you putting gold aside for Xin? You must be; Yveun would assume this anyway, my saying so would pose no extra risk. Or Cvareh's journey to Loom. Yveun seeks our brother's blood already, him knowing how his Riders were killed would not satiate that lust for violence. And he would certainly not share the truth, as the whole affair is a source of shame considering how many Riders he lost."

"No," Petra spoke quietly, stopping him before he could think of any more useless ideas. "Your words are near treason, Finnyr. You will not bargain our truths for his favor. That makes us exactly what he wants House Xin to be: loyal at all costs. If you must tell him anything, fabricate something. Tell him whatever you please."

"He will know if I am lying. He'll see it lacks no substance!"

"Than become a better liar."

"Petra, I cannot help you if you will not let me in!" A familiar hurt colored Finnyr's voice. "I cannot be loyal to House Xin if I do not know what House Xin needs."

"House Xin needs information on Rok. House Xin needs you to relay information pertinent to our success."

"And I—"

"I have spoken." Petra cut him short. She'd had enough of this tantrum. "Go back to the Dono's temporary estate and come back to me tomorrow with something tangible. Have some self-respect as a Xin'Kin and make use of yourself to our House."

"The Dono has told me that I would stay in the Xin Manor during the Court."

"The Dono does not decide who sleeps in my halls, and he would do well to remember it." Furthermore, Petra could not stand to look at Finnyr for a second longer. Not after this slew of disappointments. If he returned to the manor, she might kill him before the night was over, just so the mere knowledge of his ineptitude couldn't shame her further.

"Petra—"

"I have spoken!" Her teeth clicked together as she slammed them shut into a half snarl. "Now leave, Finnyr."

Finnyr looked at her as if considering disobedience. Lucky for them both, he retreated. Petra took a deep breath of the air that was wholly hers the moment he left.

She had somehow managed to avoid killing Finnyr for over three decades, but every time he was around her it was a test of her resolve on the matter. He was the embodiment of all that she loathed: entitlement without effort, weakness, proximity to House Rok. Petra would not kill a member of House Xin without good reason, especially not her elder brother.

But eventually, she knew it could not be helped if he continued as he was.

Petra stared into the setting sun, the gold fading in the wake of Lord Xin's hour growing nigh. Petra invited the strength of the Death-giver into her heart. So, too, would she someday watch the sun set on House Rok.

FLORENCE

"How did the Dragons save Loom?" Florence was utterly baffled. All her life, she'd felt the negative effects of the Dragons' presence in her world.

"How old are you?" Powell asked.

"Sixteen. I'll be seventeen later this year."

"And you're still an initiate?" He raised his eyebrows, referring to her outlined mark. "You should have taken the second round of tests for Journeyman by now."

Florence stayed her tongue, choosing to look out the window.

"I see." She had no doubt Powell actually did. "Revolvers, then?"

She neither confirmed nor denied the fact.

Powell merely chuckled at her silence. "Come with me, Flor."

Florence followed the Harvester away from the outer ring of windows and into a narrow hall lit by biophosphorous. She took note of the same lanterns she had seen in the tunnels below. "Does Faroe have no generators?"

The man glanced at the lanterns. "There isn't much room for anything unnecessary here. Generators take up precious space that could be otherwise dedicated to the essentials."

"I see," she mumbled as they pressed onward and upward.

The stairs wound straight up into an open second floor. Large tables made a ring by each of the windows. Men and women, all bearing a sickle on their cheeks, walked between them, stopping at smaller tables to check things and make notes along the way. Chimera sat in an innermost ring of chairs, their brightly colored ears betraying their black blood.

"This is where we plan new mines," Powell explained. "We have a bird's eye view of the immediate area. Each of the other cities in Ter.1 has towers of their own that function for the same or similar purposes. To the north, it's mostly plotting farmland. On the coastlines, they serve as lighthouses for the sailors as well."

He led her over to one of the tables that sat flush against a window, strategically picking one with the least amount of activity.

"On the maps we mark the depth and location of existing mines, as well as what they're producing."

The map was covered with marks, crossed out and marked again and again. Lines in different colored chalk wound around and between them. Dust from past coloring hazed the paper.

"The chalk is for veins and pockets of minerals, which we then—" He directed Florence to the inner table that sat opposite. "Mark and note how much is harvested. These numbers are compared against historic numbers and reports from the guilds to estimate how much needs to be pulled from the earth."

He motioned toward the Chimera sitting in the middle, engaged in conversations seemingly with their palms, fingertips touching their ears, or with the other Harvesters who walked around the room.

"Then the reports go out to the mines, as well as to another group of Chimera upstairs who then communicate with the

Ravens to see the resources are ultimately moved to where they need to go."

"How did the communication happen before magic?" Florence couldn't help but wonder.

"Much more slowly," Powell admitted. "Letters delivered by couriers. Though our overall perception on mining was different then."

"It's fascinating," she admitted. "But I fail to see how this relates to the Dragons saving Loom?" Saying the words singed her tongue; her body physically rejected the notion.

"Look here again." He tapped the papers he'd carefully spread out on the table. "This is one mine and this column is the overall output for all minerals over time."

Her eyes skimmed the years and the numbers. It went back over six decades, a virtual eternity. The figures became more reliable with time, but it wasn't until the year the Dragon King became Loom's sovereign that all the rows were consistently filled in. Despite this, Florence could see the trend clearly.

"It was a lot more before the Dragons."

"It was," Powell agreed, as if she'd suddenly understood. Florence gave him a look that said she didn't. "For generations, the mines sprawled as if the earth went on forever and the minerals we found would never run out of resources. When we found new pockets, we'd pursue. When we ran out, we dug deeper, and deeper, and deeper."

Florence was reminded of the cavernous chasms they'd crossed to reach Faroe.

"The Harvesters had produced the most addicting drug Loom had ever known: progress. We never questioned if we should, only if we could, and the idea spawned the rest of the guilds. We asked and asked, what would we find if we pushed just one peca further into the earth?"

"But because Loom had those resources, the Alchemists made medicine, the Rivets created engines, the Ravens laid track, the Revolvers built guns." She had yet to see the flaw in it.

"And all of these things enabled us to dig further and further. It was a self-feeding system, a chain linked by the need to produce."

"What's wrong with that?"

"What happens when it runs out?"

Florence looked back to the window, to the endless sprawl of mines. She tried to imagine what the land might have looked like before the Harvesters carved into it. "Can it run out?"

"Some mines have already been abandoned as barren."

"Then what?"

"Then we blast and dig until we find a new place to blast and dig farther."

"So the problem is solved."

Powell chuckled. "What happens when there are no more places to blast and dig?"

"There will always be…"

"This world is *finite*, Florence." He motioned to the records and tables. "What you see before you is all we have. The Dragons saved us from ourselves. Magic vastly reduced the consumption of resources. The Ravens now make trains that run purely on it."

"Magic travel, magic moving anything, still requires gold," she pointed out.

"Yes, but the steel only needs to be tempered into gold once. Then it can be used for an eternity," he countered. "The Dragons' existence helped, but the King's oversight of our resources was what pushed the Harvesters' Guild to not just take from the world, but truly try to understand it. We began to pay attention to mines drying up. How fast we'd run out of this or that and how much deeper or farther we'd have to dig to find more. How these scars we've made upon our earth will never heal."

"The Dragon King made new scars." Florence scowled.

"You're bitter about the tests."

"Are you sure you're not a Master?" She checked his cheek for a circle. His mannerisms reminded her far too much of a certain Rivet Master she knew.

"Not yet. My name sits with the Vicar Harvester right now on recommendation, however. It's why I returned to the guild from Ter.4.5."

"Oh…" Florence was immediately humbled. That was one thing the Dragon King had not changed. Mastership could not be tested; it was earned in the eyes of peers. Only a Master could award another Master's circle, and the approval to do so came directly from the Vicar.

"In any event," he said, "when the Dragons introduced the idea of families…" The concept made Powell as uncomfortable as every other Fenthri she'd ever met. "Which, I grant you, is an odd one. Free and unlimited access to reproduction and fertility chemicals widened our talent pools. But we could not sustain that demand on our resources."

"So the pools needed to be culled." She was one such person who was not talented enough to earn her life.

"They do." There was an appropriately sympathetic note to his tone. "The first culling happens before the children grow enough to be any real drain. The second ensures a known population. We know exactly how many people we need to supply at all the guilds. Exactly how much food to produce, how many resources to dig up."

Florence was silent. She was trying to see if she could reconcile herself to a system that would have her killed for not being a good enough Raven—despite being a damn good Revolver. But under the same logic, the Revolvers had their own quota. She didn't have a place there either.

It made her want to scream.

She settled on a scowl instead.

"I understand, I believe, your turmoil on the matter." Powell motioned to the windows and room. "But I want you to comprehend the logic woven behind the madness."

"People should still be able to choose their guild. A finite pool, perhaps, but… The Ter.0 system of learning was better. Divide the finite pools from there. Let all test for all and then separate. It should—"

He rested his palm on her shoulder, squeezing it lightly. "I don't disagree with you." The words were a balm to the fervor that had been brewing in her gut. "There are better ways to execute this system. There are alternatives that would have been more in line with our culture, our way of life. Something the Dragons have yet to fully understand."

At least he admitted that much.

"But we were a runaway train, headed for a half-finished bridge. In such a situation, you do not worry foremost about what wrong turn you took to get there. You reach for the brake and pull with all your might. *Then* you find the right way. But if we didn't reach for that brake, Florence, and make the sacrifices we made, we would have run ourselves off that proverbial ledge and into extinction."

She wanted to point out that she didn't appreciate a very Raven analogy, because he was no doubt assuming it would resonate with her for the mark on her cheek. But Florence held her tongue. She felt bitter and suddenly very, deeply tired.

"This is a lot," she confessed with a mumble.

"We may talk on it more, if you're interested in learning."

Florence considered it for a long moment. She'd learned from the Ravens, the Revolvers, and a Rivet. She'd always been so focused on completely transforming herself from one thing into another, it wasn't until the endwig attack and the weeks that followed on the train that she'd discovered the true strength of combining all parts. Why not see what a Harvester could teach her? Who knew when it would come in handy?

"I am."

"Very well." Powell motioned for the stairs where they'd entered. "Let me show you to a guest room, for now. I am tired from the train and ready to wash and rest."

"Thank you." She hoped he interpreted her gratitude on the multiple levels it was intended.

"You are quite welcome." He seemed to. "Rest up. Tomorrow, I will take you to the organ harvesting rooms."

ARIANNA

The smell of woodsmoke was etched upon her skin with his tongue and teeth. He drew long, delightfully painful lines with his canines. He followed with his mouth, his tongue, his tender kisses and delicate ministrations upon them while they healed.

Again and again, he repeated. They were a room on fire, cedar on smoke. Pain and pleasure made comfortable bedmates, etching his caress upon the steel of her memory with an endless amount of determination.

She wanted him. They had crossed every line and traversed every seemingly impenetrable barrier to arrive with him between her legs. But she yearned for every moment. She yearned for his firm grip on her hipbone, his mouth on her shoulder, his attentions bordering on the meticulous.

There was a broken-ness to their passion, a ritual sacrifice of everything they were for something they could be. Let them dive into the acidic fatalism that would forever be splashed upon their memories. They were going to dissolve into each other until there was nothing left.

She arched off the bed, his hand smoothing across her ribs and onto her back, holding her in place, his mouth upon her breast. She had forgotten the feeling of being vulnerable. Control had fought against its tether, cutting into her palms, and now she let the beast go free.

Arianna's claws trailed up his arms and shoulders, into his blood-orange hair. She watched how it splayed across her chest when she held him upon her.

"You have magic here," he mumbled into her bare stomach. His breaths ran ragged laps around her navel.

"I do." She was already stripped bare before him. There was little else to hide now.

"Where else?" He propped himself over her.

Arianna had seen his bare chest dozens of times; the Dragons weren't exactly fond of clothing. But it looked different now. Hovering just far enough for her nipples to brush his skin, it seemed to take on a different shade, a more appealing curve.

"You know the other places." Arianna slid her palms to the chest she had just been admiring. "Though, I wouldn't mind lungs…"

"You wouldn't." He pressed his mouth upon her.

Arianna sucked his tongue between her teeth, biting hard. Blood poured into her throat and she sucked hungrily, magic exploding once more. She was well and truly drunk off the man— the taste, the feeling. It was better every time and worse each passing second after it faded. She wondered what it would be like to give into every desire and lie here with him until the end of days.

Arianna smiled faintly into his mouth. *What an idealistic notion.* The things the man had done to her…

A growl rose from the back of his throat, which she also eagerly consumed. Arianna flipped them on the small cot, mounting him like one of their flying birds. His erection pressed against her and she, shamelessly, ground herself upon it.

"You witch," he groaned when she finally returned his lips to him.

"Wraith, actually." Arianna pressed forward, kissing up along his ear to the point. "And don't doubt me. There is very little I wouldn't do—especially to you."

He pressed his thumbs into her thighs, holding her in place, pushing her down. Arianna met his demands willingly. It was a war for dominance that was punctuated by winning and losing battles of submission. They took turns allowing the other to be the victor and alternated the joys and struggles of relinquishing control.

She felt the waver in his magic, the fear taking over again. He was thinking too much. The man who seemed to care for nothing but beauty and ease was giving in to the dangers of contemplating all they were and what they were doing. She appreciated the irony of wanting to tell him to let go, to let them have the moment they'd encased themselves in.

Arianna kissed him lightly, absorbing the emotion. She forfeited words for action. She slid onto him and felt that stretching, pressing, pushing, filling sensation once more.

It was for the best. He should be afraid of her—of them. The idea of him and her becoming a "they" would be the worst thing that could happen to either of them. She would consume him. She would use him for her own delight. But if it ever suited her, she would break him. She would cast him from the pinnacles of pleasure upon the cold and lonely world below.

It made her afraid of herself.

Arianna had never let herself go so far. Even with Eva, an understanding and logic had pulsed between them. They had begun as partners, scientific equals, and evolved into something more. Arianna had yearned for the woman. She had embraced the throes of passion with her now-dead love.

She had admired the woman's tenacity and determination. Similar things attracted her to Cvareh, but they stemmed from different sources. There was no logic to Cvareh. Man, woman—Dragon or Fenthri—he was not someone she should find herself with. Arianna snarled, driving her hips harder, faster, as if she could force out the conflict. She hated him. She wanted him. Shades of gray, rainbows of color—they blurred and smeared into gold.

Cvareh pulled her down and she acquiesced. She let him have her mouth, her tit, her shoulder. She heaved her moans into the pillows like curses, or prayers.

Nothing made sense, and she would have him until it did.

They peeled apart an hour, or a minute, later. Time no longer mattered. She would burn it on the passion pyre they'd been immolated upon all afternoon. With it burned her principles and her self-respect. She had coupled with a Dragon as if her life depended on it. But luckily, she had exhausted her ability to care alongside every other muscle in her body.

The ceiling came into focus; it had never been more fascinating. It was the only thing safe to look at. The room was a mess from their tumbling. Things had been broken, furniture had been moved and scratched. Blankets made mountains on the floor, the warmth of their body heat more than enough.

Cvareh didn't move either. Arianna closed her eyes. Already the feeling was returning, the want to place her mouth on his again. It had been *so long* since she had last touched and been touched—since she had even wanted to be touched by anyone. She had clearly yet to find satiation.

"Why?" Cvareh's voice was still deep and thick. It had a purr to it like a well-oiled engine that set her hand to moving, her knuckles brushing against where they'd fallen on his thigh.

"Why what?"

"Why me?"

Arianna laughed. Her voice was hoarse and raspy. "Really? *That's* your question?"

"I have more."

"As do I."

The pillow shifted next to her and Arianna turned toward the sound, meeting his eyes. The understanding that had always been there had deepened. It shone brighter, as if she could see his very magic in the air around him.

"So, why?"

"I don't know," she confessed to both of them.

"You don't know? Something the infallible Arianna doesn't know?"

"I will bite off your tongue. Don't think this changes anything."

"This changes everything." Cvareh sat. "What we are was not what we were."

She watched the muscles in his back stretch. His skin had a certain pallor in the dim candlelight. Flickering shadows danced in lines and muscular curves. Lean and strong. Strong enough to hold her up. Strong enough to support her if she chose to let him shoulder some of her burdens.

"Nothing has changed," her mouth insisted. She spoke lies, to herself, to him, to everything they were. Her body may have been ready, long overdue even, for a lover… but her heart. Her heart was another matter entirely. "We are two people merely filling needs."

He placed a hand between her arm and side, leaning toward her. His fingers brushed the line of her jaw but the touch was different than before, without haste. And yet it still possessed fire. They had not been a flash in the pan. Something burned deeper, more determined. A small flame, but a white hot and relentless one.

"You don't believe that."

"I do."

Cvareh smiled knowingly. She rose upward and kissed the expression. He'd given her no choice. There was only one way to expunge that look from between his cheeks. Still, it persisted when she pulled away.

She kissed him again. She kissed him harder. He tasted suddenly of longing and salt tears her eyes had stopped spilling years ago.

"I know you, now," he muttered upon her. "I know you, Arianna."

Resistance was futile. The man could think what he would; the more she objected, the more he persisted, the more she slid down into him like quicksand. She could hardly breathe if the air wasn't sweetened with the tang of his scent.

"I want to show you something."

"What?" She let his hands tangle in her hair, a mess from the fight and their sex.

"It's not on Ruana, so we'll have to travel."

"Where?" The idea of venturing into the unknown with him was not as frightening as it should've been.

His fingers coaxed out the knots he'd made. "Do you trust me enough to let me not tell you?"

She hated him for the question. She hated him more for the answer that already leaped from her tongue. "Yes." Arianna pressed her eyes closed. How had she arrived at that answer? It was like adding two and two together and getting yellow. "And I will kill you for it."

"I will not give you a reason to." Cvareh stepped away, hunting for his clothes. He made no effort to smooth them, only enough to patch them back together from where she'd torn at them. His shoulder pieces were hopelessly lost. Fortunately, Dragons wouldn't think twice about him walking around in next to nothing.

Arianna followed without instruction, picking through what was salvageable. She was still too Fenthri to stomach the notion of walking in nothing, even with her illusion. Still, the most important piece was the splint that helped her hold her illusion in place.

"Head upward, and tell me if you have trouble finding the departure platform. I'll saddle the boco." His palm fell on her hip, and his magic surged at the touch. It wrapped her up in a familiar embrace, already intertwined before his lips fell on her ear.

"Arhoncedov," he breathed.

It was a sound just for her and it sparked off his tongue with sheer power. He'd cast forth a tether, and now it fell on her to take it.

Arianna took a half step closer, her own arm wrapping around him. Cheek to cheek, she leaned for his ear. It had been a long time since she'd last established a whisper link. The silence that had filled her mind upon Eva's death should have been enough discouragement to ever do it again. She'd vowed not to.

"Ranhoftantu," she replied.

Magic pulled taught with a twang. Another line holding them together under tension. A step closer, when she should've taken a step further away. A yes that should've been a no. And a want indulged before a thought could be applied.

They were drunk on each other still. Their magic was still fresh, and new, and desired. But eventually, they would sober. They would wash away the sweat of sex and the heat of each other's skin. When the time came, what would they find?

FLORENCE

Nora and Derek were set up across the hall from her. Florence heard them entering in a haze, but sleep's hold was too strong on her to even cast off her covers. She would ask them in the morning how their meeting with the Vicar had gone.

But when morning came, a knock awoke her, and she found neither was waiting.

Powell stood on the other side of the door in the same, simple, pocketed worker's pants he'd worn the whole journey. Well, judging from the lack of smell and stain they weren't the *exact* same trousers. They were belted, and a loose cotton shirt was tucked into them, sleeves rolled up to the elbows.

"I woke you." His observation seemed mildly apologetic.

"I might have slept for the next two days if you hadn't." She rubbed her eyes with a yawn. He had been right, there was no substitute for sleeping in a proper bed.

"Then I'm glad I woke you, seeing as I don't know when you're leaving and there's much I'd like to show you before then."

"Well, I don't seem to have much else to do." It was nice to feel welcomed by someone, to have them engaged in her wellbeing. Nora, Derek, and the rest of the Alchemists' Guild were poor substitutes in that regard. Since Ari left, Florence had no one to look after her other than herself. "Are you sure you have the time?"

"I will until I won't. I'm at the leisure of the guild's Masters and Vicar. Whenever they reach their decision, I'll find out if I have something to do, or if I'm returning home with my mark as it is," he explained. "Here."

Florence accepted the bundle of clothes he offered. She'd brought her own, but they were still soiled from travel and the prospect of something clean was incredibly appealing. She wondered if he had paid that much attention to her needs or if this was standard hospitality for the Harvesters.

"You can wear what you want, but I thought after the organ halls we may head into the mines, so you might want to wear something you don't mind potentially getting soiled or ripped."

"These days, all my clothes can potentially get soiled." Powell didn't know the half of what she'd been through. The days of her pristine vests, matching top hats, and perfect stitching were gone. Her vests were wrinkled, her top hats lost or left behind while she was on the run, and the seaming at the elbows of every one of her shirts had been torn. "But, thank you. It's nice to have something clean."

Washed and dressed, Florence followed her new friend once more into the Harvesters' Guild hall. Powell was indeed known, as she waited once or twice for him to have short conversations with Journeymen and Initiates. There was an easy comfort about him as he spoke and answered questions. That was what had made him easy to speak to on the train and what, effectively, had forged their unconventional relationship.

Florence had always set Ari on a pedestal in terms of what it meant to be a Master. Her breadth of wisdom. Her intense respect of knowledge. Her reverence for the halls of education that elevated guilds and classrooms from mere institutions to temples of learning.

Powell embodied these things, but there was a different sort of openness to his mannerisms. He worked to include Florence in all the conversations, despite her lack of experience in these areas. He treated knowledge as a delight, rather than a sacred right.

"Sorry for the delays." He leaned toward her so the people they had just bid farewell wouldn't hear.

"It's no problem. It's nice to be included in such a positive atmosphere."

"You were not before?" He posed the question delicately.

A tired smile curled her lips. "The Alchemists' Guild is… a very different place. It suits them. But there isn't much room for a Revolver there."

He made no comment on her reference to herself as something other than her marked guild. And Florence didn't feel the slightest bit of concern at the fact that she'd openly declared it. Powell was smart enough to figure it out—had already figured it out—and she didn't see the point in insulting their mutual intelligence by masquerading otherwise.

"I am forced to take your word for it. I've never been to the Alchemists, and I cannot imagine a place where there would not be room enough for someone as eager to learn as you." His smile was infectious. "Here we are."

Florence wished she could bottle his words and save them for the next time she was struggling in the Alchemists' Guild. Or with the Revolvers… Or in general.

"We worked closely with the Alchemists to develop our harvesting processes for Dragon organs." They walked through a series of narrow halls, washing their hands along the way and passing through antechambers. "We may not know how to heal a wound, or convert a Fenthri to Chimera... But when it comes to removing the organs themselves, we're just as skilled as any Alchemist you'll find."

Florence gave him an encouraging smile at the pride he so clearly felt in his guild. It was heartwarming to see. Powell led them through a door and onto a narrow, raised walk.

Florence's smile melted off her lips.

"This is one of the viewing areas we use to see how they're progressing. There's only so fast you can harvest organs. They re-grow, but you have to make sure they're healthy and strong before you remove them, or they won't work to make Chimera and they'll be weak reagents."

She walked over to one of the glass windows that tilted away from the catwalk, separating her from the honeycomb of rooms below. Florence stared, barely making sense of what she was seeing, let alone Powell's words. A chill swept through her.

Somehow she had let herself believe the organ harvesting pits would have mimicked her experience with Cvareh when she became a Chimera. She remembered the Dragon, willingly at her side, dutiful and pleased to give her his blood.

This was nothing like that.

Dragons, mostly shades of blue and green, some red, were strapped to tables, bound with steel and leather and held prone. Some screamed and thrashed. Others stared listlessly, as though their very souls had been harvested.

Gold blood seeped from open wounds, left to face the air without so much as a bandage. A man's stomach had been carved apart, the skin still peeled back and pinned carefully to keep his innards exposed as the organ slowly grew back. *They don't even want to have to cut back into him again*, Florence realized. The Harvesters couldn't be bothered to repeat their incisions, so they let him heal while vivisected, only to have the process repeated again, and again, and again.

Her palm fell on her own abdomen.

"How did they get here?" She realized she interrupted something that Powell was saying. But she hadn't even heard him over the ringing in her ears. The hall was silent, yet somehow the screams of the countless Dragons before her were so, so very loud.

"The Dragon King supplies them."

Florence took note of a mark on each of the Dragon's cheeks, all the ones that weren't red. A crown supported by a triangle like design. Was it the mark of an animal led to slaughter? What did that make them? What were the Fenthri to this Dragon King, who was willing to condemn his own to such a fate? Just so much livestock awaiting slaughter?

"How are they chosen?" she asked.

"I don't know."

"How do you not know?" Florence tore her eyes away and in the process swayed slightly. Her head spun. "How do you not know what these men and women have done to deserve this… this level of cruelty?"

"Florence, do not think of them as creatures with emotions or will." He placed his hands on her shoulders, trying to both stabilize and soothe her to no avail. "They are magic farms. Think of them as organs and parts. Their bodies just help keep them fresh."

"No." She stepped away, shaking her head. Her mind went to Cvareh, the sometimes comically clueless Dragon whom she had given her life as a Fenthri for to see across the world. The good man who had answered the call willingly to make the blood in her veins black and give her life anew. "They are not. They are just as you or me!"

Powell arched his eyebrows. "I would not expect Dragon sympathy from someone such as you."

"What?"

"A self-proclaimed Revolver, dedicated to tools of death and destruction. One who clearly fights against Dragon systems. Coming from the Alchemists' Guild… it's not a stretch to imagine why you and your friends are here. We've heard the rumors."

Florence glared at him. She hated the truth that was bleeding beneath her and she hated the truth that flew from his mouth. There was nothing but contrasts now in her heart and they were all being brought to a head.

"I don't have all the answers," she admitted, as much to herself as to him. "But this—" Florence motioned to the rooms below her, and the carvers who continued their work upon the helpless Dragons. "This is not right. This is no better than the mining practices you told me about yesterday."

"No, the mines when depleted will not replenish. So long as the Dragons are forced nutrition and not over-harvested, they can remain for decades—a century, even."

That only served to spark further outrage. "Four generations' worth of carnage forced on a single person to endure." Florence shook her head violently, as if she could rattle the images and truths out of her ears. "No, no. This isn't right." She pushed past Powell for the halls behind him.

"Florence—"

"This isn't right!" She wanted to hear no more, see no more. There was no justification. All reason and logic betrayed what sense of morals and heart she had clung to. She wanted to believe in the good in people, but what good was there in this?

Loom survived because of the Dragons, if Powell was to be believed. They curbed Loom's wasteful practices and lessened the tax on the earth. But a new tax emerged: blood. To make the gold that powered the world while the environment recovered, Dragons paid what Florence now saw was a terrible price.

The Dragon King may have been the catalyst for the Harvesters to uncover the problem of Loom's rampant over-production. But the solutions had damaged Loom's culture and ways of life, and required that he give his own people over to darkness and pain.

Florence may not have a neat solution, but she knew she had settled on one thing: She didn't see eye to eye with Ari. That much had become apparent. Ari wanted the past without question, the days of deregulation and progress burdened only by the gates of the mind. Florence knew now that she didn't want that, not after speaking with Powell. But her teacher remained her friend and ally in both heart and principle.

The door to Derek and Nora's room slammed as Florence stormed in without apology. The two were still slumbering, wrapped in bed. Startled awake, Florence sat herself at the foot of their bed, comfortable in both their presence and various states of undress. Her eyes only saw the Dragons, still bleeding.

"I have decided something," she announced before either could speak. "At all costs, we must see the Dragon King dead."

CVAREH

The bocos were kept in stables below, where slaves tacked them and brought them up on command. But he didn't want anyone but himself touching the seat in which Arianna would sit. He was doting upon a passion most tender and new. But love felt good, especially reciprocated love. Arianna had yet to say as much, but he'd felt it.

He had been with women before, never so intimately, just enough to cross exploratory lines. But that—*that* was what it felt like to mate. They sung the sweet chorus of passion in perfect harmony, a performance that could never be denied. He'd known hands on flesh before, but it was so vastly different when one had truly found the person he was to be with for the rest of his life.

Until she was ready, Cvareh would treat the blossom of their affections with delicacy. He would see it nurtured. He'd move forward, and wait until she removed one of his toes to let him know he'd crossed a line.

So long as she didn't, he would relish every new and crisp feeling. He would do all she allowed for her, to her. He would memorize every crease and curve of her body and do it again should he ever find his memory lacking—which would be often.

He knew the feeling would eventually dull. But for now it was as sharp as a freshly forged blade and, for the first time, it was a weapon he was willing to allow Arianna to use to carve out his heart.

"Cvareh'Ryu, you stink."

He stopped, his hands on the slightly longer saddle he'd been selecting. Cvareh's fingers tensed, but he kept his claws sheathed. He would not draw them on a friend. But that tone would only be forgiven for so long, and the timer was counting down.

"Cain'Da." Cvareh squared his hips and shoulders, the tacking of the boco forgotten. "Mind your tongue."

"You coupled with her." Cain scrunched his nose, marring the line of his scowl. "You reek of sex."

"Who I choose to lie with is none of your concern." Cvareh added a cautionary note to his words. "Watch your words, Cain. We may be friends, but I am still the Xin'Ryu."

"Then act like it." Cvareh had never seen this sort of boldness from Cain. "You are endangering not just our House and future, but all of Nova with this tryst."

"Cain—"

"Cvareh, I am coming to you as your friend."

It should have enraged Cvareh more, but he did give Cain some allowance. They had grown up together and Cain had always been a good man. He had good will to cash in as he saw fit. If this was how he wanted to do it, Cvareh would allow it.

"Speak your piece." Cvareh folded his arms with a small sigh. "But know permissions like this will not be given regularly."

"You know I love House Xin. You know I love Petra'Oji. You know you shall find no one more loyal than I."

Cvareh couldn't refute it so he didn't.

"Cvareh, there is something dangerous about that woman."

"I am aware of that much." A smirk lined his mouth. "I think most of Nova is aware after her display in the pit today."

"That is precisely why I am worried." Cain's scowl only deepened. "Her blood, Cvareh."

Dread was a sobering potion that took effect instantly, dulling the lust and delight that had been filling his mouth and veins all afternoon.

"She has too many organs for a Chimera. She doesn't smell of rot. She's strong, like us. And she—her blood, I don't think that was an illusion—"

"You speculate too much." Cvareh tried to dismiss Cain from hunting Arianna's scent. "She is strong, but that is all."

"It is more than that." Cain stepped forward and his voice dropped. Even though they were the only ones in the immediate vicinity, he looked as though the very walls and leather saddles would take offense to the whispered topic. "I have heard rumors from those who live on Lysip, rumors that the Riders were seeking you for something about a Perfect Chimera. Yveun has tried to keep them hush, but the quietest of whispers are often times the most true."

"You would believe Rok bastards over your own House?" Even if the rumors were true—and damn that they were— Cvareh was still taken aback by the idea.

"Are they lying?" Cain knew him too well. When Cvareh didn't immediately answer, he continued. "Cvareh, the Dono himself fears these monsters, these perfected killing machines. They would be mightier than us. We are born with our magic; they *steal* it. One creature who could possess all forms of magic, who would imbibe without shame as you know they do."

Just the word exploded the flavor of honeysuckle in Cvareh's mouth.

"If something scares Yveun'Dono, why would we not use that to our advantage?"

"Yveun is a monster, you will find no objection from me on the fact. And I wish to see him dead as much as any other Xin, perhaps more for my love of you and Petra. But I do not know if it is best to slay a monster using an even more fearsome beast. A beast we are welcoming into House Xin with little consideration for what doing so could truly mean." Cain cautioned, "What makes you think this new terror could be contained and controlled?"

Cvareh kept his answer to himself, but not well enough.

"Her fondness for you?" Cain snorted, outright laughter churning up through his stomach. "Cvareh, thinking something like *love* can contain a woman like that is akin to thinking you can funnel the winds in a particular direction with a cup of your hands."

"I know her." Cvareh felt an ugly emotion brew like storm clouds in his chest. He did not want to hate Cain. But he also did not want a woman, a Fenthri, to make him hate Cain on her behalf.

"As do I."

"You do not." Cvareh wouldn't hear it.

"How much time did I spend with her because 'you cannot trust yourself to be in her presence'?" Cain threw Cvareh's past words from when he arrived on Nova back at him. "You never said why, but clearly it's because you can't handle her for longer than a few days before you would force yourself on her."

Cvareh lunged. Cain side-stepped and Cvareh twisted to meet him. He kept his fists balled, claws contained. He wanted to pummel Cain, but he wouldn't make his fellow Xin bleed. Not yet at least.

His fist connected with Cain's face. The other man reeled. Claws jutted from sea foam hands. Cvareh pushed forward and slammed Cain against the tack wall, pressing him into the shelves and leathers, one hand on his wrist.

"Do not challenge me, Cain," Cvareh snarled, his mouth wide and teeth bared.

"If I do, will you fight me in the pit, Xin'Ryu?" Cain gnashed his teeth back at Cvareh as he spoke. "Or will you send your Chimera? Will you have a woman from the land below do your fighting?"

He wanted to peel Cain's skin off one strip at a time. He wanted to throw the man on the floor and cut down through muscle and sinew to bone. He would gnaw on his innards and feast on his heart. Cvareh had never bested Cain before in a fight, practice or otherwise. But he knew in that moment he could. Fighting for Arianna somehow made him more vicious than he'd ever been. It gave him a reason to be more dangerous than he'd ever thought possible. Dangerous enough to kill even a Xin. *For her.*

Cvareh threw Cain away. The man stumbled but spun, ready for a continued attack. None came.

"You have made a fool of yourself with this, Cain'Da. Abandon this folly, and return to the obliging man this House needs." Cvareh straightened.

"You know the depth of my loyalty to our House." Cain waited for Cvareh to challenge. He didn't. "Do you think I would question you or Petra if I didn't think it was in our best interest?"

His heart sang the truth of Cain's words. Despite his means, the man worked toward an end he truly believed was best for their House. Cvareh sighed heavily. The fact would keep him alive. "I will keep this from Petra for now, for our friendship. For she would flay you for your disobedience."

Cain had no objection. The man might think he could handle Cvareh in a row, but Petra was another force altogether. The only Dragon foolish enough to challenge the Xin'Oji was the Dono himself. They were titans among men and women.

And they both fear Arianna. Cvareh's mind betrayed him. He snarled at the echo of Cain's words twisting in his mind. Petra feared nothing. Petra only needed an ally.

"Return to the Xin Manor, and pray to Lord To for wisdom in this." Cvareh threw a saddle on the boco at random, tightening it for punctuation. "And pray to every Lord and Lady you have breath for that I do not reconsider letting Petra know of your misgivings."

A darkness lurked over Cain's features that Cvareh had never seen before, least of all directed at him. The man had been his friend, his brother, and he was determined to dig a chasm between them so wide that Cvareh could not jump across. Cain saw one possible future, a bleak place where Cvareh would be forced to choose between his House and the woman he had come to love. He gripped the boco's reins, leading it from the stable with a flutter of wings.

"Cvareh'Ryu," Cain called. Cvareh should have never stopped. He should have not allowed any more of Cain's poison words through his ears and into his mind. "That woman will be your undoing. If you wish to damn yourself with her, fine. But for the love of Xin, do not damn the rest of us by taking her into the House's bed, too."

Cvareh did not dignify the statement with a response.

YVEUN

"S he means to make a fool of you." Coletta nursed a glass
of wine, reclining in a chaise.

"That much is apparent to anyone with eyes." Yveun
continued to pace the room. It was large and open, with
a gaping maw of a balcony and tall ceilings. It was more elegant
than he wanted to admit and befitting of his station—which
fed his anger further. Petra insulted him with one hand, while
lauding him with the other. She toed the line finely enough that
he could not challenge without seeming in the wrong to the
masses.

"What is also apparent is that you are letting her." Coletta
regarded him with eyes the same color as the drink she
consumed. Eyes that stripped him bare. Eyes that judged him
even more harshly than he judged himself.

"I have not—"

"You are the Dono." When Coletta wished to be heard,
none would interrupt her. None would sway her. She was not a
flashy weapon like most Dragons, and was all the more deadly
for it. "You only do what you wish."

"You would not have had me sit in the place Petra prepared
at the Court."

"I would not have had Petra organize the Court at all."

He loved and hated his mate all the more when she was right.

"You did not consult me before this whole affair and you took a half measure on the matter, Yveun," Coletta admonished. "You wanted to make a statement by holding the Court on Ruana. But you merely gave Petra the opportunity to show Nova what a Cobalt Court would look like. The only thing *Dono* about you today was the title servants called you as they fattened you on Xin food and drink while you sat out of sight and out of mind of the people."

His claws strained against his fingers from the tension he put them under. Still Coletta sat, and sipped, and spoke.

"You sent a half-trained 'Master Rider' into the fray, who was made into an even larger fool than you by an Anh." She straightened slightly. "I gave you Leona. I instructed you to nurse her in every way a man can. You had one of the greatest tools of our past forty years of work, and you wasted her."

"There is something deeper here." Yveun knew there must be. He would not let so much power slip through his hands otherwise. There was a variable he was still missing. "The Chimera on Loom—"

"You would blame your shortcomings on a Chimera." Coletta stood, walking to the balcony. "That is the only thing I could imagine to be worse than blaming them on Petra."

Yveun watched as the small-framed Dragon ventured out into the night. She possessed all the grace of a Dono. But Coletta had never desired the title. She couldn't win it by normal measures, so it had suited her better to attach herself to him. They needed each other in different ways.

"It is only through half measures that these things are allowed to happen." She raised her wine to her lips again, savoring the taste. "And if they continue, you will lose everything, Yveun."

She didn't say "we" or "House Rok". The statement was so pointed, it was nearly a threat. She wanted him to be made aware that the House would live without him. *She* would live without him.

He stood to lose the most.

Yveun felt like a man before a god as he approached Coletta. She stood, washed in night, like the Divine Patron under which she was born—Lady Soph, the Destroyer. He hated admitting he had erred. But if he was to swallow his pride, he would do it before Coletta and no one else. He would drink the bitter poison of her words, to save himself from anything else she might concoct.

"Did you know that the most deadly flowers are oftentimes the most delicate?" Her tone had shifted. It had taken a softer note. There was danger in the quiet.

"I would believe it."

"They are beautiful, Soph Pearls, the most delicate of all. When the tiny white flowers finally lose all their petals, the smallest fruit forms. And in this is a toxin that can slay even a Dragon with some magic in their gut."

She smiled, revealing her gray, abused gums. Worn from years of her work, from years of experimenting with flavors. From working up tolerances and immunities. From breaking down her body out of reverence for her Lady. From the belief that to create, one must first destroy.

Coletta held out the glass she had been holding. The wine sloshed, airing with the very darkness itself. The stem of the glass dripped between her fingertips like a moonbeam.

Yveun met her eyes. Coletta changed nothing in her stance. She was as still as silence personified. As ever-present as death itself.

He reached for the glass, showing no fear. He took it from her fingers and he drank. The alcohol burned lightly, cutting the sweetness of the wine. It was a jam profile, sweetened with fruit and aged in light wood. He savored the flavors, holding them on his palette, searching for anything he might have missed, before swallowing.

"Do you like it?" Coletta asked.

"It is the same wine we drank today," he observed.

"It is," she affirmed. Yveun waited patiently for her to impart the importance of having him try something he'd consumed all day. He waited for the spark of magic of his stomach churning against poison. "This is a specialty for this side of Ruana, a favorite among House Xin. So loved that it does not even make shipments out of this corner of Nova."

"I was not aware."

"I know you were not." Coletta shot him a glare from the corners of her eyes, conveying her lack of appreciation for his interruption. If such a look had come from anyone else, Yveun would have killed them on the spot. "Because you have become drunk on power, and are operating under half measures."

Something indeed churned in his gut, but it wasn't poison. No, anger at the truth his life-mate was lying before him tore at his insides. He had become drunk on power, on the idea that he was an invincible force and his rule was as inevitable as the sun rising. And tonight, that would change. There was something already brewing in the air.

Yveun took another long sip. "But you knew."

"I knew." She smiled into the blackness. "I knew, and I knew where the wineries are. I learned of each of the storerooms where the vintage is kept."

"It would be a shame if someone tampered with the brew."

Far on the streets below, the first cry cut through the night.

"Such a shame." Coletta took back the wine, helping herself to another long sip. "For the flavor is right."

More screams as Dragons fell, convulsing on the stone streets that sprawled out beneath them. A symphony of agony his Coletta had produced sang to them with all the beauty of a full orchestra.

Yveun wrapped a hand around her hip and smiled into the night alongside her. It was going to be a much shorter Court than he was accustomed to.

"There has been word from the whisperers to Loom."

"What did they say?" Yveun asked over a particularly high-pitched cry.

"Two messengers arrived to the Harvesters' Guild. They came to sow seeds of dissent from the Alchemists. They are seeking to rise against you. A rebellion has formed."

Yveun cursed under his breath. It was hardly a surprise. An annoyance, the persistence of Fenthri. At least, that was how he'd always viewed it. And that had been the problem. He had treated the men and women in the gray world below like children, poor helpless creatures in squalor, in need of his guiding light.

After all he'd done, they still stood against him.

"What did the Guild do?"

"The Vicar Harvester took their meeting. It was one of their Masters who alerted the guild's Dragon whisperer to Nova of it."

"Without order from the Vicar?" Yveun clarified.

Coletta affirmed it with a small nod.

There was only one reason for the Vicar Harvester not to immediately come to him, not to immediately take the rebels' treasonous heads: they were entertaining the notion. Or they were trying to hide it. It didn't matter which to Yveun; both were equally unforgivable.

The Harvesters had been a loyal guild. From the beginning, they had followed his laws when he had shown them the error of their ways. They had remained in communication. But the Fenthri were fickle creatures. They tried to fit multiple lifetimes in what was not even one-fourth of his.

"I have taken enough half measures upon Loom." This was what happened when one tried to leave room for the foolishness known as kindness. He had tried to be kind to Loom, and this was how the Fenthri repaid him.

Delight rose in his mate. Coletta's magic shifted to a pleased pulse that hummed against his palm. It was a wonderful physical sensation to the auditory wonders of the world falling apart around him. It encouraged him to be one step more vicious, to be wholly committed.

"The guilds on Loom are bold anew. Squashing their last rebellion was not enough, because from its ashes the Fenthri rose again. Attempting peace by allowing them their guild cultures, to allow them to teach, was far too generous. They forget too quickly, and for that, they need a firm hand."

There would be no more exceptions. No more half measures. The tree had rotted; he would no longer pick through the fruit. He would cut it down at the base, burn out the roots. He would till the soil and plant again.

"The world below is broken beyond repair. It must be destroyed and rebuilt."

"Lady Soph and Lord Rok," Coletta referred to both of their Divine patrons with a toast, continuing to pass the glass back and forth between them.

"Tell the whisperer that all Dragons loyal to me are to be pulled from the guilds. They will be moved to New Dortam, where my Riders will shuttle them back to Nova. Then, the Riders will remain on Loom and take over the Revolvers—and their weapons." The plan took shape with vicious precision. "The Harvesters are to be made an example. It will show all of Loom that I am their King, that they thrive by my will and that they will die by it too. If even the most willing and loyal guild could not resist entertaining treasons against me, they and the rest will know none are safe, from the tallest of their mountains to the deepest of oceans. The land below is mine, and they will know it in every unbroken scream."

"Merely the Harvesters?" Coletta pushed.

Yveun's magic surged, his bones hot with power that boiled over into the atmosphere. He wanted to rain magic and blood down upon Loom from the chaos he would unleash on Nova.

"No. Destroy the Harvesters without warning. Lay waste to the Alchemists before their pathetic rebellion can retaliate. Shatter the Rivets' tallest clockwork towers so that nothing may be rebuilt. Stop every one of the Ravens' trains and snuff out trade and communications. Then, when the four are destroyed in absolute, bring the torch to the Revolvers' gunpowder. Explode all those who know how to make the tools of war to disrupt this world's divine hierarchy.

"Let them cry for order from the chaos. Let them beg for a savior to deliver them from the suffering they will know."

"And you will be that savior?" Coletta asked after a long stretch.

"When I return their lives to them, I will be Lord Rok Himself. I will be their red God."

"No half measures," Coletta said with singsong delight.

"No half measures," Yveun repeated, and savored the tuning sounds of discord in the air as he stepped behind the conductor's podium for the greatest symphony of destruction ever composed.

ARIANNA

A t night, the clouds below Nova looked like a sea of silver. The garish and brightly colored world was washed clean by the pale glow of the moon, which softened the harsh tones to something Arianna's eyes were more familiar with. The stars spread out above her infinitely. On one of her first nights she had attempted to count the glowing celestial bodies, but lost track around three hundred.

They sparkled and winked, dancing in tiny streaks of light, hiding behind the glow of the great, bright moon. Certainly the sun fascinated her, but it was the celestial elegance of the night that had begun to enchant her. There was something, dare she even think it, *romantic* about it. The night sky, the changing landscapes, the sparking magic... It had all begun to fit together in her mind to show her a picture she hadn't even been able to comprehend before coming to Nova: a world defined by beauty and a people that embraced it above all else.

One such person was under her palms now. Cvareh had been cryptic about where they were going. All he had said was "off Ruana," but to where and why he had not revealed. Arianna hadn't questioned, nor forced it from him.

The man had been changing her, against her will and beyond her expectations. And, today, she had given in to it. Arianna had loved Eva; the woman had been a mental equal who pulled Arianna's mind into delightful shapes and caressed her intellect in the right way.

Cvareh was a similar force, but different. His very being was a mystery wrapped in an enigma. He needed to pose no scientific riddle or postulation. Just trying to rationalize who he was and why he acted how he did was more than enough. Arianna wanted him all the same for it.

Ruana shrunk in the distance. Smaller, floating islands drifted through the pale ocean below them. Arianna had been trying to get her hands on a map of Nova for some time, but apparently no one had bothered to make one in recent years. Over time, the islands drifted and their arrangement changed. Dragons navigated by these smaller, unimportant rocks like skipping stones or breadcrumbs that rode on the invisible current of magic that tethered Nova together.

It was as illogical as anything else was in the sky world, and she accepted it now with a grace she hadn't possessed months ago.

"We're headed there." Cvareh pointed to an island at the end of a long line.

"What's there?" She squinted at the barely visible outline of rock in the distance.

"I know you're at least somewhat familiar with the pantheon, thanks to Cain."

Arianna huffed in objection. "I studied well before Cain."

"So you know of the Twenty Gods?"

"Each of the Twenty is Patron of a month on the calendar, and each has an aspect of your world to oversee, such as Lady

Lei supplying your water." Arianna grinned faintly at the asinine nature of the idea. But the expression faded. She was riding a giant flying bird across the heavens above floating islands in a world of rainbow-colored people and magic. At this point, it was almost irresponsible to entirely rule out the possibility of some even greater magic overseeing the Dragon's every need.

"Just so." Cvareh missed her expression, guiding the boco as he was. "Every Dragon possesses two patrons, that of their house and that of the month they are born in." He paused, interrupting himself. "What month were you born?"

"The tenth." Even knowing why and seeing the brightness of the sun for herself, it still amazed Arianna that Dragons and Fenthri kept the same twenty-month calendar.

Harvesters had observed the patterns in the light of the moon long before the discovery of Nova—how every thirty days came a night of complete darkness, and every twenty months a day of total light. The Dragons had told Loom it was Lord Rok and Lady Luc heralding the new year with a flaming chariot that lit the night sky. She had always been skeptical but never had a better explanation. Even now that she'd lived on Nova, she still had no better reasoning to offer.

"The tenth month, Lord Pak, the Dark-wielder." Cvareh laughed into the open air. "That would suit you."

"What month are you?" Arianna hardly believed in legends having any bearing on her day-to-day life.

"Eleven. Lord Agendi, the Lucky." Cvareh nodded his head forward. "And tonight, his temple is where I am taking you."

"A temple sounds like serious business." She'd had enough Dragon customs today for a lifetime.

"I will be surprised if anyone is even there." Cvareh
soothed her concerns. "The supreme gods—those who are
house Patrons—and elder gods To, Veh, Soh, and Bek, have
oft-frequented temples. But Lord Agendi is too far down the
pantheon and too far out of the way for anyone to make the
journey regularly."

She certainly wouldn't have called the trip convenient.
But Arianna was in a good mood. Her body still felt afire from
the fight, her imbibing, and their lovemaking. The night air
was crisp on her mostly naked form, charging her skin with a
pleasant icy sensation.

Cvareh tugged on the boco's reigns, leading it to a wide
landing platform connected via a stone walk to a small temple
with a pointed roof and lined with columns at the opposite
end. He dismounted, reaching a hand to her. Arianna ignored
it, helping herself off the boco. Some things were never going
to change, no matter what came to pass between them.

"It'll start soon." Cvareh looked up at the sky. "We'll only
be waiting a short while."

"For what?" she asked.

"You'll see." Whatever it was, he was so excited about it
that she forgave his cryptic nature and didn't press. "Come,
let's wait in the shade of the temple."

Around the pathway, and the entire island, were long
stalks with some sort of egg-shaped growth on the end. They
swayed in the breeze, leaves whispering quietly between
each other. It seemed no other plants would survive on this
particular rock.

Cvareh reclined on a wide step at the entrance to the
temple. Arianna poured magic into her eyes to cut through
the darkness and peer within, but was generally disappointed

in what she saw. There was a statue of a Dragon man holding a box of silver, a crown of flowers atop his head. Coins and other offerings were piled into his little treasure chest, but not much else adorned the space.

Satisfied, Arianna sat next to Cvareh.

"Might I ask you something?"

"You just did," Arianna pointed out, as though he were a child making such an error for the first time in his life.

"Will you answer it if I ask?" he rephrased.

"That depends entirely on the question. Maybe I will, maybe I'll rip off your tongue." She wasn't used to her threats earning laughter. She wasn't used to being called out when her words were bark with only a tiny possibility of bite.

"Very well, I shall take my chances." Cvareh paused, sobering once more. "The woman you loved..."

Arianna stiffened and Cvareh hesitated. She wondered if he was waiting to see if she lashed out for him even mentioning Eva. She wondered why she hadn't yet.

"Eva."

"Eva," Cvareh proceeded delicately. "You and she... you two..."

Arianna sighed heavily. She didn't want to talk about Eva. But somehow, she felt as if she owed it to the man sitting next to her. The man in whose pleasures she'd delighted in for hours had perhaps earned that much truth. If she was going to talk about Eva, she was only going to do it once. She would tell him everything he wanted to know.

She pulled off the splint, releasing her illusion. The island pulsed with the quiet sort of vibration that all of Nova had. But, like Cvareh had suspected, she didn't sense the presence of another magical being anywhere.

Seeing her skin exposed in the night was instant discomfort. It was her flesh, not the illusion. But it was also flesh Cvareh had seen, that his mouth had worshipped.

"She kissed me, for the first time, here." Arianna held out her wrist. Upon it was inscribed: *20.9.1078*. So much had happened in a mere three years. "She was vivacious, full of life and challenge and heart. She loved like a dream and she fought like a sea monster."

"What happened to her?"

"I killed her." Arianna stared out into the vast sky as if the truths she'd been searching for would be there written in the stars. Stars she never could have seen if she'd never met Cvareh. More likely, the truth would be found in the man sitting next to her. Arianna stared down at the hands she'd recently acquired.

"Arianna, I don't think you should blame—"

"I slit her throat, Cvareh." It wasn't some misplaced blame. It was fact. "We met in the last rebellion. She worked with me on the Philosopher's Box. A gifted Alchemist and one of Loom's experts on Chimera research. She was the best of all worlds and somehow loved me."

Ari leaned back onto her elbows, tipping her head back and drinking in the darkness like sharp liquor. It would fuel her words and make her brave. It already had for years, if Cvareh's gods were to be believed. "She favored Sophie at first. But we were far more well-matched in mind...and in heart."

"Do all Fenthri favor their same sex?" Cvareh asked with as much delicacy as he could muster.

Arianna laughed as a Dragon would, tipping her head back and pouring forth her amusement without reservation. "We prefer what we prefer."

"But loving one you cannot have a child with is futile. You can't continue the family..."

His words trailed off as he saw the look she gave him. She wanted him to figure it out. She would wait as long as he needed, but she would judge him past a certain point if he couldn't come to the right conclusion.

"... and that's not a concern of the Fenthri."

Arianna tapped the stone next to her like it was a bell. "Ding-ding." Her sarcasm was too weak to stand against the weight of their conversation. "The Dragons, this notion of family... For over a thousand years we would head to the grounds of Ter.0 and induce fertility, breed as we needed, the best of the best, raise the children in the guilds."

"It sounds cold and sterile."

"Families sound limiting and suffocating."

He huffed in a tired amusement. "Fair enough." Cvareh looked back to the stars, as though they would give him strength to ask the question he'd been awkwardly shifting around. "Why did you kill her?"

Arianna wished she hadn't resolved to tell him everything. She pressed her mouth into a thin line, as if she could smother the words, extinguish them like a flame. But the truth remained.

"I didn't just kill her. I killed them all." She let out the bleakness of her heart's truth. "Your people should thank me. I was the hand that crushed the last rebellion against your King."

"I don't understand."

"When we discovered we'd been betrayed, that the Dragon we'd trusted was not a double-agent for us, was not an ally against the King, but a man under the King's own thumb, we destroyed it all—or tried to." The smell of burning flesh and reagents gone sour singed her nose anew. Her hands were caked in invisible blood that would never wash away, black and red alike. "I was the only one who could do it. The rest of them had been poisoned. My stomach saved me."

"So the schematics I carried..." Realization was beginning to take over.

"Shouldn't have even existed. They were stolen at the onset of our betrayal."

"Why didn't you kill yourself?" It was a fair question, based on what he knew of her, what she was.

"You know how hard it is for a Dragon to kill themselves. It's no easier for me."

"You really are, then?"

"I'm a Perfect Chimera." Arianna finally brought her eyes to meet his. She wanted him to feel the weight of the truth. She wanted him to cower in fear or see her purely as a tool. But he did something far more dangerous: He didn't change the way he looked at her at all. "More important than overcoming the logistical challenge of killing myself, Eva and Master Oliver asked me to live. She died knowing all our research, everything we'd worked for, was being destroyed. I don't expect you to understand, but for a Fenthri, there is nothing more horrible."

"You fled, detaching from everything, and became the White Wraith. You worked against Dragons," he finished, painfully simple.

"In the hopes that I would someday find my way to the man who betrayed all I loved. In the hopes that it would bring me vengeance." She felt a sudden wave of guilt. He now knew everything, and she had never even told Florence the beginning of her story. When she returned to Loom, the girl would know the truth, Arianna vowed. The girl—no, woman—had more than earned it.

"The boon?"

"Was an opportunity to find that man."

"Why haven't you demanded it of me yet?" Cvareh's confusion mirrored her own.

She stared at her hands. The moment she'd inhaled their scent—a scent etched on her memory by pure hatred—she knew she was close to finding the Dragon who'd called himself Rafansi. But she had yet to speak on it. She had yet to utter those words, *"Take me to the man whose hands these are."* If she did, she would kill Rafansi on sight. Only she now knew he was a Xin, and an ally of Cvareh. It tore at her gut on so many levels.

"I can only ask once," she whispered. "I want to make sure what I am asking for is what I really want."

"Boon or not." Cvareh sat and took her hand. "I will give you whatever you ask, Arianna."

"Don't offer me that."

"Why?"

"Because you know who I am."

"And that is precisely why I offered."

For the first time, she was at a loss for words. She didn't know if she should capitalize on all the closeness they'd shared over the day to have him bring her to the Dragon who had betrayed all she'd loved. She didn't know if she should cross the remaining distance between them and kiss him. Rusted rivets, the mechanisms that spun her world whirred and Arianna was stuck in place, no longer grasping their logic.

"His name was Rafansi," she whispered, bracing herself.

Cvareh blinked, and burst out into laughter. Arianna withdrew her hand. She didn't know what reaction she expected, but his amusement had not been it.

"That couldn't possibly be his name."

"I would never forget it," she insisted.

"Then he lied."

It was certainly a possibility, one she hadn't ever ruled out. Yet to affirm that she didn't even know the man's name yielded a certain sort of disappointment. "How can you be sure?"

"Because no Dragon parents would ever name their child that willingly."

"Why?"

"That was the name of Lord Rok's failed first—and only—attempt at the creation of life. The lore says Rafansi was a deformed and useless wretch of a creature who only earned his existence from Lord Rok's pity." Cvareh shook his head. "A life earned by pity would be the ultimate disgrace... What an awful name to even be called in secret."

"But fitting," she snapped in annoyance, at both Cvareh's sympathy for the traitor and the fact it left her without a name for the man.

"Perhaps we could find him another way?" he offered, frustratingly helpful. "Do you know his House? Was he marked? What color—"

"He was Xin."

Cvareh straightened instantly, putting distance between them.

She read him like an open book. She felt the pulse in his magic, withdrawing on instinct, reminding him that this was not a woman he should be involved with. He fought against the pull of his upbringing, though, and took her hands with renewed passion. He held her fingers tightly, his eyes pleading as if she could explain why he was doing what he was. As if she had a neat solution for everything that drove them apart.

"Be careful what you offer me, Cvareh," she cautioned grimly, with all the sorrow of an ugly reality. "Your house looks to me to be the herald of victory. But I may well still decide to watch it burn."

"No," he whispered. "I won't let you have a reason to."

Her instant rage at him arguing with her about what she would and wouldn't do was stilled.

"We will find this man, and then I will see you kill him."

"You would let me kill a Xin?" She was rightly skeptical.

"A Xin who takes the name Rafansi and works for the Dragon King against our interests should not be alive." Cvareh smiled the smallest smile of hopeful—foolishly hopeful— encouragement. "I may not be as good of a fighter as you, Arianna. But I have other uses. I can be quite good at finding information. People just say things around me they shouldn't, like they forget I'm there entirely. I will help you find this man, and I will give him to you for judgment of his crimes."

Her brows furrowed and her lips parted just enough to let out her speechless shock. The hands he held so fiercely were the very thing that would allow him to fulfill his promise. He was ready to give her everything she'd wanted since her world ended.

But if he did, would she be asking him to sacrifice one of his own ideals? Would their relationship survive her asking him to deliver one of his own for slaughter? She was afraid it wouldn't, despite his earnest insistence. Arianna stared into Cvareh's eyes, shining bright and gold against the darkness, and saw something that might just be worth more to her than her vengeance.

Those eyes were oblivious to her struggle, and easily swung away, looking to the field. "It's starting."

"What is?" Arianna looked as well, but her answer didn't come from Cvareh.

As the moon reached its apex, the whispering reeds they'd walked through to the temple slowly straightened. Their egg-shaped ends peeled away, unfurling long pedals of red, lined in gold, from within. Their wavy edges tapered to points that curved opposite their center.

A fine mist, like the afterglow of neon, clouded the air above them as the plants' superfine pollen was released into the wind. The rock before her was awash in light and magic. It soothed her weariness from the day; it gave her strength. She felt as though she could live forever if she laid among them.

Arianna stood.

"What are they?" she breathed, stepping toward the blooms. There was no mistaking it.

"The flowers of Agendi." Cvareh was at her side, but he may as well have been back on Ruana. Arianna's mind was moving a thousand veca a second, whirring with new possibilities. "They're particular about where they can grow... So they're found only here and on Lysip. They're said to bring good luck. Do you like them?"

Arianna stepped into the cosmos that floated before her, a dance of magic turned into a fog of the whole spectrum of light. They were unmistakable. Their power even more potent than the last time she'd seen them.

"*Like* isn't the right word..." Arianna trailed off into her own thoughts.

He would take her mannerisms as awe or wonder, and Arianna would let him. It was a safer assumption than the truth that now confronted her. Did she ask Cvareh for the heart of the man who had betrayed her past, at the risk of it damaging all they were, and especially when she now knew he could get her the resources she needed for the box?

Or did she give in once more and let herself dream, and perhaps even look to the possibilities of the future?

FLORENCE

The door to her room slammed open, waking Florence with a start. Powell stood in the frame, his dust-colored hair seeming to fray at the ends with stress. Panting, a mess, he crossed to the bed in a long stride.

"Florence, we have to leave."

"What? Why?" She shied away from his grip, uneasy in the man's presence. She'd avoided and outright ignored him for two days since he had shown her the Dragon harvesting rooms. She didn't know how she could feel about someone who seemed to revere Dragons for saving the world and endorse treating them worse than livestock in the same breath.

"There aren't many trains left and they're filling." He reached for her upper arm, yanking her from the bed.

"Trains?" Florence ripped herself from his grip. "I don't know what you're thinking, but you must be seriously confused." She stood her ground, pointing at the still gaping door from where he had entered. "Now leave my room."

"They're going to blow the guild."

"What?" It was as if she had half the powders needed for a canister and he was expecting her to produce a complete shot.

"We have to get out before they do. There's not much time."
Powell reached for her again and she sidestepped away. He
cursed loudly. "Pitchforks and sickles, woman, if you want to
stay, then *fine*. I didn't have to come for you anyway."

He started for the door. Florence stared at his back in a
daze. Even if she didn't fully understand what was happening,
she knew desperation when she saw it. She knew what fight or
flight looked like in someone who was struggling to fall into
their training rather than chaos and cowardice.

Whatever Powell thought was going on—right or not—he
really believed they were all in danger.

"Powell, wait." Florence grabbed the back of his shirt. She
regarded him with a glare, hoping to make it clear that she was
still very aware of the uneasy terms they were on despite their
situation. "When you say they're going to blow the Guild..."
she tried to speak slowly and evenly, coaxing him into some
sense of calm that could bring order from what seemed to be a
tempest of thoughts raging in his mind.

"The Dragon King has ordered every guild hall destroyed.
We're the first."

Florence's hand went limp, dropping to her side. She
laughed. "What?"

"Florence." He grabbed her by the shoulders, shaking her
roughly. "This isn't a joke, and we must leave."

It made no sense. The Dragon King was going to destroy the
guilds? Why? He needed them. Nova needed their technology
and their production and, at the very least, their gold.

"We have to get Derek and Nora." She was already at her
friends' door, banging loudly before entering. "Derek, Nora, we
have to go."

"Flor?" Nora rolled at her lover's side, groggy.

"What's going on?" Derek was far more alert.

"I don't know," she confessed, hoping they had enough stock in her decision making ability to trust her blindly. "But I believe we need to leave."

"And quickly!" Powell urged.

Derek and Nora, to her surprise, did exactly as Florence asked. They left the bed without further question, not even bothering to tug on more than their sleeping clothes. Together with Powell, the three hastily started down the winding halls of the Harvesters' Guild.

At first, it seemed they were the only people to know what was happening. The halls were quiet and empty; only random scampering as a person sprinted ahead of them, or someone darted from a side room with a bag in tow. But the open doors on either side of them told a different story.

They weren't the first to know. They were the last.

As they wound down, the halls began to crowd with people. They were pushing by each other, forcing their fellow initiates and journeymen out of the way. None seemed to regard Powell as anything more than anyone else, despite his nearly being at Master status.

Everyone was running. Shouting. Pushing and shoving. They funneled into narrow walks that wound tightly beneath the Harvesters' Guild in Faroe, compacting in on each other in tunnels that were not meant for the current capacity.

Elbows pushed against her, pressing her forward as the masses reached a point at which it seemed they could go no further. Florence looked to turn back, but it was already too late. More people had run up behind them, slamming into their backs as she had slammed into the backs of the people in front of her. They were part of a mass of people attempting to claw their way forward at all costs.

She felt very small, and compressed even smaller. Florence gasped for breath. Her footing was slipping out from under her. She was being carried along by the Fenthri tide. Nora and Derek were nowhere to be found, and Powell had somehow drifted out of her line of sight. She was going to die here, drowned in an ocean of panic.

Her heart raced into her throat, preventing her from even calling out. All there was to see were shades of shifting gray, illuminated by the tunnel's dim lighting. Her ears filled with the groans and grunts and cries, dizzying her mind.

A hand, sure and strong, calloused from years of work, wrapped around her forearm and yanked. Her shoulder popped and her skin bruised instantly from the force. She was threaded through the line of people—barely—to reach her friends on the wall.

Powell held her tightly, preventing the masses from ripping her away from the group again. Derek and he shared a linked arm as Derek held onto Nora with the same might. Florence gasped for breath in the small space Powell created between his chest and the wall for her.

"We have to go along the outside. There's a door ahead, a worker's tunnel, and I have the key," Powell shouted. "When I open it, you have to run. You have to run as fast as you can. Don't look back, don't think, just trust me and run. If you fall, you will be trampled."

Derek and Nora gave fearful nods. Florence looked up at Powell as he sheltered her from the writhing masses at his back.

"Run, and I'll run with you."

He gave a nod, and they pressed forward.

They squeezed in a chain, hands wrapped along elbows, along the outer wall. Derek's nose exploded with black blood as a man behind him pushed his face directly into the wall. Florence was nearly smothered once as someone tried to turn her into a ladder to see above the masses.

"Why aren't they letting us through?"

"Let us through!"

"Why isn't the door open?"

"There are still people here!"

The chorus of shouts was deafening, a cacophony of fear and pleading agony.

Powell reached the door and pulled out the key. Florence positioned herself near his side, Derek and Nora pressed behind. As soon as he saw they were all there, he disengaged the lock, and let loose the floodgates.

They sprinted. Florence didn't look back. Her lungs and legs burned, but her magic kept up. It made her faster—nearly faster than Powell, who was half a head taller.

"This way!" Powell veered left.

They followed.

"Down!" He gripped an iron ladder handle, vaulting over the edge into the darkness below as though it was nothing more dangerous than measuring gunpowder. His hands flipped their grip, his booted feet met the ladder, and he slid into the darkness.

Derek and Nora followed, Florence skidded to a stop. She couldn't see the bottom of that yawning blackness. She couldn't see where the iron ended.

But she could hear the screams behind her. The front of the pack was mere steps away. She had to make the leap of faith.

Florence jumped onto the ladder, her feet landing on a rung. She shifted her hands onto the outside, releasing her feet as well. Her stomach shot into her mouth as she free-fell and Florence had to expend every conscious thought on arching her feet around the outside of the ladder, pressing in with as much strength as she could muster to slow.

The iron burned against her bare flesh, catching and ripping. Her arches shot daggers of pain up into her calves. But she didn't stop.

She fell for a seeming eternity before she finally let out a scream. She was falling into those endless pits she'd seen on the train. The infinite strip mines that spiraled down further and further into the earth, stopping only when they had been exhausted, when the Harvesters had taken everything they could. She was going to fall to her death, and die in the darkness fate seemed determined to condemn her to at every turn.

Two hands grabbed her waist, pulling her from the ladder. They fell together in a heap of momentum. Florence opened her eyes, but was only met with more darkness, darkness so black that she couldn't even see with her improved Dragon sight.

"You're all right," Derek soothed, standing her.

"We have to keep moving," Powell stressed. "We're losing time."

They linked hands once more and marched forward into that endless blackness. The sounds of the other fleeing people began to fade as they were filtered into the worker's tunnels, splitting at forks and dividing into smaller, equally hopeless packs. Men and women were behind them, but their lead was growing. Florence chose to focus on the sound of

Powell's hand sliding against the rough-hewn walls, instead of the screams behind them, begging for deliverance from the endless black.

Florence had to put faith in the Harvester before her. This man approached these tunnels with years of knowledge and all the fearlessness of a Raven jumping into the Underground. His mind was likely spinning a mental map not unlike Arianna's would be. The latter thought gave her more hope. If Florence thought of him like Arianna, she could find the faith she needed.

She held Powell's free hand tighter.

They reached another door, this time unlocked. Light flooded the tunnel the second Powell heaved his shoulder into it. Any relief Florence could feel was abruptly cut short by the squealing hinges and the screams that rose like heat off a pyre.

The four of them ran along a narrow catwalk suspended over Faroe's under-city terminal station. Three platforms were vacant; the fourth already had a train departing. Men and women flooded over the platform, trying to press themselves against the vessel in some odd hope that they might stick. That left the fifth train, already billowing steam and clouding their vision high above as the engine began to gather heat.

"We have to make that train!" Powell shouted.

Florence's legs burned, her feet felt like rocks, but she kept pushing forward. She worked through the numbness to the point that sliding down another, long ladder to the chaos on the platform below didn't even hurt her bare feet. Powell continued to forge a path for them, Derek at his side. Florence kept her shoulder against Nora's, elbows linked.

"Powell!" a man from within one of the open cars called. "Powell, here!"

"Max," Powell shouted in reply. Harvesters flooded around them, everyone desperate for the same opening.

"Let us on! Let us on!" the people chanted and cried. They begged and bartered. But those on the car had no solution for them. To make room for those on the platform below required those on the train above to give up their spots.

Powell jumped onto the car, helping up Derek by the elbow. Florence reached for the offered hand when Nora was ripped from her side.

"This train is for Harvesters," a man screeched.

"Nora!" Florence and Derek called in unison. Their friend became nothing more than a lump on the floor, hidden under the stampede of feet.

"Let me on!"

"Nora!" Florence tried to push back to her friend. The man stepped in front of her.

His hands reached out. He was going to grab for her shoulders just as he had Nora's. He was going to take her and throw her to the ground, too. She was going to be nothing more than a lump of flesh on the floor, disregarded in the chaos as nothing more than a life less valuable than those of the people stepping upon her.

Florence reached for the holster that now never left her shoulders. One revolver, six canisters. She drew her gun and tracked the barrel right between the man's eyes.

"Touch me and I will shoot."

Fight or flight. Florence breathed heavily. *Fight or flight.* The man grabbed her shoulders. *Fight or flight, fight or flight, fight or—*

Fight!

Florence pulled the trigger, blowing off half the man's face at point-blank range. His skin exploded, curling back and away from the epicenter of the blast. The contact shot vaporized his skull and pulverized his brain. It sent blood and gore flying.

Those around were stunned into a brief moment of silence. The world stilled as everyone realized at once what they should've known all along. Every choice, every decision now, was a judgment call of whose life was more valuable. And every man, woman, and child, would always put their own life before any others, by virtue of instinct if nothing else.

"Nora." Florence took advantage of the moment, pushing people aside, stepping through the gore, grabbing for her friend. Black blood smeared Nora's body, but she remained breathing—dazed, but intact.

The people closed in again, as Florence pulled her friend toward the car. "Don't touch us," she screamed again, cocking the weapon. "Don't touch us or I will shoot to kill."

She waved her gun through the air, keeping the people at bay. She had five more shots; they could overpower her in a moment. But people seemed to favor the chance of potentially getting on the train somewhere else rather than certain death from the wrong end of her firearm.

Derek pulled Nora onto the train, then turned to help on Florence. She found her spot pressed between Powell and Derek. The Harvester's side she was flush against was too hot. It was kindling to the spark of her swift and sudden guilt.

Florence swallowed, looking at the body on the platform. She had never killed a Fenthri before. Not like that.

The train lurched to life, bringing on more screams as the people on the platform were faced with the realization that there simply wasn't enough room for all of them. They chased the train. They jumped for the vessel. Some missed, tumbling under the train's wheels with unsettling thuds. Others managed to find a hold, only to be splattered the second the train entered the narrow tunnel leading out of Faroe.

It seemed like an ocean of black and red blood was going to drown them all.

"Powell..." Florence finally began to catch her breath. "That man..."

"It was you or him." The Harvester at her side verbally recognized the fact, but he didn't look at her. He remained focused ahead, looking into the wind that carried only the darkness of the tunnel. "You had no choice."

"He was of your guild..."

"The rest were as well." Powell shook his head. "I chose to get the three of you on board."

"Why?" Florence asked.

"For Loom. I did it for Loom. The Alchemists and Ravens and Revos and Rivets—rusted sickles, they may not have gotten warning. You may be the last ones. As a Mast—As a Fenthri, knowing at least some of my guild escaped, I had an obligation to preserve the widest reach of knowledge. It was my duty..."

For now, Florence willingly chose to ignore the idea that she may be the last Raven, or Revolver, alive.

The train shot from the tracks in the dim light of morning. The world was awash in sepia tones of clay and rock. The morning seemed almost peaceful, until Florence looked back at the guild hall they were fleeing at bone-rattling speeds. High above, rainbow trails curved and spiraled. Concentrated magic glimmered down as light.

"Dragon Riders?" Florence remembered what Powell had said, but it made no sense.

Florence watched as a Dragon leapt from a high rooftop, caught by another mid-air. They began to arc and spiral away, uncaring of the trains and people fleeing. They made no effort to pursue.

No, why would they?

Florence realized the truth of it as the very evil in the air iced down the column of her spine. They wanted an audience. They wanted people to see.

She knew what was coming the moment she saw the wide canister lofted above a Rider's head. But Florence still screamed. She screamed before anyone else, because she had seen those canisters before. Hidden away one of the dark nights that she studied in the Revolvers' Guild proper, she had laid eyes on them as every Revolver should at a certain point in their studies. They were a testament to the truth of the Revolvers— that just because they could, did not mean they should.

The bomb fell like a dark omen against a silver sky.

Seconds stretched on as she watched it plummet toward the guild. It was so tiny from her vantage that it was almost as if she could reach out and pluck it from the air. But she couldn't. She could only watch, and hold her breath.

A flash of blinding light, brighter than any day. A wave of heat and air that jostled the train itself. An explosion of magic and chemicals so loud that it silenced all else in the moments to come, both demanding and earning a committed audience.

The top of the guild shuddered and groaned, toppling like the building toys of a toddler Rivet. It began to fall in large pieces as they tumbled away from what had been the epicenter of all supplies for Loom. The room she had learned about with Powell—gone. How many records of their resources, the very lifeblood of Loom, had been lost? The true shock waves of the day were going to reverberate long into the future, long after her cheeks dried and her ears stopped ringing.

But the Dragons spared no kindness. Secondary explosions rang out from deep within the guild. The walls exploded outward, tumbling the very foundation upon which the oldest city in Loom was built.

Faroe was tumbling and with it went all those who weren't safely on a train, whizzing away. Florence's mind returned to those who had entered the worker's tunnels with them, the souls who had sprinted into the darkness and would never find a way out.

The riders watched as the walls shuddered and shook. They stayed long enough to see the spiderweb fractures pop and split into existence. And then they left, as behind them the guild crumbled and burned and violently exploded, reduced to nothing more than rubble and smoke.

Florence watched with the rest of them, with every other Fenthri who screamed and sobbed and then stared silently in horror, at a complete loss for all emotions. They watched as the Dragons razed the first guild of Loom. The Dragons, who had always claimed to be their saviors, their guiding hands, demolished one of the five fundamental pillars upon which their world stood.

Florence burned the image into her mind with the heat of rage. She watched as the city of Faroe crumbled and fell into the hungry abyss that surrounded it.

ARIANNA

They spent most of the night on that island.
It had been a long time since Arianna had covered her concerns with the warmth and flesh of another. She'd never make a habit of it, but there was something to be said for it. To want and be wanted. To need, to desire, to delight in another and feel that same delight. They moved well together, for a copious number of reasons, and Arianna turned off her mind and let herself simply be.

The flowers bloomed for only a short period of time, but they didn't need light for the acts they performed. When the time came to mount the boco again, she found herself lamenting the end of the short quiet in the storm that was her life. She dared to say she enjoyed the peace she'd come to find with Cvareh.

But that was precisely the problem. They were at peace only when they didn't think about what their unconventional relationship really meant. The moment she dedicated thought to it was the moment she realized its true folly. They had pulled the trigger and the bullet could not be caught. It was shot to kill, and they would both be right in its path. The question was, did she push him out of the way, and shoulder the pain on her own? Or did she pull him before her?

Arianna rested her cheek in the middle of Cvareh's back, watching the clouds swirl effortlessly beneath them. She wished she could see Loom, however small and insignificant it was from Nova's vantage. She missed her home and its industrial sensibilities.

There had been no word or rumor from Loom. The fact didn't surprise her, given the logistics of communication between the two realms, but she worried for Florence. The girl was no doubt involved in the rebellion and the very fact put her in danger. Arianna hoped she was merely oiling guns in the Alchemists' Guild hall. But knowing Florence, the likelihood of that was slim.

The world would only ever be safe when the Dragons no longer attempted to rule Loom. For as long as they did, Loom would bend and break, rebellions would creep up, the dream of bygone days would flower into bloody conflict. She knew she had reached her decision when they landed in the manor.

"It's quiet," Cvareh observed as they headed for her chambers.

"Perhaps they are still in Easwin?" Arianna proposed, quickly changing the topic to what weighed on her. "Cvareh, I have decided that I will help your sister."

He stopped in his tracks, leaving her to pause as well, a hand on the doorknob.

"Ari?" The Dragon was uncertain, searching. It was as if she'd given him a truth he deemed far too good to be true. But all Arianna could see was that she was giving him certain war.

"It's not for her."

"Who then?" he asked tentatively.

"Florence." He visibly deflated at the name. "Helping your sister will be the best chance of this rebellion she's put so much stock in seeing success, as long as Petra doesn't betray us and try to rule Loom when she has the throne she so wants."

"Logical. I'd expect no less."

Arianna sighed softly. "It's for you as well, idiot."

He brought his eyes back to hers, hopeful.

"You don't think I actually *trust* Petra, do you?" Arianna took a deep breath and braced herself. What she was about to say would no doubt rattle them both. "I trust you, Cvareh. If nothing else I trust that you will do what must be done."

"I will, I promise you. But Petra won't betray you, either." He eagerly followed her into her quarters as she made her way to her desk.

"Good, because I will need some supplies." She grabbed for the journal that was mostly still blank inside, the others scribbled across with random notes, maps of the manor, and other postulations.

Her pen paused as she thought a long moment. What did Sophie say she needed? What would help the rebellion the most? Arianna wasn't born to be a leader and she didn't want to be. She was born to create tools and was content to let others figure out their use.

"Yes, anything. You know I will give you anything," he repeated his dangerous offer.

Arianna withheld scolding him. She would save her boon for as long as she could. She would use it when she had no other option. When it was something he wouldn't give her willingly, or tried to be subversive about.

"Those flowers, I will need them." Merely thinking about crafting the Philosopher's Box again set the hairs on her neck on end. With every pen stroke and mental note made, she felt like she was writing the world's future.

"The Flowers of Agandi? Why?"

"The traitor. He brought them once... I thought he was a simpleton, bringing back something for the sheer beauty of it, a memento of home. But it was a stroke of luck." She laughed at the irony of her word choice. "We discovered that they have a special property in their pollen that can be used as a type of tempering on gold. It helps keeps magic fresh and rejuvenated."

Cvareh's eyes widened. The man was smarter than she gave him credit for, sometimes. He was beginning to piece together why she needed what she claimed. "But it wears off when the flower closes, or dies."

"It does, but if the pollen is tempered properly, the properties stay," Arianna explained. "It keeps the blood from turning black. It removes the strain of the magic."

"This is genius," Cvareh whispered by her shoulder.

"This was Eva's genius." Arianna would never miss a chance to laud her dead lover. Eva deserved that much, and so, so much more. "She was the one to notice her reagents hadn't gone sour in the flower's presence."

"How many do you need?"

"Not too many... well, depending on how many boxes we make. But since they don't grow on Loom and you said they're particular about where they grow even here... We'll need your help getting them. They must be transported quickly and securely so they arrive living and undamaged."

"Petra and I will see that this is done." There was an awe about Cvareh's excitement.

"We will also need more gold." Arianna tried to think back to the things Sophie said were in short supply. "For the boxes, and in general. I think you could perhaps intercept some shipments here to Nova from Loom."

"Far simpler than that." Cvareh placed a hand on her shoulder with a broad smile. "My sister has refineries here, nearly in working order."

"Refineries, here on Nova?" Arianna tried to grasp what this meant for Loom. If the Dragons could refine their own steel into gold, that meant Loom was one step closer to becoming irrelevant. She stared at her supply list. Loom needed the Philosopher's Box. They needed to secure their place in the world's future.

"Not as large as on Loom. But there are even Rivets and Harvesters Petra has brought up to help."

Arianna snorted, trying to imagine the thought. But the emotion was quickly lost. After all, here she was.

"Very well, then. The Alchemists could still use more guns. And any help with transport on Loom. We'll need to leverage the Rivets to put things in mass production."

"We will help how we can." She understood Cvareh's hesitation. Their power was significantly less once they stepped off the floating islands that drifted across the stars. "I will go pass all this information along to Petra."

"I'll finish the list while you do." Arianna drew another line, thinking of any other demands she could make on behalf of her home. Even if Petra ultimately betrayed them. If she could give Loom enough of an advantage to tip the scales, it might be worth it.

Wrenches and bolts, Arianna mentally cursed herself. She sounded like the same idealistic girl who had let herself be swept up in the rhetoric of the last rebellion.

"One more thing, Cvareh." She didn't look up from her paper. "Tell Petra to ready the glider for me to return to Loom."

There was an agonizingly long pause. "Pardon?"

"I'll need to return to Loom. I'll need to return to the Rivets personally. I will still have sway there—the Masters will remember me as Oliver's student. I can teach them how to make the box. I—"

"We have everything you need here." Cvareh said hastily. "The flowers, the gold, tools…"

Arianna looked out the window. This shouldn't be so difficult. But here she was, struggling against the truth, fighting for words. "I need factories. I need other Rivets and Alchemists. I need to go home."

"Can you return?"

"Why would I?" Arianna turned to see him trapped in limbo in the doorway. She wanted to stand and walk over and comfort him. She wanted to pull him into the bed and build blockades out of blankets to keep the world at bay.

"Because Petra needs me here." The truth was more deadly than a paring knife between her eyes, though the pain may have been equal. "She won't let me go again. I can't afford the suspicion."

"Understandable. Your place is here, mine is on Loom."

"Arianna, that cold and detached persona will no longer work on me." Cvareh stood his ground, literally and proverbially. "I know you, and I know that you…"

"That I what?" she pressed, seeing if he would really say the words her mind filled in. Cvareh faltered. "You barely know me, Cvareh."

"After tonight, I think I do."

"One day of sex and a small conversation does not give you my mind, all my history, my truths. You will never understand what drives me."

"I don't have to." He smiled soothingly. "I merely have to love it."

"You're being a fool." The man was going to paint color on her gray and dreary dreams, and somehow, she wanted to let him.

"No." He stepped toward her, rather than hastening away to his sister to report that he had finally secured all that House Xin needed. "I think this is one of the few times where I'm not."

That smile, sharp canines and all, was more dangerous than it had ever been. She hooked a hand on his neck and brought her mouth to it. Arianna wanted to taste the flavor of hope again.

"I love you, Arianna. And I will not stand in your way, but I will also not let you flee from this. Reject me if you must, and that will be that. Until you do, I will see my future built with space for you in it."

She searched his face as if she could read the words he wanted her to say off it with ease. But she was tired. There was only so much change that could be expected of a single person in one day.

Cvareh eased away, but there wasn't disappointment in his motions, merely patience. "I should go to my sister."

She watched him go, still caught in the same limbo. He loved her. *Loved.* Arianna placed a hand on her chest, feeling nothing. She remembered what it felt like to have a beating heart, though she hadn't in years. Eva had cut out the heart Ari had given her, and Arianna had built a new clockwork machine to take its place.

She didn't remember anything in her designs that would allow her to love again.

PETRA

Her people, her *family*, were dying in the streets. By the time word arrived to Petra of the mysterious circumstances under which they were suffering, it was far too late to even attempt to save the majority of them. The organs from a slave squished under her feet as she paced the room. Killing the messenger solved nothing, but the scent of blood made her mind sharp and her senses keen. Killing directed her rage at someone worthless, so it didn't escape through her at the people she needed to depend on.

The doors at the far end of the hall opened. Claws out, fangs bared, Petra wheeled in place to look at who had traversed into her space at such a time. There were only about five people she wouldn't kill on sight, and lucky for Cain, he was one of them.

"Cain, tell me news. Tell me something worthwhile." She felt utterly useless, and it was a feeling Petra both loathed and feared. She was the Xin'Oji, the young warrior, the champion of blue. She knew how to fight her way out of any corner.

"Petra'Oji." Cain's bare chest heaved as he fought to catch his breath. "I just arrived from overseeing healers from Napole to Easwin. They began to try to help the living, but their medicines are failing, so they looked to the dead. They suspect poison."

"Poison?" Petra repeated out of pure shock. A shameful death, poison was only reserved for killing animals without marring their pelt or flesh, or for the ill whose hearts could not be safely consumed seeking relief. Petra tried to think of even one poison, but could not name any. "It was not a rash of sour elk? Or an unhealthy growth upon the yeast?"

Cain shook his head grimly. "When they opened the cores of the fallen, half their innards had been completely dissolved."

"Are any surviving?" Petra walked over to one of the tall windows in the hall that faced east. All that was before her were the spires of her manor.

"Only those with strong magic in their stomachs."

Petra hung her head. Her claws dug so far into the stone that they nearly snapped. This was an enemy in the shadows. It was not one she could hunt down. It was not someone she could summon into the pits and make an example of several times over.

She had dealt with a coward. She had dealt with someone who was willing to sacrifice all their ideals for the ends they wanted to achieve. Petra snarled despite herself; the irony was not lost on her. Whoever had done this knew it was a very dark way to twist the Xin motto.

"Cain, I have an important task for you." Petra thought through her next move as carefully as she could manage. But blood clouded her mind and engulfed her nose. She wanted to roar the song of vengeance.

"Oji." Cain brought his heels together, standing taller.

"Find Finnyr, and bring him to me." Petra straightened, looking at Cain's reflection in the blackness of the windowpane. "I only need him alive and able to speak, Cain. His condition otherwise matters not."

"Do you think Finnyr'Kin has anything to do with this?"

Petra was smart enough to tell the difference between true insubordination and inquiry; this was by far the latter. Cain's face was overcome with horror at the very thought. It was heartening, but Petra did not have time for it.

"No..." Petra tapped her fingers along the windowsill. "Finnyr is a Xin, even if he lives under a Rok roof. Furthermore, even if he wanted to betray us, this is beyond him. At worst, he's a worthless little slime, not cunning or devious.

"However, the man whose roof he sleeps under is both." Petra growled the Dono's name. "Yveun has much to gain from Xin fighters mysteriously dying in the night, especially after our showing today."

"I will find Finnyr'Kin."

"See you do so with discretion," Petra cautioned. "We must act carefully until we know what picture is being painted." Accusing a Dragon of engaging in dishonest battles was a high offense if it proved to be unfounded. Even if Finnyr confirmed it was Yveun, Petra still wasn't certain she would be able to outright accuse the Dono of treason.

Dawn had barely kissed the sky when Petra knew Cain had returned. She smelled the man's magic and the sharp tang of her brother's. She had done nothing but pace the room for hours and bark orders at any who entered.

The doors opened and Cain shoved Finnyr through them. Her brother tripped, nearly falling on his face. He was like a skittish field mouse trying to squeak a mountain lion into submission.

"I am a Kin of this House. I will not tolerate this treatment!"

Cain looked to her. It was a delicious feeling—another person deferring to her above Finnyr, the first born, the fallen child of Xin. Petra's claws felt ten times sharper.

"We shall see what you are soon enough," Petra said silkily.

Finnyr turned slowly to look at her. All boldness he had tried to throw around with Cain washed away beneath the shower of her judgment. She poured her suspicions silently atop him and watched as they eroded his resolve.

"Petra, what is the meaning of this?" Finnyr demanded.

"Cain, I wish to be alone with my brother." Petra didn't want an audience for what she was about to do to Finnyr. She didn't want anyone in the manor to know what she could do with her claws. The speculation over what prompted each delightful scream would be a far stronger message to warn others against disappointing her.

"As you wish, Oji." He closed the doors behind him. Petra's ears twitched as she listened for footsteps. There were none, meaning Cain had assumed responsibility as guard.

They would not be disturbed.

"Petra, there—"

"Petra'Oji," she corrected venomously. "You will refer to me by my title, Finnyr."

"There are things I must tell you."

"Oh, I imagine so." She began to advance on him. "Our House, your family, are dying, Finnyr…"

"You can't possibly think I had anything to do with it." Finnyr retreated, shuffle step after shuffle step.

"No, I know better. You're far too inept for that," she chastised. "You're weak. You think small. You require a guiding hand." Claws shot from her fingers at every flaw she named. "You likely aren't even aware of what happened."

"No, I am aware."

"Oh?" She wanted to hear him say it. She wanted him to be so worked up and afraid that he would do anything to prove himself to her. And, in doing so, he would show her his true colors.

"I hadn't come home because I was searching for answers on my end, just like you commanded." Finnyr stood straighter, like a performer in the spotlight. "I overheard a conversation that I think will be of use to you."

He couldn't overhear anything when she needed him to, but suddenly managed without a problem when it was far too late. His inconsistency was beginning to rub Petra wrong. "For your sake, you'd best hope it is."

"It was in the wine," Finnyr said hastily. "The poison was in the wine."

Petra stopped just within arms reach. She stared at her brother for a long moment before raising her hand in a quick motion, bringing its back across his face. Her claws dug long, golden lines in his cheek.

Finnyr reeled. "What, why?"

"Tell me true. Where was the poison put?"

"I told you—"

She grabbed the chain that sat around his neck, the collar the Dono made all his beasts wear, and yanked him by it. Petra placed a hand on his shoulder, tensing her fingers and dragging her claws down his bicep. Finnyr howled in pain.

"Tell me how my people were poisoned!"

"I am telling you!" he snarled. "It was in the wine."

Petra slapped him again, this time with her palm. She ripped a chunk from his ear in the process. "Where did they put it?"

"In the wine!" Finnyr hissed in pain. "Petra, the poison was in the wine."

"Where?" She hit him again.

"The wine!"

"Where was it?" Petra threw him backward. Finnyr stumbled, giving her an easy opening to straddle his feet and hold him against the wall by his neck. Rivulets of gold pooled in his collarbones as her claws dug into the soft muscle of his throat.

"The wine!" Finnyr was nearly at the point of tears. The shameful, pathetic man came undone under her fingers, the truth pouring from him like the blood from his neck. Petra could confidently ascertain that he was not trying to deceive her in any fashion.

She dropped him into a heap on the floor in disgust.

In a display of how low she regarded him, she stalked away, her back to him. *Let him lunge*, Petra seethed mentally. If he dared attack her when her back was turned, she really would kill him. Right now, his death was merely a high probability.

"Cain." Petra pulled open the door. The man was at attention. Cain was not perfect, but Petra was truly grateful to have him in that moment. "Go and have the word spread that all wine on the isle of Ruana is to be cast into the God's Line. Every last bottle, cask, and vat."

"As you command, Oji." Cain made haste away.

Petra slammed the door shut and turned with a sigh. It wasn't even sport to tear her brother into pieces. He had already healed, but he remained on the floor in a puddle of pale blue flesh. She should be done with it and send him to the refinery to function as Ruana's personal reagent farm.

She squatted before him, assessing her broken prey. Petra reached out a hand and he flinched. She slowly began to stroke his hair, as if she were soothing a skittish animal.

"Now, Finnyr, tell me whose poison it was, and don't lie to me."

"Coletta'Ryu's." Finnyr swallowed, trying to wash away his weakness. It didn't work. "It was Coletta'Ryu's poison."

"What?" Petra tried to make sense of this. The Rok'Ryu? Coletta was nothing, worthless, weak and small.

And that would be just the sort of person who would resort to such devious and underhanded means. The person who could not stand in the pit. The person who would attach herself to one of the fiercest Dragon fighters while still offering something of her own to match the bloodthirstiness of her mate.

"I know it was her," Finnyr insisted. "She is known for staying in her gardens, but allows no one else in there. Most assume it's for her privacy, to hide her frailty. But I began to suspect something else when a servant went in and wound up dead."

Petra glanced at the servant she had killed hours ago, the body now cold. She could entirely understand killing someone for being in the wrong space at the wrong time. Especially when that someone was worthless.

"The man was killed without any kind of wound. His chest, head, all intact," Finnyr clarified.

It made too much sense.

"How have you neglected to tell me this?" Petra raged.

"I did not think it important." Finnyr tried to move away but Petra's hand tightened into a fist, yanking him into place with force.

"You did not think it important for me to know that the Ryu of Rok is a shadow-master, a potion-mongering coward?" Their noses nearly touched as she verbally assaulted him. "That she is far more despicable than even her mate?"

"I did not connect the facts! I did not see what was there! Nameless die all the time."

"That is because you are an idiot." Petra slammed Finnyr against the wall. "A useless idiot."

"Petra—"

She gouged out his throat with a hand, blood pouring, bubbling as his words escaped through the open holes as gasping wheezes. Flesh strung from between her fingers like taffy, stretching until it snapped.

"You are useless." Petra let the one wound heal, pinning him down with her knees on his arms and sitting on his chest. She leaned forward, dragging a claw around his eye, watching the liquid ooze out alongside the blood, as she whispered in his ear, "Useless."

She scolded herself as much as him. They had both failed House Xin. He had failed them with his incompetence. She had failed them for depending on it. His punishment would be her claws. Her punishment would be the shame of flaying her brother in a back room, hidden from the world.

"Useless."

She reared back and struck him.

"Useless. Useless. Useless!"

She would slice him, once for every Dragon that had died this night, and then another hundred times for every Oji of House Xin he had shamed. His magic began to falter in its ability to keep up healing between her relentless blows. It reduced his flesh into little more than liquefied meat. He tried to struggle against her but Petra pressed herself upon him until she began to hear bones snap. If he died tonight, he would not die with a face any would recognize. She would see that she never had to look upon the shame of Xin ever again.

Her claws stopped, mid swing. Petra tugged, blinking from her blood-frenzied trance. A hand was wrapped around her wrist.

"Sister, enough!"

CVAREH

The woman pulled him in so many directions at one time that Cvareh was surprised his limbs were still attached. He had sensed her hesitation, her wish to withdraw, but she hadn't rejected him outright and he didn't know yet how to fully process the matter. Arianna was a woman who always knew what she wanted, what she fought for. A lack of opposition could mean support, or agreement.

Cvareh scowled to himself at the logic, dangerous in more than one way.

Perhaps she merely had yet to find the way she wished to outright reject him. It was confusing and laborious to try to reason through her mannerisms. But it was something he did gladly. The better he understood her, or tried, the better he could give her whatever it was she needed, be it revenge, or gold, or someone to whom she could finally confess the weighty secrets that she carried alone in her heart.

It would be his lot that the first woman he would design to take for his mate, his life-mate if she ever agreed to it, would be the first Perfect Chimera—and impossibly head-strong. Cvareh grinned faintly to himself. All the reasons he should find her tiresome made her all the more endearing. She had accomplished an inspirational amount in her short life. If Arianna could be all she was, then he could be a man she deemed worthy of her love.

She didn't say she loved him.

She didn't outright reject him.

Their magics and minds had been so close for the past day that he wouldn't be surprised if she began to smell of him and he of her. Even if she said otherwise, he knew more of her than she gave him credit for, and what he knew and felt gave him hope. Cvareh paused, looking down the long stretch that would eventually lead back to her room.

The mere thought of her being near brought a smile to his mouth, a smile that quickly fell when he remembered her desire to leave Nova. The pain of being separated from her was like lightning in his mind, hurt its rallying thunderclap. But love would be the rain, soothing both.

There was a solution here, he merely had to find it.

"Cvareh'Ryu!"

Cain was the last person he wanted to see, especially after the increasing closeness he and Arianna had shared. "Cain, you have yet to recover my good favor," Cvareh cautioned.

"We have far more pressing concerns," Cain's tone was grave.

Cvareh put all else aside. If it was enough to unsettle Cain, it was something serious indeed. "What has happened?"

"The wine on Ruana has been poisoned."

Cvareh didn't even have the capability to process the words Cain was saying. It made no sense. "Why would the wine be poisoned?"

"Think of who such a thing would benefit." Cain scowled with murderous intent.

"Rok bastards." Cvareh rolled another several curses off his tongue.

"All wine is to be discarded into the God's Line. I am to spread the word."

"Go with haste." Cvareh would not keep him a moment longer. "Where is my sister?"

"Her sitting parlor."

Cvareh started in that direction. He had to get to Petra. She would know how to make sense of this.

"She is alone with Finnyr'Kin."

The words made Cvareh pause. He turned to look back at the Dragon who stood several steps away now, and whose words held an unspoken caution. Cain would say no more, clearly. He had been put too far in his place of late to do so. Furthermore, it was not a matter of the House's safety. This was now a matter of family.

"Thank you, Cain."

"Walk in the protection of Lord Xin."

They went separate ways.

If Petra had called Finnyr, she suspected him to be involved, or to know something of the crime. She was dumping all wine on Ruana, which led him to believe the damage was widespread. Dread grew with his every step.

It wasn't until the sharp smell of cedar drifted through the halls of the Xin Manor that Cvareh broke out into a run. He pushed slaves out of the way, focused only on his destination. The scent of blood grew to an overwhelming, pungent stench as he neared Petra's parlor.

Cvareh broke through the door, skidding to a stop at the sight of the scene before him.

Petra was straddled atop what could only be described as the pulp of their older brother. Her claws dripped blood with

every swing, spattering around her in wide arcs. She rocked
atop his chest like death's lover, a dark and primal savagery
overcoming her.

"Useless. Useless. Useless!" she screamed the word over and
over.

Finnyr cried and gasped through lips that were sheared back
to bone. If he could make noise, then he was alive. That meant
Cvareh wasn't too late to save Petra from her own madness.

Cvareh ran to their side. He gripped Petra's wrist, stopping
her mid-swing. Petra snarled at his tether.

"Sister, enough!"

"Unhand me," she growled.

"Petra." Cvareh slackened his grip, but he still held her. He
needed his sister to feel his magic, their magic, the magic that
their brother also shared. "You will kill him if you continue."

"It is because of him that Xin have died this night." She spat
the words. "Save him and you are no better than the cowards
and butchers he works for."

"Kill him, and neither are you." Cvareh knew his sister. He
knew when she needed to be pushed. He knew he was the one
person in the whole world who could get away with it. "Did you
intend to murder him without witnesses? Without calling his
crimes? Without a proper duel? Will you stoop to the level of
House Rok?"

Petra panted. Finnyr groaned. Cvareh was left to speak
sense into the madness.

"You are the Xin'Oji. Your House needs your example."
Cvareh knelt. He focused only on his sister. "No one doubts
your ferocity, Petra."

"Move." She pushed him away. Cvareh thought she was
merely making space to strike at Finnyr again, but she stood

with a small sway. The death of House Xin's fighters and innocent alike had taken something from her. "You're right, Cvareh."

Cvareh remained silent, letting Petra speak. Just as he knew when to push, he knew when to back away. And this was a Petra who would skin anyone or anything alive that prevented her from being heard.

"He doesn't deserve to die a death hidden away." Petra bared her teeth. "Finnyr, I will challenge you at Court this day the moment it convenes. And if you run, I will still challenge you. I will leave it standing for all Dragons to hear." Petra spit on their brother as he groaned, his flesh knitting sluggishly from the tax on his magic. "So that I may hunt you down and kill you at my leisure. There will be nowhere you can run from a duel called in Court."

Cvareh did nothing to help Finnyr up as he tried to pull himself off the floor. Their brother locked eyes with Petra—one eye, the other was still a slow-healing, bloody socket—as if somehow he still thought he could fight her. The majority of his face had been scraped away down to the bone.

"I have powerful people who will stand for me, Petra," Finnyr uttered darkly.

"Who? Yveun'Dono?" Petra scoffed. "Let him challenge me. I invite him! Let us settle this like Dragons rather than the coward he is, poisoning my men and women his only means of securing an advantage."

"Do not cast me aside," their brother cautioned. "I will be your undoing."

"You undo nothing but my honor with your existence."

"You never valued what I could offer this House!"

She snorted. "There was nothing to value."

"House Xin does not need you or any information you can give us." Cvareh interjected himself into the shouting match before it got out of hand again. Both sets of eyes were on him, but he looked only at Petra. "She will produce it."

"Cvareh…" Petra gave a cautionary look to Finnyr. That was already saying too much in front of their brother. Not when they had just effectively disowned him and marked him for death. An animal in a corner could still be dangerous, even one as small as Finnyr. Especially when that corner was backed by Yveun'Dono. "You mean…"

"Yes." There was no doubt they spoke of the same thing.

"Then the night was not a total waste." His sister clapped her hands together as though she cheered for the arrival of the Lord of Death himself. "Cvareh, remove him from my sight. Keep him, tucked away where I can't see him until the Court begins. Yveun wanted him to stay in the manor? Very well, he will stay, long enough for me to kill him."

Cvareh stood over his elder brother. Finnyr glared up at him with the same coldness he'd always shown after Petra had named Cvareh Ryu over him. Cvareh wished it could have been different. He wished he need not look upon his brother with contempt. But he knew nothing else.

This was the conclusion they had all been marching toward from the beginning. This was the breaking point of the three Xin siblings. Their House only had room for two.

Finnyr stood without his help, limping away. Blood trailed behind him as he walked and Cvareh stayed at his side all the way out of the room, then closed the doors tightly behind them with a heavy sigh.

He looked at his elder brother with a weight in his chest, a vacuum left behind by the joy Arianna had placed there earlier. Petra wanted to see Finnyr locked away and then led to slaughter. It was a shameful death.

"So where will I be kept before my slaughter?" Finnyr rasped through his yet-healing wounds, blood dribbling from his chin. "Will I even have time to wash before Court? Or line my skin with the blessings of the gods?"

Cvareh swallowed hard, feeling oddly brave and very stupid. Petra would no doubt want Finnyr locked away in the sparsest, deepest room in the manor. "You will."

He led Finnyr down the halls and away from his sister to the guest rooms usually reserved for noteworthy occupants. Finnyr was his brother, and a Xin; he would present himself well before court. Even if today was the day he would die, he would die a proper death befitting a child of the House.

Finnyr, to his credit, made no effort to struggle or escape. Even if he could overpower Cvareh, Petra wouldn't hesitate to reduce him once more to a golden smear if Finnyr turned now. His brother kept his head bowed and his mouth shut, defeated.

"I'll return in a few hours, right before the Court begins." Cvareh assumed responsibility for the task. Even if Petra hadn't designed it to fall to him, it should be one of them, and she wasn't going to be in the right mindset to escort Finnyr anywhere.

"Little Cvareh, so good to his big sister," Finnyr spoke with his back turned, making a show of dedicating more effort to looking around the room than his pointed comments. "Take a good look at me, Cvareh. This is the fate that awaits you. She'll cast you aside the moment you're no longer of use. She'll destroy everything Xin for her ambition, if that's what she must. The end Petra had designed for herself will stand before all her ideals, forever. It stands before me. It will stand before you. If you don't stop her, she will lead everything you love to ruin and you will be left with nothing more than the feeling of Yveun's claws ripping out your beating heart."

Cvareh clenched his fists tightly and still his claws tried to escape. Blood pooled in his hands from his own palms, but he didn't open them. If he did, he would strike Finnyr down where he stood.

"Everything Petra does is for Xin." Cvareh shook his head sadly, reaching to close the door. "It's you who destroyed everything, Finnyr."

Cvareh shut the door and summoned a servant from down the hall to fetch the key. He waited, guarding the room, until it could be sufficiently locked. Even then, he stalled, listening, holding his breath, waiting.

There were no outbursts of anger. No sobs. No screams of anguish. Finnyr was quiet, going about his business as though his impending expiration didn't bother him in the slightest.

Cvareh gave a long sigh and stepped away. This was normal for Finnyr, being a prisoner among luxury, disposable nobility. And he was going to die as he lived—as nothing more than a captive.

ARIANNA

The list of her supplies was almost finished.

It was an extensive process to calculate out the amount of various elements she would need to get a satisfactory initial production on the boxes. For the first time in maybe her entire life, she wished she could talk to Sophie. The woman would know how many boxes were a reasonable number to produce. She was far better at planning tactically for things like that than Ari was.

But that was currently impossible, and Arianna needed to give something to the Dragons before she left. She wanted a sort of contract in hand, a written understanding of expectations. The comfort it'd give her would be literally paper thin, but it was something.

She operated under the thought that an initial run of a hundred boxes would be enough to begin to shift the tides in House Xin's favor. Then they'd move into second-stage production, where all the tooling would be perfected and the workers on the line would know the full assembly process with ease. They could make more, faster.

She hoped it would be enough.

The waft of a scent hit her nose, distracting her. Arianna paused her pen on the page. It was the smell of Dragon blood, a sharper, fresher aroma than just trace magic. It wasn't extremely close, but it was near enough.

She stared at her hands. She had decided to look to the future, not the past. She was going to craft a new world for Loom, for Florence. Arianna pressed her eyes closed. She was going to let herself hope and dream again for a future that she might design herself to be a part of.

But the smell of blood was stronger than hope, and more real than any dream. It lured her back to the old addiction known as revenge. Arianna gripped the pen tightly, as if it was a lifeline in the rip current she was about to be pulled into.

The scent grew and Arianna stood. The Dragon named Rafansi was nearby. He was bleeding. Arianna didn't know why, but she felt the immediate tug in her gut that meant if she was not the one to kill him, she would harbor nothing but resentment for the rest of her years. This man had taken her life; she would not also let him take his death on his terms.

It is better this way, she tried to convince herself as her body moved on auto-pilot. She would seek him out and have her revenge. There would be no need to involve Cvareh and, in fact, she could still have a boon from him to spend on anything he didn't give her freely out of adoration. *Yes,* she was doing this for him, as much as herself. It would be better for everyone this way.

Arianna walked to the door, poking her nose into the hall, looking around. The smell was stronger, though it seemed to be trailing away. She looked back to the desk, caught between what she had vowed to fight for all her life—a rebellion, a future for Loom—and a quiet whisper that this was the one thing she truly wanted.

The Dragon she needed dead was here. He was here, and vulnerable. She could kill him and then build a future without the shadow of the past lurking somewhere in Cvareh's home. Rafansi was close enough that she could do it and be back in her room before the sun crested the horizon, before any were the wiser.

Arianna tore at her Dragon clothes in a sprint of movement. Yanking open the top drawer of her dresser, she pulled out her industrial trousers. They fit as perfectly as they had before. No matter how much time she spent on Nova, this was the cloth she was cut from.

She was meant to walk in boots designed for function before fashion. She was meant to tighten belts and harnesses about her fully-covered torso, wrapping herself in her own clockwork designs. She was born of stronger things than colors and fanfare. She was born of steam and steel. It had never felt so right to don the coat of the White Wraith.

As she started down the hall, her hands running over her winch box, the bottom of her coat flapped about her calves and she felt like a bloody god. She would not take her revenge in the clothes of a Dragon. She would do it with every advantage she had stitched into herself during every hardship she had survived over the years.

Arianna was not seen if she didn't want to be. She'd spent days, months, slowly mapping out the Xin Manor with the same care as she would a high-paying heist. The halls were surprisingly empty of occupants, which made it all the easier.

She tracked the scent, running in parallel halls upward until she was right upon it. Arianna looked up and down the stretch, seeing and sensing no one. In the distance, she could pick up the edge of magic, but it was weak. Likely a servant, nothing she couldn't handle if she was forced to.

She stopped before the door and took a deep breath to slow her racing heart. Her eyes shot open, blood boiled. He was here. Rafansi was right in this room.

Arianna forced herself to take measured breaths. She forced her head to cooperate. But all she could hear in her ears were the dying words of Eva, of Oliver, of everyone she held dear. She could feel the tug of bloodlust pulling her under its powerful wave, and fought all the harder to breach the surface with clear thinking and logic.

She looked down the hall once more and briefly considered walking away. If she let this man go, she would reclaim control over the one force that had driven her to the brink of insanity for years. She would reclaim her future by snapping the tether of the past.

Killing him would also snap that tether.

Arianna dropped into a crouch, peering into the keyhole. Just from the bit of tension the door handle gave when her hand rested on it, she knew the lock was engaged. She reached for the small tools concealed in the belt holding her winch box.

The lock was as simple as the one on her door. She approached it with ease and familiarity. Still, sweat dripped down her neck and her fingers nearly trembled. *Nearly.* She reaffirmed her grip on the pin now slick with sweat in her hand, and held steady.

She was close. She was so close.

The lock disengaged and the sound was louder than a gunshot to Arianna's ears. She slammed down the handle, swinging open the door. Her hand was on her knife, drawing it. The door snapped shut behind her, her blade wedged into the groove to prevent anyone else from entering. She turned, her other blade already in hand.

A Dragon stared at her in shock from the center of the room. His face had paled to nearly a Fenthri gray, his jaw slack. His magic seemed to nearly vibrate with pulses of frantic terror.

Arianna stared at him. Their eyes locked and it was a spell, one she couldn't fight. Here he was, here was the man who had betrayed her. No one to get in her way, nowhere for him to escape, he was hers. Her lips curled in a guttural growl of bloodlust.

"A-A-Arianna?"

"I'm glad you didn't forget my name." Her voice was gravel and broken glass and the sum of countless hours spent screaming alone into the darkness. "I never once forgot yours, Rafansi."

He shuffled backward as she advanced.

"And now, it will be the last thing you ever say."

Arianna pushed off, unloading the tension of her knees into the floor. She grabbed for the golden chain around his neck. The tempering resisted her magic—*no matter.* She twisted, swinging him like a rag-doll down onto the floor.

He fell hard. Arianna went down with him. She panted, her knife rearing back like an adder. She had him right where she wanted him and the idiot was too stunned to do anything. She could do anything she wanted, kill him however delighted her, though nothing would satisfy her hunger for his suffering.

Did she want to scoop out his eyeballs with the point of her blade? Did she want to carve out every organ he ever gave her? Did she want to take his heart and be done with it?

Arianna wanted to scream.

None of it was enough. None of it would be enough to quench her thirst for revenge. None of it would bring back the woman she'd loved, the teacher she'd revered, the friends she'd made in the only true home she'd ever had. She could kill him a thousand times over, and it wouldn't be satisfying to her. Because what she truly wanted, no boon, no vengeance, no vision, could give her. She brought down her dagger.

His hand shot up, catching her wrist. The other swiped for her throat. Arianna caught it. They were in deadlock. Eyes on eyes, blade point and claw point at throats. She shifted her feet, ready to overpower him. She could feel it in his trembling grip— he wasn't nearly strong enough to hold her.

"Wait, don't kill me," he spoke quickly, before she could laugh or scream or even give a growl at the coward's attempt to barter for his life. "Don't kill me, Arianna. I can give you something better."

"Once a traitor, always a traitor," she snarled. Arianna swung backward, pulling on his wrist, feeling the bones pop. She curled herself and brought her feet forward, kicking out his other wrist.

"Yes!"

Her blade stopped a second time, now of her own accord.

The man's face moved oddly as he spoke. His visage was horribly scarred with markings that hadn't been there the last time she'd seen him. Arianna watched his bones knitting before her eyes. Envy bubbled up at whoever had maimed him so effectively; jealousy was quick to follow that somehow she found herself lacking in doing the same.

"Yes, I am a traitor. But it is not you I am betraying now. I can give you something better, more satisfying than my death."

"You have no idea how badly I want this." Her hand had finally given to shaking.

"I betrayed you, Arianna, but I was nothing more than a puppet. If not me, it would've been someone else. What do you get from my death? Nothing. There will be more like me who creep up from the shadows. Kill the man who pulls the strings."

"You'd betray your own King?"

"Once a traitor, always a traitor." He grinned darkly.

A shiver of malice raced down her spine. She wanted to kill him. She had wanted to kill him for years. But he was now a low-hanging fruit. She had him and she could slay him any time. She knew she could overpower him and best him in any fight—that much had already been proven in their short encounter thus far.

Yes, killing him would serve her personal vendetta. But it would mean little for any beyond her. If she killed Yveun... She would cut off the head of the snake.

"I can take you to him, right to him. I can get you in his room before the sun even wakes. No one else can give that to you, no other Dragon will." Rafansi panted softly, continuing to eye her dagger. "It's a fair exchange, my life for the life of the Dragon King. Don't you think?"

Arianna stood, glancing to the window. If she killed him in the manor, she'd have to contend with the other Xin. She could let him take her to the King, kill Yveun, then take Rafansi's life in turn. Arianna flipped her dagger in her palm, once, twice, before sheathing it.

The mere idea, even if it was a farce, of working with him again made her feel soiled. *Eva, forgive me.* But she was going to cast the die and gamble for it all, or nothing.

"Take me to the Dragon King."

FLORENCE

Why?

The word seemed to linger on the tongue of every survivor. *Why?*

They were adrift in the world, separated by the distance of train lines and the bleeding wounds that had been carved deep into their hearts. So the train continued in the only direction it could, on to Ter 1.2. No one objected. No one suggested otherwise. There was nowhere else to go.

An entire guild, an entire people, homeless and adrift.

Florence had wanted to live to see a world where people weren't tethered to their guilds, but she hadn't wanted it like this. She'd never wanted this. She would sit and listen to the wailing tears that were only smothered, not soothed, by time. She rocked silently with the train.

Powell looked equally shell-shocked, numb. The truth of what he had been saying since he had woken her two days ago echoed in her mind, underscoring the parted lips and drifting eyes that now made up his face. She waited for it to wear off, but she could only wait so long before her burning questions threatened to immolate her fragile sanity.

"Powell," she whispered, hoping to get his attention without disturbing any who dozed around them.

"Florence?"

"You said the Dragon King ordered the attack." His silence was affirmation enough. "How did you know?" She didn't ask him why. If the man knew why, his state over the past two days would've been different. He would've been angry, frustrated, regretful. But he seemed as confused as her in that respect.

"There was a whisper." His voice mirrored the word. "From the Revolvers' Guild. It was a warning that the King's Riders had taken over. That they demanded explosives en mass. That the Harvesters were to be the first example."

"'The first example'?" Florence repeated. "You don't think the King means to attack the other guilds, do you?"

"I don't know." Powell's shoulder rubbed against hers with the swaying of the car. "And we have no way of finding out now."

All the Chimera with whisper links in the Harvesters' Guild had been killed. It had been an impressive hub of communication, one that could rival even the Ravens'. Florence's stomach turned sour. A guild had been destroyed, possibly the first of many, and the world didn't even know. Injustice and pain that went unknown hurt all the more, she had discovered.

Nora and Derek tried to ease her into sleep, but Florence refused. She sat on the edge of the train car, watching the world go by and the distant mines appear and vanish along the dawn-colored horizon, none the wiser to the fact that their world was burning. She envied that distant point, a place beyond the edge of the world where she now lived.

They were the fourth train to arrive in Ter.1.2. That was a relief to all. The people who greeted them on the platform were already equipped with knowledge, and prepared to manage the survivors. They were shuffled along, unburdened by the need for thought, into various inns and temporary encampments that had been set up throughout the too-quiet city.

"I think this is where we part."

Florence was startled to attention by the sound of Powell's rough, solemn voice. She grabbed Derek's arm, preventing him and Nora from disappearing ahead in the flow of people. Florence turned her face up to Powell's, demanding an explanation.

He sighed heavily. "The Vicar did not survive. So there must be a vote for who will assume the mantle. Only four Masters seem to have made it out, however." Pain flashed hot on Powell's features. "The Master Harvesters were all called in on my behalf, to vote."

"This was not your fault." Florence gripped the man's forearm. She tried to push magic into him, despite the fact that he was a Fenthri. She tried to push in her truth—that she, too, stared survivor's guilt in the face regularly. "Powell, look at me: This wasn't your fault."

"No…" He sounded unconvinced. "Anyway, seeing how four isn't enough for a quorum, they voted to grant me my circle and make me a Master for the vote."

"You would have been awarded it anyway." Florence couldn't imagine being awarded Mastery under the current circumstances. It made her heart ache for the Harvester before her.

Her effort brought a small smile to his mouth. "I like to believe that's true." She knew he would always wonder.

"Powell." The other Master Florence had met on the train, Max, called from a short distance away. The circle emblazoned on his cheek around the Harvester's sickle seemed almost like an omen of sorrow now.

"I'm coming." Powell turned to leave.

Florence held fast to his forearm. "I'm coming with you."

"What?" It came from Powell and Nora at the same time.

"This was what we came here for," she explained to the Alchemists. "To speak with the Vicar Harvester about the rebellion."

"The Vicar Harvester was undecided," Nora reminded her.

"That Vicar Harvester is dead. And in light of recent events, I think we have a better case to make." Florence squeezed Powell's forearm. She wanted him to feel her strength and certainty. She wanted to be as strong as Arianna was when the woman had pulled her from the depths of the Underground and told her everything would be all right. "Powell, we would like to request this of the Masters."

He looked back to Max who was halfway to them, no doubt having heard the better portion of the conversation. He was tall for a Fenthri or Chimera, nearly Arianna's height. His sharp blue eyes assessed her.

"The vote won't be a place for a Raven."

"I'm not a Raven," Florence replied on instinct.

"What are you, then?"

She stopped short of her usual response of "Revolver." Instead: "I'm Florence."

The man raised his eyebrows. But his response was interrupted by a solemn bell toll from a nearby assembly hall. He pulled out his pocket watch, inspecting the time.

"Very well, come along. But they sit in the back," he cautioned Powell, as if the man was now solely responsible for the three of them. Judging from the train, it wasn't an unfair assessment.

Usually, a filled hall would seem like a joyous occasion. The rising of a Master, the appointment of a new Vicar. Every seat was packed with journeymen and handfuls of initiates.

But nothing had ever looked sadder than the three men and two women who were seated in the center of the floor. No one spoke for a long minute. The room was as still as a tomb.

Max stood. "Today, on the thirteenth day of the eleventh month, in the year one thousand eighty-one, we, the Masters of the Harvesters' Guild, have been called together to elect a new Vicar Harvester from among us."

Florence shifted her weight from foot to foot. She was short enough that she had elected to stand in the back of the room on a small box to be able to see. Plus, even if she didn't fully agree with them, Max's words stayed with her. While she believed that any Fenthi from any guild should be able to witness the changing of a Vicar, this did not impact her in the same way it did the journeymen and initiates who lined the room. They deserved to be closer.

"Do any have a nominee from among us?"

The first journeyman stood. "I nominate Maxwell."

"I second." Another stood as well.

"I nominate Theodosia."

"I third Maxwell."

"Second Theodosia."

"I nominate Powell."

Florence watched with more interest the moment Powell's name was added to the ring. Whoever the other two Masters were, they didn't seem to have the same type of fervor wrapped around them. Eventually, the only names that mattered were Powell and Theodosia.

When it was clear that the room was split, the two stepped forward, away from the Masters, to face their peers. Chosen from a select group, supported by the guild on the whole, now the most experienced men and women would cast their votes for who would lead.

"I vote for Powell." Max was the first to cast his ballot.

"I vote for Theodosia," the second woman decided.

The final man thought it over a long moment. Florence wished she could ask him what ran through his head. What did one think while they were deciding the future of a guild? How did someone even approach a situation like that? It was a skill Florence wanted to imitate and learn.

He took a deep breath and made his choice. "I vote Powell."

Max stood again, as the woman at Powell's side stepped away. "Powell, Vicar Harvester, so voted on the thirteenth day of the eleventh month of the year one thousand eighty-one. Lead with wisdom."

"Lead with wisdom," the room repeated, Florence included. Even though she had never seen a Vicar voting ceremony, she had read about them. And, while this was certainly an unorthodox situation, falling to convention felt right. It harkened back to the old days of the guilds and the traditions they kept—the things the Dragons could only take from Loom if the guilds let them.

"Sow and reap." Maxwell placed his hand on Powell's shoulder.

"Sow and reap." Theodosia did the same.

"Sow and reap." The other Masters spoke the words and joined as well. Soon, the room was one large, spoked wheel with Powell at its center. "Sow and reap" filled the air and connected the Harvesters as much as their physical contact.

"Sow and reap, Powell," Florence whispered, apart from the group. To her surprise, Derek and Nora echoed the same.

It was a dark stroke of luck, but a stroke of luck all the same. Florence leaned against the wall, content to let Powell have his moment and to let the Harvesters find comfort in it. For she was no longer worried about finding time or sympathy from the Vicar Harvester.

YVEUN

Yveun was awoken with a sharp knock on the door. He gave a low growl from the back of his throat, expressing his discontent at whatever fool would dare disturb him this early in the morning. He chose to ignore the offender. Instead of flaying them, he curled toward his queen.

Let no one claim he wasn't a benevolent ruler.

There was another knock. Another low growl. And a voice that changed the pace of the early hours of dawn.

"Dono, Dono, I have returned from the Xin Manor." *Finnyr.*

Yveun narrowed his eyes in the dim light. Finnyr of all people would not be so bold before him. Which meant whatever he had learned at the manor was worth risking Yveun's ire. He bared his teeth in the twilight dawn, as if the scent of wine and poison could still waft through his open balcony.

Coletta stood without a word. She drew a sheer vermillion robe around her that floated like an aura of freshly broken sunlight as she excused herself without word into a small side room. They rarely let themselves be seen together, especially fondly. It suited their image better when the perception was the fearsome King and his unwanted Ryu.

Yveun stood, walking to the door. He paused briefly. There was a different magic in the air. Muffled by the door, it was hard to make out. But, judging from its ferocity alone, it was certainly not Finnyr's.

He eased open the door. His posture was relaxed, but every muscle in his body was taught and primed, ready to explode. The claws of the hand behind the door were already unsheathed.

"Who is your guest?" Yveun asked directly, narrowing his eyes at the unfamiliar Dragon at Finnyr's side.

There was no time for Finnyr to formulate a response.

The illusion over the woman rippled the second she moved, too complex to maintain over the bulky clothes she wore. Yveun crisply heard the sound of bone breaking and the slicing of flesh. The scent of cedar assaulted his nose as Finnyr coughed blood.

With a spray of gold, Yveun watched as the careful play he had been orchestrating for years was cut down before him. Finnyr, his toy, his opportunity to slice Xin down and seat a loyal shadow in the Oji's seat, could not be killed here and now. They were too close, Petra too weakened, to stray from the course.

Rather than reaching for the woman, Yveun reached for Finnyr. He gripped the man and pulled forward, un-impaling him from the woman's blade. She twisted her knife through the empty air with a snarl, its mark gone. Yveun threw Finnyr behind him, hoping the wordless Dragon would muster enough sense to crawl from the fighting. All the worthless Xin had to do was keep himself alive, yet Yveun was unconvinced if he'd manage that much.

The woman lunged for him, all teeth and growls and golden blades. Yveun dodged, letting her momentum carry her into his den. He slammed shut the door as she turned.

Two bright lilac eyes stared at him, nearly glowing in the first sunlight of morning. She was gray, bland, swaddled like a babe in industrial garb. A Fenthri turned Chimera. Unmarked. Addressing him like she was a champion.

Yveun wanted to laugh, but he recognized something in her eyes beyond their oddly familiar shade. It was the same look Petra had when she stared at him. It was the same look he saw in the mirror.

A broken lust for something that you would drown the world in its own blood for twice over.

He didn't announce his attack. He didn't throw a threat. He didn't give her the opportunity to know he was about to claim her life. It didn't matter how or why she was here; she was an agent working against his goals and that was all he needed to know. Fools threatened. Killers moved.

But his claws didn't meet flesh. They met a golden dagger that sprung to life seemingly with its own consciousness, like some kind of barbed tail tethered to a line. His hand pushed against the weapon in surprise, cutting to bone on the edge of the blade.

The blade twisted, deepening its bite onto him. One hand closed around his wrist, pulling him in one direction. She landed the first hit square onto his face with claws.

The dullness of shock wore off quickly. Yveun dipped down, pushing the blade and her hand back. He reached with his teeth, sinking through all the mess of fabric and leather to her shoulder.

Most Dragons never attacked with their fangs out of the taboo associated with imbibing. But that made such attacks the perfect opportunity because they were unexpected. The woman gave a grunt, biting in a yell of pain. She let go of his hand, reaching for his neck. His claws gouged into her side and they both drew blood.

But the slit across his throat was enough to make his jaw relax. She leapt away, her dagger lashing out. Yveun parried it with his claws effortlessly.

It was then that he noticed the blood pouring from the wound on her shoulder. The taste it left lingering in his mouth. As gold as his, she did not bleed the rot of a normal Chimera. On his tongue was the taste of honeysuckle, the faint essence of Finnyr, and the recognition that didn't require the other man's obvious interjection.

"Arianna! It's the Master Rivet, the engineer. The one from the rebellion!"

The woman turned to Finnyr, momentarily distracted by who she wanted to kill more. Yveun sprung for her when she was caught in her own loathing, barreling into her like a bull. Arms around her waist, he dug into her. He felt her knife stab into his shoulder.

Golden blood poured over his hands like an omen of all his worst fears.

"The Rivet who claimed to make the Philosopher's Box." The scent of blood made him feel alive, woke his senses and gave him power. Yveun gave an extra push and she tumbled under his weight. "I'm sure you've confused many a Dragon with your trick of bleeding gold."

Arianna rolled away from his violent slashes, her blood leaving a trail on the balcony. The spool on her hip spun and the line whipped forward, keeping him at bay. Yveun ducked, narrowly missing it wrapping around his neck. She panted, reclaimed her feet and kicked, spinning midair, seeking purchase against him with feet or claw or wire.

But Yveun dodged her.

The woman was good, that much he'd admit. Yveun began to laugh, which only seemed to whip her into more of a frenzy. He could see how this creature had killed his Leona. It made so much more sense than the unambitious and untrained Cvareh. He had seen these movements in the pit, another explanation settled just by watching her attacks.

Cvareh was not mighty. Xin was not mighty. It was this girl, this prodigy of two worlds, who threatened him time and again.

As he dodged an attack, Yveun felt the line of a wire wrap around his ankle, pulling. The world fell from under him as he slipped back. She lunged forward, her knee digging into his side. Her blades above him, he didn't even struggle, he merely kept laughing.

It was delightful.

"I expected more of a fight from the Dragon King," she snarled.

"I've no further interest in fighting you, my pet." Yveun relaxed, noting movement from the corner of his eye. "You are more valuable alive, at least for now."

"You've lost." She raised the dagger in triumph.

"And you wasted the chance to kill me like the child you are."

Coletta loomed behind the Chimera who thought she had him pinned. In her hand was the smallest of daggers, little more than a letter opener. Without a single expression crossing her features, she dug the tiny blade into Arianna's neck.

Arianna's spare hand rose to the wound as she turned in shock. But her eyes were already losing focus, the artery quickly carrying Coletta's poison to her brain. The Chimera twisted her blade in her hand and swung backwards.

Coletta stepped back in an effortless dodge.

Off balance and sluggish, the Rivet tipped sideways, landing in an undignified heap at Yveun's side. Her eyes held awareness still. The only thing capable of attacking him. But looks couldn't kill, and Yveun stood.

"She had you on a few attacks," Coletta both teased and chastised.

"I merely didn't want to kill her," Yveun explained.

"I reasoned." Coletta leaned forward, drawing the dagger from the woman's neck. "The poison will wear off within the hour. Move her before then."

Yveun watched with both fascination and chilling horror the gold blood that dribbled from the hole. This was what Fenthri could be capable of, if they were left to their own devices. The ability to become mighty enough to slay Dragon Riders and challenge even the Dono himself. All from the might of stolen organs.

"Your insight is unparalleled." Coletta began to collect her things after nothing more than a cautionary glance that showed she had heard him. Yveun looked to Finnyr, knowing the source of his mate's discomfort. It was very rare for them to have a guest in their chambers. "You have many words to tell me," he spoke to the pasty blue Dragon.

"I will tell you all of them." Finnyr thrust his face against the ground at Yveun's feet. "But we have more pressing matters. Petra has sworn to challenge me today in court."

And Petra would win.

Yveun sighed. The blue sack of flesh before him sometimes seemed more trouble than it was worth. As easy as it would be to off Finnyr once and for all, doing so would be a half measure, the easy route. He had cultivated Finnyr for too long to throw away the effort.

"After yesterday, there need not be another day of Court," Yveun announced. "She will not have a chance to challenge you, as we will be on Lysip within the hour. I will announce the Court ended."

Yveun stared at the unconscious engineer, the woman who had single-handedly caused him so much trouble. There was information he needed from her. But for once, he was going to have the time to extract it. And Yveun would do so with deliciously slow, full measures.

FLORENCE

The room began to clear and Florence bided her time. She would not endear herself to Powell by taking this moment from him. Plus, it was the silent observation that freed her mind time enough to think.

She had come here on behalf of the Vicar Alchemist to secure the loyalty of the Harvesters. Florence glanced at Nora and Derek. Well, she had come here as an escort to those appointed to secure the Ter.1 guild's loyalty.

But a rift was slowly growing between her and her Alchemist friends. Not one of the heart—in that respect they were as close as ever. The rift was one of purpose. Nora and Derek were still being pulled along by the mechanisms of fate and chance. Florence had seen those gears spin too many times. There were two types of people in the world: those who loaded the gun, and those who pulled the trigger.

Florence wanted to be the latter.

She didn't want to live another moment in a world of the Dragons' making. Certainly, there were some Dragons, like Cvareh, who were genuine and peaceful and kind. But the more interaction Florence had with the race, the more she saw that Arianna had been right all along. The Dragons were vicious, destructive creatures that had no true regard for the world. No matter what Powell said, Florence couldn't believe their intentions matched their actions. They were compassionate only so long as it suited them, and even then, it was the Harvesters who found the solutions to the problems Loom faced.

Florence pushed away from the wall, starting for the ever-thinning center of the room. There were only a few journeymen with fully inked sickles on their cheeks, and the Masters. It would be as good a time as any.

"Congratulations, Vicar Harvester," Florence commended sincerely.

Powell's coal colored eyes met hers, offset by the mess of long hair that was perpetually determined to hide his right eye. He looked haggard, they all were. But the man had aged nearly to double his life in an hour. His cheek had yet to be tattooed with a Master's circle and he was already the Vicar.

"Tell me of the rebellion." Powell wasted no time. He knew what they were there for.

"The Alchemists are working toward a Philosopher's Box." Derek stepped forward. "If we have the appropriate amount of gold and organs—"

"A Philosopher's Box?" Max snorted in amusement. "We need solutions, and the Alchemists give us dreams."

"It is quite real, I assure you," Derek responded faster than Florence could.

"Your guild has been claiming such since before you were born." Theodosia stepped forward. "But we have yet to see the product. Stitching together a Chimera with that much magic without falling is impossible."

"We have a solid lead." Nora joined the fray, as if to prevent Derek from being outnumbered by the Harvesters.

"Leads and lies." Max turned to the new Vicar. "Powell, we have other more pressing matters to concern ourselves with. We have to reorganize the guild. We have to rebuild Faroe. We are responsible for what remains of the Harvesters."

Powell's eyes never left hers. The room buzzed around them, yet Powell remained focused, searching, silently calling out to something in Florence's soul that he may have felt all along. What within him had made him speak to her on that train? What connected them with such faith?

"I know where you can go." The idea came to her in that moment, thinking of the fundamental essence that joined every Fenthri at the core. It was the essence that Loom so desperately needed to recover. "I know where you all can go."

"Where?" the elder asked.

"Ter.0."

"From the fisher's hook onto his spear!" Theodosia threw her hands into the air in exasperation. "We have our own wasteland here. We don't need to go to another."

"This is our home," Max agreed. "We won't abandon it."

"I'm not saying abandon it." They didn't understand yet. "I'm saying go to Ter.0, and meet with the other guilds."

"You want to hold a Vicar Tribunal." Powell was the first to realize.

"A Vicar Tribunal? There hasn't been one in over a decade," one of the journeymen interjected.

"Exactly." Florence remained focused on Powell. His decision was the only one that mattered now. He was the Vicar. "The Dragons split us apart, forced us to be silent. They bred animosity between the guilds where there was none. They separated us as children, forced us to learn apart, to compete. They fostered silence with magic. Whisperers may make it faster to converse, but there is no magic that can compare to seeing another's face, truly hearing their plight with your own ears. Anything less is separating, impersonal, dividing. It makes us think the only way we are strong is with their help.

"But Loom was strong long before the Dragons." She addressed the elder of the group, the man who should remember best the bygone days of another time when Loom was free. "We stood together. Links in a chain. One strong, unified, force.

"We gave the Dragons technology. We gave them gold. And, yes, they have given us some insight," she begrudgingly admitted, thinking about Harvesting practices. "But that does not make them our saviors. They did not find the solution; they merely identified the problem. We are our own saviors and we must—"

Powell held up his hand, cutting her short.

"Enough, Florence." He sighed softly, pressing his eyes closed a moment. Florence's heart raced, not just from her risky declaration, but from truly not knowing what Powell's reaction to it would be. The tiniest of smiles curled his mouth when he opened his eyes again. "The Harvesters agree to a Vicar Tribunal."

"Really?" Theodosia shifted uncertainly. "The Dragons torched the Tribunal hall and the rest of Ter.0 in the war. They said if we assemble again, they will do worse."

"What could be worse than what we have already witnessed?" Powell asked. All were silent. "We have no more guild for them to destroy. Faroe has burned. Our mines are stalled. Our fields will go unplowed. Our fishers may be moored for who knows how long, while we attempt to recover what was lost. What more can the Dragons take from us?"

"Our pride, if we let them." The question was rhetorical, but Florence wanted to drive the point home. It was an almost Arianna-like quip and she was instantly proud of herself for thinking of it so deftly on the spot.

"And the Alchemists will not let them," Derek said, lending his support.

"The Vicar Alchemist will support the Tribunal?" Powell asked.

"I have no doubt," Derek affirmed. "Vicar Sophie wants to see the rebellion to power. She wants it for Loom. I'm sure she will stand at the Tribunal."

Powell seemed satisfied by the response. "We will get word across the narrow strait then, to the Rivets in Ter.3. They are connected by land to the Ravens, who can then get word to the Revolvers."

"How quickly can we hold the Tribunal?" Strong words aside, the reality of their situation was becoming very apparent to Florence. Communication systems, in all forms, were down. They didn't even know if there were Vicars left to meet with. Perhaps the Harvesters had been the only ones warned with enough time.

The idea was only kindling to the pyre of Florence's rage. The Harvesters had been a fluke, with all the Masters in the guild at the time. The other guilds had their Masters positioned throughout the territories. They would regroup. And if word spread far enough and fast enough, they could do so at the Tribunal.

"Two months, perhaps?" Theodosia begrudgingly suggested at a silent behest from Powell. "That would give messengers enough time to get all the way to Dortam, and for the Vicars to travel."

"Spread the word like wildfire," Florence suggested aloud. "Invite all of Loom."

"What if the Dragons choose to attack again?" Max was still clearly uneasy at the idea of gathering in one place.

"We have the numbers on them. Even with Chimera alone, we have the numbers." The fact had been known since Nova was first discovered. The sky world was a much, much smaller place than Loom. "The only way they will overpower us is with our own weaponry, coronas, and gliders. And how will they get that weaponry when there is no one to build it?"

"We cannot make a real stand against them," Max pressed.

Derek was quick to speak up again. "Not without the Philosopher's Box."

"You keep saying that, boy, but you have no evidence."

"We do." All eyes were on Florence. "We do," she repeated without hesitation. "We have the person who made the very first Philosopher's Box."

"Lies."

"Her name is Arianna, and she is my teacher," Florence spat venom, protective at the mere round-about accusation against Ari. "She will make the box for the rebellion."

"Arianna, Arianna the…"

"Rivet," Florence finished for Max. "A Master Rivet, at that."

"Who appointed her?" Max asked with squinted eyes.

"Master Oliver." Florence had only heard the name a few times before, and prayed she had it right. Judging from Max's reaction, she did.

"That's impossible." The man shook his head. "Master Oliver was part of the Counsel of Five—the fools who died in the last rebellion. His student, Arianna, she perished with him."

"Except she didn't," Florence insisted. She was exhausted the moment the defense crossed her lips. Standing for someone whom everyone seemed to know more about than she did was wearying. The first thing Florence would do the moment Arianna returned would be to demand an explanation of everything. "She is alive and well, and is securing the resources to make the box," Florence lied, perhaps. What Ari was doing was anyone's guess.

"We will expect to see the box, then, at the Tribunal." Powell's tone left no room for question or interpretation—it was now a caveat. "Once the Vicars see the Philosopher's Box working, we will stand behind the Alchemists' Rebellion."

"I don't know…" Derek started uncertainly.

"Done." There wasn't time for hesitation. Derek shot Florence a look from the corners of his eyes. "Can we count on the Harvesters, two months from now, in Ter.0?"

"I will be there to see the Vicar Alchemist and her Philosopher's Box," Powell affirmed. "And I will personally see that the other guilds come with me."

"Thank you, Vicar Powell," Florence said sincerely.

"The best thanks you can give us is holding up your end of the deal," he cautioned.

Florence nodded. "We will return to the Alchemists' Guild with haste, on the fastest train out."

They didn't have anything to pack, so the three of them made their way toward Ter.1.2's main terminal directly from the hall. Florence knew Derek would have something to say about what they had just done, but it took him longer than she expected. When at last he spoke, the words he found were also unforeseeable.

"Florence, Sophie will stand for the Tribunal, but the box…"

"I don't think she'll want to share it with the other guilds," Nora finished.

"That's lunacy." Florence shook her head with a small laugh at the comical notion. "How would she see the box built en masse without the Rivet's tools and factories? Or get the supplies without the Harvesters and Ravens?"

The two exchanged a look. Florence waited for their nonverbal dialogue to end. When it did, Nora linked one arm with Florence's and Derek linked the other. They walked together as one tight-knit group toward the station.

"Whatever happens, Florence, we're with you," Derek spoke for the both of them.

"You may be the worst navigator we've ever seen." Nora gave her a toothy grin. It slipped when their eyes met and Florence desperately wished she could see what Nora saw in that moment. "But so far, you seem to always get the people who stick by your side where they need to be."

It was a compliment that rang fundamentally Raven, but not. Either way, for the first time, Florence looked beyond the guild affiliation associated with the words and really distilled their meaning. For the first time, she didn't try to correct any link between herself and the transportation guild of Loom.

CVAREH

As the first light of dawn winked into existence, Cvareh realized he hadn't slept a wink in what amounted to nearly a full day. Even as a Dragon, he was beginning to tap into his magic to find energy. And another day at the Court awaited him, a day that was sure to be awash in blood. The only relief he found was in the thought that the Court would not possibly sustain a full three days, as was the average. After all that had happened, he'd be surprised if it ran a full two.

He dragged his feet toward his room. Even if there wasn't time to sleep, there would be time to wash and dress in something clean. Cvareh never underestimated the power of a pair of well-stitched trousers or a fashionable vest. He would feel far more like himself if he wasn't coated in the blood of his sibling.

His room was intentionally far from Petra's. They could reach different sections of the manor faster and could easily meet in the middle in instances of emergency. As such, it also meant that most of the aesthetic had been catered to his tastes. Thousands of gemstones were inlaid in a dark ceiling, shining like the light from Lord Agendi's flowers. How he had loved them and their magic, only to have his sentiment surrounding them forever clouded by the events of the past day.

There was irony in nearly everything that encompassed him. The woman who was sharp as a dagger and more abrasive than pumice was his lady of flowers. She smelled potently of honeysuckle, a scent he had delighted in long before they met. Her skin was the color of Lord Xin's veil, her hair the shade of Lord Agendi's path. She had been the first woman to so consume him that he had taken her before his patron to mate.

And yet, it had been those same well-loved flowers that had changed her life as well. Had the Dragon who betrayed her never brought them to the rebellion, she may have never found the solution to the Philosopher's Box. Her lover may well still be alive, or maybe they would have perished together.

Cvareh certainly would've never met her, and that would have spared them much confusion at the very least.

Yes, it all seemed to come down to that Dragon's singular act, a man she had named as Rafansi. Cvareh knew he should loathe him in a stand of solidarity with Arianna. But, guiltily, he appreciated the man's dark hand in her life. For it had so clearly driven Cvareh and his Fenthri lover together.

He ran his hands through his clothes, trying to carefully select his ensemble for Court. He did not want to run the risk of re-wearing anything too similar, resulting in a fashion crime he would hear about for years to come. It was a therapeutic process that freed his mind, allowing it to wander.

Arianna had claimed this "Rafansi" was a Xin. *Perhaps a nameless from below?* Cvareh mused. He had neglected to ask Arianna how she'd known his House—if it had been the man's skin shade or if he'd had a tattoo on his cheek. The Dragon could've been someone loyal to Rok originally.

Now, *that* would make more sense. By the time Petra had even heard of the rebellion from Finnyr, the Dono had already begun putting an end to it. The traitor must surely be Rok, or someone with ties into that House.

Cvareh crossed into the bathing room attached to his dressing area. The water was hot on his skin and the steam cleared his head. He perfumed it with rose and hickory, trying to overwhelm his senses with heat and scents so foreign that they would inspire no further thoughts on anything. But it was a futile effort.

Arianna was certain that the man who had betrayed her had been Xin, not Rok. The woman wouldn't have said anything if she was unsure, and she knew enough about Dragon culture now to be confident in such a claim. He didn't think the Dragon she had dealt with was marked, not after Arianna's surprised and curious reactions to the House tattoos. Even if she didn't know the meaning years ago, she did now.

He closed his eyes, sinking deeper into the smooth porcelain of the soaking tub.

Her eyes stared back at him. Tam purple amid a stormy sea of ashen skin. They looked through him, seeing right to his core, as though he was nothing more than a child's riddle. But they hid her truths just as deftly.

Cvareh mapped the curves of her face. He tracked the soft line of her jaw, the surprisingly feminine arc of her cheek. Her hair, the color of pure snow. Had she ever worn it long? Had she always kept it cut just below her shoulder as it was? These were questions he may never know the answer to and the fact shouldn't have stung him so.

Yes, he was enamored with her. Her differences. All her contrasting pieces that made up a whole that could be none other than Arianna. Even the pieces that weren't hers: the eyes, the hands, the ears—

Cvareh's eyes snapped open.

The hands. The ears. He repeated it again and again in his mind.

He stood from the tub, his heart racing. The ears she had possessed as long as he had known her. They were an older part, from when she had first become a Chimera—a *Perfect* Chimera—more than three years ago. She had never detailed how she had acquired them, and Cvareh had never asked. He'd assumed it to be some horrible harvesting ring that chained his people and turned them into meat factories. He hadn't wanted to think on it.

But what if they were given willingly, by a Dragon who had been seeking to earn her trust? Cvareh remembered Arianna's accusations when they first met. The fragile stitches he had ripped off the gaping wound within her heart at the fact that he carried her schematics.

He hadn't really listened to what she had said then. He thought her anger had stemmed from the fact that they had been stolen, and her general distrust of Dragons. But no, the woman had mentioned he was merely trying *again* to earn her trust. To betray her *again.*

Cvareh barely had time to towel dry before he was moving out the door, still dripping from his hair, still naked.

If her ears were given to her by the Dragon who betrayed her, that meant he may have given her other things, like her stomach or blood. That meant he had been the Dragon she thought was Xin. Her betrayer, her organ provider—the man was from his House.

"No," Cvareh breathed, and began to run.

Arianna had nearly attacked him when he delivered the hands. Hands that matched her ears nearly perfectly, when he actually stopped and considered it. Hands that smelled of cedar, a scent she had enough organs and perhaps blood to also possess, alongside the much more favored and potent sweetness of honeysuckle.

Finnyr smelled of cedar.

Finnyr, a man of House Xin who lived under the Rok'Oji— loyal to House Rok.

Rafansi, a failed creation of life that lived under the pity of Lord Rok. A name Yveun Dono would not doubt delight in using at every turn, at forcing upon a once-Xin'Oji.

He arrived at her door, panting. He wanted to find her in the room. He wanted to tell her that he had put together everything she had been telling him—and not telling him—all along. That he knew who had betrayed her and, even better, that she could be the one to give the man death.

It would've been perfect. Petra wouldn't have to kill their brother. They could make up another claim for Ari to make in the Court. Yveun wouldn't stand for Finnyr, not when Petra could then stand for Ari and they would be forced to face each other in the ring. No one else would dare step forward in a seemingly Xin-on-Xin duel. It would've been a neat solution to all their problems.

But Cvareh knew, the moment he saw her ajar door, there would be no neat solutions.

He entered the room silently, as if by doing so he could sneak up on the truth and tear it apart with his claws to craft a new reality. He looked hopefully to the bed, though it showed no signs of being slept in. Her Dragon clothes were strewn about the floor. Some tears in them had been made by Cvareh's hands earlier, but new ones tore his hopes asunder. Ones that told him they had been discarded in haste. That their wearer didn't care if they could ever be put on again.

His eyes fell on an open drawer. It was empty. Cvareh's heart may well rip through his chest trying to drown out the ringing of horror in his ears. He pulled out the next drawer, throwing clothes onto the floor, clothes Arianna may have never worn.

He darted to the bed. Feathers filled the room as he threw aside the pillows, his claws unsheathed. He was out of control. Anger, heartbreak, denial, frustration, exhaustion—it all had worn him down. He trashed the room, at first in his search, but then just out of anger when he realized he wouldn't find what he was looking for.

Her daggers and coat were gone.

That meant the White Wraith was now on Ruana. Arianna was at work. And he did not think it chance that this disappearance followed the one night Finnyr himself had returned to the manor.

Cvareh collapsed into the chair, the weight of inevitable truth compressing him into a small, weak being. She had never trusted his family. He had barely begun to earn that fragile gift. *And now...* Cvareh groaned, burying his face in his palms.

It had been his brother that had betrayed all she loved.

With a snarl, Cvareh slammed his fist into the desk next to him, spilling a bottle of ink and sending pens rolling. He looked at her soiled inventory. It had been going so well. Petra had been getting all she had ever wanted, and somehow, Cvareh was getting all he ever needed. But Arianna had yet to find either.

Cvareh was back on his feet. He might still be fast enough to stop the momentum spinning the wheel of fate that threatened to crush them. She had no doubt smelled Finnyr's blood; given her last reaction, his brother's room wasn't far enough to protect him. Really, he should be surprised it took the woman so long to put together the pieces. But the same could be said for himself.

Cvareh prayed to the Twenty that he was not too late in realizing what she had been trying to tell him from the moment they first met.

He collapsed to his knees in the open doorframe of Finnyr's room. The wrinkles in the rug and splintered wood of the door latch told the story of what happened as plain as the daylight breaking through the window. He had failed her by not being fast enough, by not being smart enough. She and Finnyr were gone, no scent of blood to betray a kill. Which meant there was a chance they both left alive, and that was a truth far more horrible than having to deal with the body of a Xin'Kin slain in a duel without witness. Where Finnyr went, the Dragon King—the true orchestrator of Arianna's heartache—was sure to follow. And there was no way Arianna would not take the opportunity to challenge Yveun.

She was going to get herself killed.

He practically jumped back onto his feet. He was on the move again through the halls. But rather than heading to his room, he headed for Petra's corner of the estate.

Petra would know what to do, he insisted to himself. Her mind would've cooled enough that she could think logically, and she would force it to for the sake of the woman who had promised her the Philosopher's Box.

She would do it for the woman Cvareh had chosen as his, he wanted to believe.

"Petra!" He banged on the door so hard the hinges rattled.

"Enter," she called in reply.

Petra was halfway dressed for Court, two servants attending her.

"Leave us," Cvareh demanded.

Petra arched an eyebrow, clearly trying to decipher what had worked Cvareh to a frenzy. But when she gave no question to his order, the two slaves left, closing the door behind them. Cvareh crossed to his sister.

"Arianna is gone." If he wasn't just out with it, he may lose all courage.

"Gone?" Petra repeated.

"She found Finnyr, and she, they, he—she's going to make an attempt on Yveun's life."

"Finnyr?" The mere name elicited a snarl on the back end, rising up from the throat. "Why?"

Cvareh launched into his explanation without thought. Arianna may have kept the matter private. She may hate him for speaking her truth. But it was Petra. This was his sister. His flesh and blood, the woman in whom he had nothing but faith.

Petra was seething by the time he finished. "You should have come to me sooner with these truths. I would've never let Finnyr stay under this roof had I known."

"I did not form lines between them until just now, until she told me enough yesterday."

Petra cursed, knowing he was right. His sister gave him a once-over. "Dress, for the sun has nearly risen and we will head to Court. He will no doubt be keeping her and Finnyr close. We will find them during the Court's distraction," Petra vowed.

Cvareh did as his sister commanded. He was thankful he had already set out his clothes and they were waiting, because for the first time in his life, he didn't care about fashion. He wanted to jump on a boco and fly across the island as fast as he could. He wanted to try to find Arianna before she found Yveun. But a torturous pragmatism whispered that he was no doubt already far too late.

He suspected as much, but he didn't know until Petra and he were standing on the platform about to take off. Cain landed to meet them. Angry lines marred the man's face and Cvareh knew what had been the best day of his life was only going to steadily become worse.

"The Dono has left Ruana," Cain cursed. "Out of kindness to the mourning of House Xin, and to protect members of House Tam and Rok from the sudden illness, the Court has been ended early."

Cvareh turned to Petra, only to find his sister staring back at him.

There was only one reason the Dono would cancel the Court: He deemed it no longer worth his time. And why would he? He had already killed most of the Xin fighters. Finnyr was marked for death and would be far less accessible to Petra on Ruana.

And he now had the only Perfect Chimera in Nova or Loom. He had the woman who could make the Philosopher's Box. He had the key to shifting the tides of fate.

He had Arianna.

ARIANNA

She fought a losing battle with consciousness. On the edges of her awareness were the simplest of sensations: cold, hard, damp. Arianna tried to pull together the scattered shards of her mind. They lingered out of her reach, jagged and crumbling when she tried to put them back in place. The picture would never be what it once was.

Vengeance, in its own way, had been her greatest hope. The belief that there would be some great justice in the world to be dealt by her. Arianna screamed at herself in the recesses of her mind, at the foolish, idealistic girl she'd never stopped being. It escaped as a raspy groan from split lips.

Reality filtered in around her, breaking through the darkness and alighting the edges of her misgivings. She didn't know what she would live for any longer. She didn't know if she would live at all after this.

All she knew was that she'd lost.

That was the first true thought that returned to her. She'd been bested by the Dragon King. She had fought and trained her whole life, and when the time came, it hadn't been enough. Not Arianna, not the White Wraith, not the Perfect Chimera. She hadn't wanted the mantle, but damn if she hadn't tried to live into it once it had been thrust upon her. Not for nobility, not for honor, just for Eva.

Eva shone brightly in her memory in all her effervescent beauty. That picture was still perfect. But perfection was fleeting, a sight that wasn't long for mortal hands or mortal minds. The woman was like one of the falling stars in Nova's sky.

She faded into darkness.

The darkness was what was real. In that blackness, she fought to find light. She fought for the sake of fighting, for everything left undone. She might be broken, but so long as she drew breath she would pick up the splintered pieces of all she was and use them as shanks between the ribs of those who had crossed her. She'd lived for that one desire before, she would cling to that tether again.

Arianna opened her eyes.

She was face-first on a marble floor. The wide, thin-grouted tiles carried up the walls and onto the ceiling. A room of white illuminated by the light of a single window behind her. It was nearly blinding and Arianna's vision blurred, her senses returning sluggishly from the prison of her mind.

A man slowly came into focus, seated against the door across from her. His powder skin was nearly gray in her hazy sight. Almost gray enough to be mistaken for a Fenthri, almost the same shade as Cvareh, and the same color as her ears and hands.

"I see you're finally awake."

Arianna's lips curled back into a snarl. She moved to push off the floor, her hands weighted by shackles. The chains snapped taut as she lunged in spite of them. Arms bent backward, chest pushed forward, she stuck out her neck and snapped her jaw like a dog, snarling and growling for one more inch of slack. She would rip him apart with her teeth if she had to.

"You can't break those chains," a different voice spoke—familiar, but less so. Arianna turned to find another Dragon leaning against the wall behind her, no doubt just out of reach as well. The Dragon was the color of Fenthri blood, as though the lives of all he'd shattered from Loom below had been poured and hardened into a ruthless mold of irreverent destruction.

She looked down at the shackles around her wrists and ankles. Gold and tempered, she could feel the magic within them object to her attempts to force their locks to disengage. Arianna straightened, swaying slightly with the remnants of the poison that still chilled her veins.

"You have tried to shackle me my whole life. You have yet to succeed," she addressed the Dragon King with a growl.

He looked mildly amused. "Finnyr told me much about you. It's a pleasure to see the Rivet genius for myself."

"Finnyr." The mention of the man's name brought Arianna's attention back to him. The traitor. Underling of the King. "Finnyr Xin."

"You've finally learned my real name. No need for Rafansi any longer then." His lips moved oddly as he spoke, long scars marring them straight to his cheek. "Stupid little Fen, never probing deeper, taking from my open palm eagerly, never questioning what was in my other hand. Your idiot rebels never saw the dagger coming."

Arianna merely curled her lips in a snarl. She hated this man with every thread of her being. She loathed him to the point that he didn't even deserve scalding words. This rage transcended them. "I will kill you," she swore.

"Go ahead." He stood.

It was that simple to goad her into lunging forward. Closer, close enough that she could smell him. That his shirt was ruffled by her breath. But he was still too far for her snapping teeth or tethered claws. Arianna let out a scream of agony.

"Did you really think our great King would let me die? That I would lead you to him if I thought your pathetic attempts to kill him would succeed?"

Arianna questioned everything, all her decisions, and the hubris that had led her to this. She had thought she could take the Dragon King on her own, when so many others had failed. It was arrogance in perfect form, befitting more of a Dragon than a Fenthri.

"I never expected to find you on Nova, not to mention in my family's home." His voice deepened at the mention of the Xin manor. "Did you come with my brother?"

Cvareh. The name ripped from her chest and shot straight to her eyes. Arianna blinked, furious with herself. She had let her mind cloud and her eyes go blind to what was before them. This was the price of love; this was her punishment for dreaming.

"How did you survive the poisoned organs all those years ago, the rot from too much magic exposed to your pathetic Fen frame?" Finnyr asked, oblivious to her plight. He raised a clawed hand and dragged it along her cheek, drawing a line in gold. "Is it because of this, because you actually did complete the box? Is that what made you strong? Tell me, Arianna."

Magic laced his tongue. He was trying to use power to influence her. That was an easy trick on Fenthri and weak Chimera. But it was nothing more than a sizzle of annoyance in the back of her mind.

"You will not sway me." She straightened, gathering her height, nearly as tall as he. "My power is far stronger than yours."

"But still falls shy of mine." The Dragon King reminded her of his presence and Arianna turned abruptly, readying some whip of a response.

It was never said.

The moment her eyes met his she felt the icy grip of magic smothering her. She wanted to blink, she wanted to look away, but she was frozen in his stare. It started from her fingertips and swirled into her chest. It trickled up her neck, pressed behind her eyes, whispered through her ears, before it sought entry into her mind.

"Tell me of the Philosopher's Box, Arianna."

He was trying to penetrate her thoughts, to own the recesses of her brain. He wanted to crack it like an egg, scramble its contents, and pour them out to pick the information he needed from the plasma. Though neither moved, she felt him pressing on every part of her. He was smothering her, drowning her. It was like his hands were on her throat and his body weighted her down. The only way out would be to give him what he wanted.

Let me in, the magic whispered. *Give it to me.*

"No." Her jaw ached from gritting her teeth. Her lips formed a series of unintelligible sounds that followed, but she did not allow words to come. There was nothing she would say other than "No."

"How many have you made?" He pressed harder, straightening away from the wall.

Arianna wanted to blink. She tried so hard to break that stare, though her body refused all commands. She was trapped and wanted to scream for relief. But she would not give in. She would not stop her struggle. Her magic pushed back harder. She focused on her lips, making them hers. He would violate the rest of her with his presence, but he would not gain her words. "No."

"What do you need to make it?"

She could no longer speak; she no longer trusted herself to. Every ounce of magic in her screamed at once in her mind to give him anything he asked for. His magic poisoned her more than the other Dragon's dagger had. Her stomach turned to sickness. Her forehead grew hot with fever. Her body rebelled against the presence of the foreign power and slowly began to turn septic.

But she would not give in. She would not forfeit to this man. She would die before she did. She would spit up blood from her stomach decaying. She would bruise across her skin from her magic depleting. She would go deaf and blind and have all her fingers snap.

Her hatred was more than all the pain combined. And her desire to sow malice across his land was stronger than his magic would ever be. She would fight against the Dragon King until her last breath because she was Arianna, the White Wraith.

"Tell me how you make the Philosopher's Box!" Golden tears streamed from the man's eyes.

"No!" she screamed in reply.

Yveun shut his eyes, tearing away his magic. Arianna collapsed to her knees. She inhaled long, gasping breaths, gulping for air, for the taste of freedom. Her body shuddered and felt like a room ransacked. Everything was there, but nothing in its place, and all bearing the mark of a stranger's touch. It was merely the pain of bruises from her blood exhausting, but they created phantom impressions in her arms and shoulders and back as if she had just been beaten for hours. As if his hands had actually been upon her.

She was the first to look at him, throwing the gauntlet silently. She gave him her eyes again to try if he so dared. She kept her muscles tense, ready to fight, warding off the trembling that rumbled across her with the aftershocks of being so violated.

The King snarled down at her. "I will gain what I seek."

"You will not."

"I will return and I will try again." He stepped forward.

"You are welcome to." Arianna watched his movements carefully on the edges of her vision.

"You can die peacefully, or screaming like your dear guilds below as they all burned on my command." He squatted down, his knees bending forward. "But either way—"

Arianna pushed off the ground. Her shoulders popped and every last bit of slack the chains had was consumed. One finger on the hand he'd placed on his knee was in range. Just one.

She bit it off in a single bite, spitting it at his feet.

"You Fen trash!" The Dragon King stood with a snarl. He pounced on her, pushing her off-balance.

Arianna tried to bring up her hands or feet to defend herself. But she couldn't find enough movement in the chains in the way he had her pinned. He gouged at her throat with his claws.

She felt as tendon and muscle were shredded. The vibration of the skin ripping was sound in her ears. She coughed, sputtered, and choked on her own blood.

Even still, she smiled. She smiled at the frightened King. She smiled as he retreated. She smiled at his yet-recovering eyes. She smiled as the door slammed shut and her throat began to heal. She smiled until her jaw popped.

Because smiling held in the screams.

YVEUN

This was the danger of what the Fenthri sought. This was what he needed to fight against—how their science disrupted the natural order of the worlds the gods themselves designed. The woman was not a Fenthri, not a Chimera, not a Dragon; she was wholly monster and entirely dangerous.

Yveun flexed his still-healing finger, a soft pink from newly mended flesh and still re-growing. The tiniest of claws was begin to form next to the bone, magic strengthening it steadily. He had given the woman half a breath's distance too close and she had taken it.

He wanted to admire her for it, but this was even too much for Yveun. Even he—obsessed with power as he was, and struck by the lack of half measures a Perfect Chimera represented—could not stand for this. If she became even the slightest bit stronger, if she imbibed, if she gained an organ she didn't already have...

There was no way even he would be able to stand up against her.

"Dono, I do not think any more of the boxes have been created." Finnyr scampered along at his side like the worthless rat he was. "She seems to be the only one."

Yveun gritted his teeth. He needed something that could stand against other creatures like that monster. To assume that no more boxes had been made was to welcome the death of everything he stood for. It would be the end of Nova.

"I think we should merely kill her," Finnyr suggested. "If she's only made one box and used it on herself—"

"And who is to say it couldn't be used on others?" Yveun stopped, rounding on Finnyr. "Who is to say that it isn't in the hands of those disgusting Fen rebels as we speak, slowly turning them into something that can challenge even me?"

Yveun held up his hand, showing his finger for emphasis.

"Dono, no one can challenge you," Finnyr sputtered.

The King roared with bitter laughter. Finnyr was still playing a game, a child holding onto an ideal. No matter how many times Yveun drove the point home, it seemed the weak little man never understood. So few could fathom his shame from the mistakes he'd made. He'd only revealed his regrets to Coletta, Leona, and men like Finnyr, who were close enough to his movements that they needed to understand the full gravity of all his risks. For the risks Yveun took rarely ever held consequences only for him.

"Finnyr, I assure you, I am very much a mortal man. While it suits me for the masses both on Loom and Nova to think otherwise, it does not change the fact." Yveun stepped forward, impressing on Finnyr's personal space, trying to make him feel as insignificant as he actually was. "And if I die, Finnyr, so do you. You live only by my grace. You exist only because I protect you and permit you to. Do you think Xin will ever show you love again without my support at your back? The only way you will ever leave here is as the Xin'Oji, and that cannot happen if I perish. Your life is mine."

The man cowered for a satisfying moment. Yveun watched him struggle to steady his voice, but appreciated the struggle all the same. Finnyr would never be a great Dragon, but Yveun needed something from him more important than greatness: obedience.

"Yes, Dono." The man lowered his eyes. "It is an honor that my life is owned by one such as you."

"See that you do not forget it." Yveun straightened away from the smaller Dragon, starting off in the opposite direction. "Now, if I were you, I would find somewhere to hide for the next while until you are needed again. Your use has been exhausted for now, and you will only risk earning my ire if you linger."

He paused at the end of the hall. "Furthermore, your sister is out for your heart. If you think being on Lysip will keep her from hunting you down, you underestimate her."

Finnyr glowered at the mention of Petra, but he didn't object. Yevun continued away, trusting in Finnyr's cowardice more than anything else about the man. He would continue on for the sake of his self-preservation above all else. Yveun had more important things to worry about.

Dragons would not be enough to stand against the threat of the Perfect Chimera. To fight a beast, Yveun needed a more fearsome creature of his own. He needed Dragons that would have no shame in stooping to any level for power and strength. Even if that meant imbibing.

But something even further than consuming the flesh of other Dragons was working through the back of his mind. Fenthri could have the flesh of Dragons cut into them. They had no taboos and no fear of exploring such things. If he found Dragons who would cast aside those inhibitions as well, could they receive the organs of other Dragons? Could he sew together his own Dragon warriors from the strongest parts there were to pick from?

Yveun licked his lips with a morbid sort of hunger.

"Coletta." The heady scents of earth and foliage assaulted his nose the moment he crossed into her domain.

Coletta's world was enclosed by a tall wall, cleverly designed right into the aesthetic of the estate. Large sun shades allowed in light for her plants, but helped conceal the true nature of her gardens from the casual observer on the back of a boco. For any who looked too close would see the ominous crimson spikes that scaled up some of her flowering plants, or the unsettling aroma that lingered beneath the heavy perfumes of unnatural sweetness.

"Yveun," she stood from amid the plants down the path from him. The woman wore nothing, allowing the poisons to brush directly against her skin. Yveun had thought her a fool for it in the beginning. She was sick constantly, frail, always afflicted with horrible boils and rashes. But with time, her body had developed immunities. Now, he would dare argue that she had become the strongest of them all, and no one but him ever saw it.

"Leona. You knew of her well before she lived in our halls."

"And how to pull her strings to tie her to us as something useful." The woman knelt back down, returning to her plants as though they spoke of little more than their preference of meat for dinner that night.

"Your little flowers budding everywhere, they were the ones who gave you such knowledge, no?"

"They did." She resumed her business, plucking flowers as delicately as a hummingbird drawing nectar.

"I have someone else that I need you to find." Yveun didn't enjoy going to Coletta for help. While he wouldn't begrudge his mate the enjoyment of knowing she was needed in his world, Yveun wanted to provide. He did not want to be seen as lacking or half-measured when the woman did not even know how to breathe without giving the act everything she possessed.

Coletta smiled, lowered her eyes and gave a small dip of her head, an elegant curve that offered him subservience—visually anyway. Her chest remained upright, her body strong, her back straight; she relinquished no real power to him. She was a study in contrasts: strength from weakness, beautiful and hideous, dangerous and so tender at the same time.

"She is an unnamed."

Coletta crossed over to a work table next to him, dropping off her basket among a variety of distilling beakers that would make an Alchemist of Loom envious. "I know of whom you speak."

"You do?"

"I told her to stay away until you had solved the matter of Lossom." Coletta spoke lightly while her hands remained busy. "He was a fine temporary recovery for you after Leona. I didn't want you running into the training of a true replacement for our lost girl until you were ready to do so properly."

"Coletta, I would—"

"Remove the growl and spare me the bravado, Yveun." She narrowed her eyes to a dagger's edge. "You cared too much for the girl. Her death affected you, made your head soft. All you need to do is look at your delicate actions following. The fact that Cvareh Xin is even still alive."

Yveun's lip twitched in a rage that was directed more at himself than his mate. He wished she had spoken this truth sooner. But if she had, he may not have been yet ready to hear it.

"Trust me," Coletta breathed delicately, a spell made from spun glass. She stepped forward, resting her hand on his cheek. "I have always seen to it that the path is clear for you to walk. Trust my designs."

His mate was a shadow master, well versed in the underbelly of Nova. Most never realized how deeply her roots stretched while she enjoyed the sun of the world above, and it seemed Yveun had forgotten as well. The death of his riders had turned him into a reactionary beast. He had to trust the hand that rested itself upon him to pull him back on course and chart a route that would lead to their conquest.

"Go under. Find her. She will come with you now." Coletta's instruction was a borderline command. She abruptly returned to her work, the tenderness gone.

"Now?" Yveun clarified.

"*Now.*"

Yveun paused for only a moment. There was more to this than what Coletta was letting him see. He took her hand and pulled her face toward him. She set her jaw in determination, clearly expressing her opinion on his attempt to draw out any additional truth or facts.

He leaned forward and placed a gentle kiss on his mate's mouth that transformed the ambivalent line into a thin smile.

"I love you, in no half measure," Yveun whispered. When the world was falling apart, it made him appreciate the pillar of her ruthlessness all the more. She brewed death at her fingertips and reaped it with words over claws. Most other Dragons would see cowardice, but he saw a stunning commitment to all she was.

Yveun left his Ryu, his true mate, to start for the world below—and to earn his new Master Rider.

FLORENCE

"Something isn't right." It was the fourth time Derek had said so in the past day. The train made due course from Ter.1.2 to Keel along the main tracks.

"Take your pick from the garden of Everything Is Wrong. There's no shortage of bounty in the field." Florence settled in the plush seat of the train cabin they'd been given on Powell's behalf. But even if Powell hadn't asked it of the train, they still could've each taken their own cabin if they wanted. The vessel was at less than half capacity and most of the travelers kept to themselves. A heavy weight kept heads down and mouths quiet.

Nora gave Florence a tired look at the discourse repeating itself.

"There should be more Dragons along the checkpoints. They've been monitoring all trains going in and out of Keel for months, looking for an illegal transport of supplies," Derek clarified. "But we haven't seen a single one so far."

"I suppose they only have enough time to burn Loom and not dance on its ashes." Florence folded her arms.

"I don't know why they're not here..." Derek leaned his forehead against the window, watching one of the aforementioned tunneled checkpoints that kept the endwig at bay through the Skeleton Forest whiz by. It was dark and unmanned, so the train continued on.

"Yes, you do." Florence wouldn't stand to see fear and shock dull Derek's sharp senses. "You know why they left."

"No, they still need to…"

"To what? To guard the transportation of goods? Derek, there has to be a guild for the goods to go to."

"There's no way they would do that to the Alchemists." He couldn't even say what "it" was.

"The Harvesters are more essential to Loom than the Alchemists." Derek and Nora both gave Florence incredulous stares at the notion, but she held fast. "If they'll do it to one guild, they'll do it to any."

Or all, Florence thought but didn't say. The more she had time to mull over everything that had happened, the more she realized there really was no other alternative. After what Powell had said, after what the Dragons had done… It was to be total warfare between their worlds.

"The Alchemists have fought off the Dragons for years. We're the only guild to refuse to allow them in."

"They don't need to be 'let in' to reap destruction."

"Enough, both of you." Nora pinched the bridge of her nose with a heavy sigh. "Derek, Florence is right, something must have happened. But until we get there, we won't be able to see exactly what." She shook her head and looked out the window.

Florence let the topic drop. She hadn't had a home for most of her life. She was born five years before Dragon contact was made. Her vague memories of Ter.0 were nothing more than the ghosts of emotions and the hazy remnants of bygone dreams. She had been moved to the Ravens, arbitrarily, as part of the Dragons' restructuring following the end of the brief war. There she learned, and she failed, earning a few friends rather than a sense of belonging to a guild. When she left, she did the bidding of the Wraith of Dortam, and was little more than a transient ghost herself.

Florence leaned against the door on the opposite side of Derek and Nora, watching them. She had always found more family in people than places or things. But they were different from her. Their place was their identity, and they belonged to the Alchemists.

So, while all three felt heartbreak the moment they arrived in Keel and learned the Alchemists' Guild hall had been destroyed mere hours after the Harvesters, Florence's pain was of a different sort than her two companions.

The streets of Keel were full of Alchemists, not unlike how Ter.1.2 was now the de facto hall for the Harvesters. However, unlike Faroe, the Alchemists Guild Hall was far enough from the city that the majority of the capital city of Ter.2 remained unharmed. Physically, at least.

Their train was the first to arrive from Ter.1, so carrying the burden of truth was their responsibility. Men and women alike collapsed on the platform. Screams of sorrow harmonized oddly with cries of relief as people embraced in both pain and joy. Some survived, some didn't; their world had been thrown into a shaker and then spilled back out upon the land. Now, it remained to be seen what was left.

"James?" Derek called from halfway down the platform to an Alchemist directing the flow of people.

The man, James presumably, looked around before finding Derek's eyes and giving a wave. "Derek! Nora!"

They met each other in the middle with a reserved clasping of hands in relief at seeing each other again.

"We thought you for dead."

"We nearly were," Derek confessed. "The new Vicar Harvester got us out in time."

"It really is true then?" James's voice took a deeper, heavier turn. "The Harvesters as well?"

"What happened here?"

"Vicar Sophie suspected something was amiss when the day before all Dragons were pulled from Keel. Mysteriously, the King's men who had been so intent on becoming our official liaisons and staying permanently in the guild decided they had tired of the job.

"The Vicar sent a team of men and women to investigate. While they were here in Keel, they were approached by a Chimera living in the city, a graduated journeyman. He manages a store that sells dried fish from the coast, near Ter.1.3. His supplier contacted him, informing him of delays as a result of the attack on the Harvesters' Guild."

"Did the Vicar Alchemist not try to fight the Dragons?" Derek asked hopelessly as they traversed the platform.

"With what weaponry?" James sighed. "You know how it was: there was barely enough gunpowder to make a spark."

The image of that giant canister plummeting through the sky toward the Harvesters' Guild came back to Florence. There wasn't much fight to be had. The Dragons had set out to make a statement about the helplessness of Loom and so far, they had succeeded. They had traveled and killed using Loom's technology.

"How much of the guild escaped?" Florence asked.

"About two thirds."

The three words formed a single golden lining to an otherwise terrible situation. It put the Alchemists in a better position to remain the spearhead of the resistance if the other guilds were in a state that was anything like the Harvesters. But James didn't seem to share her reasoning. His mouth formed a scowl at the news.

"Then it should be no trouble for us to see the Vicar?"

"Sophie is quite busy." James's pointed look at Florence's right cheek was missed by no one. No matter what she did, she would be seen as an outsider to them.

"She'll want to see us," Derek insisted.

"Derek, you may want to wait," James cautioned.

"It's urgent."

He had the right credentials, and James begrudgingly led them out of the station and into Keel proper.

It was Florence's first time in the capital city of the Alchemists. Much like Faroe was different from Dortam, which was different from Holx, this was another city where the Rivets had put to use the natural resources and terrain to optimize structures. Pine buildings, no doubt constructed from the trees that were cut down to make room for the city itself, were stacked on top of each other around what trees remained.

Metal pipes funneled steam and wires among them, winding across bridges and trailing down walls like eager, industrial roots. It glittered in the early evening light as biofluorescent lanterns sparked to life, swirling like Dragon magic caught in jars. The heavy tree canopy, the narrow windows sparkling with seeming magic... it felt the way Florence expected the secretive city of the Alchemists to feel—dark, but full of promise.

James led them down a wide street to one of the towering trees that was nearly smothered by all the structures built against it and on top of each other. Plumes of steam mingled with an odd trail of red smoke that curled in the air around its upper levels, piped out from what Florence could only assume to be a laboratory within. James stopped just shy of the door.

"Vicar's inside."

He pointedly turned on his heel, starting for the station again. The three of them watched him go with a mindful note. There was no denying the haste with which he had wanted to get away from the place. Combined with his earlier hesitation…

Was he avoiding Sophie? Florence kept the question to herself.

"What now?" an incredibly disgruntled Vicar snapped the moment they walked in. Sophie tore her eyes away from her paper, dropping it onto the desk. They gained a different sort of clarity, however, when Sophie saw exactly who sought an audience. "Derek? Nora?" There was a long pause. "Florence."

"We've returned from the Harvesters' Guild, and have spoken with the Vicar there." She got it out of the way first. Florence didn't want any question as to what they had accomplished, especially given the terms she'd left on. It had only been a few months, but it felt like years.

"You actually made it?" Sophie narrowed her eyes in apparent skepticism. "The Vicar Harvester is dead."

"We were there when they elected a new one in Ter.1.2," Derek explained. This seemed to satisfy Sophie for the time being.

Florence was getting rather tired of needing Derek to step in to validate her claims to Alchemists.

"How did you survive?" Sophie's tone shifted to genuine curiosity rather than outright interrogation.

"Florence made friends with the man who is now the newly-elected Vicar on the way to the guild. Because of that, he worked to get us out when the Harvesters received word of the attack."

"Did you?" Sophie's eyes were on Florence again.

"Yes." Calling Powell her friend seemed rather forward. Their relationship had been up and down, odd, and short, but he had gone out of his way to save her life. If that didn't make him her friend, she didn't know what did. It had worked for Ari, at the very least.

"Will he be sending the supplies we need?" Sophie addressed Derek, but Florence couldn't stop herself from answering.

"After what happened to Faroe, I don't think much will be coming out of the Harvesters for some time."

"I didn't ask you," Sophie said casually, not even bothering to look at Florence when she spoke.

Florence clenched her fists in frustration but held her tongue.

"I believe he will help us…" Derek was beginning to look uncertain now. "But circumstances have changed."

"They have not changed in the slightest." Sophie frowned. "Now, more than ever, we must launch an attack against the Dragons. Loom has seen the danger they bring."

"Exactly." Florence saw her opening and took it. "Loom knows of the danger—all of Loom. Every guild is unified once more and will all fight together."

It was like Florence was speaking a different language, there was such a look of confusion on Sophie's face. "We do not need the other guilds to fight."

"What?"

"We need their supplies, certainly, but we do not need their involvement." Sophie scoffed at the very notion.

"How—how can you say that?" It flew counter to everything Florence believed the resistance stood for. Everything Sophie should know. Hadn't this woman been Arianna's friend?

"The Dragons see us as weak."

"And we should show them we are strong."

"No." The word was said so quickly that it punctuated Florence's sentence. "We must let them think we are weak and divided. Wait for them to make a mistake, then strike."

"What if they don't?" Florence shook her head incredulously. It was sheer lunacy. "What if this is merely the beginning?"

"This is a scare tactic, one you seem to be falling for. If we unite, they will merely respond with more force. However, if we show weakness and open doors, they will come down among us to rebuild, just like after the One Year War. *Then* will be our time to strike."

"That could take years. It could never happen! Who knows what they will do to Loom while we wait and do nothing?" Sophie was gambling with Loom's freedom rather than taking it. It made Florence want to scream and stomp. The Dragons had attacked them in cold blood. They had set Loom afire simply because they could. And now? Now Sophie wanted to roll over before them, continuing what had amounted to a pathetic quasi-rebellion in secret.

"And if the rebellion fails, as it did last time, all of Loom will live to fight again if we conduct ourselves quietly. Past failures can still teach valuable lessons, Florence." Sophie remained undeterred.

"Arianna will never go for this. She wants the Dragons dead."

"Do you really know what she wants?" Sophie challenged. "After all, she's been on Nova for some time doing who knows what."

"It has something to do with the Philosopher's Box." Florence prayed that everything she knew about Arianna remained true. She was betting not only everything that she had, but Loom itself, on the fact. "Ari will come back, and she will go to the Vicar Tribunal."

"Vicar Tribunal?" It was Sophie's turn to be incredulous.

"There is a Tribunal happening on Ter.0 in two months. The Vicar Harvester is spreading the word to the other guilds. They expect a demonstration of the box, and the Vicar Alchemist in attendance."

If Florence could pack the look Sophie was giving her into a canister, it would be the most deadly shot she'd ever made. After several long breaths, the Vicar slowly dropped her hands to the desk, standing slowly. She rose to her full height, a head taller than Florence.

"Florence, a word of advice," Sophie spoke as soft as a knife point dragging across flesh. "Be wary of who you speak for. Because you have made promises that you were not permitted to give on behalf of two very, very powerful women."

It was the nicest thing Florence had ever heard Sophie say about Arianna. And it was being used as a pointed threat. She wanted to rebuke the notion. But the fact was, Arianna was just as likely to be angry with Florence for her decision as she was to be obliging.

"It's the only way."

"There are lots of ways." Sophie rounded the desk, running her hand along its edge. "You are young, and you see the only solution as outright warfare."

Elise Kova

"What else is there? Your plan to lure the Dragons into some false sense of triumph?"

"That, and many more strategic approaches that wouldn't result in hundreds, thousands, of Fenthri deaths."

"The strategic approach hasn't worked."

"Neither has outright warfare." Sophie referred to the quick failure that was Loom's last war. "Perhaps when you are older, when you have lost more, you will understand this."

"Do not say I have not lost." Florence took a step forward, barely stopping herself from outright attacking the woman. "You know nothing of me."

"I know you are still a girl, quick to ire and stumbling in the pitfalls of pride." Sophie remained poised. "I know you have yet to see the merit of strategic sacrifice to attain one's goals."

"You *must* go to the Tribunal."

"You may not tell me what I must do." The Vicar Alchemist shook her head. "Derek, you will be on the first train back to Ter.1.2 in the morning. You will tell the Vicar Harvester to call off the Tribunal. You will inform him that the Alchemists will not be working with the rest of Loom, and encourage him to call off this ridiculous notion of a demonstration against the Dragons. Denounce all knowledge of a working Philosopher's Box as the misinformed whims of a child."

Derek looked between Florence and the Vicar of his guild helplessly. But Florence knew what his decision would be. She knew it as clearly as the two interlocking triangles on his cheek.

"Understood, Vicar."

"Good." Sophie returned to her chair, waving them away. "Now, the three of you... get out of my sight."

Nora stepped away and Derek followed, linking arms with her. Florence hesitated one moment. Venom poured from the glands in her mouth instead of saliva, and the brief, challenging look Sophie gave her was almost enough to made her spit it all out on the woman's desk.

But Florence made for the door. She would heed Sophie's words and apply them that very moment. She would make a strategic sacrifice of her pride in the form of a tactical retreat. The Vicar had won the battle, but Florence would not give her victory in the war between them.

PETRA

P etra clenched the reins of her boco so tightly that she had to consciously remind herself to ease her fingers so she didn't accidentally snap Raku's neck. In the span of a day, the world had been given and taken from her. She had been ready to kill Finnyr, she had the box, she had the loyalty of Loom. And now, Finnyr was out of reach, the woman—the *only* woman—who held the knowledge of the Philosopher's Box was in Yveun's hands, and that fact threw the loyalty of Loom into question.

Petra bared her teeth into the wind. She was going to get it all back, and then some. She hadn't devoted most her life to a dream the world had told her was futile since she was a child to see it taken from her now. She was born to be the Dono of Nova and there was nothing she wouldn't sacrifice to see that come to pass.

Cvareh rode stiffly at her side. Worry fogged his magic and made the air around him so thick, Petra wondered how he even saw where he was going. He focused ahead, past the late afternoon sun, to Lysip. The islands of Nova floated below them, guiding their track. Eventually, they would deviate and fly around the back of the island, regrouping before launching their plan into action.

The future weighed on Petra's shoulders. They had one shot. Failure meant House Xin would lose everything.

The watercolors of the sky were turning into strong pastel by the time they landed their bocos behind a far hill on the back end of Lysip. Wildflowers and grasses were their only greeting party. Cvareh dismounted, confused when she did the same.

"Aren't you—"

"Yes, yes," she cut him off with a wave. "But I wanted to speak to you first."

"Every moment we waste is another Ari spends with Yveun."

"And he will not kill her." Of that, Petra was certain. "He needs her as much as we do. He needs her knowledge, at the very least, before he could even consider removing her."

The tall foliage brushed against her hips as she reached for her brother. Her hands wrapped around the back of his head and she placed her forehead against his. Petra closed her eyes, imagining their minds as one. Her little brother, full of so much potential, the tool she had kept at her disposal. Sometimes clumsy, but always out for the best of House Xin.

"Your mind is noisy. You must silence it," she cautioned. "I know you are worried for this mate you have chosen. But Arianna is strong. Worry no more for her than you would for me."

"I worry for you plenty."

Petra pulled away with a smile. "All I want you to worry for now is yourself. Focus on what we're here to do. I will make sure to create quite a stir. I'll keep Rok's attention on me for as long as I reasonably can, but you must make haste while I do."

"I will."

"Ends before ideals," Petra reminded him. "Do what you must for our House, Cvareh."

"I will," he repeated.

Satisfied, Petra wrapped her arms around his shoulders, pulled him tight for a brief moment, then mounted her boco once more. They had always been playing a dangerous game, but the stakes never let up. They grew with each passing moment, each passing day. Everything had come to a head so quickly that Petra knew every decision they made from here on would govern the future of their House—and perhaps the future of Nova itself.

Cvareh moved forward on foot, and Petra watched him leave.

She waited long after he disappeared over the hill. She gave him time, stiff in her saddle, impatient but forcing herself to remain. They had landed intentionally far from the Rok Estate. It wasn't a distance he could traverse inconspicuously with any speed.

When the sun hung low in the sky, she took to the air once more. The shifting grasses and swaying, spindly trees below caught the sunlight, shining as if the world itself was aflame. Petra scanned the ground, flying at leisure, satisfied when she finally caught a glimpse of Cvareh. He was near the edge of the estate, entering through the homes where Yveun's political wards lived. It was an area Petra had made sure he was familiar with by having him visit Finnyr often enough.

How he would find Arianna once inside was up to him. She had more important things to concern herself with. Petra landed in the field designated for guests' bocos and summoned a face of pure ire. It wasn't hard given the circumstances.

She stormed for the opening of the Rok Estate, claws out, teeth bared, the very image of an Oji scorned.

"Where is Finnyr Xin?" she barked to the first Rok servant who had the ill fortune of greeting her.

"Xin'Oji, we were not expecting—"

Petra gouged out his throat. It was risky to spill *any* blood on the Rok estate, but the smell of one of their own bleeding would send every Rider running. It would draw all eyes to her.

Sure enough, the soft clicking of the beads of a Rider neared, rounding the corner as an apple-skinned woman stopped at the far end of the hall. She sheathed her claws the moment her eyes fell on Petra. The Court was too fresh in every Dragon's mind for any to be inclined to challenge her, any other than Yveun. Especially not over the death of a no-name slave.

"I demand my brother." She spoke loudly, for all who were gathering. "I demand Finnyr Xin."

"Finnyr is a ward of Yveun Dono." Petra mentally commended the Rider for maintaining a strong and level voice in the face of her rage. "The Dono would need to approve Finnyr's departure."

"The Dono can keep him." Petra snorted. "I merely want to kill him."

"The Dono would need to approve a duel..."

Petra advanced on the Rider. She could smell the fear in the air around the woman. Her dilated eyes, her barely stable hands. The Rider was ready to fight, but they all knew who would win. It would be a life wasted.

"This is not the Court. This is a House matter. Yes, we are on Lysip, but as I, the Xin'Oji, am demanding a duel with a member of my House, it should fall under *my* jurisdiction, not the Dono's." Petra lorded over the slip of a Dragon. For now, she didn't actually care if she was given Finnyr. She would kill him someday, and someday soon. But the longer they stalled, the more of an opportunity she had to raise a fuss over the fact and the more time Cvareh had to find Arianna.

"You are quite right." A new voice stilled the room with its whispering tones.

Petra straightened away from the Rider, looking with curiosity for the source of the sound. A small, frail-looking Dragon had parted the gathering mass of people with her presence alone. Petra had seen the woman before at Courts and a few special functions, but she was as rare as raindrops otherwise. The mere sight of her sent a whole new wave of rage across her skin.

"Coletta'Ryu." Petra had to think quickly or she'd lose all reason to anger. She didn't expect the Ryu to greet her. Yveun wasted no time glowering over her at every chance. What did it mean for this woman to be standing in his stead? He was no doubt somewhere delighting at having the butcher of Petra's people greet her. "Will you see Finnyr fashioned for me?"

"Certainly." The woman gave a thin-lipped smile, submissive and demure. Petra wondered what the Dono saw in her at all. She was nothing more than a coward. "Please, Xin'Oji, come with me. Lysip is a far ride from Ruana and you must be tired after such tragedy has struck your House."

Petra's hands vibrated from the tension her muscles were under as the Rok'Ryu had the boldness to mention her plot against Petra's home. She wanted to rip the woman limb from limb. But that pursuit of revenge would have to wait. She only had Finnyr's word to go on, one Yveun would vehemently deny. As the Rok'Oji, his word was law in approving all duels for the members of his House, and he would not see Petra's claims against Coletta as viable for a duel.

Killing Coletta'Ryu was going to be a much longer game.

"You are too kind." Petra smiled as wide as she could, her lips curling back, her fangs showing.

"House Rok is quite invested in the future of House Xin. We have been for many years," Coletta spoke as she led Petra down a long hall. The Riders and half the staff followed them. Petra knew any would say it was to ensure they were waited on hand and foot. But she knew the truth—it was a visual reminder of Rok's strength. No matter how skilled a fighter Petra was, if she attacked the Rok'Oji, they would show her no quarter. "We would not want to move against your ends."

Petra responded to lies with lies. "And House Xin is nothing but loyal in no half measures to House Rok for their kindness."

Coletta smiled falsely in reply. They were both speaking the same language.

"We can wait in here." Coletta motioned to a lavish parlor that overlooked a private garden. It smelled strongly of the woman and had a lived-in look. Petra bristled at the realization that she'd been led into the asp's den. "Yeaan, please fetch some appropriate refreshments for the Oji and me. Topann, please see to finding the Oji's brother. The rest of you, please return to your duties. There is no need to overwhelm the Xin'Oji."

"Coletta'Ryu, the Riders would like to stand guard," the woman from earlier insisted.

Petra wracked her mind for how to make sure they did indeed stay. The more people who were around, the fewer could run into Cvareh. But she had no reason to demand an audience.

"I don't think it necessary. Let us not insult out guest by even implying that she may do something underhanded." Coletta smiled almost sweetly. "I am perfectly safe with the honorable Xin'Oji."

Petra wanted to tell her she was anything but. However, there was truth to the words. Petra respected the Dragons' ways. She would not lower herself to killing a Ryu outside of a pit; she was better than this woman at least in that respect.

"It is the wish of the Rok'Oji," the Riders insisted.

"Very well, then outside with you so we may relax."

That seemed to satisfy their wishes, and the Riders assumed their places on the other side of the door. Petra listened closely after it closed for footsteps walking away, but heard none. So her presence tied up the Rok'Ryu and the Riders. It was something, at the very least.

"Thank you for your hospitality, Coletta'Ryu."

"It's just us, Petra'Oji, you don't need to pretend any longer." The woman tilted her head to the side in amusement. Something about her demeanor shifted. It was like a cat had grown into a lion in mere moments. Where there had been something unassuming before, now stood a menace.

This was the woman who had killed her House in cold-blooded shadows.

"I'm afraid I do not know of what you speak."

One of Coletta's servants, Yeaan, returned with a tray. She crossed silently to the center of the room, laying out a small assortment of fruits and cheese with two wine glasses. One vessel was set out for Coletta, the other placed on Petra's side of the table.

Petra stared at the offending liquid. The woman before her was a monster. Putting in front of her the means she had used to kill her people like a trophy. Petra's nose scrunched at the scent of the wine.

"What is this?" Petra motioned to the glasses, unable to keep the comment to herself.

"Wine from Ruana. I wanted to make you feel at home."

Was this woman so bold that she would really kill an Oji behind closed doors? Petra approached the unassuming vessels as though they could fly off the table and strike at any moment.

"It is quite safe, I assure you. A different vintage than what was consumed at Court."

"A strange happening, that," Petra said quietly. "How all of the wine, from different vineyards, different wineries, was so deadly."

"Truly an inexplicable tragedy."

"One could explain it as poison."

Coletta turned, the fading light of day catching the red of her eyes and making them glow ominously as she assessed Petra. She smiled again. This time, the edge of a canine crept from behind her lips. "You speak of dangerous things, Petra'Oji."

"I believe I stand before a very dangerous woman." It was a dance of words, neither wanting to cross the line into overt threats.

"I *am* the Rok'Ryu." Coletta hummed quietly, walking to the edge of the table. "And Petra, I have been watching you for some time."

Petra bristled at the lack of title attached to her name. That was something, almost enough of something, to challenge the woman on. But still, they had no witnesses to the offense and plenty of people who would lie and object, and stand for the Ryu. As much as she desired it, Petra reminded herself that she would not be killing the Rok'Ryu this night.

"You're a dangerous woman, too. You seek out what you want, you pursue it with a reckless passion. You are relentless." The Ryu took both glasses in her hands, inspecting them carefully. Petra never let them leave her sight. Coletta poured the wine from one glass into the other, filling it to the brim. She repeated this a few times, back and forth. Mixing them completely. "All of Nova knows you seek Yveun's throne. Why haven't you taken it yet?"

Coletta held out one glass. Petra regarded it hesitantly before accepting. But she did not drink. She would not drink before the Ryu did; she knew better.

"I am not in a position to." It was the most honest thing Petra had said to a Rok in a long time.

"No, you're not," Coletta agreed. "At least not honorably, not by Dragon law."

"And I would never be recognized as the Dono, if it was not done through Dragon law." Petra followed Coletta over to the wide window that overlooked an expanse of foliage. It was the only visible window down into the garden.

Petra wondered if this was the place where the poison that killed her House had come from. None of the plants were familiar to her. She couldn't even guess where half of them grew originally.

"I sat quietly, for many years, watching Yveun do as he would," Coletta spoke to no one in particular. "But you changed things, Petra. And left me with no choice but to join the fray."

Petra watched as the Ryu raised the glass to her lips and took a long drink. She waited several breaths, and nothing happened.

"I am beginning to believe that I have more reason to fear you than the Dono."

"Then you are as smart as you seem." Coletta turned to Petra. "I will give you one chance, Petra. Leave now, and remain the Xin'Oji. Give up on your dream to become the

Dono, swear true fealty, and I will let House Xin remain as it has always been."

The very notion was ridiculous, and Petra made sure Coletta was aware of the fact with her unrestrained laugher. "You cannot threaten me or my House, Coletta."

The woman's eye twitched at the lack of title.

"And I will never bargain with House Rok. Not when I hold the cards."

Coletta huffed softly in amusement, raising her glass in the light of the orange sunset. "Then, to war."

"To war." Petra clinked her glass against Coletta's, and finally drank alongside the Ryu.

A side door opened and Topann reappeared, Finnyr in tow. Petra snarled, setting down her glass heavily on the table the moment she saw her brother. "I declare now a duel, before the Rok'Ryu, for your life, Finnyr."

"Under what claims?" Coletta asked, per the script.

"Actions against his House." Killing Finnyr was going to be a fringe benefit of the night. Petra's claws shot from her fingers.

"I approve this duel."

Finnyr tried to make for the door the second the Ryu spoke the words. Topann closed and stood before it, preventing him from leaving.

"Y-you, the Dono still needs me," Finnyr pleaded with Coletta. "You can't let me die like this. He would not allow it!"

"Look at you, Finnyr, pleading to a Rok for your life." Petra spat at his feet. "You pathetic little coward."

Petra pulled back her hand. She was done dealing with her brother. She would go right for his heart and end it once and for all.

A chill swept through her, swift and sudden. It shot up her spine and into her stomach, pouring forward as blood from her mouth. Her knees knocked and her lungs burned.

Petra shuddered, and fell.

No. The word seared her mind. Coletta entered her blurring field of vision, looming over her like the Lord of Death himself.

"H-how?" Petra stuttered. Nothing made sense. "I-I am an Oji."

"You think a title will protect you, Petra," Coletta spoke down to her. "That has been your greatest flaw. You put so much stock into titles and rank that you forget what gives them power—fear."

The woman squatted next to her, narrowly avoiding the blood Petra was spitting up as she gasped for air.

"You failed your House. You, who should believe in whatever means necessary to achieve your ends, never even thought that I would kill you here."

"You drank from the same glass." Petra tried to defend herself in what she knew were her final moments.

"And you know nothing of poison." Coletta smiled, wide and open-mouthed. Her teeth were dull and small, eaten away beyond her young years. Her gums were worn and gray, curling and tired. Her breath smelled of death. "But I do. I know of poisons well. My body, too; it is strong with them, invulnerable to them. I also know that you do not have magic in your stomach."

"F-F-Finnyr," Petra growled up at her brother. She wished she had the strength to stand, just enough to kill him. If she was going to die, she would take one of them with her to the halls of Lord Xin.

But she didn't have the strength.

Her body was in revolt. Her magic surged but couldn't keep up with everything failing at once. If anything, the effort to heal resulted in her organs wearing out from magic depletion. She could feel herself turning septic, growing rotten with each passing moment.

"You should have taken my deal, Petra." Coletta stroked her hair like a child. "It's a shame to lose a woman on Nova as strong as you." The Rok'Ryu stood with a sigh, as though the matter actually did cause her strife. "Finnyr."

Petra rasped with laughter. Between the blood and death's heavy veil she could still see her brother tripping over his own two feet to get to her. Even when he was handed carved meat on a platter, he couldn't find the knife to spear it. Her mouth curled in an expression that was part snarl, part grimace.

"Y-You will ne-neh-never stand as O-Oji," Petra forced from between chattering teeth.

"It was mine all along." Finnyr knelt beside her. His hand wavered.

"Cvareh w-w-will kill you." Petra bubbled up laughter through the blood in her throat. "You were never meant to stand as the ruler of House Xin. You—"

His hand plunged into her chest. She felt her brother's fingers close around her heart. Petra closed her eyes; death was upon her, and there was no point in fighting it any longer. She would watch her House for the rest of time from the halls of Lord Xin. She would watch, gleefully, as Cvareh finished what she started decades ago with Finnyr.

She would see her younger brother kill the elder, a task she should've done years ago.

Petra Xin'Oji To's last discovery in life was the sensation of what it felt like to have her heart ripped out. The act she had done to many was finally performed upon her. With her final breath, she embraced the veil of the god she so loved.

CVAREH

Petra was counting on him. Arianna was counting on him—even if she didn't know it. The future of House Xin was counting on him.

It was the same sort of weight he felt the last time he had crept through the Rok Estate for the schematics. Now he felt it in triplicate, looking for the woman who created those same drawings. There was a twisted and cruel sort of parallel drawn between them that had started long before they'd ever met.

Cvareh knew the moment Petra had arrived, since every man and woman who had been milling about the halls quickly sprinted off with eager whispers. His sister was always cause for attention, and the Xin'Oji calling for the blood of one of her kin was added fuel to that particular fire. Cvareh just hoped she kept her word from back on Ruana that she would not actually kill Finnyr.

He had promised that honor to Arianna and, after all Cvareh had come to know and realize, she well and truly deserved his brother's blood.

In the fading sunlight, the Rok Estate was undeniable in its glamour and overpowering in its lavishness. Rooms of grandiose proportions dwarfed him, glittering with gold and gemstone. He used the scale to his advantage, keeping his head down and the scarf of the drab, humble clothes he wore high around his face. Peeking out just above the fabric was the symbol of House Rok. He'd inked it shortly after sneaking into the estate, using an idea he borrowed from Arianna.

He wasn't known on sight here. Petra had kept him from many a Court and function across the years, making his appearance only vaguely familiar to any not of Ruana. Once more, Petra's foresight served them well when another head-bowed servant crossed paths with him and paid him little more than a glance at his cheek.

Cvareh knew his general headway to the holding pens of the Rok Estate. Most Houses had something of the variety for containing Dragons awaiting a duel—or for when the Oji couldn't decide if a duel was even merited at all. It was where he should've taken Finnyr, rather than putting him anywhere remotely close to Arianna. Usually, the pens remained empty; Cvareh had yet to meet an Oji would couldn't make a split-second decision on such matters.

He heard the shifting of beads from around the corner and stopped his progress, listening carefully to the movement. Without doubt, a Rider was stationed at the door. If he needed any further proof that Arianna was likely being held in one of the rooms in the hall beyond, that was it. They wouldn't exhaust a Rider on something so trivial, otherwise.

Cvareh leaned against the wall, stilling his breathing, trying to slow the very beating of his heart so he had time to figure out a solution to his predicament. Did he try to draw the Rider away and then circle back to the door? If he attacked, the scent of blood would draw others. He pressed his eyes closed and uttered a quick prayer to Lord Agendi and Lord Xin. He asked the first to cast his gaze on this endeavor, and the second to do the opposite.

Cvareh rounded the corner.

The Dragon looked up from inspecting her claws. The woman had only two beads and Cvareh didn't instantly recognize her. If she wasn't at the Court, she might not know his face either. Cvareh adjusted his wide scarf and hoped the mark he drew on his cheek was clear enough and hadn't smudged.

"What do you want?" the woman sneered at the very sight of him. But she didn't attack.

"Your presence is requested upstairs." Cvareh kept his voice level and his eyes lowered. He hated taking his sight off the woman, who could decide to lunge at any second, but he had no choice. The more suspicion he raised by acting out of character, the lower his chances of getting inside. "To deal with the Xin'Oji."

"The Xin'Oji is here?" The woman sighed heavily. "What trouble is the blue devil trying to make now?"

Cvareh kept his mouth shut. It served his image, and if he didn't, he might have spit out a hasty defense of Petra. He'd learned the hard way to keep his mouth shut in a train station on Loom in a confrontation that now seemed an eternity ago. It was a mistake he wouldn't now repeat.

"You sure you don't want to go back to her and beg for your place in House Xin? They may invite you to their tea parties and wine tastings if you do."

"My loyalty is, and always will be, to House Rok." Cvareh forced his mouth to make the words when his heart revolted at their very thought.

"Good boy." She patted his head. "Make sure no one goes in. If you do, I'll rip the muscle from your bones."

"Yes." He assumed his place against the door.

The woman started down the hall. Cvareh's heart raced. As soon as she was out of sight, he was going to find Arianna. He was going to get them out of there. He kept his eyes focused on the Rider's feet.

"Oh, what did you say your name was, Xin traitor?"

Cvareh looked up on instinct, anger flashing hot at the mere mention. Their eyes met and she tilted her head to the side, staring at him with more intent at the spark of resistance. Cvareh quickly lowered his face.

"My name…" he hadn't thought of a name. "Rafansi." Cvareh cringed instantly at the first thing that came to mind.

"Rafansi?" She started back toward him with a snort of disbelief that echoed Cvareh's reaction when he'd first heard the name. "Look at me, Rafansi."

Cvareh had no choice but to oblige. The illusion was melting around him and he'd only add heat to the flame if he resisted. If he was careful, he might be able to save the situation.

The woman stopped. "What kind of a name is that?"

"Any wonder I tried to get away from my parents on Ruana?" he tried to jest.

"Say, *Rafansi*, were you at the Crimson Court?" She leaned forward.

Cvareh shook his head, amazed he could while under the tension of his muscles.

"Shame. You could've watched the pampered prince of Xin cowering behind an Anh to do his fighting for him." The woman stepped away, shrugging. "I wonder if he could even stand up in a fight."

"Better than any Rok could." The words flew from his mouth like caged birds escaping at the first opportunity.

The woman froze. "I thought you looked familiar," she snarled.

Twenty gods above, I didn't learn anything on Loom. Cvareh chastised himself as he watched her muscles tense from her knees to her lower back.

Cvareh lunged to the side, expecting the twisting strike. His claws unsheathed, he pressed forward and up into the armpit of the Rider.

"Xin coward," she snarled, pushing him away, raking her claws along his arms in the process.

Blood spilled to the floor, a warning call to any Dragons in the proximity. Cvareh cursed aloud. There was no time, no point in subversion now. He was going to fight his way out alone.

The Rider lunged for him and Cvareh side stepped. He countered; she thrust right for his chest. Cvareh twisted out of the way of her wicked sharp claws. The Rider wasn't half as fast as Arianna, Cvareh realized in delight. He had been training for weeks with a creature far more deadly than some two-bead.

They came together, twisting, snarling, spinning, and splitting apart once more. Cvareh stumbled, falling to his hands, his feet wide in a crouch. He pushed back then lunged forward, wrapping his arms around the woman's waist. She slammed into the door and it swung open, the lock broken.

They tumbled into a narrow hall lined on one side with doors. Cvareh pinned her to the floor and sunk his teeth into the soft flesh of her neck. Blood and magic exploded into him. But it was a sour taste, fuel for what he needed to do and nothing more. There was only one woman whose blood could make him hunger, could make him lust.

His hand sunk into the Rider's heart, ripping it from her ribcage with brute force. Cvareh tossed it aside with a dull splat, uninterested in eating it. His mouth was already filled with the unwelcome tang of the foreign woman.

Motion from one of the rooms sounded like rainbows and fireflies and the brightest of magics against his ears, against his body. It sparked life into the dim corridor. Cvareh sprinted for the last door on the left, swinging it open. The smell of his mate assaulted his senses and Arianna looked up at him like some deadly, caged predator.

"Ari..." he breathed in relief.

Her lip curled in disgust at the mere sight of him. "You will let me out of these chains so I can properly kill you."

"I can explain but—"

"He was your brother!" She lunged. She must have known full well the range of the chains, but she did it anyway. She was jolted to a stop, just short of where he stood inside the door. She chomped and foamed at him in rage, a rabid wolf at the end of its leash. "He was your brother!"

"I know." That only served to make her angrier. "But I didn't know then. I didn't figure it out."

"You idiot, he was your *brother!*" The woman he admired for the equal ferocity of her mind and body was reduced to animalistic rage, functioning only on instinct. And those instincts now told her to tear him apart. Lord Xin give him strength, because if what she needed to be made whole was his heart, he would tear the organ from his body himself and serve it to her on the finest silver platter. "You didn't tell me. He was your brother. You supported him. You—"

"You didn't tell me!" Cvareh snapped back angrily. "Surely you knew when I brought you the hands, but you said *nothing.*

Did you not think I would help you? Could you not trust me? I offered you everything!"

"He was your brother!"

"And I want to see you kill him."

Arianna stopped all movement, stunned.

"I want to see him die by your hands, Arianna."

He placed his hands on either side of her face and crossed the line of safety into her reach. He pressed his mouth against hers. She stilled all movement for a long moment. He felt the warmth of her breath on his cheek, the heaving of her chest on him. It was life and everything good in the world. Finnyr would be a worthy sacrifice for this woman's pleasure.

Her head twisted and she tore off his bottom lip with her blunt teeth.

Cvareh reeled backward, holding his bleeding face. Arianna spit his flesh at him. Anger still consumed every inch of her. But she was no longer raging.

Twenty gods above, this woman was the only creature he'd ever met for whom tearing off his flesh was a step in the right direction toward the return of stability and sanity.

"You think *now* is a good time to be kissing me? Bloody cogs, your incompetence is only rivaled by your idiocies." Arianna shook her head at him, standing strong on her feet. "Now, free me so I can kill you properly after we escape."

He should've left her there. Had anyone else spoken to him that way, they would've been promptly killed and forgotten, especially given her prone state. But Cvareh found himself inspecting the locks at her wrists.

"I don't have the key."

"You don't have the key?" She sighed heavily. "You really are useless for this whole rescuing thing."

"I didn't—"

"I know, you didn't think. Hardly a surprise." She was a vicious sort at the moment. But he'd take verbal lashings over physical ones. It was its own kind of progress. "I need gold, untempered gold. They took my harness and tools."

All the ornate trimmings of the Rok Estate came to mind instantly. "A moment."

Cvareh sprinted out to one of the earlier rooms. For now, it seemed the bloodshed was far enough away from other Dragons that it had yet to attract attention, but he was certain their luck would run out. Lord Agendi only had so much good spirit for him, and he kept cashing in prayers daily.

Using his claws, he ripped out a chunk of the ornate gilding, bringing it back down to her. "Will this do?"

"Well enough," she admitted, begrudgingly awarding praise. Arianna focused on the gold and her magic filled the air.

Cvareh watched as it lifted itself from the wood, isolating the strip of metal. She took a deep breath, and the sliver turned hot. Arianna didn't even wince as she burned her fingers to blistering on the molten metal, shaping it into a fine and slightly curved point. Her fingers had healed by the time she tested the pick in the lock, only to be burned as she adjusted the shape a second time, and a third, until there was a soft *click*, and the shackles fell away one by one.

"Now we need to—"

She lunged for him. They fell to the floor and Arianna had him pinned in a mere breath. One hand was at his throat, claws pressing into his neck, drawing blood. The other hand was drawn back, ready to attack his chest.

Cvareh didn't struggle. He submitted beneath her, gave her the control she so clearly craved. If she needed to physically see his heart to know it didn't beat against her, he had already decided to permit it.

"Tell me why I don't kill you."

He stared at her, his tortured lover. Her soul had belonged to another. Eva had broken it into pieces with her death. It was not meant for his hands to fix.

"Tell me!" Arianna screamed. "Give me a reason, Cvareh. Tell me why I don't kill you!" Her hand quivered like a shackle was still attached, holding it back from diving into his chest.

They were running out of time, especially if she kept drawing attention with noise and blood. "Because I love you."

Arianna's face twisted as the invisible soldiers who fought wars in the dark battlefields of her mind plunged their claws into her all at once. "That's not good enough."

"Because I love you, and because you love me in return."

Her eyes shot wide open. "I do not."

"Why didn't you kill me then, on the airship? Why not after? Why not on Nova, when I avoided you because I could no longer stand being in the same room as you without touching your skin? Why not when I brought you my brother's hands? Why not a moment ago? Why not now? *Why?*" He needed to hear it as much as she needed to say it. They'd been dancing around it for so long, a waltz on the deck of a swan-diving airship.

"Because... because I want my boon."

"Then why haven't you spent this precious boon?" he pressed. She was too logical for this.

"Because I don't know what I want."

He sighed softly. "Yes, you do. You want this. You want me."

"I only wanted you for a night." Fallacy colored her magic.

"You wish that were true."

"Damn you, Cvareh." She cursed loudly. "Damn you!"

Arianna pushed away from him, swaying as she stood.

"You want to kill my brother. I want to see you do it. Petra's already marked him for dead! You want to free Loom from Dragon rule, and Petra will give that to you. I will help."

"I—"

"No more objections, Arianna. You know it's true just as you've known all along that the man who betrayed you was closely connected to me. Perhaps, somewhere in that brilliant mind of yours, you'd already deduced the possibility of our familial ties." Cvareh appealed to her sense of logic, her sense of reason. She was too smart not to have put it together. Even if she hadn't consciously admitted it, she knew it was true.

"Everything has changed," Arianna whispered.

"Nothing has changed," he insisted. "There's not much time. Come back with me to Ruana."

"This isn't about you," she said sharply. "The King, he said something, something about destroying the guilds. I have to return to Loom."

"Yveun Dono would never."

"You're clearly delusional if you really believe that he would not resort to whatever extreme he deemed necessary." The very statement made him wonder if she somehow knew of the poisoned wine.

"We'll be stronger together."

"I don't even know if I want to look at you." The raw honesty of the statement cut him low. "I'm going to find a glider, and I'm going home."

Arianna started for the door. Cvareh reached out, grabbing her wrist, stopping her. He couldn't let her leave, not like this. She, the woman who had so claimed his heart, was leaving, and he honestly had no idea if she would ever return to him. If she would ever let him return to her.

She stared down at the offending hand, clearly waiting to see if he was going to willingly remove it or if she needed to cut it off. Cvareh chose the former.

"Ari, I'll wait."

"For what?"

"For when Loom is ready to join my House in this fight." He pointed to his ear, reminding her of the whisper link they established and that either had yet to break.

Arianna stared at him with her violet eyes for one long moment. They scanned his face as if memorizing its every curve and edge. He wondered what she saw in him.

"We don't need you," she whispered. "You'll only betray us again."

"Do not lump me with my brother's sins because it is easer for you to remain angry!"

She started down the hall once more, ignoring the comment. Cvareh watched as the first and only woman he had ever loved marched willingly into the hornet's nest of enemies that was House Rok. He wished desperately to know what she was thinking, just once.

Arianna paused and spoke without turning, "Don't whisper me first, Cvareh. Or I will know that everything was merely for your House, and Loom will never side with you."

Cvareh stared long after she was gone, the image of her back imprinted on his eyes. To most, the statement would seem like the definitive end of all possibilities. But not to Cvareh. He'd come to know something of the White Wraith's logic. And in the smallest corner of his heart, it gave him hope.

For if she cautioned him against an action that would make her not work with him, it meant that despite everything, the woman still considered him her ally. She still regarded *them* as a possibility, perhaps even an inevitability if nothing further was damaged between them. Repeating this fact to himself, Cvareh started back through the estate, making haste through every hallway, killing the two servants who saw him.

Petra was doing an exceptional job of keeping the place busy, for he hardly ran into anyone on his way out.

ARIANNA

There was a swirling tempest in her chest. Its winds caught pains old and new, blending them with loves familiar and yet to be fully realized. The longer she spent in his presence, the greater the likelihood it would tear her apart.

She didn't want to love someone at the cost of her ideals. She didn't want to need someone attached to the murderer of the last person she needed. She didn't want to set her heart free in a world that was slowly shifting closer and closer to the end of days.

She had spent too long on Nova. She had let her mind be swept away by music and paintings. She had let her body grow fat with magic, let her mind languish. She needed to return to Loom. There, everything would make sense again. She would remember who she was and what she needed to do.

Arianna gouged out a Dragon's throat with a grunt of frustration. Her claws severed the spine and she cast the body aside, continuing onward.

The truth continued to stare her in the face every time she caught a glimpse of the blue of the nighttime heavens. The hue reminded her of the curtains in her room at the Xin Manor, reminiscent of the color of the sky when she and Cvareh set out for the temple.

She *did* love him. Despite everything, it was true. Of course, if she was going to fall in love again, it'd be a Dragon. And would she pick just any Dragon? No, she had to pick the brother of Rafansi. The traitor. *Finnyr.*

Arianna slammed a Dragon against the wall. It was a tiny thing, and had been trying to avoid being seen at all. The boy let out an almost-squeak at the feeling of her claws pressing into his chest.

"Gliders, where are they?" she snarled.

The child nearly wet himself.

"Gliders." Her claws bit through his flimsy Dragon clothes and into his skin. "Maybe I'll let you live if you tell me where they are."

"Up those stairs." He pointed. "Down the hall, second corridor, and out."

She dropped him and continued upward. There was one thing that seemed to be similar across all races of life: the need for self-preservation.

The gliders were exactly where he told her they would be. Some Dragons attempted to block her passage, but they didn't put up much of a struggle. Arianna saw Chimera looking on from the edges of the platform, golden chains looped around their necks. The gold reeked of the same scent as her chains had, tempered to the King's magic alone. Arianna couldn't break them if she tried. Chimera slaves bound to do the Dragons' bidding.

Yet they moved as one to the sides of a glider, doing nothing to bar her access.

Arianna sprinted over and mounted the vessel. She rested her hands on the handles, feeling magic surge from her fingertips through the interior channeling of the glider and into the wings.

"You won't be able to fly it."

"Yes, I can." Arianna shifted her weight.

"Only Dragons can." The man seemed tired, like he'd had this debate countless times. "Chimera don't have enough magic."

Arianna held up her palm and drew a claw across it, showing them her gold blood. It mattered little now, keeping her secret up on Nova. Let them talk. Let the Dragons know she was real and she would come to kill them with an army of Perfect Chimera just like her.

The Chimera looked on, stunned, like she was one of the Dragons' gods come to life. She wished she could tell them that she was, and that she had the power to save them, but they were lost causes. She couldn't bring them back to Loom with her and she had no doubt that when the Dragon King fell, he would take everything he could with him—assuming they weren't killed for not barring her access now.

"I can't save you." She felt compelled to apologize.

"We know," a woman replied. There was some comfort in hearing the tones of Fennish spoken again. "But we can save you."

"What?" Arianna asked in confusion.

"Go. We'll see to it that you can't be followed." The Chimera closed in on the other gliders with tools in hand.

She pushed her magic into the wings, strong and even. Arianna focused her will and commanded the glider like an extension of herself. *Up*, she demanded mentally, and the glider took to the sky.

Arianna soared on her own for the first time. There was no illusion of another Dragon, no airship captain, no bird-like beast propelling her upward. Just her and her magic. The sight of the glider caused quite a stir, but by the time she was noticed, she was too far for any of them to reach her.

She leaned forward, shooting across the hills and towns of Lysip to its far edge. The Chimera might be on her side, but she couldn't have absolute faith that they would dismantle every glider before some Dragon got to them. Arianna pushed hard over the edge, spiraling around the underbelly of Lysip.

Finnyr's face seemed carved into the shadows of the clouds beneath her. She was deliberately leaving her opportunity to kill the man behind. Arianna swallowed, and let it go. She'd waited years; she could wait longer. Charging in recklessly had failed, so when she returned for his head it would be with an army at her side. It would be with his brother helping deliver him to her justice.

Ari began to gain speed, and braced herself for the winds that rippled the surface of the clouds below attempting to bar her entry home. Arianna pushed more magic, steadying herself, sparking a magical corona to encase her. She was ready. She would—

"Stop." The shout was laced with magic that sizzled across her mind, penetrating the vulnerability of surprise and fractured focus.

Arianna looked toward the source, following the trail of magic back toward Lysip's underbelly. Her eyes met a pair of fire-red orbs that seemed to glow with raw power in the distance. *Let go*, they urged her. She stared, vapidly confounded by the presence of the King of the Dragons in the underside of the island. But there he stood on a ledge, holding her eyes and mind in his sway.

Let go, he mentally urged again. Her hands shook.

Between the shock and magical exertion, Arianna's fingers uncurled. It was only a second—the feeling of air rushing between her digits and over her palms—but she was jolted back into awareness.

A second was all it took.

The magical trail that had been following her the whole time dimmed as the glider lost its fuel. Arianna found herself spiraling in the air, trying to grasp for something that was never where she expected it to be. Her other hand ripped off the remaining handle with the force of the wind.

The clouds were coming fast and she had only one chance to try to get to the glider and form a corona that might be her only shot at survival. She twisted her body in the air, trying to swim through nothing toward the one life raft that would save her from an ocean of death.

Her fingertips touched gold as the clouds engulfed her with their howling winds.

FLORENCE

The forest at night was cool, despite summer encroaching on them. Faint light from the gray sky above was almost completely smothered by the tree canopy. The leaves rustled in a faint wind, echoing the restlessness of the Fenthri below.

Florence had followed Derek and Nora to a group of their friends. She recognized James from earlier, but the rest were vaguely familiar faces, a tight-knit group of Alchemists that had no interest in allowing a wanderer to penetrate their ranks.

Perhaps that was the problem with Loom. They had all been told to stay in their place, to follow their guild marks, to not question when it had been their nature for so many years to question everything. The older generations resisted, but Florence's age and younger? They knew no better. They had grown up accepting the idea that Loom was as it was for some unknown reason, even if they didn't fully agree with it—even if history didn't agree with it.

That was the danger of Sophie's plan. She spoke of sacrifices, but the sacrifices she was risking encompassed the very future of Loom. The longer they spent accepting the Dragons' rule, the more they would all forget. It was easy for Sophie to say otherwise from where she sat; she was of the last generation. Her heart had been hammered into shape before the Dragons had ever ruled.

The young ones who sat among them now were still taking form. Florence watched silently from her seat at the far end of the table, closest to the open window, as the younger initiates slowly trickled from the room. When they were older, would they even remember a rebellion? What world would they inherit?

"You've been quiet," Nora noted, tearing some bread off the loaf in the center of the table and shoving it into her mouth.

"Just hungry," Florence lied. Well, it wasn't a complete lie. She *was* hungry. But that had nothing to do with her silence.

Nora hummed, clearly unconvinced. "Does it have to do with what the Vicar said?"

"What else?" Florence mumbled, wishing the conversation would change. She had yet to work through the best response to Sophie's decision.

"You spoke with the Vicar Alchemist?" one of the women seated at the other end of the table interjected with surprise.

"When we returned," Derek affirmed.

"What did she have to say for herself?" The woman stabbed at the food on her plate with renewed purpose.

"In regards to…" Florence left the question hanging. She wanted to see how the woman would finish it. Her tone was too similar to the one James had spoken with when they asked about the Vicar earlier that day.

"Killing her own guild."

Everyone at the table suddenly found everything else in the room far more fascinating than the Master speaking, or the three people she addressed.

"Explain yourself." Derek was visibly uncomfortable with the narrative being constructed before him.

The master exchanged a look with another circled man at the table, as if tacitly asking—and being granted—permission. "When we learned of the Dragons' plot, we made to evacuate the guild as fast as possible. But our Vicar didn't want to risk alerting the Dragons to our attempts. She didn't want to see Keel attacked in place of an empty guild hall, or in addition to."

The logic was very real, and instantaneously uncomfortable.

"She wanted to give the illusion that nothing was amiss."

"She left a third of the guild in the hall." It escaped Florence's mouth the moment she thought it.

"She told them we were moving in groups to prevent suspicion. The first group left. Then the second, her with it. It wasn't until we reached Keel proper that any of us realized her intent..."

"... and by then it was too late," Nora whispered.

Florence rested her elbows on the table, her chin sinking into the heel of her hand in thought. The reasoning, however horrible, made sense. No one would ever really know if Sophie's calculation had paid off. Keel wasn't attacked, but who could say if that was for Sophie's decision or merely because the Dragons never had any intention of destroying the city?

"You went to Ter.1 to seek help for the rebellion, didn't you?" One of the Masters asked. If their trip had been a secret, it wasn't any longer. "We must see an end to these Dragons."

The tiniest sliver of light appeared on the floor of Florence's mind as a door of opportunity cracked open.

"We did go to Ter.1 for help with the rebellion," Derek started delicately.

"And? Were you successful?"

"Not quite…"

Florence was going to smash through that door with force if she had to. "We were successful," she said, injecting herself once more into the conversation. "Not only the Harvesters, but the rest of the four guilds of Loom want to align with the Alchemists. This is Loom's fight, and they will stand with us, give us the help we need." It was a bit of an embellishment, but Florence believed it to be nothing but truth. There could be no other way for the future to unfurl. Surely, the other guilds would see this logic.

The two Masters exchanged a look of relief, and a surge of power flowed through Florence. She had always seen tools of destruction as the way to gain control. Hope was a much more dangerous weapon.

"Florence—" Derek urged her for silence, but she ignored him.

"The first Vicar we spoke to was uncertain. But after his untimely death, the current Vicar Harvester was all too happy to agree to a Tribunal at Ter.0."

"A Vicar Tribunal?" The Master sat back in his seat. "I never thought I'd live to see the day."

"Well, you may not…" Florene gave a heavy sigh, picking at her food anew. "The Vicar Alchemist refused to attend, demanded the Tribunal be called off."

"What?" the woman gasped. "Derek, is this true?"

Florence felt mildly guilty for the position Derek was put in as he looked between her and the Master. "Well, yes."

"Why?" the entire table seemed to demand at once.

"Vicar Sophie said that it is best for the rebellion if we submit to the Dragons, for now. Lure them into a false sense of security, strike when they're not expecting."

The Master stood so quickly his chair nearly went tumbling behind him. He slammed his palms on the table in visible rage. "She still has her head in the clouds from the last rebellion. There is no Council of Five to lead us any longer, not unless we make one by banning together. There are no great minds to lead us through this dark night. If we do not ignite the flame of our own lanterns, we will lose the way."

"What do you think should be done?" Florence asked, as if she had never even mentioned the Tribunal.

"The Vicar must go to Ter.0. Sophie must work with the other guilds. The Dragons have asked for war; we must give it to them."

Whispers of agreement turned into murmurs that then gave birth to outright spoken affirmation.

"There is no way Sophie will agree." She tried to muster all the delicacy she had.

"We must make her agree."

"And if she still doesn't?"

The Master sat heavily, suddenly deflated. "If she still doesn't, then we will honor her wishes. For the world will slip into true anarchy if the guilds begin to go against their Vicars."

"Who would have suspected the Harvesters were lucky for their Vicar dying," Nora whispered.

"It was certainly convenient for them," the Master agreed, most of the table echoing the dangerous sentiment.

Florence remained at the table until the lamp glow was dim and the food had long since been finished. She listened to Masters and journeymen alike lament their situation. She listened to how they would want to do things differently.

By the time the last of them finally broke away, her mind was made up.

She knew where gunpowder would be kept. She'd know it by logic and looks alone. All good Revos were trained how to properly store their explosives.

"Florence," Derek called after her, arm in arm with Nora. The two exchanged a look, and Nora gave a small nod, breaking away and starting in the opposite direction. Derek sprinted the distance between them.

She looked into his dark eyes, searching, waiting. She would not say the first word, not this time. He had sought her out, after all.

"You're walking a dangerous path."

"I'm walking the only path." She shifted her weight, still assessing if they were, indeed, talking about the same thing. "Will the rest of them see it that way?" She gave a nod in the direction of the now-empty hall.

"I can't say for certain..." The very idea of it made Derek uncomfortable, but he was not objecting. He had yet to speak a true word against it.

"Say for you." Florence took a long step toward him, their toes almost touching. She ran her hands down Derek's forearms slowly, encircling his fingers with hers. The touch demanded his attention. It was slow, but not quite sensual; demanding, but not quite heated. There was a certain life-changing weight to it that almost negated the need for a link mark. "Here, now, no one is around, Derek... What do you want, as an Alchemist?"

"I want to fight," he whispered, as though the words themselves could damn him in some way.

"Good." Florence squeezed his fingers.

For the first time in her life, she thought about kissing someone. She thought about closing the gap between them and placing her mouth on his, about crossing the line of familiarity into desire. It would be easy to do, almost too easy, and somewhere inside herself, she knew it wouldn't be unwelcome.

"Why do you stand with me?" she asked, holding them in place, letting the world fall away in the gaps between her words.

"Because you see the world differently. You have a connection to the greatness that Loom was, like the elders... But you look with eyes like mine, like Nora's, to how that will change to make a future for all of us. You've seen so much." Derek swallowed. "Because you're as undeniable as a pulse."

"Stay with me, Derek. Stay with me. Tether the rest of them to you, and stay with me."

"Are you sure you want this?"

"This is what I was made to do." She let him go, allowing him to reach his own conclusions. She was satisfied.

The rest of them were chained to something: love of a guild, loyalty to a Vicar, memories of the past. Florence did not live in bondage. She had struggled for so long trying to find a place where she belonged that she had never stopped to see the innate benefits of belonging to nowhere. She could do things no one else could do. She could be things no one else could be.

Florence helped herself into the room where they kept the gun powder. The lock hung open on the door. A quiet invitation, the first "accident" in a series of many to come in the following minutes and hours.

The canister she made was simple and small. It would be a quiet shot, one with the power it needed and no more.

As she continued silently back through the city, across bridges that spanned the trees and through spiraling outer staircases, Florence cemented her resolve. She wondered what Arianna would think. The woman would undoubtedly find out. Would she be angry, or proud?

In the end, it didn't matter. Florence wasn't doing it for Arianna. She was doing it because she believed it was right. Because it was what Loom needed, and in the name of a cause she was willing to die for. She had set the future she thought the world needed in motion; she would accept the responsibility that came with keeping its momentum.

The door to the Vicar's chambers was unlocked. Florence rounded the desk from behind which she had been reprimanded mere hours before. Behind it was another door that led upward to a makeshift laboratory. Magic hummed quietly in the air. The bubbling of beakers over tiny torches masked her footfalls. There was a power in sneaking, in moving unknown to all. It was a predatory rush and she wondered momentarily if Arianna still had the same feeling when she donned the coat of the White Wraith.

Florence opened the door to the uppermost level over the course of several breaths. It sighed softly, but the speed silenced any squeals from the hinges. There, sleeping under the moonlight filtered through the clouds above Loom and the thin curtain, was the Vicar Alchemist.

Florence adjusted the grip on her revolver.

Now was not the time for second guessing. Now was not the time for hesitation. There was one future before them, kill or be killed. Any who didn't see that were a risk to the rest of them.

Strategic sacrifices had to be made.

Florence crossed the room in a few wide steps. A floorboard creaked from her unhesitant movement and the Vicar stirred. Florence raised her arm.

Sophie's eyes opened to the barrel of a gun. Florence didn't give her more than a breath. Her pupils barely had time to dilate in shock, to register what was happening, before it happened.

Florence squeezed the trigger.

A single shot echoed through the streets of Keel. It was the first bell to usher in an assembly the following morning, in which the Masters of the Alchemists' Guild appointed a woman named Ethel—a woman who had been seated at the opposite end of Florence's table the night before—as the new Vicar Alchemist. The transition was smooth, simple, and well received by the guild entire.

No one spoke of the mysterious departure of the not-Raven, not-Revolver, who had been in their midst for months. Not one Alchemist searched the airships headed for Ter.4 for a coal-skinned, ink-haired girl. No one even breathed a word about finding the assassin of the former Vicar.

Sophie's death was a mystery, and the culprit was nothing more than a whisper on the wind.

YVEUN

It was not long after Yveun descended beneath the surface of Ruana that he was approached. He always knew what Coletta's little shadows looked like, when they chose to show themselves to him. Coletta dried and lacquered flowers for each of them, which they wore as pendants. His mate was too particular to assign the different buds and colors at random, but whatever system she used, he'd yet to decipher it.

It was merely another layer to his Ryu, a mystery cocooned in the delicate webs of her mind. Yveun was content to let her keep her secrets, for doing so both afforded him freedom, and odd benefits like the one that now stood before him.

"You will take me to her?"

The figure nodded.

There was no further exchange. It was one of the many unspoken rules he'd picked up along the way and followed with ease. He never tried to see their faces or otherwise uncover their identities. They would not speak, only gesture yes or no to questions with a nod or shake of the head. He never asked anything unrelated to the task at hand.

The woman led him into the dim, dank depths of the underworld. The condensation on the walls combined with the general filth made it appear as though they were actually oozing, as though he was in the innards of some kind of grotesque beast.

They shimmied through passageways and wandered around storerooms that connected to equally unappealing alleys. They stepped over the remnants of carnage and the destruction left from illegal duels. The stench of blood and rot quickly became so potent that Yveun had to mentally keep his hand at his side, lest he end up walking with his nose covered the entire time like some kind of delicate Fen.

He adjusted his wide hood as they entered the imbibing parlor. The man behind the counter looked up but stopped shy of addressing them. His guide held out her pendant. Just the sight of it silenced the owner and dropped his gaze.

The shadow woman lifted her finger, pointing toward the end of the hall.

"The last door?" Yveun whispered in a higher note than he usually spoke.

The woman nodded.

Yveun left her and the man behind him. He had what he had come here for. The door ended up being not a door at all, but a heavy curtain that was well framed. Still, he didn't knock, and he didn't announce his presence.

His Master Rider was laid out upon a lounging chair. Arms and legs stretched every which way, muscles cutting out from underneath the skin. She was naked, save for the thin coating of blood that seemed to cover most of her body.

But the blood wasn't hers. She had engorged herself to the point of her stomach growing fat and her eyelids heavy at this little illegal parlor. Her body moved slowly to life, her eyes opening just enough to see him.

They were a bright purple, the color of lilacs, and seemed to nearly glow with power. It gave him pause. They were so similar to eyes he had only recently lost a battle of wills and magic against.

A smile crept upon his mouth. It pleased him that his new Rider and the Perfect Chimera known as Arianna would share similar eyes. Let them both be monsters.

"I was told you would be coming again," she purred, a fat cat on its bed.

"You're House Tam." He focused on the expansive and unbroken display of her emerald skin.

"That's what you choose to say?" She laughed at him.

She laughed at *him*. This was going to be a very different Master Rider than his Leona had been. He couldn't wait to discuss with Coletta what methods she'd suggest he employ to ensure the woman's loyalty.

"And you're not marked as loyal to Rok."

"I haven't had a reason to be."

"Marked? Or loyal?"

"Now you're asking the right questions." She slowly drew herself to a seated position. Her hair was short and as wild as she, spiking in every direction. "Let's say both."

"And if I give you a reason?"

"It's what I've been waiting for." She stood, as tall as him.

Yes, this woman will do nicely.

"I was sold the idea of coming here by one of the flower women. She told me there could be an exciting opportunity for one such as myself, but that I had to wait until the time was right."

"So you made your own excitement in the meantime."

"I did, though I'm getting bored." The Tam woman sauntered over to him. "Tell me, King, is the time right?"

"It is." He let her put her hands on him. He let her slip her palms under his vest, over his chest, and onto his shoulders. She touched him fearlessly and without reverence. She touched him like an experienced lover who knew exactly what she was looking for. "I want to make you strong."

"I am strong." She gave him a coquettish grin.

"I want to make you stronger."

"Will it feel good?" she breathed into his ear.

"The best you will ever feel." Yveun smiled into her neck. She had no idea what he had in store for her. He would find Alchemists and bring them to Nova. They would sew and stitch until she was the Perfect Dragon.

"Will there be blood?"

"So much blood."

She quivered, whimpering softly as if his words had put heat straight to her groin. The woman smelled of fallen Dragons and freshly healed wounds. Coletta had done a good job identifying this one for him. Yveun's palms fell on her narrow hips.

She straightened away. "Now?"

It took him a moment to realize she was talking about imbibing. But when the woman raised a clawed finger to the top of her breast and carved a golden line down to her nipple, blood dripping off its peak and onto the floor, the point was made well and truly clear. She smelled sweetly of dewy honeysuckle. She looked like some kind of dark goddess, bleeding both life and pleasure from her tit.

"Not now," he refused, though the thought was certainly appealing. His hand cupped her breast, thumb flicking over the nipple to smear the offered blood across its surface. It hardened at his touch, a rigid point coated in gold. "For now, I wish to take you to the surface, and find you marked as mine."

"If I must." She raised a hand to her cheek. "I think I'm far more appealing without any tattoos on my face."

She had a sharp chin and a crooked nose. He wasn't inclined to agree that anything could harm the overall aesthetic, or lack thereof, of her face. But Yveun didn't argue. The appeal of this woman was not feminine curves or pleasant features. She was raw strength. She was wild and carnal, danger personified as flesh, and it was rare for Yveun to find anything that set him to throbbing more.

"Come, my Master Rider."

She grabbed for her tattered cape, throwing it over her shoulders.

Yveun paused in the door frame. Looking over his shoulder, he asked, "What is your name?"

"Fay."

Master Rider Fay. It would work.

When they left, neither the flower woman nor owner of the establishment was anywhere to be seen. Yveun and Fay helped themselves out, she no doubt skipping on the bill. They didn't speak much up the pathways. It wasn't until they were halfway up that he heard the certain *zip* a glider made when it took to the skies.

Yveun raced down a narrow walk, heading for the glimmer of sunlight he saw at the end. It was a precarious balcony, but a good enough vantage for him to see the rider shooting by. It was not a Dragon of his, but the Rivet. Yveun growled in rage. She had escaped. And not only had she escaped, but she'd stolen one of his gliders and was riding it better than any of his own Riders.

"Stop!" He shouted, his voice echoing with magic, as Arianna gave a wide turn and spiraled down toward the Gods' Line.

The Chimera stilled. His influence reached her. Yveun knew it wouldn't be enough to truly sway her in any way. She was much too strong for that. But all he wanted to do was give the word enough of a jolt to gain her attention.

Once he had it by virtue of her eyes, he wasn't letting go. Yveun poured every ounce of will and asked for something very, very simple. The more complex a command, the easier it was for the person he was commanding to refute it. This was a simple wish. Two words. Just the mere distraction they would cause could be enough.

Let go.

When he saw her fingers uncurl, he knew he'd won.

The girl flopped through the air like a fish out of water. She was a rag doll that had been cast aside, headed toward its ultimate demise. If he could not have her knowledge, no one would; he would see her dead. The woman plunged into the clouds a mere hand's width from grabbing the glider.

To have even a hope of surviving, she'd have to find a way to reach it and then summon the magic, mid-air, to muster a corona. She'd either have to sustain that magic, or fly it again to survive landing.

Yveun cursed aloud.

Had it been anyone else, he would've taken them for dead. But not Arianna. He had been trying to kill this woman for years, and yet she persisted.

"Who was that?" Fay asked, caressing his forearm as she pressed her breasts into his triceps.

"The first person you are going to hunt down, kill, and consume."

The woman on his arm shivered in delight and it was enough to bring a small smile back to his lips. He had tried to hunt Arianna before. But it had always been in half measures. He hadn't known the girl, not really, to issue a full command. But now they had both seen each other. Now he had a Master Rider worthy of the name, and he would not stop halfway when molding her into the perfect killing machine.

Let the Rivet return to her bleeding world, Yveun thought darkly. Let her know only hopelessness, before her imminent demise.

LOUIE

What a time to be in the organ business. Dragons blowing guilds up. Guilds blowing themselves up. The world had gone crazy and there was only one thing he was certain of: everyone could use a little bit more magic right about now.

"King Louie, we have received reports that a glider has fallen into the remnants of Dortam."

After the destruction of Mercury Town, Louie had decided it was time to invest a bit in the real estate business. Dortam had always been dangerous, but it was taking a new turn with the past year's events. He found a comfortable spot down along the main train line out of the city. Close enough that his men could pop into the Revos' world whenever they needed something, but far enough away that he was well removed. Conveniently, it also positioned him better to run down the line in the opposite direction to Ter.5.2, which opened a whole world of opportunity for exporting.

Business had been going so well that he was considering moving operations permanently in that direction. Or even onto Ter.4 altogether. He'd been contacted by two very interesting Ravens at the behest of a certain girl he once did business with for the infamous White Wraith of Dortam. It almost made him feel bad for selling out young Florence to the Dragons. *Almost.*

But all was well that ended well. The girl clearly survived and was none the wiser to his decision to trade her for a few organs. Organs he never got.

"Would you like us to investigate?" Ralph asked.

Louie took his eyes away from his personal harvesting operation. "Let's continue this upstairs. The smell is overwhelming."

Ralph followed him upward. They switched back in a half dozen flights of stairs up to ground level, and a few more to Louie's new "throne room". The depth helped hide the scent of harvesting, so Louie had purchased the building immediately when he had discovered the depth of its underground portion. Bloody cogs, how he loved the Revolvers and their need to build a bunker into everything.

Not to mention, it had an excellent view of the mountains of Ter.5 that turned into a front-row seat to watch Dortam burn days before.

"Has there been word on if it took off again?" he asked.

"No reports of such."

"Any Dragon activity?"

"None seen."

Curious, Louie thought to himself. He had good instincts. It was part of what made him so effective for so long. Good instincts, determination, and the proper amount of ruthlessness to tie it all together. They lived in a cold world, no point in rewarding it with warmth.

"I shall go investigate myself, I think." Louie slipped on a pair of leather gloves, carefully selecting the proper goggles and mask to match. Dortam was a smoking wasteland.

"Do you think that's wise?" Ralph folded his arms.

"My men work harder when they think I could appear at any moment," Louie explained. "Furthermore, there's something odd about this one. A Rider returning alone?"

"Perhaps they were checking to see if the guild was truly destroyed?"

"That explosion rattled the world itself." Louie chuckled and shook his head. "Even if that were true, why has the glider not left yet?"

"Perhaps it has, and was unseen."

"And, if such is the case, I will just be checking to ensure my men are leaving no stone unturned, no valuable untaken, and no organ left to rot."

Ralph knew better than to continue objecting when Louie had made up his mind. He knew who paid his salary, after all.

Trains had long since stopped running along the main tracks into Dortam. The only engines that went in and out were small vehicles fashioned for single-track runs. Fast little things lifted right from the high-speed thoughts of the Ravens themselves. Louie didn't know the first of how it worked, but the two Ravens, Will and Helen, had agreed to supplying schematics for his Rivets to reproduce as a sign of good faith in their business agreement to funnel weaponry to them from the Revos. What two Ravens wanted with the guns, Louie didn't know nor care to find out.

He, Ralph, and two others kept on retainer whose names Louie never bothered to learn, sped toward Dortam in the late night.

The center of Dortam, where the guild used to be, was nothing more than a smoldering crater. Louie had kept his ear to the ground, following the destruction, trying to make sense of the presence of Dragon Riders and sudden silence that seemed to sweep across Loom. He was slowly gaining a picture that explained why the Revolvers would blow their own guild five ways to rubble.

The refinery still burned, keeping other parts of the city aflame with it. Buildings still tumbled. Smoke still darkened the air in all-too-quiet Dortam.

Louie couldn't be bothered for any of it. The days slipped from one to the next, and people struggled. Everyone fought so hard for everything they thought was so important and, in the end, what did it get them? Piles of ash.

"Ralph, tell your men to seek out my other excavators and have them all report here with their current findings for my review," Louie instructed. "You will lead me to where this supposed glider landed."

Ralph did as he was told, sending off the other men and starting through the carnage in the general direction of what was once Mercury Town. Louie was winded within minutes, and questioning his decision to come out at all. It was hard work scaling all the rubble. He had people for this.

But the prospect of a Dragon glider was far too enticing. Technology he didn't get his hands on often, at least not until the first glider crashed in New Dortam months ago. If he had a few more mostly-intact machines, he might be able to finally reverse engineer the mechanics the Rivets kept under such careful lock and key. That would really accelerate his business in new and exciting ways.

It was nearly enough to make him giggle with glee.

"According to the reports, it should be somewhere around here." Ralph helped Louie onto the top of a fallen building, trying to get a better vantage.

It was hard to see through the darkness, even harder with the perpetual haze that clouded the air. "Do you see anything?"

"No, I—" Ralph stopped and pointed. "Over there."

Louie followed his finger, looking through the night. He squinted, trying to see what his right hand man had seen. Just when he was about to regard it as nothing, his eyes caught a flash of gold.

"Yes, yes!" He clapped his hands gleefully. *Oh this was fun.*

They made haste across the remaining distance. Ralph was his strong arm, pushing materials out of the way and clearing a path for them to get to the glider. It was further than he expected from their previous vantage. But the trip would be well worth it, Louie kept reminding himself whenever his clothing snagged on a metal snarl or he had to climb over a particularly steep chunk of concrete.

They approached the glider, and both stopped at the same time. Louie didn't need to ask if Ralph saw what he saw. For there was no denying the spot of white shining in the faint moonlight as if protesting the inky blackness that tried to close in around the figure.

The glider was half atop the woman, a Chimera by all appearances. But there was something different about this one. Louie stepped forward.

"It may not be safe." Ralph stopped him.

"Anything worthwhile rarely is." Louie grinned madly, brushing him away.

Ralph stayed in his place.

Louie approached the semi-crushed figure with interest. For the first time, he saw the creature up close. There was no mistaking it—the unique coat alone was proof enough—each detail met every first-hand account perfectly.

The White Wraith was a woman.

But that was not Louie's most important revelation of the day. No, there was something far, far more curious about her. A spear of iron was stabbed directly through the side of her stomach. Her body was, no doubt, struggling to heal the wound despite the presence of the foreign object. But no magic could remove the iron, so blood continued to ooze around it before slowly fading into the night air.

Louie squatted next to the unconscious woman, touching his fingertips lightly against the wound. Sure enough, the blood was warm. It was truly coming from her. He had encountered many valuable things over the years and dealt in everything from secrets to organs, weapons to schematics. But Louie had never found something so rare, so precious, and so dangerous that it could change the world.

He grinned, already thinking of the possibilities for how he was going to work this discovery to his advantage. Not only did he have what he well suspected to be the infamous White Wraith of Dortam in his clutches, he also had a Chimera the likes of which Loom had never seen. Though he didn't understand exactly how, he knew the creature before him would shake the very foundations upon which their world was built.

He had what guilds wanted and Dragons feared.

He had a Chimera that bled gold.

The story continues in...

R*The*EBELS
O*f* G⬤LD

COMING DECEMBER 2017

The WORLD Of L⌀OM

Pronunciation Guide

People

Arianna	Are-E-ah-nah
Cvareh	Suh-var-ay
Florence	Floor-in-ss
Leona	Lee-oh-nah
Yveun	Yeh-vu-n
Louie	Loo-EE
Petra	Peh-trah
Sophie	So-fee
Agendi	Again-Dee
Finnyr	Fihn-er
Dawyn	Dawn
Coletta	Koh-let-tah
Soph	Sah-f
Luc	Luke
Theodosia	Thee-Oh-doh-sha
Faroe	Fuh-row
Topann	Toe-PAh-n

Places

Ter	(Short for Territory)
Lysip	Lisp
Holx	Hole-ks
Keel	Key-uhl

Ruana	Roo-AH-na
Easwin	Ees-win
Abilla	Uh-bih-luh
Venys	Veh-nis
Napole	Nah-pole-Ee

Things

Peca	Peh-kah
Royuk	Ree-yook
Fennish	Fehn-ish
Dunca	Duhn-kah
Boco	Boh-koh
Endwig	Ehnd-wihg
Glovis	Glow-vihs
Raku	Rah-koo

Dragon Houses/Titles

Xin	Shin
Rok	Rock
Tam	T-am (same as 'am' in 'I am')
Oji	Oh-jee
Ryu	Re-you
Dono	Dough-no
To	Tow
Bek	Beck
Da	Dah
Vicar	Vih-kur

The Five Guilds of Loom

Harvesters   Alchemists   Rivets

Ravens   Revolvers

Guild Brands

Found on the right cheek, tattooed guild brands were imposed by Dragon Law to designate a Fenthri's rank and guild membership. The tattoo is elaborated upon as new merits are achieved.

 Initiate

 Journeyman

 Master

Dragon Houses

All members of Dragon society belong to one of three Dragon houses. Ties into the House can be by blood, adoption, mating, or merit.

Rok

Tam

Xin

Dragon Names

All Dragon names follow the structure:

[Given Name] [House Name]'[House Rank] [Societal Rank]

Shortened names are said as one of the following:

[Given Name]'[House Rank]
or
[Given Name] [Societal Rank]

House Ranks	Society Ranks
Oji – House Head	Dono – King/Queen
Ryu – Second in Command	To – Dono's Advisors/High Nobility
Kin – Immediate Family to the Oji/Ryu	Veh – Nobility Chosen by the Dono
	Soh – Upper Common
Da – Extended Family	Bek – Lower Common
Anh – Vassals/Lower Members of the Estate	(nothing) – Pauper, Slave, Disgraced

Acknowledgements

NICK—I wouldn't have made it through this manuscript without you. I push, and you push me harder. Your thoughts, suggestions, insights, were all imperative for me to make it through this story that demanded so much of me. Thank you for having both the strength to demand the world of me and hug me hard enough so I keep it together when I may crack under the pressure.

ROBERT—thank you for all the inspiration you gave to me, however inadvertent. You're an exceptional friend and a role-model for me on how to be a decent human being (even if I'm pretty sure I regularly come up short). Thank you for being a parallel river of temperate waters.

MY EDITOR, REBECCA FAITH HEYMAN—there should be a saying that behind every marginally decent author is an editor who's ten times more amazing. Thank you for working with me on this manuscript and helping me from throwing ideas around to cleaning up my structure when it needed it most. I am so, so glad we met and are getting to have this experience together.

KATIE—as always, thank you for keeping me sane. You give me something no one else does in your unique blend of encouragement and love. I would've long gone crazy if I didn't have you to get turkey clubs and fancy tea with.

JEFF—Thank you for all the love and support you gave me over the years and throughout the writing of this novel. You were there when I needed you and supported me through this crazy dream.

2

your continued belief in me and, you know, not deciding I'm
not worth your time. It's been a delight to work with you and I
can only hope wc continue to bring worlds into readers' hands
together.

THE TOWER GUARD—my dear street team, thank you for
everything you do! You're always there when I need you and
such a great group. I'm so honored to be surrounded with
people who really take care of their own.

About the Author

ELISE KOVA has always had a profound love of fantastical worlds. Somehow, she managed to focus on the real world long enough to graduate with a Master's in Business Administration before crawling back under her favorite writing blanket to conceptualize her next magic system. She currently lives in St. Petersburg, Florida, and when she is not writing can be found playing video games, watching anime, or talking with readers on social media. She is the author of the Air Awakens Series.

Subscribe to Elise's mailing list for the latest news and updates:
http://EliseKova.com/Subscribe/

CONNECT WITH ELISE KOVA
http://www.EliseKova.com/
https://twitter.com/EliseKova
https://www.facebook.com/AuthorEliseKova